Chronicle of Stolen Souls: the Legacy of Fathers

Craig L. Andrews

Alternative Book Press
2 Timber Lane
Suite 301
Marlboro, NJ 07746
www.alternativebookpress.com

2014 Paperback Edition
Copyright 2014 © Craig L. Andrews
Cover Illustration by CL Smith
Book Design by Alternative Book Press
All rights reserved
Published in the United States of America by
Alternative Book Press
Originally published in electronic form in the United
States by Alternative Book Press.

Publication Data
Craig , L. Andrews, [date]
Chronicle of Stolen Souls: the Legacy of Fathers/ by
Craig L. Andrews.—1st ed.
p. cm.
1. General (Fiction). I Title.
PS1-3576.C73A537   2014
813'.6—dc23

ISBN 978-1-940122-16-8
Printed in the United States of America
10 9 8 7 6 5 4 3 2 1

Table of Contents:

Craig L. Andrews

Chapter 1

William Rinehart started to back his tiny car out of his driveway, lamenting another workday awaiting him at the State America Committee, SAC, headquarters. He was an Industry Equalization Manager, one of many who possessed the worthless title. It was Tuesday morning, a steel-gray, chilly day in October of 2054.

As usual, he had crawled into his little car about seven. His assigned SAC, bus pickup parking area waited for him four and a half miles away, essentially the only destination allowed him with his car, other than a trip to the area SAC market. From there the government vehicle transported him and other human-automatons to their offices in the SAC building in downtown Washington. It was no longer the District of Columbia. The bus, with covered windows to prevent passengers seeing the countryside, took an hour from Fairfax, Virginia and his SAC bus collection area.

He backed out of the garage, taking no notice of the light frost that had dusted the small patch of grass at the front of his home and left it glistening like a fallen silver shield. At the end of the driveway, he stopped, twisting his head, checking the street behind him. Suddenly a black v-tran flashed in the corner of his eye. He jammed his foot on the brake, the inertia throwing his head back slightly. He held his breath for a moment. V-trans were the government's cross between a van and a seven passenger utility car, and only the SAC had them. Everyone dreaded the vehicle. In spite of his fear, a perverse curiosity compelled him to follow its path. As he looked out of the corner of his eye, his fear slowly gave way to resentment for its presence violating his family's residential sanctity. The v-tran's presence portended the arrest of someone in his housing area. He watched the ominous black transport, trying not to turn his head too sharply or watch for more than a few seconds. They could have come for a mass arrest, one in which they would scoop up all the people of a single neighborhood. The SAC had formulated an efficient solution to one of their problems, collecting all alleged the members of a conspiracy with one quick operation, thereby stopping all rumors and negative ripples in the emotional sea. Illegal stories circulating through the n-zecs, all workers below a section head level told how the SAC would swoop in and swoop back out like black ghosts. William held himself still as the v-tran rolled toward a house down the street.

Out of the corner of his eye, he watched the horror of the SAC unfold before his eyes, as if it were a movie and not part of his reality. After a few moments, he looked away and backed his car another foot. If he were to gawk too obtrusively, the men from the black v-tran could arrest him for spying.

He didn't know the people living where the v-tran had stopped, which was two houses down from his family's small home. Within

6

moments, the SAC protectors, law enforcement officers, led a husband and wife from their home with their hands restrained behind their backs, their heads hung down as if recognizing the futility of crying out. The protectors marched the couple out to the waiting v-tran. The two gray-uniformed protectors pushed them into the backseat with a casual flair, chattering and smiling as they slammed the door closed. Up on the home's small porch, William saw a small brown-haired boy of perhaps five years and a taller young blonde girl who could not have been more than eleven years old. The girl held the hand of the crying little boy as they watched their parents disappear. As the v-tran sped away, the children walked off the porch toward the street. Both stood there crying.

William's chest shuddered as he envisioned his own children on that porch. A rare tear ran from his eye, which he brusquely wiped away. They could have been his Stefan and Marie. Abruptly, a second v-tran appeared, swept up the children and disappeared like a phantom following the first v-tran. The image burned into his brain. It was then he acknowledged the last arrest from his housing area had been back in June. William knew all too well that the SAC didn't need any reason to sweep a citizen into their net.

William Rinehart walked wearily up the slope of a gravel mountain road. It was week after the DPP, Department of People Protection, protectors had swept the parents and children into one of its black v-trans on his street. He walked out in the open, exposed to the life or death judgment of an armed underground conspirator who was in hiding from the SAC. Fearing what would happen if he failed his assignment, he kept lifting his tired feet against his fatigue, hoping that his task would soon end.

He was just an average SAC office employee and not in any way prepared for what they had ordered him to do. Why? And even though he shouldn't think it, he hated the government forcing him to do their dirty work and taking him away from Lynn and the kids.

From the horizon of his memory came Lynn's recent reminder about the couple living down the street. That incident added enormously to the mystery of his selection. By all rights, the SAC should have arrested him and for that matter, her. He had pushed the incident to the back of his mind, Lynn buying black market flower bulbs from the woman taken by the DPP, the same mother whose little girl and little boy were left at the curb. Why hadn't the DPP arrested Lynn and him instead of picking him to walk up a mountain?

He couldn't have refused the SAC, ordering him on this unusual assignment with the DPP. If he did, the SAC could terminate him. However, in lieu of death, leniency was possible. In such a circumstance, they could hand out a ten-year sentence to an SAC government hard labor camp. No one ever wanted to go to any of the labor camps, the places from which no one ever returned.

Section Head Karl Steinhoff had told him the SAC had selected him for an assignment, with a contemptuous grin, and to stand outside his house ready to go when the v-tran got there to pick him up. From his home, the DPP, led by Protector Captain Rogers, drove him to Durand Airport in Washington where their plane departed for North Carolina. At the base of the mountain in North Carolina, Captain Rogers had ordered him to walk up the gravel road until he encountered a bunker. At the bunker he was to persuade the members of the underground, to surrender.

If he failed, the SAC could accuse him of purposefully failing the assignment to help a criminal against the State.

Knowing how Steinhoff hated him, he wondered if Steinhoff had influenced the SAC to select him. On second thought, looking at the selection logically, the order for William's involvement likely originated a level above Steinhoff, with Director Helmut Kauffman, the shadowy head of the SAC intelligence section, SACI. For some strange reason the SAC had connected William and the conspirators, and considered the undergrounders incredibly vital, otherwise the SAC would have just obliterated the top of the mountain.

For nearly all of his adult years, the years following his schooling, he had followed the rules like everyone else working for the SAC, choosing to accept the tradeoffs for having a modicum of comfort above the N-SACs, the non-SAC workers. If you didn't work for the SAC, the State, a person's life was harsh, and essentially a survival existence. His family's living conditions were above that of the N-SACs, who depended on the government-run factories, farms, and labor camps, and who the SAC had assigned to general housing centers, which were old apartment buildings and homes commonly in ill repair. Among the government population centers, the major cities where the SAC had moved masses of people, the area around Washington was the best.

When the SAC tightened the screws on freedom, he had used his education to grab an opportunity working for the SAC. With the lack of jobs in the country, it was the safest route he could take, and it had stability. Initially he had relied on his mentor-SAC, and for several years, had blindly believed in what it professed. In those days, despite the growing restrictions on people and only obtaining information about his country from the SAC,

9

he had believed the SAC provided everything the poor needed, and he had accepted how it orchestrated the wealth for equal distribution and welfare. Of course, he also embraced the SAC's mantras, which was required of all trusted employees and he had passed the yearly lie detector allegiance testing.

The arrest of the family on his street came back to his thoughts, and the image of the two pitiful children standing at the curb watching the DPP taking their mom and dad from their lives. What was their crime? Was it the black market flower bulbs? *He was thinking of arrests again.* Well, it was a frequent event. William looked out though the trees, wonderful trees, trees without cameras, a forest of majestic wood spires, ornamenting the hillside with radiating searching limbs, limbs reaching out with skeletal hands. A few stubborn leaves of October clung to the bony limbs. The barren woody arms made a framework about which shorter adolescent splotches of green pines provided accent. The limbs reached outward and upward unencumbered and free, going freely in any direction they wished.

A mixture of pine, fallen leaves, and damp wood fragrances floated on the breeze, tugging on his memory, taking him back to his childhood. He threw his head back and pulled in the forest air with an unencumbered breath. The smell was a perfume, a heartwarming scent. He smiled. The free chilly air coursed through his nostrils, stinging slightly, electrifying his brain, spreading tingles in his face, arousing a bold clarity of mind, throwing a switch, resurrecting dangerous questions related to freedom.

Life away from the constant government gaze was a dream. *What would it be like living in a forest?* His eyes roamed unhindered, although he couldn't disregard the nagging feeling that the SAC might be watching— somehow. Even though the SAC probably didn't have cameras, vid-cams, watching, he felt the effects of the rat-in-a-maze conditioning, always needing to look for the electronic eyes pressing down on him. Sadly, the act of breathing air and the act of searching for vid-cams held equal importance in their daily lives.

His thoughts returned to his walking. The plodding extension of each foot onto the gravel-littered clay road, dragging him forward, seemed to take him past tiny milestones of his mission. The boots on his feet fell awkwardly to the earth, feeling more like lashed weights, relentlessly pulling his feet down.

"Manager Rinehart, this is Captain Rogers, it would be nice if you would walk a little faster." The captain's flat voice bored into William's com-link, a black kidney-shaped device plugged into his ear.

"I'm doing the best I can," William replied with a labored breathy voice. "Can't you tell me why I'm here?"

"I have my orders just like you. Just walk. You're not refusing to support the SAC are you?"

"Absolutely not. I'm a loyal supporter of Chairman Durand's plan. I welcome the chance to serve him and the SAC."

"That's what I thought."

It was possible they were using him as a sacrificial lamb. There he went again. Just thinking about not wanting to be there was a thought violation. Over the past year he had violated that law so many times he'd lost count. He questioned the unquestionable when he was alone, on his drive to and from the bus pickup area in his government allocated car. He had violated the SAC mental programming, violated how they had wanted him to react, and violated a promise to surrender himself for mental rectification if he found himself using a faulty mental process, basically disagreeing. Of course, he never would surrender himself for mental rectification. Curiously, even though he now detested the SAC, his years as a zealous servant undergoing its programming probably conditioned him to feel anguish and guilt for thinking negatively about the SAC. If the SAC discovered his faulty thinking, they would arrest him and off he would go to the labor camp or worse.

It wasn't until a year or two ago he had accepted the reality of the labor camps, the really bad ones. Up to that time, he had thought they were merely normal farms. The SAC had announced on the vid-net, their television system, the death camps were stories created by terrorists and undergrounders. And that was another problem. *My mind is wondering.* Other than fear, they maintained power by controlling people's thoughts and controlling all information. Possibly, they controlled people's thoughts because they couldn't send everyone to the labor camps. The SAC needed slaves to survive, bodies for the human gristmill. *Watch your thinking.*

To avoid issues with the facial watchers using vid-cams, he used the SAC mantra to keep mental control, focus, and right thinking, the detestable sickening tool that circled in his brain like a bad rhyme. *Wrong thoughts, wrong mind, bad thoughts, no bad mind of any kind!* In addition to functioning as an initial indoctrination rhyme, the SAC used the mantra as a maintenance tool to recharge the blind belief in their regime. When he had begun seeing the demonic character of the SAC more thoroughly, two voices began battling in his head, and since then it had gotten worse. Now one voice recited the SAC mantra and the other one protested he was a slave to the SAC. *SAC loves us. SAC gives life.* More words suddenly popped into his head. *Wrong thoughts, wrong mind, bad thoughts, no bad mind of any kind!*

He swept his eyes from the trees on the left to those on the right, looking for protectors or an underground conspirator, or even a vid-cam. He didn't see anything to cause worry. He looked up at the gray sky and listened for a moment. He couldn't hear or see any drones. Three had flown over his house, each on a separate occasion and they were essentially silent, emitting only a humming sound similar to an electric motor. He wondered why the SAC didn't have one up here.

The use of drones and their impact on SAC control made him think back to his family's future. His awakening, which he also envisioned as a curse, had started with one crystal moment months ago when he obediently followed procedures assigning an old couple in their seventies for relocation to a steel mill in Minnesota. The SAC labeled the old couple as DOS, destructors of the state. When he read the age of the old man and woman, it was clear the SAC was sending them to their death by hard labor. He had no choice but to issue the order, and even though he had made thousands of assignments before, he had nightmares about it for weeks afterward. The DPP had scooped them up along with, according to the file, fifty others. In a brain-freezing moment, William knew the DPP, or rather the SAC, had charged them with some inane charge.

The DPP probably grabbed the old couple and it was an agency the people didn't discuss openly. The words, street police, popped into his brain automatically. It was the term average citizens used for protectors, the officers of the DPP. Everyone feared the DPP. They arrested people in the middle of the night when they were helpless, they didn't hesitate using their black batons on people's heads, and if they hit someone too hard it was one less person to worry about.

The DPP wasn't the only factor gnawing at the collective mentality. Around him and his family, fear permeated every citizen's life in one manner or other. Living for years under such circumstances had made every citizen nearly numb to the dangers in order not to go insane. Citizens merely hoped to live one day longer. In a sense, people wore blinders and tried to look the other way when a black v-tran appeared on the street. The SAC evil was like an unseen vapor that would encapsulate an unsuspecting citizen, who, without his knowledge, had attracted the persecuting eye of the DPP.

He still saw nothing of any conspirators lurking behind a tree or rock.

After seeing the DPP taking the mother and father last week, he had seen a vision of his children's future. He sat in his usual chair after dinner, watching his children playing, when in a daydream, he saw the DPP pick up the two kids from down the street. What would become of his children in future years? How would the SAC treat them when they got older? The SAC could send them to a labor camp. He now knew the government for what it was a soulless monster and they were living within the SAC's mental barbed wire. *Why was I stupid and weak in the beginning? Wait. That's wrong thinking. You are a loyal SAC citizen-comrade. What am I saying?*

His eyes consumed the wholesome vision of trees and falling leaves. How wonderful a life could be with his family in a forest like this. That was a wasted thought. Freedom from the SAC was impossible, unless you escaped the country and that was impossible. Nevertheless, the SAC had sucked him into their diabolical collective, and somehow he had to survive with his family. What alternative did he have? Perhaps all he could expect was a dream of freedom for his children.

He stopped and watched a black squirrel rummaging through the leaves near the base of a hickory tree and then continued. He looked up at the sky, at forest on his right, and then to the left. He liked looking deep into forest past the trees that were near the road. It was like exploring. He looked for animals. He envisioned himself walking freely and deeply within the trees. He marched on.

Where in the hell was this bunker? The pastoral nature so remote from a sizeable city seemed the only explanation for the absence of video cameras. It only made sense that they could scan and communicate from every square foot of the country's surface. *Wrong thoughts, wrong mind, bad thoughts, no bad mind of any kind!* Why again?

Why did the State America Committee, the inscrutable group of dictators, pull him from his job to confront conspirators on the top of a mountain? It didn't make any sense. The assignment was ridiculously foreign to his daily SAC office job. A DPP protector sneered at him as he prepared William for the mission, handing William black mid-calf, DPP military boots, and a DPP uniform made up of a gray shirt and pants. Then, after barking at him to lace the boots up properly, William got a surprise. The man handed him a bulletproof vest for under the gray wool, SAC winter coat.

"Manager Williams, stay alert," Rogers whispered into William's ear, startling William. "This isn't a Sunday stroll in the woods. You make this happen and maybe you'll be allowed to go back to your life."

William didn't know if he was to answer or not. "I'm walking as fast as I can. I'm not used to doing this." *Just march my ass up a gravel road and make the people walk out of the bunker. Right.* "Maybe I should stop and catch my breath."

"You stop, and I'll report you for aiding a conspirator."

"I'm walking."

He braced himself against the late October breeze, lowering his head, and squinting away wind-made tears. The cold's icy hand slapped him across the face, nearly snatching away his breath. The emaciated trees thrashed about, struggling against the invisible current under the angry clouds, forewarning snow. The dank chill seeped through his coat and into his body.

He stopped. *This is not right.* He covered his nose as he sucked in a long breath, then he puckered his lips and let out his breath so that it made a slight whooshing sound. "Captain Rogers, this is William Rinehart. What am I supposed to be looking for? I have no damn idea what a bunker might look like." William kept walking, looking around as he waited for a reply.

"Look Rinehart, it doesn't look like a damn tree. It's something made out of concrete you idiot. Keep going. We want to get this over sometime this year."

"How far?"

"Don't be an ass. Keep moving until you see it. You'll see it after you go forty or fifty yards . . . maybe more. Keep your eyes open."

He slowed his walk, sucking air deep into his lungs, trying to satisfy their demand. The beads of perspiration on his forehead, chilled by the air, felt like drops of ice.

"Only a brain-dead nutcase would be hiding here," William muttered nearly in a whisper.

"What was that Rinehart?"

"Nothing, I was just talking to myself."

"Stop it."

The whole thing stunk. What to hell. *I do labor equalization work. That's what I do. I push computer keys, shuffle papers, and write reports.* Wait. *Wrong thoughts, wrong mind, bad thoughts, no bad mind of any kind!*

"Manager Rinehart, stay alert. You should be getting close to the bunker."

"What am I looking for?" William whispered into his com-link. *Maybe I'll know it when I get shot.*

He stopped, sweeping his eyes over the wall of trees to the left and right of the road, pausing to penetrate deeper through the curtain of leafless hardwoods and green pines. He chewed his lower lip for a moment, listening for any sound, listening to the wind through the barren trees, catching the sound of the rustling of leaves tumbling across the forest floor. He walked on.

He saw nothing of the operations support personnel from the DPP. He supposed that was normal. That was their profession, staying out of sight.

"Captain Rogers," William whispered.

"Why are you on the com-link?" Rogers snapped.

"How much farther do I have to go up this road before I see something?"

"Get off the com-link and do your damn job. If you don't, I will report you for obstructing the operation."

"Maybe I should have a gun."

"If you have a gun, they might shoot your ass. Now get off the com-link."

He sucked in a breath and released it. His thighs had started to burn. The time on his watch, 10:46 a.m., disappointed him. He had hoped to get home yet today, to be with his family, to remove his wife's burning fear. *Damn Steinhoff for taking me away from home.*

Suddenly, William felt the object hanging around his neck swing across his skin. He reached up and touched the silver cross hanging from a chain under his shirt, thinking of his wife, Lynn, giving it to him before he left home. His kids had stood there with questioning sad faces and then came Lynn's fear-stricken gaze, which had nearly brought tears to his eyes. Then she gave him the cross. He had never traveled away from home before. Knowing the SAC policy discouraging such objects, he placed it where the SAC people couldn't see it. A piece of metal in that shape hadn't been in his life for years. The SAC had discouraged employees from wearing such, antiquated symbols, as they called them.

He peered through the invisible wintry wall of air, looking for an object or something moving. He thought he might see a glimmer indicating a weapon pointed in his direction. The road, scarred by a few tire tracks at this point, barely had the width for a car. There was a massive rock at the side of the road, an enormous chunk of granite, the largest rock he had seen, and the only one that was red.

A gust of wind pierced his coat. He tugged at his collar, pulled his stocking hat down, and sent his hands into the pockets of his waist-length, DPP wool coat. *It will soon be over and I can get back to my office.* He felt the DPP force, even if he couldn't see them. They were probably drifting through the woods like flies searching for a carcass. He looked behind him with a sweeping glance. No movement by the operations people. They worried him as much as his target—simply because one of their trigger-happy idiots could shoot him in the back by accident. He didn't trust them any more than their Section Head Karl Steinhoff.

Off to the left, ahead of him, a flock of birds shattered the silence with their flapping wings, rising up like swirling smoke until they cleared the treetops where they scattered. He walked across a patch of loose stone lying over the hard clay, crunching it under his field boots. A few straggling leaves of autumn fluttered down into the brush, tumbling from one branch to the next, landing on the bed of their predecessors where they were secure. He smelled the mountain pines again. It reminded him of when he was a kid and when his father left home. *The bastard.* When he and Lynn first got married, he promised himself he'd always take care of his family better than his father.

Wait. What's that up ahead?

His eyes struck an open area in the trees. A manmade structure extended out from the natural rock of the hillside, like a small alcove; it was a concrete arch filled with shadow. He stopped and studied it. Where was the door? He had barely picked it out from the background of trees and shadows. Its wall was mostly green with fungi and moss, and it looked as if it had been there forever. He looked up to the sky, suddenly realizing they hadn't used any of those infamous black helicopters. It had to be a stealthy ground operation, although the SAC had silent choppers.

He walked slowly, not taking his eyes away from the structure. The concrete was more massive than he imagined. The visible portion of the wall, about ten-foot high, ran east to west for fifteen yards before it merged into the side of the mountain rock, as if it had grown out from the natural stone. Nearby trees, even though most were only skeletons now with their leaves on the ground, formed nearly perfect camouflage along the outside of the structure. There were no vehicles.

He nudged his bulletproof vest up around his neck even as he doubted its protection.

"That's far enough," a man barked.

William flinched and froze where he stood. His heart pounded against his chest. "I'm unarmed," he replied, his voice thick with fear. From where did that voice originate?

"That's too bad. I have a thirty-caliber Winchester aimed at your chest and even if you have on a bulletproof vest, it will hurt like hell when it knocks you on your ass. Of course, I could go for your head."

"I'm only here to talk." *Yeah, I shouldn't even be here. I should be in my nice warm office.*

"That's bullshit. You know it and I know it. There's a DPP special operations force down the slope from you, spread out like flies on a dung pile. I have some explosives hidden down there, which can blow you people all to hell if you so much as breathe too deeply. My old monitoring system still works and I heard you crunching the gravel on the road a mile back. That's why the military built this outpost here back in the sixties. Back then, they were worried about the Soviet Union."

William tried to think of something he should say, something to inch toward his assignment without alarming the man. "Can I talk with you?" He gestured easily with a hand, palm up and fingers spread, as if pleading. "I swear I'm unarmed. I'm not part of the DPP or SACI. I'm supposed to talk with you to get you to surrender. They don't want to kill you. They want to talk with you. That's all I know." He suddenly remembered the com-link in his ear.

"Oh, I'm sure they don't want to kill me, at least until they have sucked everything I know from my brain. The SACI is no better than the old KGB under the Soviets."

William thought he heard a curious character in the man's voice. The tone reminded him of someone fatigued and resigned to a disastrous end. He took a step forward wondering if the man would shoot him. He paused. He took another step. "I'm coming up. You can shoot if you want, but it won't do you any good. I don't have any weapons. I'm not DPP."

Something metal creaked and then screeched as if it had scraped across stone or concrete, sounding like a heavy metal door. The long barrel of a rifle pointed at him from the man's arm, while the man's face remained in the shadow, nothing but a gross dangerous outline.

"All right, but if I see anyone else move in this direction the fireworks will start," the man said, his tone giving warning that contained satisfaction. Then he yelled loudly. "You hear me down there in the trees, you DPP assholes? I will blow the shit out of all of you if you move."

As he moved onward, William didn't know what to make of the structure. No matter the label placed upon it, bunker or something else, the concrete structure looked quite impregnable. From his perspective, it was an excellent hideaway, allowing the complete view of the approaching mountain road, and he doubted if the DPP could break into it. William took two more steps, looking into the alcove, penetrating the challenging shadows, as if a weak light had been turned on, but he still couldn't see the man's face. He paused not more than four feet away, assessing the man's demeanor, wondering if he would face a burst of violence. The light changed as clouds moved overhead. A faintly illuminated face appeared. It wasn't what he expected. Although only a little light brushed it, the face appeared aged, and not that of an irrational conspirator against State America. This person gave him a strange feeling, something other than a twinge in his nerves. The man's voice troubled him, something more than the age-worn edges of his words, something more than the timbre, and something other than its pitch. An irresistible inflection in the tone caught like a thorn in William's ears.

Then the man stood before him in clear view. William gawked at him, speechless. The man looked back at him with alarm-widened eyes. The conspirator surprised William, not by his unflinching manner, but by his age. He was an old man. He wondered if the old man knew about DPP weaponry. The man didn't have headgear for protection from the DPP microwave guns, the M-guns, which with one shot to the head would scramble the brain. From his lack of uniform, William concluded the man wasn't connected to any organized underground military. The old fellow didn't hold the rifle like the DPP, properly up at his shoulder, although he gripped it fearfully.

"Hold where you are."

There it was again, the voice. William stopped. The character of the man's speech sounded less like a backwoods hero and more like someone well educated. On top of that, his gun looked quite old. William studied the man, their eyes challenging each other, assessing threats and movements. The man's eyes were alert and penetrating, the type of intelligent eyes you'd see directing an office of workers at the SAC building. The man had to be near his seventies. A feeling in William's gut told him this man was no ordinary conspirator, although he didn't base his conclusion on any experience. If the man were an ordinary underground conspirator, the SACI would have gotten him themselves. They always captured the people they wanted. Always. Dead or alive. *Somebody wants what this man has in his brain! But, why me?*

William looked up, wondering if a satellite was staring back down at him with a big eyeball, documenting his every move. Regardless of SAC's technology, it hadn't been a satellite eyeball that picked this guy out the crowd. It was an ordinary vid-cam. Captain Rogers had eased his tongue to divulge that little tidbit on the trip down from Washington. William suddenly had an image cross his mind, the broadcast appearing on the national vid-link nearly every night, declaring the vid-cams saw every crime, making people safe from crime.

Okay, all I have to do is bring this man back alive.

William wondered if his boss, Director Aldrich, would write something positive on his record, since fulfilling his obligation on this mission. He turned and glanced back down the dirt road, mindful of a possible friendly-fire bullet in his back, or just as bad, the goons hitting him with an M-gun.

The man in front of him snorted and laughed at William. "Don't forget to look up and smile for the camera up there in space. And—don't try to play dumb with me. I know about most of their technology, including the M-guns. I may have been here for a long time but I wasn't without communication to the outside world—such as it is." He paused, moving his tongue around in his mouth, as if it were making a decision. "You know," he said with a caustic smile, "I just about shot you in the head a few minutes ago. So you might consider yourself lucky."

The man remained partially concealed by the massive metal door, a monolithic slab of steel with splotches of rust replacing faded dark-green paint. The door had to be more than eight inches thick and worthy of an explosive. From the way the man position himself he clearly feared exposing himself past his doorway, not that William could blame him. Even with his head barely visible, a good DPP sniper could have terminated him.

William took another step. The man flinched and moved back a step.

William could now see the man was about his height, although with a slender build, possibly thin from not eating or age, but he definitely was not a military survivalist, one of the weird people the SAC wanted to eradicate. Speculation had floated around from time to time about a few survivalists still in hiding, but he never believed it. It had become the folklore of the hopeful.

"From the way you're breathing you must sit on your ass all day. If you're not DPP, then you must be one of the other SAC slaves." The man's voice came with an inflection of amusement.

The steel door inched open, as the man seemed to be considering taking William inside. "Can we talk?" The man's face drifted back into the shadow of the opening.

"Why are you here?"

Again, the voice reminded William of someone he'd met, teasing him with its impossible familiarity. "Like I said, I'm supposed to talk you into surrendering peacefully. I'm not DPP. They don't want to kill you."

"Why mess with a harmless old recluse like me?"

"Honestly, I have no idea. I was just ordered to come up here and talk with you."

"I'm not talking out here where one of those idiots can take a shot at me," the man grumbled. "Step in so I can sweep you for a transmitter and any other electronic junk they may have hidden on you."

"They have orders to give me time to talk with you." William leaned his head in one direction and then in the other, trying to see the face again.

"Okay, step in here and don't make any funny moves while I close the door behind us." The man reached for William's arm. "Get in here." He pointed his gun down the tunnel. "Move this way. Quickly."

As William moved around the man, the light caught the man's cheekbones and chin for an instant, before he felt the rigid pressure of a gun pushed into his ribs. "Not so hard," William groaned.

"Stand easy. Another gun is trained on you from down the tunnel." The man set his rifle against the wall and pulled the door with his weight leaning heavily toward William as he pushed with his legs. The door screeched against the concrete as he pulled it closed. A painful metallic groan with guttural resonance erupted from the door when it contacted its framework. The painful sound echoed down the tunnel where distant darkness swallowed it.

William's eyes fought to adjust to the meager light inside the concrete burrow. The inside simplicity of stark concrete walls and floor, and the lifeless space surprised him. A single incandescent light shed only enough tarnished light to expose the interior expanse and the path for walking. What he saw confirmed what the DPP had told him about the structure, that a military force had used it as a bunker at some point in its history. The arched concrete tunnel reached upward about fifteen feet and stretched across to more than fifteen feet at the floor. Along one of the walls, a three or four gallon fuel container was marked for diesel. The old man certainly found one hell of a secure fortification, William thought to himself.

With the door securely closed behind William, the undergrounder had just imprisoned him. The only avenue available was talking and trying to achieve the surrender. With the labored motion of a elderly citizen, the man moved past him, his steps precise but obvious in their absence of any youthful spring and rhythm, and then the man stopped and stared strangely at William, as if wondering about the next step in their encounter. The man's motion didn't match William's preconceived image of a conspirator. The man seemed rather awkward and unschooled in maneuvering his rifle, especially for a so-called underground soldier.

At last, the man stepped into the soft light, turned, and faced William. William washed his eyes casually over him, staying conscious of his facial reaction. William posted his weight on one leg, trying to appear nonthreatening. He had to take care with his choice of questions and remarks, purposeful not to excite the man into violence or suicide.

"Well, I'll give you one thing, you don't look like DPP or SACI," the man said.

"I'm not," William replied, eyebrows raised, feeling as if he were guilty of something, feeling himself shaking a little.

The man pointed his rifle down the hall toward the dark. "We're going down the hall a short distance so we can talk. You lead the way."

"That's fine." William started walking toward the shadowed area of the tunnel.

This person, who the SAC so desperately wanted, wasn't anything like an angry undergrounder with rippling muscles, and wasn't anything but an elderly man. The man's hair was mostly gray with dwindling streaks of brown. It was cut about two inches long and appeared to have miniature mountain peaks and valleys, the likely product of an unsteady hand, William guessed. The flesh of his face had sunk inward as if the water of life had drained from the muscle, and the bones of his hands had seemingly grown almost visible through a translucent film serving as skin. His years had left him with sagging skin under his neck and a valley in once youthful muscle at his chest. Leanness of his face and hands betrayed his malnourishment and his rounded shoulders not only spoke to his years but also indicated he had done hard labor at some time. William wondered if this man had escaped a labor farm. William did not see his expected ferocity and anger, even though the man stared at him with sharp and piercing eyes. He couldn't help wondering about the man's origin. How had the guy ended up in a bunker? *Do the job and get out! You don't want any trouble with the SAC.*

He couldn't relax his guard yet. Danger might wait down the tunnel. The man could fly into a rage at any point, and become an angry and unbalanced person intent on killing for the sake of making a statement. Down the hall, another meager light hung from the ceiling at the junction of a tunnel going off at a ninety-degree angle. The weapons the DPP had asked him to identify didn't seem to be anywhere, except for the rifle, but he had no reason to doubt they weren't somewhere in someone else's hands. *Vid-cams.* He couldn't see any vid-links or vid-cams, which told him the place had existed for decades or someone had cleaned it of the technology. The vid-links would have been easy to see with their monitor-screen and attached camera-eyeball. With the variety of small vid-cams used by the SAC, a person could never feel safe that one wasn't concealed somewhere.

He turned toward the man for a moment as they walked, noticing the limited range of motion of his steps and the effort the man expended. *This man is old. What harm can he be?*

"Keep walking," the man said, sounding more bored and irritated than angry.

A musty odor from the dank old bunker made its way into William's nose. The odor slowly overpowered the fresh air that had followed them from outside.

The man jabbed the gun into his back again, just above his belt. "You're slowing. Turn right here. No games and you'll stay alive. Keep moving." The man cleared his throat wretchedly, and spit off to the side.

They continued walking deeper into the bunker. The gun jabbed William's back sporadically, possibly due to the man's irregular pace. The man exhaled audibly through his nose, as if he were having difficulty breathing. William felt a different pressure on the bottom of his feet from the tunnel floor, and realized it was angling slightly downward. After several yards, they came to a metal door, some sort of blast-resistant barrier, beyond which was a dimly lighted area with a table and three chairs along the wall. Barren concrete walls and ceiling formed the inhospitable room and inadequate light.

"Stop at the table. We'll sit there."

"Okay," William replied softly, thinking the man sounded less aggressive than minutes ago.

"Say something else, will you."

William thought the man sounded as if he were searching for a clue to something. "Okay. What?"

William stood near the table, waiting for the old man's next instruction. On the wall above the small square, wood table accompanied by two chairs, hung an old calendar for the current year, 2054, and it curiously showed the month of August instead of October. On the table sat a small gray, electronic box. A short distance from the calendar a two-foot high, gray, metal box hung on the wall, looking like the enclosure for communications or electrical power breakers. He noticed a path worn into the concrete floor by the occupants, as if they were animals leaving trails in a forest. Again he smelled the unmistakable dank odor, hovering everywhere, permeating everything, and with every breath, filling his nose. A few feet from the table, down along the wall, sitting on the floor, sat three wooden crates, each about two-feet square. As he brought his gaze back to the table under the light of two dingy bulbs encased in protective wire frames up on the wall, he found words scratched crudely into the concrete: "After you give them your freedoms, they will take your soul." He wondered who was losing their soul.

Still attempting to form a picture of the man, William's gaze pursued the old man as the supposed fearsome conspirator leaned his rifle up against the wall with the challenged movements of an elderly person. The man clumsily removed a handgun from his worn canvas coat adorned with strings hanging from the sleeves and placed it gun on the table as if sending notice of a his commitment defend himself with violence. William looked at the man's build again, at trousers torn at the left thigh and, like the coat, had stay threads dangling from his cuffs onto his scarred and cracked leather boots. From the table the man picked up the small gray, electronic box, checking its meter before he flipped its switch.

The question of how this old man could threaten the SAC popped into William's thinking. Of course, he could have massive connections to people in the underground, but if so, why have a computer data manipulator get involved?

"Take the com-link out of your ear and hand it over."

William pulled the com-link plug from his left ear, and dropped it in the man's wrinkled hand, which appeared remarkably clean, especially for someone living in such a dismal place.

"Okay, hold your arms up while I sweep you for other SAC electronic snooping devices."

William raised his arms. "I'm not bugged, as far as I know."

The man moved the detection meter slowly over William's body and just as he waved it past the back of William's neck, it chirped. The man pointed a warning finger at him, lifted the collar of William's coat, and removed a black disk the diameter of a small coin. The man dropped the disk and the com-link on the floor and crushed them under his boot.

"Okay, we're going to sweep one more time." The man waved the scanner around William's body, around William's head, past William's nose, past the left ear, and then past the other.

"I don't have any implants in my skull if that's what you're looking for," William snapped indignantly.

The old man laughed satirically. "I'm surprised you don't have one of those internet computer terminals in your skull." He grinned as if he knew the secret of the ages.

"I don't think that technology has been developed completely, despite what you may have heard somehow. Besides, I don't believe in the bastardization of the human soul with technology."

"I'd say that was prudent." The man frowned and waved the signal detector over William again. "Okay, I'm not seeing any signals coming from you so I guess you're clean." He stopped, cocked his head, seemingly thinking about something, and then he smiled quizzically. "I wonder what someone would do if their blasted computer brain implant went out of order . . . on the fritz. Call a repairman. Hellfire, they quit repairing things decades ago." He laughed with a strange snort.

What a quirky old guy. William looked the man in the eye. "By the way, I didn't know that bug was there."

"I'm not surprised." The man paused, not moving his gaze. "You look . . . never mind." He shook his head as he frowned at William.

"What?" William studied the man's face in the wash of light. An unsettling impression swept through William's brain, tickling him again with the sensation that the man was familiar to him through some impossible connection. "Now that I can see your face . . . you . . . you look like someone . . . I don't know . . ." William squinted at the man. "Can you tell me your name old man?"

"Don't be preposterous. Of course, I can tell you my name. I'm not afraid of your employer. It's Henry." The man coughed, looking as if his chest was collapsing, and then he roughly wiped the corner of his mouth with the back of his hand. He gathered in a ragged breath.

William could almost feel the man's discomfort from the grimace on his worn face, which held a pain-ridden expression exceeding what should come from a trivial cold. He analyzed the voice, sending it around in his mind over and over, trying to pull back a recording filed in his brain's audio archives. Along with the voice, there was a familiar character about the man's face. He continued staring obtrusively for a moment, shot his gaze down at the floor, over at the gun on the table, and then back to the man's face. "Are you married?" William asked plainly, trying to avoid any threatening tone, as a question was forming in his brain. Suddenly, he hesitated voicing it.

"Yes, but I won't let you torture her, if she's still alive. I'll die before I give you her name."

William's gut wrenched as a collection of nebulous memories suddenly began sticking together. "Was . . . was her name Katherine?" A lump lodged in William's throat.

The man's eyes exploded with his utter shock and confusion. "My God, you're William. You're my son!" Motionless, Henry's eyes flooded with tears. "Oh my God, they've sent my own son after me—and you didn't know it. Those bastards! Those rotten bastards."

William stabbed the air with an accusing finger. "You bailed out on my mother, left her to take care of us kids and survive on our own. She had an enormous load to handle. You rotten son of a bitch." William had been thinking what he would say if he ever caught up with the old bastard and he had finally done it. A memory shot though him of the time he worshiped his father, looked up to what he did for a living. He remembered the pain that stabbed him when his father left. He remembered his father playing ball with him, working on model planes with him, and helping him with school work, but when his father ran off, those memories burned like salt in wound.

Henry clutched his mouth, his face showing utter bewilderment. "You don't know anything about the period or the circumstances that caused me to leave the family." His head sank as he brushed away tears on his cheek. "I had to protect Katherine and you kids. God, I loved my family and it ripped out my heart to leave like I did, but I had to. They would have killed all of us. I couldn't let them kill my family. I had to leave, to cut myself off from you guys, and go into hiding." He sobbed into his fist, his eyes closing as his brow wrinkled in anguish. His voice fell to a murmur.

"I'm so sorry. I never intended any of it. The government fabricated events and charges so they could issue a criminal indictment. I became a threat to the government. I never did anything illegal. My only crime was that I knew things and I believed in something called the Constitution." He looked up at William. "Never! I never did anything illegal." His chest shuddered. "I never wanted to leave you."

"You've been here all those years?"

The man nodded, the lines on his face hanging in a sorrowful apology.

William shook his head side-to-side, unable to believe the old man, unable to break with the bitterness that had festered inside him for years. "I don't understand." William looked at him, wondering what he should do, what he should say, other than cursing the man. "I feel like beating the shit out of you."

"I can understand. Go ahead if it will make you feel better. I'm too old to bother fighting."

William shook his head disgustedly, disappointed he was losing his anger and ferocity, something he'd cultivated for years. He had used his hatred to feed his ambition and drive to take care of his own family. Seeing this man tired and worn sent his mind swirling in a wind of confusion. Like rising sun, William realized he needed to know the reason behind the man's abandonment, the man's story, told by the man he had hated for years, even if it might be a lie. But why would it be a lie now?

"Come over here to the table and sit down," Henry said, sounding out of breath, the softness of his tone conveying hopefulness for the opportunity.

William looked at him bitterly, stubbornly, fighting with himself to remain defiant. "I'm supposed to collect you for the SAC and the DPP force waiting outside. Remember?" Remarkably, those words tasted sour in his mouth as he realized he needed information from a capsule of time, answers that only this man could provide, and the answers he might lose forever.

Henry gestured toward an old wooden chair. "Please sit. Please. I'll tell you everything."

Section Head, Karl Steinhoff spun around in his chair and straightened his tie that dangled down his baggy white shirt. He faced the three-foot by two-foot gray vid-link screen on the wall behind him in his Washington, SAC office. He took excessive pride in his second floor office of SAC Building Two. Without thinking, he drew his mouth into a determined line. "Vid-link on," he said mechanically, barely containing his agitation. He folded his arms on his chest as he draped his right leg over the left. He rocked his right foot up and down in place like a metronome, knowing he had to keep his nerves under control in front of his field people at the other end of the vid-link connection. The DPP field operations bothered him. He hated his dependency on his team of protectors. He saw them as nothing more than crude and unreliable instruments made to fit into precision situations. This operation was vital. He could not allow the opportunity within his grasp to slip away, not if he was to maintain favorable consideration by his boss, Kauffman.

"Vid-link, ready," a monotone computer-generated voice replied.

"Call, Captain Rogers."

After a moment, a scratchy noise, as if someone were shuffling papers, emerged from the vid-link. "Sound available only," the computer voice stated.

"This is Captain Rogers, sir."

Steinhoff cleared his throat with a short burst of breath. "Captain Rogers, has the operation commenced?"

"Sir, say again. The communications is acting strange."

"Operation status."

"Sir, the operation is underway. Manager Rinehart has walked up the mountain road and has entered the bunker with one of the conspirators."

"Very good, Captain," Steinhoff said, sounding as if his comment was conditional. "Captain."

"Yes, sir."

"This is a no fail operation. Make certain you bring the conspirator back alive."

"Sir, are you aware Manager Rinehart may be in danger of being shot?"

"Make certain the conspirator comes back alive. If Rinehart is injured, we'll deal with it. He's expendable—the conspirator is not. Make certain to give him time to negotiate with the people in the bunker."

"Yes, sir."

"Vid-link off," Steinhoff said angrily. He turned around, facing his desk, a subtle calculating smile creeping over his mouth. He rested his lean angular frame back in his chair, feeling its powerful embrace, as if it were one of his weapons the hierarchy of the SAC had given him. Behind his desk, his personal command center, he orchestrated lives of the worker class with his DPP.

He ran a hand back over his coal-black hair, verifying its smoothness and that it laid perfectly in place, maintaining his image in case directors or other executives called him on the vid-link or were spying on him from a hidden vid-cam. He held his left elbow in his right hand, pulling his gaunt cheeks between his thumb and forefinger, stretching his face slightly before releasing. He ran scenarios of situations and opportunities around in his head, squinting his steel-gray eyes past his boney nose and off across his office, wondering about the identity of the conspirator. He wondered what would happen when Rinehart came home and they interrogated him. Maybe he'd talk to someone he shouldn't and then he could be charged with a crime against the State. He went back in his mind to those first days with the SAC, competing against Rinehart. *Rinehart is done.* "Vid-link on," he said, snapping his chair around so he could face the vid-link screen on the wall.

"Vid-link, ready."

"Call DPP Coordination Center, Protector Sergeant Rooney."

A uniformed man appeared on the screen. "Sergeant Rooney, sir."

"Sergeant Rooney, I want electronic surveillance set up on Manager William Rinehart's home, and an invisible observation established on everyone in the family."

"Children too?"

"Yes."

"Very good sir. If you can give me a moment I'll . . . sir."

"Yes."

"Section Head, I'm finding a previous order in the computer for surveillance."

"Who requested it?" Steinhoff snapped, before remembering to moderate his tone, in case a section of SACI had him under their view.

"Sir, it has been in place for four years and the authorizing person is listed as secret.

"Very well, arrange for a review of procedures and add one more protector to the detail.

"Very good, sir."

"Vid-link off." Steinhoff turned slowly toward his desk, thinking he had Rinehart right where he wanted him. He squeezed the arm of his chair, as if he were squeezing Rinehart's neck, but quickly released his grip, remembering that eyes could be watching him right there in his office.

Chapter 2

Henry stood motionless and silent, seemingly searching William with glassy-eyed amazement. He gestured at the chair again, waiting for William to remove the chair and sit before he would drop his hand. He smiled hesitantly, as if fearing he'd enrage William. "Please sit, William. Please."

William frowned at the old man, moving his hand to the back of the chair.

"It looks as if you're taller than me, maybe six feet, but with those muscular shoulders you're built like your grandfather," Henry said, lightly, pride filling his eyes. "He was a big man with massive hands and big chest, although your chest isn't as bulky. Just as well, you don't want to be too heavy. Can I see your hands?"

"I think my shoulders are average. Actually, I'm five-eleven." William pulled back the bruised and faded wood chair, and slowly eased himself down onto its edge. Uncertain how to react, other than with the rage he had cultivated for years, he directed his eyes toward the stained and worn table surface. *Calm yourself. You have to talk with his man.* He held out his hands palms up, resting them on the table.

"Yeah, just like your grandfather, big hands . . . I mean long fingers. But, I think you have your mother's rounded chin. It's a firm chin, not a weak one. You look like you mean business."

William shrugged and rubbed his hands together. He feared what the SAC would say if he wasn't tough enough. He opened his coat, and rubbed his cold nose with the back of his hand. The way the man regarded him with eyes sagging at the corners, as if he were beaten down, made William wonder again, why the SAC considered this man dangerous or valuable. Now, in the light, such as it was, William detected gentleness in the man's face and a soft character begging him to listen. He couldn't remember many details from when he was twelve, except that his father always seemed patient and had never yelled at him. He was never afraid of his father punishing him, because his father had a nurturing way of talking to him and his sister.

William's eye ran to the gun on the table, and then to a small wooden box turned on end next to the wall that held six books. He quickly read their spines: *Constitutional Law: Principles and Policy, Cases and Materials, Writings of Marcus Aurelius, Works of William Shakespeare, The Bible, The Gulag Archipelago, and Albert Einstein's Theory of Relativity.*

The old man grinned at William. He steadied himself with a hand on the table and studied William. "Your face has some of the character from when you were twelve but it's really changed, definitely in the eyes, and you've got the Rinehart, German and English ancestry in your face. You have your mother's narrow nose instead of a big thing like mine. Your voice sounds a little like your mother's with that breathy ending on your words. Your face is somewhat oval, like your mother's face. Your green eyes are also like your mother's and they are as clever as hers are, sharp and moving, picking up details as if they analyze things before sending data off to the brain. But your hair took after me. I used to have my hair cut a little longer than yours is cut, so I could use a comb. Mine was actually blond when I was young and then it became darker brown. You turned into a handsome man, your good looks obviously coming from your mom." He grinned. His eyes grew glassy for a moment and then he swallowed with pronounced difficulty. He became still, not just in body, but his eyes became motionless, as if he were suddenly massaging and analyzing data in his mind. He wet his lower lip as a tentative expression formed on his face. "I knew there was something else . . . something I was trying to remember, but I couldn't put my finger on it until just this minute." He nodded, almost to himself. "You still look like honesty searching for an answer to the world's questions or seeking to drill into a question for the honesty of truth."

William flashed his eyebrows and fought back a smile. "I don't know about the hair. The SAC has rules on hair." He looked down the tunnel into the darkness. "You're here all alone?"

Henry squinted, which was like a confirming momentary look, before turning from William's face. "Yes, I'm quite alone. Been alone for more damn years than I care to count. It's a wonder I haven't gone totally loony."

"What do you eat?"

"When they built this place they stocked it with rations to feed at least hundred people for four months. When Adam Haggerty and I arrived we thought we'd found heaven, but the variety is horrible. So to add variety we would go out and gather pine nuts and some wild things."

"Where's Adam now?"

"He died about four years into our stay. I think it was cancer. He was a great friend. I could have gone nutty when he died, but I had a duty."

"Okay, dammit," William snapped, "I want to know why you left home."

Henry's brow arched wearily. "Here's what happened to our family." He drew a slow breath and sighed. "I left you in 2028. You were twelve. God, you were a great kid, curious as hell though, taking stuff apart, hooking things together, and very creative. You talked about dinosaurs, planes, and of all things, people like George Washington, Lincoln, and Eisenhower, all amazing heroes for a twelve-year-old." He looked off in the distance. "When you were small we couldn't get you to drink much milk and we worried about your bones, but I guess it wasn't a problem. In your early school years, the teachers worried about you paying attention in class, but you always got your work done and even got excellent grades. Your sister . . . Mary Louise was nine. She was the sweetest, singing all the time, and fantastic at drawing flowers and bugs and houses. God, I loved playing with you kids. I still see your faces at night, your bright eyes and puffy full cheeks, just as you were, as if you were frozen in time. In my dreams, you're still twelve and Mary Louise is still nine. I can't tell you how many times I've cried about not being there with all of you, but they would have killed all of us if I hadn't left."

"Mary Louise is dead . . . killed five years ago."

"I know, son. I heard. Through my channels. It came in one of my last communications. The SAC killed her."

"That's not true. She was sick and had a reaction to medicine."

Henry dropped his head. "My connections told me she was working with people from the underground. At the time, she worked for a food distribution section of SAC. Louise and another person in her office got into SAC secret files. She printed off Durand's ten-year plan, including their ideas for Bruner's takeover as Chairman. The document exposed their plans to implant every person in the country with an electronic device that could be used for tracking, mental control, and termination." Henry stopped, sighed almost imperceptibly. He studied William. "William, they plan to control people's minds, people's thoughts, people's emotions, the very soul that makes us human."

"She did work at the food distribution section, but . . ."

"She was a fighter. The SAC traced the computer access to her colleague and they tortured him for a month until he confessed her name. She was so idealistic. God bless her. Before they picked her up the SAC watched her drop off a package for her contact. He also belonged to the underground group. He swallowed his cyanide capsule before they could use him to drill deeper into the underground organization."

"You've been hiding in this bunker too long," William barked. "That's bullshit!" *There can be only one truth!*

The man looked up at William solemnly. "How do you reconcile men like Lincoln, Jefferson, and Adams with someone like Adrian Durand? When was the last time you saw what the country is like outside the city?"

"Times have changed. We all belong to the collective family."

"Bullshit. The moral reason to do what is right doesn't change with the times. Are you willing to listen to the truth, willing to hear the real history? Are you willing to use an open mind, or are you going to be just another SAC stooge, listening to their programming bullshit? The SAC has stolen your freedoms and turned you into a slave?"

"I'm not a slave." The words came out of William's mouth automatically, as if his brain were detached, but he didn't really believe them.

"Really? From the look on your face and the tone of your words, I'd say you are scared everyday you walk out the door. Do they still send people of to the labor camps?"

"Why should I listen to more of your historical fantasy? Frankly, I'm not interested and I don't have time. You are to surrender to the SACI."

"Listen to me you dumb ass. Back before the country turned to shit, you could go to a grocery store and buy white bread, brown bread, grape jelly, fresh strawberries, or peaches, or oranges, on any day of the week. What do you have now? When I was a kid, we had Sunday dinners with the grandparents, sometimes with fried chicken and mashed potatoes with gravy. In school, we would say the pledge of allegiance to the flag of the United States of America and not to the leader of the country, now called State America. History in school was real history, not buttered over propaganda created to make the State America Committee sound good. We learned about the real people who built the country, not the striped-down version highlighting only members of the old NFP. You could take a drive out in the country on a Sunday afternoon, just to see the trees and smell the air, or go for an ice cream cone. We took a few drives when you were toddler jabbering in barely coherent phrases. People could even sit on their asses and watch any number of sports on television, which came before the vid-net you watch now. Tell me if you can, do any of those things now . . . please! You're lucky to avoid being arrested for thinking negative thoughts about the SAC."

"Tell me why you left."

"Answer my question first."

William knew the answer but couldn't get it off his tongue. "You still haven't told me why you ran off."

"I said I'd tell you everything." Henry took in a tired breath. "Hopefully, if you listen, I'll save your life." His voice dropped to a whisper. ". . . and this country."

"What?" William demanded, sitting up on the edge of his chair. *Please, no more trouble.* He just wanted to get this over and go back to his family.

"Nothing." Henry gazed off at nothing, and then down at the table, his eyes now gravely heavy, as if a weight pulled at them, and something had taken life from his aged cheeks. He raised his eyes to William as if the gesture could hammer his coming message. "Don't you want to know why you were sent here to capture me? They're using you! Can't you see it? It's because of my past, who I knew—and what I know."

Competing voices buzzed in William's head, voices of SAC compliance, and voices urging freedom of thought, and then a voice urging safety for his family. Perhaps he could compromise, even though he had been doing that for years. "Okay, old man, but time is short," William replied tiredly. "I can't be here very long or the guns will come. Besides, how do I know you're telling the truth?"

"I have nothing to gain by lying. Why would I lie to my own son? You can't do anything for me. I need for you to hear how I was ripped from your life."

"That seems logical." William wanted to hear that explanation more than anything he could ever hear. He had spent his life trying to answer that question.

"I have to believe that every day you surrender a little bit of your soul. As the years go by it must to chew into your sanity and swallow you."

"I know my place. I know I'm no more significant than one more potato on a truck from a government farm bound for a city food distribution center."

"You aren't alone. There are millions of other hopeless faces, sharing the hateful taste of being controlled by the SAC."

"Stop it. Every citizen-comrade must believe in the SAC. Wrong thoughts, wrong mind, bad thoughts, no bad mind of any kind!"

"Listen to yourself. You're sick. That's a form of brainwashing."

"No more of this vulgarity."

Henry pressed his hands together in front of his face as if making a prayer, sliding them over each other for a moment as he slowly sent his eyes from William's face to the table. "But first, how is Katherine?" Henry's voice came out thick as he began to choke.

"She's doing fairly well, although she refuses to move in with us, even if I could make it happen. We communicate by mail and I think the SAC is checking our letters. I've asked her several times about coming to live with us. I don't understand how she got there, but she's in an SAC housing unit for non-working seniors up in Carlisle, Pennsylvania. She's being fed okay. I don't know about medical care. She hates the SAC section meetings where they are required to sort and cut clothes for recycling. She says she misses us. I can't get permission to drive to see her. She's saddened by working on the clothes."

Henry winced. "You know why she's not in one of those hell holes for older people?" He glared at William. "She's married to me. The government criminals think there's a chance I'll try to see her or communicate with her."

"What?"

"I'll get to it in a minute." His shoulders sank. "She's okay?"

"Yes. I think so. They are allowed free access to a walking path for seniors."

"She's not a senior."

"She's a senior by the current guidelines. I haven't heard from her for a month or two."

"As long as I'm alive she will probably be okay."

William cocked his head to one side not wanting to agree.

Henry grinned. "How's her health?"

"She says it's pretty good, although she confesses her memory might be slipping a little."

"She needs to do puzzles or something," Henry said. "I really miss her. I wish to hell I could see her again, one more time."

"Maybe you can see her when you come with me."

"You don't really believe that and I sure as hell know that would never happen."

"Oh, I don't know," William said hesitantly, realizing he wasn't fooling the old man.

"First things first. We should go back to the outer door, yell down to the creeping infestation of yours, and tell them we're talking about my surrender. Maybe it'll buy some time."

"Why should I?"

"I thought we resolved that question." Henry cast a disgusted frown at him. "You don't have anything to lose. If you want to be pissed at me the rest of your life it's fine with me, but knowing your mother, she probably told you to use your brains. And frankly, if you don't give a fair evaluation to what I have to say, she'd be disappointed. She was always a very bright lady, nearly a perfect four-point in economics at Vanderbilt. Did you know that?"

"Yeah, I think I did." He sighed tiredly, his eyes closing for a second. "You haven't given me much of a reason to keep listening. I have to assume you did something bad, else you wouldn't be here."

"Like I said, dammit, I will tell you things that just may save your life."

"Like what? Save my life from what?"

"From the government for God sakes . . . from your slavery."

"Yeah, yeah." William smirked, but it was as much at himself for not acknowledging his agreement. "There's nothing you can tell me I don't know, and you can't save me from the government." Suddenly, William was afraid to hear the old man's revelation—and he feared what the SAC might do if he did. "I can't even save my family. No one can save the country now!"

The old man looked toward the outer door, pushed himself up with the help of a hand on the tabletop, took a step, and then turned to William. "I suppose you already know you're a pompous ass—although I think I might see a twinge of concern in your eyes. So maybe there's some hope for you." He paused. "Get up. We're going to the outer door."

William rolled his eyes disgustedly as he stood. He followed the old man to the outer door, where the man threw back the bolts and began leaning against the door, trying to push it open. Seeing the old man barely

47

moving the monstrous door, William felt a twinge of shame for standing there and not helping. He stepped up to the door. "Okay, get out of the way old man."

"Bullshit, it's my door."

William laughed under his breath and leaned with both hands against the door, joining the old man, the two of them pushing the door, sending screeching echoes down the tunnel again.

William stuck his head into the doorway and yelled, "Captain, I need more time. The underground person . . . he's telling me important information before he surrenders. Please hold your positions. Do you hear me?" Nothing moved as far as William could see, but he knew they were still there. They were always there, just like the SACI and vid-cams. "Captain, please give me a confirmation."

A distant ghostly voice drifted through the trees, "Affirmative."

William pulled the door closed. "Okay, old man. This has to be fast. They won't wait long before they try to blow their way in here."

"I'll go as fast as I can."

William followed the old man back down the dingy tunnel to the small table. They sat as before, William staring at the old man as if waiting for an invisible barrier to come down between them, feeling a little confused, feeling pressure to complete his SAC orders, but telling himself he needed to listen for his family's sake. *Wrong thoughts, wrong mind, bad thoughts, no bad mind of any kind!* He had to be careful. He couldn't allow the SAC see him capitulating to a conspirator. He wondered how long he would have to listen before they could leave. He folded his arms on his chest, leaning back in his chair, waiting. "What will help my family?"

The old man's eyes fluttered tiredly as he dropped his head, and sighed. "I'm excited and pleased my last bit of time is being spent with my son, one of my true joys on this earth. I couldn't ask for a more appropriate person to receive this chronicle, to carry it on to others. However, I do have a wish . . . really two wishes. Call them last requests, if you will."

William frowned. "What?"

"First, you should do a little research and try to learn how the government evolved into a monster that destroyed our freedoms. You need to know how you became a slave. I know they have indoctrinated you over the years, and most likely, the information I will tell you will seem like poison to your brain. You need to fight the poison. You your logic."

"Doing research is impossible. The books that still exist are controlled and all have been revised by the SAC. I can't even drive into the countryside with my little car. No one can. People who have managed to get out into the country are quickly shipped off to a labor camp."

Henry shrugged painfully. "I know a lot of records and books have been altered and are destroyed, but give it a try. You're resourceful. You are your mother's child. She was wonderful at research. She could find anything on the old internet or in a library."

"And second?"

"The other is to remember two things. Remember, man must exist for his own sake, not forfeiting himself to others or asking others to yield their interests to him. It's freedom! You are a free man." He stopped as if suddenly deeply troubled. "I hate to tell you what I have to tell you, but the country is nearly dead. Maybe someone like you can save it. Remember, what we want is frequently right under our nose—things like freedom."

"Huh . . . wait."

"I hope and pray it will benefit you in the future. That's all I can say."

"Okay, give me something I can try to verify, to prove you're not spouting lies. Although, this is a wasted gesture. I probably won't be able to check what you say."

"The death started with the systematic attack on the freedom of speech by the National Freedom Party, the NFP, and the president of the United States. Then a poisonous rain of fraudulent votes poured over the country, giving the NFP control of the elections. Along with freedom of speech, they attacked the second amendment right to keep and bear arms, making it illegal to own a gun. This prevented armed revolution against them. These may not sound like much but by controlling information, the NFP manipulated truth and told the public whatever fabrications they wanted. They covered up their corruption, had complete disregard for the constitution, and because theirs was the only party in control they couldn't be impeached from office."

William jumped in. "What's wrong with controlling speech? The SAC does that now. There are no protests. Like said before, they read our letters."

Henry shook his head. "Research the year 2007 and review history for the following years, and then you should be able to confirm that I'm not a drooling old fool. This is probably all esoteric compared to your world, but it's the beginning of their control and our loss of freedom. I'm sorry this is boring and tedious. And just as I see your eyes glassing over now, the public's eyes glassed over then. The public gave little attention to the piecemeal demise of their freedoms."

"What you ask is impossible and, by the way, merely reading such material will get me sent to a labor camp."

"I know how bad it is," Henry replied, closing his eyes and sighing. "You have no freedom." Henry paused for a moment and then he arched his brow. "Come to think of it, I have a book you can take and read. I can't believe I didn't remember it until now. It doesn't enumerate the causes of the country's collapse in an unbiased view like the one I have recorded in my writings but it will help. You must take the book."

"No, no, I couldn't."

"You can hide it."

"I can't, I'll be sent to a labor camp. You don't live out there with the vid-cams."

"A lot of what I'm going to tell you is based on events that slowly destroyed the country."

"Dammit, I can't read that material. They'll find out. They have vid-cams everywhere."

"Do you have any guts at all?" Henry asked as he got up, sounding more disappointed than angry. He walked over to a wooden crate by the wall, fumbled through newspapers and books, returned to the table and pushed a book in front of William. "Take this. Hide it in your pants and read it when you get home. If they catch you, you can always claim you collected it for the SAC."

William looked at him, not knowing what to say. "I have a family that I have to protect."

"When the government controls your voice or the media, they control you. If people with opinions contrasting with the government can't express those opinions, the government controls what you learn, and what you know—and ultimately what you believe. They control your mind like they are doing now. You must see that! That's what happened many years ago. You must read about the past to understand the present."

William grimaced and shook his head. "I don't know. Damn! I want to, but it's risky."

"I know it's hard. But at least take the book."

"Okay, I'll take the book."

"Thank you. Just try to read it," Henry said softly. "Now you must clear your mind."

The solemn cast in the man's face warned William again that the information he might receive could place his life danger. Knowing the secrets behind the SAC power was not allowed. It was obvious to him now, the SACI and its Director Helmut Kauffman wanted the vital information in this man's brain. What a contemptible trick to send him to fetch his father. Obviously, the SACI figured the son would have the best chance to collect the man alive. The SAC task with which they had drafted him had transmuted into a torture at the outlying region of his thinking, a conflict of his State indoctrination and programming with fierce survival needs, with the opportunity for retribution for sins against his mother, and with a basal compassion for a fellow human.

"What in the hell did you do that made you such a high priority target for the SAC."

"I'll answer that question. It's related to what I just told you."

William drilled his gaze at the man, tortured by the mystery.

Chapter 3

Section Head Karl Steinhoff's office had a windowless purity, which was part of the security design, but now, as he frequently did, he sat in solitude strategizing with only the light from a desk lamp. It seemed to close out the world, but he knew he wasn't alone. No one was ever alone. The lamp, not quite illuminating the gray walls around him, carved out a pocket of light. He stretched out his legs, resting his feet against the interior wall of his desk. He spread his fingers over his face and pulled them downward over his cheeks. He had been envisioning how events would play out under his control. He identified situations that would reward him with visibility. He had to become more trusted in the eyes of Chairman Durand and Director Kauffman. The next position could be a directorship. Each member of his staff under him was his tool and his pawn. He envisioned how to move them across the SAC chessboard under his deft and usually surreptitious manipulation. *I need to know what's going on down there on that mountain.*

It had been around thirty minutes since he called Captain Rogers. *Why haven't I gotten an update from the operations force?* Perhaps he would have to move someone to a labor camp to set an example.

He tilted his chair back, holding his hands palm-to-palm at his chin. The most pressing event tumbled in his mind. Important assignments were like food for him and he consumed them with a carnivore's relish. This assignment carried the weight necessary for high visibility and an effective demonstration of managing a high-level responsibility. He had hungered for assignments such as the one on the mountain. The current operation was a critical information gathering campaign with no room for mistakes. Director Kauffman would be greatly displeased if it turned out poorly. Getting on Kauffman's bad side wasn't something he wanted to face.

He laughed to himself. It was ironic, he had finally gotten a chance to get even with William Rinehart, supervising a mission utilizing Rinehart, sending him into harm's way to capture a conspirator, and yet he couldn't allow him to get killed, at least not until the conspirator had been secured. He needed Rinehart to accomplish his task. It was strange how Rinehart had been a thorn in his ass ever since the SAC entry testing and their employment at a manager level under Herbert Vogel doing finance work, just after starting with SAC. He remembered how people had liked Rinehart and they had not liked him. The hatred of the situation had fired him to do whatever was necessary to win. What really made him feel like shooting Rinehart was how the bastard out performed him during entry tests. He laughed to himself.

In the end, it didn't mean anything. He remembered laughing at Rinehart. *Yes, Mr. Rinehart, brains didn't mean a damn thing.* SAC administrators taunted candidates with the performance of their competitors to cause dissention and unrest, and they made a special point to tell him Rinehart was better than he was. The SAC selected him precisely because he tested behind Rinehart. When they told him of their goal, building loyalty to the inner SAC, he understood, but had considered the system strange. And— he could give a shit about proper thought. Regardless, he was willing to play their game. He laughed under his breath. It was all a game and he knew how to play. *Remember the vid-cam is watching.*

Thinking of the game he played reminded him of more bitterness of his youth, playing with imaginary people to survive the place where he lived—a lifeless depository for children. He hated his life within a children services group. The bitch who ran the place on the outer edge of Hartford, Connecticut, had her favorites, kids who would run and blab about the slightest offense, and kids she loved to punish. She took every opportunity to punish the ones she disliked, whether the person was guilty or innocent. *Just like the SAC. She pulled my hair so many times.* He remembered it hurt like hell. He wanted to cut it off so she couldn't grab it, but she would have beaten him for that, too.

He could still see the bitch if he closed his eyes, a round-faced chubby woman, with too much red rouge on her cheeks and short brown hair that seemed pasted to her head in strings. Of course, he had been guilty as much as the biggest of the bullies. He recalled how he had learned at an early age, how to send his mind away as the yardstick cracked against his back, promising to himself with every blow to get even someday. That he did. He grinned. He had fixed the old bitch good.

He saw himself working in the kitchen washing dishes. One day his chance came. His job in the kitchen turned from being a chore to an opportunity when the cook went shopping for supplies one day. In a separate pan on the stove, he cooked something he knew little about. He dropped his surprise into the old witch's bowl of soup on the way to the dining table. He was naively amazed how well his recipe worked. It wasn't until later he learned more about castor beans. It was strange how he had gotten the idea one day when he was outside in the back lawn where he learned the beans were poisonous. The authorities questioned the cook and eventually arrested him for the crime. Two children sealed his fate by reporting they had heard him complaining about his pay. The plan had worked amazingly well. It seemed to fade into a blur after two years and he had departed the hellhole for college. He'd almost forgotten about what was going on in the world in his early college years, except he'd gotten into college free under a government program, which the government eventually discontinued. He got his business degree and pushed away memories of his childhood without parents.

He gazed into the shadows toward the door to his office. He couldn't wait to see Rinehart's report on the mission collecting the conspirator. The corners of his mouth curled a little from the thought of placing Rinehart under the caustic SAC scrutiny where a stumble would be disastrous. He wondered if Rinehart had progressed past the naive misconception about the SAC operating as a logical machine. Based on what he'd read of Rinehart's file, it looked as if the well-educated manager was still blind to events, policies, and the SAC's manipulation of the people? He laughed to himself. Rinehart's flawless record indicated a man trying to maintain favor with the SAC and survive. Perhaps he really was aware of the true nature of their world—and was scared like millions of other people. Time reveal that story.

He looked down at his desk, at his book-size computer consisting of a horizontal paper-thin panel. The panel computer lying on the desk displayed columns of numbers but didn't see any data on DPP operation status. He stared at it contemptuously for not having any update. He checked the time on the computer. He should have had an update by now. His DPP force had always carried out orders to the letter. He liked to think of them as unfed and mistreated wild animals, each one eager to chew on a piece of citizen-meat. He rubbed his hands together, noticing his perspiration. He laughed to himself about his eagerness.

When his DPP force got back from the mountain with the conspirator, he was certain Director Kauffman would take the man to SACI headquarters for debriefing, and immediately inform the three Vice Chairmen and Chairman Durand. He could see Kauffman's stern angular face, see him brushing his salt and pepper mustache with the same finger he always passed over it, and could see the diabolical curl forming at the corner of his mouth before pronouncing a stern decision. He wanted that job.

If only he could become part of the briefing process, he could capture more exposure with the chairmen and directors. The conspirator's interrogation would be crucial. He needed to be involved. If he could listen to the important information, which with all the resources expended to acquire it, was a chunk of golden knowledge that would feed his image. It had to be something seriously vital for Kauffman to be so involved. He wondered if there was information on an underground military or a failure in the SAC system. The only protocols used heretofore for criminals had been the hunt and kill procedures, unlike this live-capture operation. Why in the hell was this person so important? What was the intelligence in the man's brain? It irritated him, not knowing. Kauffman had insulted him. Someone should have filled him in on the details. Information was power.

He leaned back in his chair, bringing his hands together, sliding his fingers between each other, folding them in a confident mesh. "Yes," he whispered, thinking about his opportunity.

He would pressure his people to make certain his DPP operations force did its job and reported all intelligence to him. If his people failed, he could find himself in one of Kauffman's little gray rooms answering questions until his eyeballs were burnt by a white light controlled by Kauffman's specialist, Doctor Conrad Beucher. Kauffman would not tolerate a failure in securing such an apparently valuable person, one certainly destined to occupy Doctor Beucher's intelligence extraction chair.

A faint glow flickered off the walls as a soft chime sounded from the vid-link behind him. "Section Head Steinhoff, this is Captain Rogers at Roan Mountain."

"Go ahead, Captain," Steinhoff replied as he swiveled around to the vid-link screen, this time showing a flickering fuzzy image of a protector's head.

"Sir, we are holding cover while Manager Rinehart completes his debriefing and negotiations with the target."

Steinhoff stared at the screen, initially irritated, and then he concluded the operation still held full potential. He hoped Rogers was one of his more competent assets. "Captain Rogers," Steinhoff replied coolly. "This operation was an extraction, not an opportunity for declaration of complaints. We want the conspirators. They must be brought in for interrogation—and alive!"

"Yes, sir."

"How many people are in the fortification? What kind of weapons do they have?"

"Sir, we don't know. Manager Rinehart did not brief us. His com-link quit sending. The bug you ordered placed on him has also become inoperable or was destroyed."

"How do we know Rinehart hasn't been killed?"

"Sir, Manager Rinehart stuck his head through the door of the bunker a few minutes ago and yelled his status to us. He advised us to stand as we were and that he was getting some information from the undergrounder before the person would surrender."

"His voice could have been fabricated."

"True, sir, but I'm confident it was genuine."

"How long have they been talking?"

"Sir, about fifteen minutes."

"Give them ten minutes more." He hesitated, thinking of the potential for problems. "Then approach the bunker. Use force if you have to. Do not kill the target."

"I'll check back," Steinhoff barked. "Get me results and get me answers. Vid-link, off."

No sooner than Steinhoff ended his call, the vid-link on the wall chimed again and a man with a stern face appeared, wearing a gray uniform, and standing behind a podium. "This is an announcement for SAC staff only. Message begins after sixty seconds to facilitate removal of non-secure personnel." An animated clock appeared on the screen with a sweeping second hand and after a few seconds, the man reappeared. "The SAC military has moved fifty thousand troops into the western Pakistan area in a joint operation with the Russian Socialist Union forces. This cooperative operation is part of State America's agreed support as part of the last nuclear missile reduction treaty with the RSU. The operation is to preempt an estimated one hundred thousand troops from the Muslim Brotherhood-Al Qaeda coalition for Jihad, the MBAQJ forces, from overrunning Afghanistan. State America and the RSU believe the MBAQJ forces are using Afghanistan as a staging area to invade a southern region of the RSU. They are believed to have at least two tactical nuclear weapons launchable from trucks. The casualties incurred had followed the statistical projections. Discussions with the RSU on biological agent dispersal have been rescheduled. All executives are to follow the usual disclosure protocols for subordinate staff and non-SAC citizen-comrades. No fatalities are to be acknowledged as usual for all foreign campaigns. Chairman Durand will do so if he deems it appropriate. The SAC will make a public announcement this evening on national vid-net. May the SAC and Chairman Durand preserve State America." The vid-link screen went gray as static, white noise, continued spilling into the office until the vid-link connection completely died.

Steinhoff decided he'd forget about the announcement. He didn't expect to talk with anyone in the next two hours. It was just another one of those operations, an SACI concocted diversion, he told himself. A meat-grinder to help with population control. *Why in the hell do we have to help the RSU? Well, on second thought, they still have first-strike capability, and they do help keep the Chinese off balance.* He remembered and old cliché? The enemy of my enemy is my friend.

The vid-link screen flickered and chimed.

The image Steinhoff saw surprised him. The mustached face of Helmut Kauffman, Director of the Department of State American

Protection (DSAP), filled the screen, the man directly in charge of the intelligence division, SACI, and to whom he reported on the daily operation of his DPP. He sat up as he straightened his necktie. *Control your facial and body movements.* In Kauffman's presence, he was always aware of his body and reactions, controlling himself, suspicious of what lurked behind Kaufmann's silent countenance, remembering the SAC's chief intelligence man's background in psychology and counterintelligence. He could see it in Kauffman's eyes, in their constant evaluation of his every word, gesture, eye movement, and even his respiration rate.

"Ah, good day, Karl," Kauffman said, his tone carrying a surprised inflection. He ran a finger across his salt and pepper mustache, as his black bullet eyes shot harshly out of his longish, rectangular head, as if shooting out from the screen like a light beam directed at Steinhoff. The old man of six-five still could send his fury Steinhoff noted as he felt Kauffman's full evaluation.

Steinhoff doubted if Kauffman was surprised and he was almost willing to bet a year's food coupons that the intelligence sleuth knew all his habits, including his comings and goings, and even how many times he and his wife had made love in bed. Steinhoff flashed his eyebrows and leaned forward, looking up at the vid-screen, trying to look eager. "How can I help you, sir?" Steinhoff asked, his words flavored with an energetic modulation. *Control facial muscles. You must be pleasant but businesslike.*

"I'm concerned about the conspirator in North Carolina. The person down there is extremely important to our intelligence effort and Chairman Durand. Our background information on this man indicates he has been in hiding longer than any of the original undergrounders."

Steinhoff cleared his throat as he rested his elbows on the arms of his chair and clasped his hands together. He studied Kauffman's face for any neuro-lingusitic signals. Even if he was a little nervous, he had to show his awareness and control. "I just talked with the protector in charge. The DPP operations force is waiting and watching. Manager Rinehart has been talking with the underground conspirator for about fifteen minutes, tying to get him to surrender peacefully. I advised our forces to approach in another ten minutes."

"No! Dammit." Kauffman's snapped uncharacteristically, shaking his head violently, firing his eyes at the vid-link. "I don't want anything exacerbating the situation. No gunfire whatsoever. I want this undergrounder captured alive. He has vital information. Vital! Alive! No failure on this."

Karl tried to conceal swallowing hard. He asked with calm. "What intelligence does this person possess that merits such priority and scrutiny? Is he connected with other underground groups?"

"I cannot share that information outside SACI. I mean no disrespect, especially since you do an excellent job running DPP for me, and it's no reflection on your security level either. You are one of the best administrators in my division. I can foresee you moving into a director position someday. But please make certain this happens. I want you to personally control the situation."

"Yes, sir." Karl paused. "What about Manager Rinehart position in this situation?"

"Yes. I can see it in your face. He's to be supported as much as possible, but not at the expense of the conspirator. He is expendable, but only if the situation dictates such action."

"Sir, why was Rinehart chosen for this operation?"

"Very well, I will share that detail with you. The conspirator in the bunker is Rinehart's father. You should know—we have been watching all of Rinehart's family for years, ever since we learned his father was involved with the underground many years ago. After the father disappeared, we continued watching William's family. Rinehart was brought into the SAC and given his position just so we could watch him."

Steinhoff fought a smile as a voice in his head screamed at him to hold a stone face.

"I thought you'd like that little touch," Kauffman continued, his head bobbing a little with his amusement.

"Understood, sir," Karl replied, pleased tremendously, but angry with himself for the facial signals he had sent Kauffman about his satisfaction. "Sir, may I suggest that we continue watching the wife and children after the operation has concluded."

"Feel free to add or adjust the monitoring we established years ago anyway you wish, but please work with my SACI, as they have already established routines, as I believe you have learned. Your additional oversight shouldn't be a problem. Please work with them."

"Yes, sir."

"Thank you for personally insuring the success of this operation."

"Thank you, sir." Steinhoff didn't like Kauffman's tone. There was an unspoken threat hanging on his words and it stung.

Steinhoff's vid-link went gray. He sat back in his chair and pulled on his chin, wondering how he could eliminate any chance of failure. Wait. If Kauffman has been watching Rinehart all this time that meant his life was about over. Steinhoff laughed under his breath at the quirk of fate. He never had to worry about Rinehart after all.

He grinned as he turned his chair toward his desk, thinking how enjoyed the way the SAC operated in their own diabolical manner, with the SAC crushing some people, elevating some, and making the manipulations in a seemingly random fashion. The planners giving an assessment on the coming final phase, as Chairmen Durand called it in an executive conference, predicted they would need more intelligence personnel and activities than they currently had deployed. Luckily, he was already in position, running the current version of population monitoring with his DPP forces, poised for advancement, and he'd wager it would happen after Rinehart was finished. *Rinehart will be eliminated after he's served his purpose.*

He wondered if his DPP force could secure, question, and acquire the conspirator's information, before Kauffman could arrange for Doctor Beucher to extract it with brainwashing. If he could get hold of vital information, he'd have real leverage, and it would give him an opportunity to demonstrate more of his executive skills. Everything seemed to be going his way.

However, Kauffman's confession bothered him. Kauffman had not thought him worthy of knowing the details about conspirator's background or his threat. It irritated him not knowing why Rinehart's father was so valuable. Why hadn't someone briefed him? If he was a section head, he should have had a full dossier to review, to use in planning, to analyze for possible secondary incidents from the underground. The question gnawed at his guts. He hated Kauffman for not considering his capability and the benefit exposure to State vital situations would provide for his SAC growth. Suddenly, he remembered he could be in the lens of a vid-cam in his office, watching and sending pictures back to an SACI monitor of his facial reaction to the director's orders. Maybe he should do what Kauffman expected as cleanly as possible and walk away from it. He could still keep an eye open for any opportunity to acquire vital intelligence.

"Director Kauffman is right," he whispered for the benefit of any camera. "I have to do everything I can to make certain this conspirator is brought back alive and well." *There, for any hidden vid-cam.*

Something strange struck him. If Rinehart heard the vital secret that Kauffman was trying to acquire, Rinehart would also become a security risk to the SAC, which would hasten his demise. *Maybe I can get the information from Rinehart before Kauffman cleans his brain.*

Setting inside an abandoned sewer facility in Harrisburg, Pennsylvania a young woman with delicate cheeks, black-framed glasses, short red hair, green eyes, and wearing headphones suddenly sat up straight in front of her desk covered with electronic equipment. She frantically scribbled on a pad of paper and when she stopped writing, she sat motionless for a second. She turned and yelled toward an open door. "Harrison, get your ass in here. I've got a message that needs to be dealt with right now."

A man of thirty-five sauntered into the room carrying a cup of coffee. "What's the problem, Cheryl? I haven't been gone that long." He walked over to her, looking down at her with a jaunty, flirtatious gaze.

Cheryl jammed the paper at him, her eyes narrowed with a take-no-crap squint. "This is important. Run it to Colonel Austin, now."

"Lighten up," Harrison said as he took the notepaper, grinning as if it were a game to tease Cheryl.

"Dammit, Harrison, if you don't do your job I'll personally kick you right where you won't like it. Go!"

Harrison handed the note to Colonel Austin, who was standing next to a map labeled the United Sates. The room was another of the made-over sewer tunnels, which included, in addition to the maps on the wall, two large tables, an old manual typewriter, and stacks of white paper. Two other officers in Army utility uniforms sat at the table.

Austin read the note and turned to his colleagues. "We just got a message from Washington. It says a DPP operations team flew south. A civilian went with them." He paused, gazing off for a moment. "What are they up to? I wonder what has stirred them up enough to muster a DPP team. They don't go to that effort for someone breaking their laws. It has to be important."

"You going to notify General Wilcox?" asked the Lieutenant Schroeder.

"Not until we get more definitive info."

Chapter 4

With each passing minute, William felt like ants were creeping up his leg. A voice repeated in his head, telling him he was taking too much time. What would the SAC think of his lingering in the bunker for so long? Nevertheless, it was impossible to rush out of the bunker with this man. Now, the only thing helping him fight his nerves was an unsatisfied hunger to listen to this old man and learn his incredible secret. If the old man told some amazing facts, possible state secrets, what would he do? Maybe the SAC would reward him. Doubtful. Even the most loyal members of SAC could fall in disfavor. Maybe, since he was a manager, this assignment was his chance to shine, to prove he was loyal. *That's stupid thinking! I've been used!* Regardless, he needed to complete the assignment for his family. It was extremely difficult to believe his own . . . that this old man had connections to something so strange, so dangerous, and so valuable to the SAC. Perhaps the SAC was simply trying to collect a missing undergrounder. The old man's innocence didn't seem likely from everything he had heard and seen. The man must have done something extremely bad.

William checked the dark area of the tunnel, looking again for vid-cams. He didn't want to appear too soft on his target, if a vid-cam was watching. *No vid-cams in here.* He relaxed a little. He thought of the children at the curb after the SAC had taken the parents.

"Okay, go ahead," William said abruptly. "But keep it short. We can't take much time."

"God almighty, you are paranoid. I don't know what you were looking at. There's nothing down there in the dark. There are no vid-cams in this tunnel and there are no listening devices. You are really brainwashed aren't you?" Henry grinned a little. "That's really kind of sad, son. The SAC is constantly watching your world. The people are always looking to see if they are being watched." He laughed. "Are the watchers, watching if they are watched?"

"That's bullshit, old man." Was the old guy right about him? Was he paranoid? Probably most of the population was just like him, always wondering if the SAC was watching.

"Okay, okay. At least I would like you to hear what caused my leaving your mother and you kids, otherwise you won't understand the gravity of the situation or the terrible danger we were in."

William rolled his eyes. "Make it short."

"So be it," Henry said, his mouth turning into a determined line. "My dream was to work in the Department of Justice, to help guarantee the rule of law. I was like most young men out of law school, an idealist believing in the Constitution. I believed legislators were shining pillars of democracy, looking to only serve the best interests of the people and nation, and I believed legislation was made purely on its merits instead of on the basis of greed and power in backroom negotiations, which were as crude as the world's oldest trade—prostitution."

William nodded dismissively. *Here it comes, the tired complaints of an old man.*

"You must realize," Henry continued, "I also believed in what the Justice Department had stood for over the decades. But—I eventually learned politicians lied to the people. The politicians, the Var-Docs as I call them, made the people believe the illusionary promise they would use the people's mandate to act on behalf of the populace, and they would create a nation of utopian splendor. But, I'm getting ahead of myself. I need to start before 2008."

"That far back?" William blurted. "We don't have time, dammit. Wait a minute. What is a Var-Doc?"

"Variable doctrine. It's actually the person or a political party holding ambivalent views that are, shall we say, based on a self-centered benefit and not necessarily bound to any lofty principle or ethic. The Var-Docs populated the National Progressives Party, the NPP, which later changed its name to the National Freedom Party or NFP. The conservatives were the CLP, the Constitution Libertarian Party."

William puffed, "I understand. I understand." He shifted his position on his chair and ran a finger across his upper lip, wiping away perspiration.

Undeterred, Henry continued with new strength in his voice, "The country was begging for a change from the burdens of Islamic terrorist threats, from the infiltration of Muslim extremists who were surreptitiously promoting Sharia law, from the concerns over climate change, from overloaded social services by massive illegal immigration, from the loss of manufacturing to other countries who manipulated currencies under the noses of our weak government officials, from exploding unemployment, and from a host of other issues. Leading up to the 2008 election, the NFP played a devil's opus on the heartstrings of the ill-informed, the uneducated, the poor, and the lazy complacent voter, promising to solve all the country's problems, if only they were given the total freedom to act. The people's cowardly surrender was largely facilitated by a heavily biased news media. The NFP promised to cut taxes on the middle class and make the wealthy pay more taxes, and in so doing, they created class animosity. Of course, this made the poor people feel as if they had found a white knight. The NFP lied to the people to get votes, knowing they would do as they pleased once the people elected them, voting totally opposite to their campaign promises. With the genuflecting mainstream news media, the NFP could deny having made the false promise, and never have to account for it. The politicians used the election dance, the same dance they had used for decades. The elected NFP representatives and senators treated the average citizen with disdain, looking at them as merely a source of tax money that could be allocated to their own get rich schemes."

William glanced at his watch, bouncing his left leg nervously under the table. "That sounds extremely biased against what I heard about the founders of the SAC. I may not agree with the conditions in the country now, but this sounds . . . I don't know. The SAC and Durand had to form our new country to save it from the disaster. I read about it while in college. Everyone had to read about it. The SAC brought control where there was none, made our society uniform, productive, and more fair." He expelled a breath of frustration. Just then, he realized he had just spouted the SAC propaganda.

"And look at your prison camp now!"

William looked down at the table. He couldn't explain why he had defended the horror that was now his country, other than they had conditioned him well.

"It's horseshit. Look William, the so-called, 'common good' of the organized mob, the collective, or state, has been the source of tyranny throughout history. It's the justification used so despots can rule men. The murderous enslavement of men in all of history has been made for the glorious altruistic objective. When a government starts taking your freedoms, it's preparing to enslave you for a 'common good.' Dictators and despots around the world were as accomplished in floral speech as they were in brutally killing their citizens, and both in an equally sincere manner."

Just then, something the old man said echoed in William's brain, but he couldn't hold onto it. "Please move along."

"Very well. The 2008 presidential election was the milestone of our downward spiral into the slime of greed, lies, and corruption." Henry glanced off, his face showing dreary blankness, and then his wrinkled eyes slid tiredly closed. He then stared at William. "It was the death knell for the country." Henry stopped and coughed, releasing a wracking bark from his throat as he bent over to the side of his chair. The next moment he found William as if nothing had happened. "As I was saying, the people gave total freedom to the NFP party in the blind hope the promised government changes would give them national security, guarantee their retirement, provide free national healthcare, form warm alliances with foreign countries that would eat us alive, continue generous welfare programs, and make the sunshine and the flowers grow." Henry let out a long breath. "Did you know I got my Doctor of Jurisprudence Degree from Yale in Constitutional Law?"

"Yeah, Mom mentioned it. She also said you died on a foreign trip for the Justice Department and they weren't able to ship your body back because of bird flu contagion."

Henry grinned. "That's one of her classics. You know, that was her idea."

"Get on with what you have to say, before the DPP break through the door after you. Wait a minute. Why do I need to hear this? How is hearing your rambling discourse going to save my life? Just tell me why the SAC wants you so badly."

"You didn't listen, son."

"Don't call me that."

"I'll tell you. First, do you know how you became a bug under the SAC microscope? Do you know life was once free? Did you know people could choose their destiny many years ago? Actually, it was that singular very significant piece of human existence that brought your life to this level of slavery."

"What's that?"

"Freedom of choice! That, plus the corruption of the human soul brought you and me to this time—this shitty moment in our country's time."

"Come on . . . please," William frowned. "I have freedom." He glanced at the ceiling.

"There are no vid-cams here. Look at yourself, constantly worried about vid-cams. Your mind is not free and you are not free."

William turned away.

Henry looked down his nose and winced as if in pain. "It's all horribly complicated how I got where I'm at." He wiped his fist crudely across his mouth catching a little saliva. "Please give me some more time." He drew a breath and cleared his throat.

"You can continue until they give us a warning." Continuing was probably a mistake but William had to appease the old man. He could have gotten forceful but getting nasty wasn't in his character, as Lynn had told him.

"The NFP candidate, Thomas Norman, won the election of 2008, becoming the most troubling president ever elected after FDR and Wilson. While his voiced views were initially sympathetic with those of the economically depressed and the uninformed lower income people of the country, a large portion of the population so believed in the integrity of their elected representatives and so hoped for better days, that they cast their fate blindly behind him. However, for many their hope resulted from a virus that had taken a foothold. The virus was the 'entitlement mentality.' The disadvantaged people, who were only takers, believed they should receive compensation equal to people who generated jobs, employed people, produced products, and created new technology. With the sickness in the background, the NFP whispered a siren song that entranced them. Surreptitiously, the NFPs used their unchecked freedom to take the country in a catastrophic socialistic direction—and it will continue unless people do something to stop it. It's nearly too late now!"

"How is it too late?" William frowned.

"In the election, and frankly for years prior, integrity had been trampled in the marble halls of the once noble city of George Washington, Jefferson, and Adams. On the floor of the House, the NFP claimed they

73

would use the mandate of the people and guarantee everyone would be living in harmony, security, and sharing in the wealth—and they declared the Constitution was irrelevant. Furtively they began to implement the means, through scalpel-like taxes and special fees, to take money from one hard working person and give it to one who either didn't work or didn't make the same level of income. They pandered to uneducated workers seeking a higher minimum wage, workers who erroneous expected to make a life working in the fast food industry flipping hamburgers, instead of seeking a good manufacturing job. The NFP promised to raise wages. Concurrently, millions of people obtained welfare payments, early slavery to the new NFP government. The people on welfare became a new classification, a homogenous disadvantaged economic population, a collective. The low-income people who paid no taxes, received government tax rebates. Like a thief in the night the NFP began taking measures to regulate radio and television programs carrying political content, trying to kill programs voicing opposition to their views or opposition affecting their control of public opinion, which would weaken their grasp of power." Henry stopped and stared introspectively at the table. "After you give them your freedoms, they'll take your soul. And that's what they did. You're proof of it! Look at your world."

William looked up at the writing in the concrete above the table, twisted his mouth, and squinted skeptically. "I've neither," William started and hesitated, "lost my freedom nor my soul."

"That didn't sound very convincing."

William stared at the old man defiantly, wondering how bad his doubt showed on his face. The old man's words caught like seeds in his brain, sprouting in his fertile searching conscience. How could he continue to ignore the less fortunate people struggling to survive in the labor camps? The ghosts of the little boy and girl standing at the edge of the street haunted him again. He possessed no power for a correction. Their lives were beyond his reach. *Wrong thoughts, wrong mind, bad thoughts, no bad mind of any kind!* He couldn't devote attention to this old man's disruptive discourse, even if he knew he should.

Henry continued, sounding as if he were breathing hard, "The printed news and the electronic journalistic news media, which were at one time the watchdogs and pillars of democracy—willfully abdicated their responsibility in favor of their own political philosophy, which was sponsored by large benefactors, benefactors who thought of themselves as the enlightened elite, an elite who never envisioned themselves as anything less than future manipulators of a state collective system. The elite, enamored with the cliché, 'for the public good,' align themselves behind the socialists who were drooling with the idea of converting America to a socialist or worker-run state. This news media never asked themselves what would happen if they didn't carry out their constitutionally granted free speech obligation fairly. They turned a blind eye to the excesses of the socialist maneuvers and attacks on the Constitution, caving in to arguments that the old Constitution needed revision. Without a second thought the congress passed legislation they knew was unconstitutional and no less than the female Speaker of the House, Marcella Gooch, laughed sickeningly and said the Constitution was out of date and irrelevant."

"That can't be true. That's SAC wrong-speak, false history, and not what was in the books I read in college."

"I'm not surprised. The SAC strictly controls the flow of information. Notice I didn't say the flow of truth. It wasn't as precious then as it should be now. If your life doesn't rely on the truth, you don't miss it so much. Open your eyes. Look at the country around you, at what it has become, the devastation of buildings, businesses, homes, roads, and God help us— all the lives. No one owns any property any longer."

William breathed hard as if it were in exasperation. "I haven't seen any devastation to speak of, although, no one is allowed to travel out in the country—except special SAC people. No one is allowed to see outside my SAC bus windows." William felt a burning uneasiness. People, even senile old men, couldn't make those statements now. If they did, the SAC would brainwash them or eradicate them.

"I think it's time you looked beyond the bus." With wide mournful eyes, Henry studied him. "Your face tells me you're distressed. Actually, I find that a good sign. Maybe I've struck a nerve."

William ran his gaze down the dreary tunnel, looking down where the illumination surrendered to the dark, running his survey along the ceiling and the walls, a habit to which he was chained like a prisoner. *My paranoia, again.*

Henry laughed under his breath. "Again—there are no video cams here and no microphones. You are safe hearing what I have to say. I'm about out of time. I know that."

William nodded, looking out of the corner of his eye. "The DPP could come in the door at any time."

Henry grinned. "I doubt if that will happen. I've triggered my grid of land mines."

William's brow arched before he realized his accidental homage to Henry's defiance. "Look, I want to hear your chronicle, but we have to leave," William demanded, his words carrying an apologetic tone. "They'll try to blow their way in at any time and something stupid will happen, like one of us getting shot. I have a family."

As if he suddenly remembered something, Henry blurted with a grin, "Do they still call their people, protectors, instead of officers?" His eyes brightened as if amused.

"Yes, they do."

"Talk about an oxymoron." Henry nodded and then he grimaced. He hung his head, capturing his brow in his hand. He went on talking more rapidly, although somberly, "They'll never blow their way through these walls. This place was built to withstand a direct nuclear blast."

William stood up from the old table, staring at the old man, confusion running rampant in his head. He couldn't get the clock ticking in his brain to stop.

"You're . . . you're scared out of your mind, aren't you? And you should be." Henry started to cough, and after three wrenching explosions, his convulsions stopped. He released a tired breath. "Okay, I'll make it easy on you. I'll give you my notes, my chronicle. I should call it the last testament, because it's the last thing I'll ever write. But if you'll read it, you just may save your family." He stopped. "Wait! Your family . . . do I have grandchildren?"

"Yes," William answered cautiously, as if it were a guarded secret.

"Tell me their names."

"My wife's name is Lynn. My son's name is Stefan and he's twelve. My daughter Marie is nine."

"That's fantastic," Henry said and then hesitated, contorting his face a little. "What do they look like?"

William gazed across the yellowed space at nothing. He had never had to describe his Lynn to anyone and suddenly felt it a breach of privacy. "Okay then, Lynn is very pretty, dark blonde hair, which is not quite to her shoulders, and she has blue eyes, freckles, a delicate chin, and a pouty wonderful mouth. She has a funny little tight smile she throws at me, as if she knows everything I'm thinking. She's fairly serious, sensible, more so than me. She has a cute nose and she's about five-seven. She loves to plant flowers if we can get seeds. She's wonderful with our children, a model of patience. When we met, she dazzled me with her knowledge, world awareness, and quick thinking. She was more informed on the world upheaval than I was."

"She sounds nice."

"She could have been anything in college . . . if the country . . ."

"I'd love to meet her. What about the kids?"

"Stefan and Marie both have brown hair. Stefan has blue eyes like his mom, and Marie has my eyes. They're really good kids—and smart. Stefan is a bit of an engineer with an artistic flair. Marie . . . I don't know . . . I guess math is her thing."

"You should check Marie for a tracking implant . . . probably located in her back."

"What?" William shot back bitterly, envisioning his daughter with an electronic pill under her skin, and then he examined the old man for the hint of deception on his face. "You can't be serious." He knew the answer before he made the challenge.

"Just scan her sometime, just to be certain. Okay, now tell me a little about yourself, before we have to go."

As William wondered how he might start, and even whether he should, the old man's eyes seemed to conceal a thought or revelation, almost as if a joke was forthcoming, but William couldn't make sense of it. William sat back down on the edge of the chair. A voice in his had badgered him on how long he should humor the old man before dropping the dreaded news, the certainty that the SACI would brainwash him until he was dead. "I have to know why you're so valuable to the SAC. They could have come here and blown the shit out of you, and instead they sent me. Why? And—why do I need to hear your prolonged boring story?"

Henry's eyelids slid closed as a tranquil satisfied expression came over him, giving him the warmth of a blanket. "Because it's the last thing I'll ever pass on to you. It may be your family's last chance." He drew his eyes purposefully to William. "The reason you need to hear what I've recorded is because . . ." he started and sighed tiredly. "It's the precursor, the beginning of the end."

"To what?"

Henry looked at him gravely, silently, as if what he might say was too horrible to utter.

"I don't understand old man."

"Now, please, I want to hear about your life."

Outside the bunker, a member of the DPP force crawled on the ground through the burnt-red and rust-colored leaves, along the base of the concrete wall near the bunker entrance, dragging a black bag behind him. He stopped ten feet past the steel entrance door, pulled wire from a supply spool in the bag, and placed two rectangular bricks of plastic explosive against the concrete wall.

In the woods, twenty-five yards from the bunker entrance, Captain Rogers spoke into his helmet com-link. "Corporal Stevens, report."

The soldier working on the explosives at the bunker wall stopped. "Sir, I'm still making connections. I'll be done in a couple seconds."

"I don't know if you have—" Rogers began.

An explosion shattered the tranquility of the woods. Ahead in Captain Rogers's field of view, where Corporal Stevens had been diligently preparing his charges to blow up the bunker, boiling smoke, fragments of trees, and dirt rained from the sky. Captain Rogers searched with his field glasses for Corporal Stevens, running his vision along the bunker wall, fearing he'd lost his best explosives man. A dark coloration on the bunker testified that his man had exploded a weapon of some sort. His man wasn't visible. Out from the base of the bunker the explosion had cut an incision into the earth, the kind characteristic of a landmine.

"Operation team," Captain Rogers said sternly into his com-link, "this is Captain Rogers, hold your positions. The approach to the target is mined. I repeat, mined. Wait for my orders."

A deep rumble vibrated the bunker walls. William shot to his feet, sending his chair tumbling over, hitting the floor with a startling crack, which repeated on vaporous echoes down the tunnel. "What the hell was that?"

Henry frowned, cocked his head toward the entry tunnel, listening for a moment. He nodded as if agreeing with himself. He flashed his eyebrows before pressing his mouth into a line. "Judging from the location and the sound, I'd say it was your people creeping around the outside of my bunker. One of them must have activated one of my mines. I warned them. I hate for someone to die but I warned them."

"I think it's time to go."

"Sit back down, William," Henry directed.

"Someone was blown up?"

"Probably. I'd guess one of the bastards out there was trying to get into the bunker or perhaps, and more likely, plant an explosive on the bunker. He was probably blown to shit. They'll not move again for a while."

"Damn, you killed a man?" William said, picking up his chair and sitting down, staring at the old man not knowing what to think. *What kind of responsibility will the SAC throw at me for that?*

"Yes, a man may have been killed by my mine. How many innocent people has the SAC killed for their hideous prison state? Millions? That's right up there with a guy named Stalin." Henry stared at him with docile eyes. "I warned them. I feel bad for the poor slob the SAC suckered to do that job. He's just like you, one of their slaves."

"They'll kill you."

Becoming still, Henry considered William with a face that could have been admiring works of art in a museum, tranquil and absent of stress. "Yes, I know. That's precisely why your coming here is a blessing from God."

Henry's words bewildered William with their tone of finality.

Henry continued in a patient voice, "Please, tell me about you."

"I don't think so."

81

"Come on.   Please . . . when did you start working for the party? What's the government look like now? Did you go to college? How did you get into the SAC? I want to know about your life before I die."

William found the man's comment about death starkly soul gripping. He shrugged as a gesture of compliance, finding it difficult to get the man's knowledge of his own approaching death out of his thinking. The ramifications of failing to get the man to surrender were . . . were unthinkable. There was a voice in his head telling him wrong-thoughts. He couldn't explain it, but he had a strange feeling about turning the man over to the SAC, as if he might be preventing some special event from taking place, something destined by divine providence, if such a spirit existed in the universe. Not knowing what was lurking in the man's brain was twisting his thoughts. What was behind the SAC wanting him alive and him fleeing to keep the family safe, decades ago? What was behind all of it? The old man didn't appear the violent type. The SAC voice in William's head screamed the programming at him that he had to finish the SAC job to avoid punishment. But now, there was something else taking place. He felt a connection with the old man. He saw a selfless humanity in the old man's tired eyes and soft-spoken manner. Perhaps he was genuinely interested in what his son had been doing in life. William found it hard to believe.

"Alright, if I must, I began in 2041. I was about twenty-two. It's been thirteen years. I had just gotten married. I joined SAC right out of engineering school at Georgetown. Months later we had Stefan."

"Why not go into engineering when you had your degree?"

William puffed with irritation. "Engineers were cheap, what with the flood of engineers from a dead auto industry and slowing military defense industry. There were no engineering jobs. I recognized the warning signs.

The only people working were in the government. I heard the SAC had some jobs so I took a shot. With a wife and family, I needed a damn job, just that simple. Now that I think about it, I had an easier time getting in than a lot of other applicants." He paused.

"They may have known who you were."

"You mean, your son?"

"Precisely."

"Regardless, my decision was totally divorced from politics."

"I understand."

"I began working for Director Aldrich. Section Head Steinhoff also began at the same time. He later moved under Director Vogel at the Department of Treasury."

"Wait a minute. Pretend you're lecturing a school class and tell me about each piece of the SAC pie, nice and easy . . . for an old man. And why did you mention this Steinhoff guy?"

William sighed and frowned. "Okay. At the top is Chairman Durand who runs the executive committee of the SAC and the policy department. Essentially, he is the SAC, the absolute head. Director Kauffman runs the Department of State America Protection, the DSAP. He oversees the Department of Peoples Protection, the DPP, and the State America Committee Intelligence, the SACI, which includes domestic intelligence. Section Head Steinhoff runs the DPP for Director Kauffman. The Department of State Protection, the DSP, is run by Director Fournier. He also has foreign intelligence."

"Wait, isn't DSP the military?"

"Yes. Also under DSAP is the Department of Facts and Fairness, DFF, run by Director Devlin. The Department of Treasury, DT, is under

Director Vogel, and the Department of Employment, DE, is under Director Aldrich. Then we have the Department of Wellbeing, DW, and it's under Director Carol Sullivan. And the last is the Department of Living Security, DLS, which is run by Director Lonigan. Now—are you satisfied?"

"Yes . . . uh, one more thing. Where are they located? I heard they were in new buildings, in addition to the one Durand had built years ago."

William tightened his mouth showing his impatience. "That's correct. The top people like Durand and the other chairmen, treasury, and policy, are in a fancy building simply known as Building One. Apparently, you know about it. Then there's Building Two, which holds DFF, and all of DSAP, including DPP, the military DSP, and SACI. The rest are in Building Three, where I'm at. These are monstrous buildings. I work in a plain room filled with cubicles, like little cells made by honey bees, each of us contributing almost anonymously to the unified community." He smirked a little. "Happy?"

"Yes, thank you. You know the security department is phony, as is the Department of Employment and the Department of Wellbeing. The Durand government sends people, like cattle, to where they need strong backs. These people may get coupons for food but they live the life of a slave, never able to divulge to the general population what they have seen, since they never return." Henry shook his head miserably. "The DPP is the street police, right?"

"Yes."

Henry frowned and squinted, gazing off for a moment before bringing his eyes back to William. "Uh . . . are they still cloistering people into population centers and preventing people from seeing what is happening in the country? Are they still blacking out the windows on buses?" He paused and began quickly. "You know I saw one. It looked like a hearse for the dead."

"The buses are covered and yes, people mostly live in the population centers."

"Used for cracking heads."

"What?" William exclaimed with confusion.

"The DPP. They are for cracking heads, mass arrests, and installing vid-cams. They are the animals while the SACI uses the less obtrusive destruction of the individual's brain by conditioning, in addition to their intelligence gathering, propaganda and mental re-training. Right?"

"I can't say."

Henry laughed. "Never mind that. I can see Kauffman is still the big cheese."

"What?"

"Kauffman's one of the key men running the whole thing, other than the maniac, Durand. And there's no DOJ."

"What's that?"

"There's no Department of Justice or Supreme Court."

"Do we really need them?"

Henry gave a mocking laugh. "So where do you fall in all that shit?"

"In 2047, I was promoted under Director Aldrich, to Industry Equalization Manager. I administer quotas on some commodities like coal and wheat, balance the workforce with industry needs, and relocate people to balance the population with the jobs."

"Wait, wait a minute. You relocate people. Is that right?"

"Yes. I review the needs for laborers and manufacturing people and assign people to jobs for which they are qualified. I also have to replace workers who die. I allocate people to different areas of the country to satisfy the workforce and production quotas, and to fulfill the policy of the SAC."

"Do you ask these people where they want to go?"

William shrugged sheepishly. "No. If I did I'd probably get moved to sweeping floors."

"Maybe you should quit," Henry replied. He shook his head slowly, not agreeing. "I'm sorry, I know you can't. You have a family. I was thinking of your soul."

Like a creeping fog, his encounter with the records of the old people he hadn't saved from the steel works flowed into his brain, and then another case clawed its way into his thoughts. The latter was a man who had come across his desk, a man with a back problem. After fighting himself over the SAC regulations stipulating he could not give any preferential or unauthorized consideration to the case, he relocated the man to a laborious factory job. Afterward he had felt sick, just as with the old man and woman he had relocated.

"My chief enemy, Steinhoff, has people watching me, no doubt waiting for me to make a mistake so he can get revenge for me out performing him on the SAC entry testing. He was moved up to Section Head under Director Helmut Kauffman at the DSAP and has powerful connections."

"Ah, yes, Kauffman, again. I heard he developed a special brainwashing group several years back. They still have it don't they?"

William nodded hesitantly, dropping his eyes to the table. "Yes, I believe so. I've thought about becoming a director but the party apparently thinks I'm more useful where I am. Although recently I've . . ."

"You have what?"

"Nothing."

"I'm glad to hear you've figured out how to survive in the oppressive country that Durand has created. Do you have a mistress?"

William stared indignantly at the old man. "Of course not, I love my wife. I don't covet any other woman and I don't believe in the SAC enticement."

"Good. It's interesting you used the word, covet, because 'wanting' is what the SAC is built upon, coveting power, and coveting control over your fellow man." His voice tailed off as his eyes went off across the bunker, and then they returned to William. "But, as I was going to say, the mistress is not for entertaining you, they're to see what's inside your head, your thoughts, fears, complaints, and your loyalty. The party will orchestrate sleazy opportunities, hoping you'll succumb to temptation. So don't ever."

"You know—after you surrender, they will send you to hard labor if they don't want what's in your brain."

Henry coughed. "My time has run out. The idiots outside will soon try to blast the doors again and I can't have you getting hurt. I need to fill you in on some last details, but you'll have to read them in my chronicle when you can escape the vid-cams. I need to explain why you were sent after me." He coughed wretchedly, his hand gripping his mouth.

William said softly, looking at the man's wrinkled eyes. "It's . . . it is possible . . . the SACI might let you live."

Thud, thud, thud.

"I don't think it's very likely. They're at the blast door now."

"I'm sorry, we have to go," William replied with a touch of reluctance, looking away at the wall. He now regretted what he had to do. He hated what the SAC was making him do.

"They just need to know we're still talking, and you're not dead like the soldier I blew apart." He pointed to a box on the wall. "Step over here. This box goes to an outside speaker. Maybe you can get them to relax for a couple minutes. I have a couple things I must to tell you quickly before we go."

At the gray box on the wall, William took the black palm-size microphone in hand, studied the antiquated device for a moment, and watched as Henry flipped a switch, which caused the box to release a low frequency hum.

Henry nodded. "Go ahead. It should still work. Just push the button down on the microphone to talk."

William depressed the button on the back of the microphone uncertain what he would say, but resolved it had to be firm. "To the outside DPP forces, this is Manager Rinehart, please hold your positions, and please stand at rest. I'm still in the middle of my interrogation of the target. Everything is progressing toward a nonviolent surrender. Please communicate our status back to the director. We are making progress and we will be exiting the bunker in a few minutes. Thank you." He handed the microphone back to Henry and listened for more strikes on the door.

Henry turned off the speaker system.

"Your time's gone," William groaned. He gazed absentmindedly at the table thinking of reaching the end of their conversation.

"If you want to shoot me go ahead, but you'll not get information you need to save your family."

"I don't want to shoot you for God's sake. I was just wondering how this was going to end and you horrible secret." He didn't move for a moment. "Besides, the SAC protects my family. It protects the managers and staff members." William wondered if the old man detected by his tone that he was lying or that he didn't truly believe what he had just declared.

"That's right, you move people around against their will." Henry's head slowly dropped. "I'm sorry, but it doesn't sound much like real freedom or a life for that matter."

"It's necessary to . . ." William began. He squinted and twisted the corner of his mouth. "Let's get back to why I'm here. Frankly, you haven't told me anything sounding worthy of all this fuss by SACI. You haven't told me why they desperately want to capture you alive." He didn't think the old man was stalling, but he was wondering if senility had crept into the man's logic.

Steinhoff, disregarding the observant vid-cam likely watching him, tapped a finger on his desk for several moments, hating every minute passing by, detesting the time that expired with the pace of grass growing, all of the mountain operation beyond his control. He detested waiting on anything, least of all a military operation that had to function like a fine machine. The capture of Rinehart's father was an opportunity he wasn't about to miss. He took some papers from the side of his desk, fumbled through them, looking at the action required, his eyes catching only a few words, their purpose not fully registering within his brain. The big question about Rinehart's father pestered him like a bad case of gas in his bowels and the extraordinary interest of the upper level executives. Why were the executives, and most notably Kauffman, keeping the conspirator's importance from him?

The vid-screen on the wall chimed, brightened from a black to a light gray, which flickered a little accompanied by the sound of static. One of his soldiers appeared on the display. The picture flickered as if it were going to go blank and then it displayed a solidified picture.

"Section Head Steinhoff, this is Captain Rogers at Roan Mountain."

"I can see you. Go ahead, Captain."

"Sir, Manager Rinehart just announced over an external speaker system he would be coming out in a few minutes. Frankly, sir, I think this is a deception. I suggest we make another attempt to gain entry and blow the door."

"Another attempt! What in the hell are you talking about?"

"Sir, we lost a man trying to place an explosive charge on the bunker. The ground around the bunker appears to be mined."

"Weren't you told to hold your positions and not to attempt any breach? Captain, you are to wait until Rinehart comes out. If you disregard any more orders you'll be working in Alaska above the arctic circle for the rest of your life."

"Yes, sir."

"Captain, you are to take no action. You are to hold your position. You are to bring Rinehart and the conspirator back to me and Director Kauffman alive, and in such a state of health he will be viable for interrogation by SACI."

"Yes, sir. Is that all sir?"

"Yes."

"Rogers out."

The vid-screen flickered and went off.

Steinhoff slammed his fist down on to the top of his desk, vibrating a pen and small framed picture of Chairman Durand. He looked down at a folder and as he read the label in the lower corner, the tab identifying the dossier covering Lynn Rinehart, a delicious dark hunger for revenge and malevolence dropped over him. He pulled out a picture of a woman and leaned back in his chair allowing his hand to rest on the desk holding the picture. He let his eyes trace the image. She was a nice looking woman, dark blonde, and quite wholesome. She could be his, if he wanted. It was within his power. The SAC allowed such things as long as there was an agreement between partners, but in this case, he would have to remove the husband.

Once Rinehart returned from the mission, he would have knowledge of an operation that the SAC wouldn't want spread throughout the country. Rinehart would be a risk. Steinhoff had no doubt that Kauffman would keep an eye on Rinehart, if he didn't terminate him. Of course, the SAC could lock Rinehart up forever, but then it couldn't use him for bait to attract stray members of the underground. It was curious. Why wasn't Aldrich aware of Rinehart's clandestine connections? Maybe he was.

What a way to extract his revenge, remove the man, and take his wife. Steinhoff thought for a moment; his own wife was almost as good-looking and certainly more voluptuous. No. Too much visibility in front of the upper level executives. A couple of them were a little old fashion. He didn't want to give the chairmen any excuse for passing over him when the time came.

However, even if he did play around, he doubted his own wife would ever leave him. She was too smart for that. An executive working for the SAC had the best life. And he had to admit she was the ultimate wife when it came to understanding. She was no one's fool; she was also practical and knew where life was easy. She would never betray the home they had, especially with her flower garden in the back, the special food, and her precious children, the two girls he rarely saw. If she wasn't married to him, she would have been living in assigned housing located almost anywhere. Chances are Rinehart's wife would like the same accommodations once Rinehart was gone. Maybe he could make secret visits. Then again, nothing was secret from the SACI.

He wondered if Lynn Rinehart had been to the executive spa with her children. He pulled up a file on his computer, looked through the records, and saw that the system hadn't scheduled her yet. It was time. Perhaps he should have his people question her too. Husbands often confided in their wives, didn't they?

On the top floor of SAC Building Two and at the opposite end of the building from Karl Steinhoff, Helmut Kauffman poured himself a cup of coffee from a stainless steel carafe on a counter in the corner of his office. He sat at his desk, took a sip of coffee, closed a file in his computer, and turned his chair around toward his vid-link screen. "Vid-link, on."

"Vid-link, ready," a mechanical computer voice replied.

"Connect to Chairman Durand."

"Connecting."

The vid-link screen flickered and displayed a silver haired man sitting behind a large, red mahogany desk. He occupied a large padded chair, sumptuously covered in dark brown cowhide, which seemed to enwrap him as if he were a child in size. It added, Kauffman immediately noticed, to Durand's fragile appearance, a worsening condition Kauffman had observed over the last two years. Kauffman studied Durand's posture and his reactions to his phone call. Whenever he saw Durand, he made mental notes on the chairman's health, which he used to extrapolate how long the chairman would be running the State and how long he should be running the State. The chairman was getting up in years, somewhere around eighty years, but sometimes it was hard to see the years. He had thought several times that Durand had one of those faces that defied age and ignored the years. His roundish face with a smallish odd up-turned nose was topped by a youthful full head of long silver hair that he combed straight back and seemed to gleam magically. Durand's eyes were set close together above puffy pink cheeks. A deep valley ran down from each corner of his catfish shaped mouth. The way Durand looked fixedly with his deep-set gray eyes, out from under his bushy, curled-up eyebrows, which were oddly still brown, always impressed Kauffman.

For an instant Kauffman was reminded of his own father back in Pennsylvania, back when he was a boy. His abusive father, Johann, had untidy long gray hair and worked in an underground coal mine. The Saturday night beatings his father rained upon him after his father consumed the better portion of a whisky bottle were always hiding in the shadows in his memory and easily tethered to the present. In those early days, he had hated not being in control. The memory of his father tasted as bitter as ever. His father and his mother, both kept him from sports and forced him to work, to bring money home for more booze. Durand only cared about the survival of State America and Kauffman respected that.

As Kauffman studied Durand, he recognized the glint of complete awareness in the old man's gaze and determination still in the line of his mouth. *Watch for shaking.* He tried to decipher facial movements as part of his analysis and gathering knowledge. He tried to identify what every subject might conceal. It was a test he enjoyed and one of his amusements from his intelligence training.

"Ah, Director Kauffman," Durand said, squinting a little and tilting his head as he looked at the vid-link and Kauffman. "I was thinking of you and our little problem. Any word yet? I know the vice chairmen are likewise eager to hear the results."

"Sir, I have gotten calls from Vice Chairman Bruner, Radford, and an actual paper note from Vice Chairman Snider."

Durand grinned mockingly. "Yes, he does still cling to the past with his use of paper. I can't really blame him, there's something about reading and touching a real piece of paper. It even smells and a lot better than these shiny computers." He folded his fingers and rested them on his lap.

Kauffman saw Durand's head shake with a microscopic movement of unsteadiness. "Sir, I agree and—"

Durand interrupted, "Helmut, you look tense. You have to learn to relax after all these years. We all like and respect you. I chose you. Remember?"

"Sorry, sir, that's the way I am. I expect nothing but the best from myself and I suppose it shows on my face at times."

"What's on your mind, Helmut?"

"Sir, our conspirator has been contacted by Manager Rinehart. Rinehart is having some sort of discussion with the man. From the time they've taken, the conspirator seems to be doing a lot of talking and we have no way of confirming the subject. He could . . . well, share vital information with Manager Rinehart."

"Why on earth would he do such a thing?"

"We sent the man's son to collect him, to increase our chance of bringing him back alive for interrogation. As you know, he may be the last one alive with information on the location of any bombs."

"You sent the man's son? Rinehart's the man's son?"

"Yes."

"Helmut, that's a stroke of genius. How on earth did you accomplish it?"

Kauffman smiled. "We have our ways, sir. Actually, we've been watching the family for few years."

"It sounds like you have the situation well in hand. I assume you've made provisions to bring the man in for our special interrogation; otherwise, we're back where we were. I'm not allowing a bunch of terrorists destroy what I've nurtured from a mere spark of an idea."

"Yes, sir. I have Section Head Steinhoff on it."

"Good. I like him."

"I've made him aware that this man is vital."

"By the way, Helmut, what do you think of Leon's announcement about our troop action?"

"Sir, I wouldn't think to question Leon on how he runs his military, any more than I'd expect him to question what I do with our intelligence operations and the DPP. The administration of foreign intelligence matters is his responsibility and mine is domestic, and I'm happy with the arrangement. However, I owe you an answer. I believe his operation is excellent and it supports our new initiative to maintain a diversion for the population. It gives us a place send those who would be trouble for in our manufacturing and some of the camps. I assume the RSU appreciates our help. It keeps them from losing only their men. One of our studies confirmed the use of a conflict for helping to focus public aggression away from SAC officials, disruptions in food supplies, and the limitation on travel. On a related note, my people are working on creating two terrorists icons that will be posted on billboards around the country so the population will have a face with which they can identify. We are also creating a composite face which will be used to represent the Chairman of the SAC."

"Me?"

"Yes. Our researchers believe we should display a fatherly photo representing you—to engender warmth, a feeling of being protected, and a feeling of gratitude. It wouldn't be safe to use your actual photo, although some of my staff specialists thought your face was excellent. Our best analysis suggests placing the single word, father, under the picture would promote a feeling of security for the citizens. It will also help with the transition to your final phase."

"I guess I fail to see the necessity. Since the utilization of our labor camps and vid-cams as deterrents to anarchists and undergrounders, and others who think they can return to the past and the inefficient democratic republic, we have had few problems. Correct me if I'm wrong."

"You're correct. Some of the thinking is an image should facilitate the formation of a tranquil population, ameliorating hostilities arising from citizens having limited mobility."

"You mean after the implantation phase has been completed."

"Yes. Even with the implants, it is possible to have disruptions. We need a workforce with a modicum of efficiency. Repetitive punishment goes only so far."

Durand nodded. "I suppose that has some merit."

"Shall we keep the program?"

"Yes, it won't hurt anything." Durand paused and looked into the vid-link, his eyes like dark spears shooting toward Helmut. "So, Helmut, how do I look today?"

"Sir?"

"Look Helmut, I know you study my physical condition every time we talk. It's in your DNA. That's why you're my spy master, my intelligence chief."

Helmut looked directly into the vid-cam with a piercing stare. "You look pretty well. I did notice a slight shake a moment ago."

"Parkinson's?"

"Too early to tell. Perhaps." Helmut pursed his lips. "Have your doctor give you an injection, just in case."

"Excellent work, Helmut. I look forward to the implementation of the final phase. Thanks."

"Secure the State."

"Yes, Helmut, secure the State."

He waited for Chairman Durand to ring off the vid-link, thinking how the old man never ceased to surprise him.

"Vid-link, off. No, wait. Vid-link, on.

"Ready," the vid-link voice replied.

"Connect to Karl Steinhoff."

A moment later, Helmut viewed Karl Steinhoff. "Karl, do you have an update?"

"Currently we are giving Rinehart all the time he needs to complete the information exchange. The operation captain reports he's still

97

interrogating the conspirator. We don't know exactly what he's talking about since he is inside the bunker but we're not moving. We don't want to risk losing the opportunity to take the target alive."

"Good. Chairman Durand is very concerned about this person and our opportunity to debrief him. He may have invaluable information. If he gets killed, it will be bad for all of us."

"Yes, sir. I understand and I have given strict orders to take the man alive."

"Maybe you should have gone out there yourself—with Rinehart."

"Possibly, sir. But we didn't want to spook the conspirator."

"I do believe the person had been hiding for a long time and probably more inclined to hunker down. How many people are hiding out with the conspirator?"

"We've not gotten any headcount from Rinehart."

Kauffman squinted coldly. "Keep me informed. Vid-link, off."

Chapter 5

William slid to the edge of his chair, resting an elbow on the table, holding his chin, watching the old man across from him, waiting with a skeptical ear for a life changing chain of words. Absentmindedly he bounced his right knee as if keeping tempo with the seconds flashing by. Despite the old man confirming his fears about a future life within the confines of State America, he doubted the man would tell him something that could save his wife and kids. Where was the earth-shattering disclosure? *Come on old man, get to it.* Of course, if he heard anything related to state security those who sent him expected him to report it to the SAC.

He wondered how he would feel when the situation culminated with the man's surrender. A memory or buried moral fiber argued against feeling abusive toward the old man. *Wait a minute.* How would he present this man to the DPP? How should he say goodbye to the man who was his father when the DPP operations started to whisk him off to a brutal interrogation? He sensed in his heart that this man had been honorable and did not deserve what had descended upon him. This person connected him to the past, to his people, to his family origin, and not to the artificial and corrupt SAC people.

The old man squeezed the back of his neck and rub it a little, seemingly signaling the time for the secret had arrived.

"William, I have written down all the information I must pass on, a complete history up to the current time, all chronicled for you to read and the soldiers of freedom. I wrote it in the hope it would be passed on to a patriot—if I could find one, to teach the lesson of what happens when people don't value their freedoms."

"Who were you going to give it to if I hadn't come along?"

Henry coughed into his hand, turned away, bending over at the waist, and coughed brutally toward the floor. Turning back, he wiped his lips with a shaky hand. "My final venture was going to be an attempt to deliver my chronicle to a patriot in a city. I was going to try making my final contact with my underground by using an old shortwave radio I have and something called Morse code. After I wrote the chronicle I realized I may have let my egotistical delusion overpower my commonsense, a delusion that I could actually record the demise of a society and country—the blinking out of a beacon, a once guiding laser light of civilization. Anyway, my chronicle is in a simple three-hole binder, labeled, *The Destructive Durand Years*. The binder is all I had for containing the pages. I've placed several pages of idiotic ranting and stupid charges against Durand in the front section of the work, purely as a diversion from the blank pages at the back. On the blank pages, I've written my memories as factually as possible, using a special ink, which isn't visible until it's exposed to a little heat. I figured using an ancient cryptographic method to conceal my writing was better than writing it on a memory chip which could be found during a routine DPP electronic scan."

"If the ink was invisible how did you write it and know what you had put down?"

"I actually wrote on a copy before transcribing it to the invisible version, besides the ink is visible for a few minutes before it dries."

"Where's the copy?"

"Down one of the tunnels in a remote part of this bunker."

"No one will ever see the second copy—I suppose."

"Wait a minute. How were you updated if you've been hiding in this bunker all these years?"

"I went to a little library a few miles from here for a few years. I retrieved coded messages from the classified advertisements in newspapers in the early years, received brief messages by shortwave radio, and went to a country bar and listened to farmer's conversations. The best came from satellite, which originated in Canada. Of course, the SAC jammed those within thirty minutes to an hour, but you can get a lot of information in that time." Henry stopped, cocked his head a little, sending his gaze to the ceiling for a moment. "Even though it has been a few years back, I think my face may have been recorded at the library by a hidden camera. You know, they have had facial recognition systems recording every person in the country for decades. Once your face appears on a vid-cam they can eventually sift through scenery to find you." Henry pointed to a pile of newspapers several feet down the corridor. "See those."

"Yeah."

"Those are the newspapers that I got for the first ten years. The shortwave messages were excruciatingly tedious. I couldn't use the shortwave for any longer than a few seconds since the transmitting signal could be located if left on too long. It would take several sessions over several frequencies to complete one message."

"Did you work with anyone?" William found the whole idea of the underground fascinating, against the law and counter to the SAC, but exceptionally interesting nevertheless. He wanted to hear more on how it worked. In the back of his mind, he saw the underground saving his family by such clandestine means.

Henry waved a finger. "As a matter of security we never knew anyone from another group or where they were located. In the early years, someone knew where I was or else I wouldn't have gotten some of my updates. If you think about it, the various avenues of communications such as newspapers, internet, the old postal service, television, and radio are vital to freedom. Once they are controlled or monitored, you become a slave and that's what the SAC did. I knew a few people in the beginning but after that, I only ever saw two or three people more than once. Even meeting people was risky."

The old newspapers lying on the floor touched something in William, brought the question of what was missing from his world, and why it was missing. *I haven't seen a newspaper since college.*

"William."

"Yes," he replied sounding as if he'd been startled.

"Will you take my journal, my chronicle, and read it? You can take it with you. You can remove the blank pages, keep them safe, and turn the rest of the binder over to the SACI. They would never know about the missing pages."

"What do you expect me to do with it after I've read it? You want me to take a book and now a binder. I'll get caught."

Distress and disappointment hung heavy on the man's face. "I don't know, maybe you'll learn you actually care about what happened to our country." Henry paused. "I can give you my tiny shortwave radio, the contact frequency, and the code. It might help you escape the SAC. If you're careful you could perhaps get my writing to the underground."

"There isn't any underground, old man."

"Who told you that?"

"The SAC."

Henry grinned and laughed under his breath. "There has always been an underground. Damn, they've programmed you right down to the bone, haven't they?"

William listened to the man's assessment of him, the words slicing as if they were a knife cutting into his flesh. This poor broken-down old man had little reason to lie at this point. William had prostituted his intellectual integrity for survival, right along with millions of the other slaves. Had he allowed the SAC to coerce him because of needing to protect his family?

"There's a protocol you can use. You can try asking around for a Rachel York running a clothing shop in Leesburg, Virginia. Of course, it's not a real person. It's a code for seeking contact with the underground. You ask a person if they know Rachel. If they say she runs a clothing shop for babies then you know you've made contact. I can't tell you more than that. Of course the procedure may be out of date."

William nodded, not saying anything. Again, he felt nervous about what the man told him. He didn't think he could keep anything from the SAC.

"About two, maybe three years ago, the shortwave messages stopped. I assumed all my contacts in the underground were killed." Henry dropped his head and released a shuddering sigh. "I never had much hope of ever seeing you or your mother again. Down deep I hoped you'd someday read my words."

The man's words penetrated William as if they were a solvent cutting through years of burnt-on hatred. "I . . . never," William began weakly. "I never thought I'd see you again." He almost called the man, Father, but still couldn't say it.

Henry cleared his throat and stuck out his chin as if plunging forward in battle. "No one else could have written what I put down. I was inside the government at the time. In addition to the chronicle containing information documenting the destruction of our republic, my chronicle explains why I was forced to leave my wonderful family. It also explains why the SAC wants what's inside my brain, which I can't tell you now. Besides, they'd run a brain scan on you and get the information, which must not happen at any cost. The information in the chronicle must get to the underground at the very least. If it doesn't all is lost. There is a hidden message in the chronicle." Henry stared piercingly at William.

At that instant, as William connected eyes with the old man, he saw the past written on an old man's haggard face, the wrinkles and crevices formed by the years, the man's character hanging heavy in the tarnished light.

Henry coughed from deep in his chest, dropping his head, hacking repeatedly, and clutching his mouth, trying to control what refused to be contained. He grimaced as he swallowed. "I thought of you several times as I was writing the chronicle, I guess harboring a faint hope you were still alive, hoping it would help your life. I know that's a little strange but it's true."

William asked himself why this man was telling him this, although he hadn't heard the diamond he expected, some fantastic information worthy of negotiation with the SACI. The man looked as if he were tired of hiding, tired of life, and tired of fighting a losing battle against the SAC.

With a raspy throat Henry began, "Remember, I said I'd tell you things to help save your family if you would indulge me telling you some background. Now's the time." Henry's face became a grave expression of concern.

William felt the hair on his neck stand up.

Henry went on, "You know, Durand has his replacement ready. Apparently, because he's around seventy-nine or eighty, he's been preparing Bernard Bruner . . . actually starting several years ago, preparing him to take over as SAC chairman. There was a warning in my last communication about Bruner and his probable move further toward absolute control. He's not nearly as levelheaded as Durand is, if you could ever stretch the definition of levelheaded to cover Durand. In fact, he's sociopath and a masochist. A few years before I left the Justice Department, I saw something written in a magazine about Bruner, who was young at the time. He was the head of a radical political group at Columbia University. The university board of regents was in turmoil over allowing a political group that preached government control of everything—including the universities, to influence tenure for conservative professors. He's a Marxist nut with leanings toward dictatorship. His father and mother were communists and brutal. They beat him for not getting top grades in school and a host of other trivial things. He mentioned in a speech early in his political career that the scars from his parents had galvanized his discipline. Well, he took good care of his parents, according to one account."

"What?"

"While he was in college they were killed in a home gas furnace explosion. A professor stated he was in class at the time, but one theory proposed he used a double to take his place in class. If you ever wondered how bad Durand was, Bruner will set new standards for a totalitarian, easily worse than Mao or Stalin. Apparently, Durand liked his philosophy and thinking, and pulled him into his organization."

"I've not heard much about him."

Henry laughed. "The guy's got a degree in ethics from Columbia. How's that for a paradox?"

"Strange."

"Quickly, before we have to leave. In 2051 I got a communication reporting on lower level SAC personnel and their family members being sent to a resort spa under the pretext of a holiday, supposedly a place for massages, soaks, and a pleasant time, but instead they were implanted with an electronic device." He paused, his mouth open, as if a question were trying to escape. "Have you ever gone to any SAC spa?"

"No . . . but we were put on the list to go. What's this about an implant?"

"Listen to me. If you go, they'll stick an implant in your head or somewhere in your body. This implant is believed to cause the brain to release endorphins, dopamine, serotonin or some combination and possibly some sort of controlling radio frequency. It is targeted toward broad population control, coming under Bruner. In their early testing, they used it to pacify some samples of the general population to reduce threats of riots against such things as a reduction in government food coupons or food supplies. The signals triggering these devices are being sent from vid-screens installed everywhere and in some cases from outdoor-lighted road signs. My contacts reported seeing people going into some sort of trance after walking near signs displaying a picture of Durand. They would suddenly begin smiling as if they were experiencing a pleasant sensation, which was a burst of conditioning. The SAC plans to control the whole population, making punishment labor camps only unnecessary to provide examples as a deterrent or for the people they want to torture. Also, related to population control, eventually they will select women to have babies and may even select the sperm donor. They know they need to replenish people or the country will disappear and their power with it. So they can also selectively activate devices of special people, for example a pregnant woman whom they value. Some devices are merely used as a threat to insure total loyalty of the SAC employee. In addition to the raw control, these people support the SAC by functioning as seeds for mass demonstrations. These people are used to help incite crowds when they think the populous needs to vent frustrations, to deflect thoughts of revolt, as well as making the people thankful for the smothering SAC embrace of protection. Some of the early implants were lethal, causing a type of addiction. In addition to that, the SAC has been cataloging the DNA of every person since 2015 so it can change the population. The ultimate control device, which they've begun testing, is the TS-V. It causes pain or death."

"That's bullshit," William barked, shaking his head incredulously. He hated what he was hearing, fighting with his own logic, which was telling him it was probably true, horribly true. A battle raged in his heart and mind, between commonsense and programming installed over the years by repeating SAC slogans and lies.

"Have you ever seen more than one person standing in front of an outdoor SAC sign with a picture of Chairman Durand, or one stuck to a wall inside a building?"

"Sure I have, but it doesn't prove anything."

"Now, please listen to me. Quit fighting the analytical part of your brain. Don't you or any of your family go to any government run spa, especially since you've been assigned to my capture. Your family is now at a terrible risk."

William looked fixedly at the man, trying to make sense of what he was saying, trying to ignore his SAC programmed brain and its mental filter, trying to make himself be objective about unbelievable things, the glimpses of dark elements he'd barely noticed and chose to disregard. "Ridiculous," he said weakly. The single word stuck in his throat and barely formed.

"In 2049 the SAC started implanting all babies with tracers. They were inserting them between the shoulders. The SAC uses a signal from a satellite to energize the implants—for tracking and who knows what else."

A voice in William's brain told him it was probably true, but it was too horrible to believe man would treat other men as cattle. The labor camps were nothing but places to slaughter people. In anguish, he snapped back. "Where did you get this garbage?"

"Listen to me dammit! People can disable these devices using a strong alternating electromagnetic field, like from a motor but more concentrated. You locate them with an old fashion metal detector. The report I got said the SAC inserted the first brain implants into a sinus cavity, and from there they are nearly impossible to remove without a very competent surgeon.

They may also implant them behind the ear. Once you get one of those things in you, it's a big problem . . . except it can be disabled."

"You're telling me my daughter, Marie, has one of these tracking things in her back?"

"Yes, if she was born around the time they began using them, or after." Henry bit his lower lip as his face turned grave and pale. "Remember, what we want is frequently right under our nose. Never forget it. Forgive me for saying it."

"What . . . what was that?" William frowned, thinking the old man made a strange comment that possibly marked the point of mental instability. *Is he going off the deep end? Is this all a waste of time?*

"Talking about the implants just made me think of something else. The SAC has people everywhere who just listen to what people say. They've been around since 2011, although at that time they were working for the NFP. The SAC has these listeners standing in hallways, sitting on buses, lurking around SAC markets, sitting in propaganda meetings, or merely drinking at a water fountain. They suck in everything people say and if you say anything counter to SAC policy or propaganda, they arrange for the street police to come and collect you. They are called speech watchers. I forgot to mention Durand's plan for making all religion a crime against the State. It seems religion and the idea of God, promotes hope in one's soul and defeats their effort to kill the individual's spirit."

"Come on, I've heard something similar but it's a myth."

"Regardless, beware." Henry coughed into his hand, looked at it, and quickly wiped it on his trousers. "I'm sorry, but most likely they'll brainwash you after talking to me. However, if you remember what I've told you, the final word can be yours. Remember what I tell you—in relation to the chronicle. What we want is frequently under Durand's nose." Henry looked down, sighed and plowed forward. "You should also look out for brain scans. Uh . . . a few years ago I got a report about the SACI working on a scanner for the brain. It's used to determine if a subject has seen something or not, as well as whether you've heard some particular words. So, if you read my chronicle they'll be able to determine if you know important information. You'll have to decide when to read my notes, the warning I've written. Listen to me. You can't read the chronicle until you're interrogated, brain scanned, and released. Do you understand?"

William rolled his eyes tiredly. "You must be joking. I'm an SAC manager."

"Makes no difference. You are a small fish. You know it. I see it in your eyes. Listen to me. Don't trust them. They'll brainwash you because you love your family more than them. It's your weakness. They'll exploit it. If you don't tell them what they think you know—they will torture your wife and kids in front of you to get information from your brain. You must prepare your family and get them to safety. I would suspect they've been watching you for years, possibly even gave you the position in SAC so they could keep a close eye on you. I wouldn't be surprised if they haven't hidden one of their damn cameras in your home. For God sake, get your family to safety! Don't wait."

"What?" William grimaced. "How?"

"They never stop looking for people and they've been looking for me for years. They probably expected me to try finding you or your mother at some point before I died."

He starred pensively at the old man as he tried to digest the warning, the caution already intertwined with, and fighting, the SAC programming in his head, along with things he should say in his report to the people who sent him. The grain and cracked varnish on the table found his gaze as he thought about the diverse dangers within the words.

"William, this country is an abomination to God. Someone must perform massive surgery to cut out the cancer, or everyone will be slaves forever, no better than cows, controlled by a few elite with bastardized minds. I know you will tell them what I've told you. You must! When you tell them what I've told you, you can't hold anything back. If you keep something back they'll kill you." He paused. "Only the people in my core underground group knew about the bomb."

William snapped his eyes to the old man. "What bomb?"

"I'm telling you now. It's a big firecracker, around a thousand pounds of fertilizer, fuel oil, and the other stuff people use to make such things. It's so old now it may not even work."

"They'll dig it up." After William replied, he realized his words expressed an undercurrent of sympathy for the man, a bit of sensitivity, and he didn't know why. *Why am I feeling differently about him?*

"I know they will. You can't stop them. Even if the bomb exploded, it wouldn't do much damage located in the floor of a sewer. I think it was originally employed more for making a statement than doing damage. Now listen. It's in the L25 sewer running parallel to K Street. Maybe if you tell them, they'll let you live. The bomb is at Seventeenth Street, right at the northeast corner of what used to be the campus of George Washington University. It's where the SAC head office is located. You go down the access portal at the corner of Nineteenth Street and K Street, take the tunnel to the right, going east, until you come to a sewer tunnel at Seventeenth. At that junction, you turn right for about fifty-five paces, and

111

there you are. My people told me the name, Thomas Norman, is scratched into the wall opposite the location of the bomb. Fitting poetry don't you think, the name of the progressive socialist president who started all this destruction?"

"Why didn't anyone use the bomb?"

"The groups became fragmented, key people were executed, and then no one could get past SAC security. I don't know if anyone is still out there hiding like me. I hope and pray—for your sake, that someone's out there. I'd bet the only person who could gain access to the sewer now would be an SAC person, which reminds me of the other important thing I wanted to tell you. If you take the left tunnel at Seventeenth Street and walk thirty paces back south from the junction, you should find Durand's picture. The underground placed it there. The two locations were separated so an explosion of the bomb wouldn't destroy the second location. If I recall correctly, the picture is supposed to be an old campaign poster made from some sort of non-deteriorating plastic film or composite fabric. They attached it to the brick or concrete wall. It is supposed to conceal something that can save the SAC slaves, some sort of . . . uh, secret information or map. I hate like hell to ask this, but if you can somehow make it into that sewer, please take a hard look at it for me. While you are there scratch my name on the bastard's nose. Going there just might help with your family's freedom. It might break up the years of brainwashing lingering in your head."

"You must be crazy telling me this," William snapped, surprised at the valuable information he now had to carry and then letting himself feel sympathy for the man. He had initially imagined cursing the man in the final moments as he watched the DPP force come and take him away, but now, this man had drained his hatred, and replaced it with something that felt strange in his gut. "Is the bomb the reason the SAC wants you so badly?"

"No. But, right now, my only wish is for you to save your family, which you may facilitate someday by going to that sewer. It will be a heavy sacrifice but please go and look at Durand's picture on the wall. Please remember me—and how much I loved all of you. They may try to do something to your family so you must get your family far away to safety before you go to the sewer wall. Use the shortwave radio. The SAC will watch you. Remember . . . oh yeah, please, please, please, scratch my name on the wall right in the middle of Durand's nose. If you agree to do that to remember me, I'll go to my death a happy man. Will you do that, not for me, but for your wife and kids? Will you promise? Even if you hate me."

"Yeah . . . I'll try . . . I'll do it, if the SAC will let me."

"Promise, dammit!"

"I promise." Of course, there was a big 'if' involved with trying to get down into the sewer. He didn't mind agreeing to what this old man asked of him, but some things sounded as if they were coming from a feeble mind. Strangely, the old man looked incredibly sane, although seemingly more haggard by the minute. Visiting a sewer was a crazy request, fulfilling a type of closure, seeing an ancient memorial. He laughed to himself. He had no idea whether the SAC would give him the freedom for such a visit. He doubted it. He had never considered himself a brave man, one who would go against authority, or anything remotely similar to a patriot. Perhaps he had always been more of a survivor, a coaster, a person who just tried to get along with the system. It seemed he had let his integrity die. He hated the way he had been living, but he told himself again it was because of his family. Regardless, he thought he might try to fulfill the man's request, if it wasn't too dangerous. At least his family still had a life.

"Just tell them you want to remember how you helped save the SAC and Durand from a big bomb. You could also tell them you want to look at the wall with Durand's name for a lasting memory and obedience to Durand's SAC." Henry looked at the table as he rubbed his hands together, and then turned toward the door. "Now, young man, you have to exit this situation looking like you've managed the whole thing as well as could be expected. Otherwise, you're immediately dead when you get back. Wait a minute, one more thing. To survive their brainwashing with a portion of your intellect still working properly, you must remember to set realistic goals, recognize they will do anything, and so you must do and say whatever you must to survive, even if it means saying you hate your wife and kids, and that you love Durand. They'll try to make you feel helpless, throw surprises at you, build doubt in your values, and make you feel guilt. I've done some research and these things can help. So believe in yourself and God."

William nodded sadly, bewildered by the man's tone. "You should probably walk out in front of me with your hands up."

Henry's eyes darted around, as if they'd come alive with new energy in the last few moments. He pulled on his lip. "First things first."

"What?"

"I have to put on a little vest I've made," Henry said, pushing his chair back.

"What are you doing?" William got up from his chair and watched the old man suddenly come to life in a distracted manner.

114

Henry walked over to the knee-high crates and piles of newspapers on the floor. He bend over a crate with a withered paper label on its side for the Jessup's Fruit Company, the one containing a clump of tangled wires beside a canvas object. The other crate also from the same fruit company, caught William's eye with all the books it contained, a huge heap filling it to the top, books he longed to open and allow his mind to search. Henry removed, what looked like a fishing vest or a hunter's vest with a number of objects shaped like one-inch square sticks of margarine spaced evenly across it. A small black box, perhaps two-inches square, with two buttons was attached at the lower edge of the vest.

"Are those explosives?" William asked, surprised.

"They are my farewell song to the SAC."

"What on earth are you doing? You're not going to . . ."

William stood there stunned, watching as Henry slid on the vest of death, buckling it, picking up a palm-sized cylindrical object connected by wire to one of the explosives. Henry located his thumb over a red button, wrapping his fingers tightly around the crude trigger constructed with a winding of black tape, and then he looked at William with an odd expression of satisfaction.

"What in the hell . . . you're a walking . . . a walking bomb," William stammered. "You're not going to . . ."

"This should work fine," Henry said. "Don't worry, it's not activated yet." He let the trigger mechanism hang as he opened his grip.

The remaining fragments of William's cold detachment abandoned him. His brain raced. Was the man going to leave William's life as abruptly today as he did all those years ago? *My father is going to die. How can this be?* He had seen something he hadn't expected to see, even after learning the man was his father, something more basic than the blood relationship, something not seen in a man's face, something visible only through the window of tribulation—a man's soul. This man valued integrity, courage, and freedom like gems. Never had he suspected his father left home because of integrity, much less courage. Even when his mother had told him not to judge his father, he had been unable to rise above his immature and selfish view of the world, a perspective feeding his youthful arrogance. Of course, at that young age he knew all he needed to know as did most young people. It was a common affliction. Obviously, his view at that time poisoned his logic and critical questioning.

A somber pall covered William, a cover woven with threads of appreciation for a man who had given so much of his life for an idea, a cover made with threads of admiration. In a way, he was embarrassed he hadn't hungered for human dignity, integrity, and justice the way this man had yearned for it. Perhaps now he understood. Indeed, he now believed Henry had left home under horrible anguish, for a cause greater than himself. William believed he would have done the same for his Lynn, Stefan, and little Marie.

Henry went to the second crate, moved a few books aside, removed a black three-ring binder, and handed it to William, his eyes coming to rest warmly on William as a little smile formed at the corner of his mouth. "Please remove the blank pages at the back and push them in your trousers, along with the book on the table, before we walk out. Those are the most important pages." He again reached down into a crate and picked up a small black box no larger than his hand. "Here is a shortwave transmitter. It's old but it works fine. You don't talk into it. Instead, you key in a code called Morse code, which is listed on the back. It should be fairly safe to use it as long as you don't transmit more than several seconds. Remember, only seconds. Otherwise, they'll track you. Set it on only 2500 kilohertz. Remember the frequency. Start your Morse code with the letters, RACHEL, then send the number sixteen, the letters, IE, for information exchange. Then send the letter N or S and the first three numbers for your latitude, and E or W and first three numbers for your longitude. Send your last name. To end, sign off with, ET, for end transmission. Turn off the transmitter immediately and don't use it again. You can only use it once, so you should destroy it after you've used it. It signals the underground, whoever's out there listening, and tells them someone needs help. The underground designed the protocol to provide protection of everyone. Eventually someone will find you. The technology may sound old but it will work. You must use the radio as soon as possible to get your family to safety . . . the clock will be ticking the minute you leave this mountain."

William hesitated, asking himself how a transmission lasting seconds could bring help, asking himself if he should risk smuggling the device home, and then extended his hand. He pushed the radio into his right coat pocket.

Henry starred at him with irritation. "Now the binder."

With Henry watching like a mother hen, William lifted the binder cover, fanned the pages until he found the beginning of the blanks pages, and carefully removed them. When he walked out of the bunker, the soldiers would be watching his every move. The only way to conceal the pages and the book was to do it now as the old man said. He opened his bulletproof jacket, folded and stuffed the blank pages down inside his shirt, wedged the history book in against the pages and reclosed his coat.

Now, as he seemed to be surgically removing parts of the man's life, he couldn't help looking apologetically at him. He didn't know why, but he was now sorry for this man, and what he felt was different from sympathy.

"Listen to me, William, don't read the chronicle before they run their brain-scanner on you. In fact, don't read any of the pages until you think they are completely done working on your brain. There's something there you don't want to know with your family around . . . connections. I can't say more, but promise me. Please read them. Promise me."

"You mean about the fertilizer bomb?"

"No. More . . . I can't . . ."

"What if I do some checking and I find what you told me is all true, just what in the hell am I supposed to do about it? I would be just one man against the SAC."

Henry smiled in a bemused manner and then his eyes somber. "Maybe it would then be your time to dig down where you have never looked before, and find a special type of courage. Someday in the future, if you get an opportunity to do something for the good of the country, please search your soul before you decide what to do. Will you do that? Do it for your mother and your family. Maybe you'll discover the hero my twelve-year-old son used to read about in his books. The decision will be hard, but I'm not worried. I know you'll do the right thing when the time comes. You are your mother's son, every bit of her. She always had courage. She was the rock I leaned on."

William found Henry's eyes soft, tired, imploring, and disturbingly thankful. "All right, I promise." William wondered what he had committed to do. And—he always did it. He kept promises. Promising something was always a solemn oath, particularly with Stefan and Marie, and his Lynn.

He studied the man for a long moment, watching the man's eyes change into a blank stare, and then his eyelids, like smooth, relaxed blankets, slid closed and opened serenely. The wrinkles on his face seemed to melt into his brow. He appeared the essence of tranquility.

"William, sometime soon sit down and ask yourself what the fundamental elements are that you hate about your life, no freedom, no self-determination, or being powerless. In slavery, you are powerless to control anything. Part of the parasitic anathema that takes a person and a society to a condition such as the current totalitarian prison is not having access to information, not having the concern to seek it out, and not taking the responsibility to read and critically analyze the information about the world around it. Information control is a key to totalitarian slavery."

He looked at Henry with a bored gaze of rejection, and realizing it, he immediately pushed it away with a nodding face of acceptance and apology. "I will try. I promise to really try."

"Thanks." Henry hesitated with a quickly smile. "So now, I will walk out behind you. We must then get some distance between us. When we are separated by a few yards, I'll stop. I'll demand you run down to your forces. I'll demand to turn myself in alone and I don't want anything to do with my vile son, who is a filthy pawn of the SAC. I'll scream you are no longer my son and start counting to five."

"You're not going to do something stupid, are you?"

Henry looked at William blankly. He shook his head slightly and then coughed to the side. A little blood oozed over the left side of his lower lip.

William couldn't take his eyes from the blood, realizing what he saw wasn't trivial. The man had to be terribly ill and he had been concealing it. But—was he surrendering or not?

Chapter 6

Once more William helped Henry push open the bunker's blast door, its hinges protesting loudly, as if it were warning of danger beyond its protection. William stepped out first, chilly mountain air splashing his face, sharpening his senses as his eyes adjusted to the daylight. Out into the woods he drilled his eyes, urgently consuming movements and shadows, searching the area for the concealed lethal DPP force. He feared unpredictable shots from their weapons, anxious weapons that had been waiting with hands nervous and hungry to carry out every SAC order. He immediately raised his hands high above his head. "Don't shoot," William yelled.

William took three hesitant steps with his hands high and paused. On the nearby tree trunks burnt discoloration documented the blast and the failed effort to breach the bunker. He looked down from the trees and saw blast debris strewn on the ground near his feet. A bundle of wires, now partially exposed, ran from the bunker and disappeared into the soil a few feet away from the bunker. Off to his right, leaning against the base of a small tree he identified evidence of the grizzly human price, a dismembered bloodied hand. He checked the woods in the distance.

"Captain, we're coming out," William yelled. "There is only one man and he is surrendering." A DPP soldier slowly stood from his position of concealment behind a large stone amidst mountain evergreens. The man pointed his rifle at William in a threatening combat posture. "Take it easy, soldier," William said in a low deliberate tone. "Soldier, the target is following me. He's afraid you'll shoot him." More helmets moved in the woods, helmets keeping cover, not willing to stand, and not willing to relax their vigilance. Electricity of fear and mistrust saturated the air. William took two steps, anxiously hoping the captain would come forward to discharge the tension.

"Okay, lead him out," a soldier yelled from the trees. "We have orders not to shoot him. Tell him he's safe."

William turned around, checking on the old man who still waited at the blast door. Blood had seeped from the corner of the old man's mouth. William thought the man's face had somehow deteriorated, as if his tortured life had caught up with him. Clearly, the tired old man wouldn't last long under the SACI's brutal brainwashing procedures, an experience he wished upon no one, least of all this curious and honorable man from his past. "Henry, are you okay?"

"I am now, now that you asked. Thank you for asking. You better turn around and face them or they'll get suspicious. Please tell Katherine I love her and that I'm sorry. Please do that for me, will you?"

"I will."

As William turned back to the woods and the DPP force creeping forward, a wave of sadness washed over him, unexpected feelings for the man behind him who had been trapped in a maze of the country's strange history. His grief surprised him. He stepped toward the woods two steps.

Henry hesitated as if uncertain how far to venture forth and uncertain what William was doing.

William snapped around for a quick glance at Henry's progress. He feared what part the explosives might play and what would happen to the elderly man? A pall of loss and regret fell over him. He wanted this enigma of a man, his father, to keep living.

"William," Henry whispered, "Don't turn around, but listen. I'm dying from lung cancer from exposure to the asbestos in the bunker or maybe it's tuberculosis. I can barely tolerate the pain. I've been coughing up blood for quite some time. I can barely breathe. My living time has run its course." He coughed. "I want you to run down the road and I don't want you to stop until you get past a massive red granite rock that's at the edge of the road. It's down there about a hundred yards. You'll know it when you see it. I'm going to blow myself apart and I'm blowing the top of this mountain all to hell, so you make certain to get past that point. I don't care if you take soldiers with you or not." Henry coughed and spit, leaving blood on his lip. "I'm very happy I got to see you before my end. I'm terribly sorry I wasn't there to enjoy all your triumphs and to help you with your trials while you were becoming a man, but I like what I see. Please give your family freedom if you can. It may be the hardest sacrifice you have ever done. The love of a family is very precious. I love you dearly. Please remember to go to the sewer and what I told you—what we want is right under the nose." He coughed grotesquely and gasped. "Now run!"

"Father," William murmured, tears forming in his eyes.

"Thank you for calling me that."

"Dear God, Dad, I'm sorry." William swallowed hard, looking at his feet, trying to make peace in his mind. He whispered, "So the SAC sent me after you because you knew where an old fuel bomb was planted? Is that it?"

Henry sighed with a peaceful composure. "No, not entirely. But you'll find out."

"What . . ."

Henry yelled, his voice straining, "I demand to surrender alone!" Henry's voice went soft. "Now run. I'll count to five before the first explosion. Goodbye, son, I love you." He sighed and yelled, "Run! Get out of here."

There was a sudden spark in William's brain and then he burst into run. He ran with all he was worth, something he hadn't done in years. *Dad!* He heard the soldiers yelling at each other, screaming orders about standing ground, about holding fire. *I'm leaving my dad behind!*

"Manager Rinehart, what are you doing?" yelled Captain Rogers, standing at a position twenty-five yards into the woods away from the bunker entrance, his weapon pointed at Henry.

"He won't surrender," William screamed breathlessly. "He changed his mind."

"What?" Rogers screamed. "I didn't hear what you said." Rogers cupped his hand over the mouthpiece of his com-link. "Attention all operation personnel, situation is unstable. I repeat the situation is unstable. Be alert. Hold your positions. We must take the target alive. No firing! Hold your fire!"

Henry yelled, "One." He looked up at the gray sky. A hawk glided overhead, swooping and lifting on the air current. "The hawk's free and now I'll join him," he murmured. He shouted, "Two." Three soldiers crept from the woods into the road, but didn't advance. "Three." He looked farther down the path and saw William just as he started around a bend in the road. "Four," he yelled with all he was worth. "Good luck, son!" He whispered, "God, please help him put the clues together." Henry looked up at the sky again. "Five!" He pressed the button on the black device near his waist, closed his eyes, and released his thumb from the spring-loaded switch in his hand.

Running down the road William barely noticed his lungs burned for air. Suddenly the rumble from a large explosion struck him, startling him for a second, until he told himself to keep running. An icy hand of sorrow gripped his heart. *My dad is gone! I barely knew him.* Knowing an explosion had obliterated his father was far worse than learning his father had left the family. Now all he had was memories—and his dad's chronicle. Remembering his father's instruction, he pushed himself harder. Just as he passed a large clump of pines, he found the large red granite rock. His feet hammered the gravel road trying to cover as much distance as possible, waiting for the unknown of another detonation. With the large stone marker now behind him several feet, the ground abruptly vibrated under his feet. He stopped and looked back, a mixture of pride and sorrow holding him. A massive explosion rumbled at the top of the mountain from where he had come, spewing its horror into the air. Smoke boiled with his father's anger up into the sky above the trees. William felt a new emptiness. It was as if the pieces of wood and dirt raining down all over the forest were part of his father's soul, falling back to eternal rest on the mountain. The caustic smell of the explosion drifted through the trees on the blast wave, poisoning the fresh mountain air with its horrible confirmation. He continued running down the mountain.

William speculated whether there would be many survivors from such a monstrous explosion, but he wasn't going back. The DPP troops could handle it, couldn't they? He didn't like to see anyone killed, but the SAC had sent the operation and had caused the death of his father, directly or indirectly. According to his father, the government before the SAC had broken William's family. *To hell with them!*

He did hate the SAC. He now could cleanly admit he hated them. None of the voices in his head talked back to him at that moment. He walked down the mountain road toward a future the SAC would fill with inquisition, uncertainty, and quite probably pain.

Steinhoff and the SAC had certainly extracted their price from his life. His father was gone, obliterated in a blast of heat and light, and given the circumstances it was the path with the least amount of suffering for his father. The SACI would have tortured him to death. Nevertheless, his father was dead. He hated to think it, but perhaps it was best. It occurred to him that his father had not yelled that William wasn't his son. For years, he'd told himself he would never feel anything for his father, but now that his father was gone, those brief minutes with his father compelled him to know more of the man. He wished his father had more dawns and sunsets, giving them time to get to know each other. Now—perhaps he had information to save his own family. *I have to stop my damn programmed thinking. I have to question what was and what is.* Events had pushed him into a maze just as they had his father. He was now at the point where his life was secondary just as his father's had been before Henry fled his family. How much time did he have to act? What could he possibly do? First, he would do research, if he could.

Steinhoff returned to his office after grabbing lunch at the cafeteria. He sat down at his desk and began flipping through the pages of a progress report on the vid-cam surveillance campaign, studying the numbers of new installations, comparing them against the monthly goal. The vid-link chimed and then a hum came from its speaker. Steinhoff spun around to the vid-screen. The picture flickered and then displayed a soldier with a dirt-smudged face and beads of sweat hovering above his eyebrows. The soldier ran the back of his hand across his brow as he gasped for his breath. Steinhoff felt a flash of alarm.

"Sir, Sergeant Beaumont . . . reporting . . . from the Roan Mountain DPP communications truck," the soldier said, his voice erratic and labored.

"Where's Captain Rogers?" Steinhoff snapped sternly, glancing at the 1:15 p.m. time in the corner of the vid-link display.

"Sir, he's dead. Sir, twenty are dead. Only five of us survived the blast. We were covering the rear, further down the mountain, away from the bunker. It blew. The whole top of the mountain blew all to hell."

"What in the hell happened?"

"Sir, I only got a couple words from the captain. He said the target blew himself up. Then before Captain Rogers could say anything else, the top of the mountain blew apart. When we got there, we found the area leveled. The target must have carpeted the whole place with explosives. Somehow, Manager Rinehart survived. He said the undergrounder told him to run for his life. He said the target changed his mind on surrendering and no one knew what was happening. Prior to the first blast, I heard Captain Rogers issue an order for us to hold positions. The target blew himself apart, like I reported."

"The target is dead?" Steinhoff asked, stunned.

"Sir, not only is he dead, we can't find any of his remains. He was totally incinerated by the blast."

"Anything left of the bunker for us to search?" Steinhoff felt himself getting anxious. He couldn't sound like a fool with his man or in front of a vid-cam. He couldn't lose his composure. He thought of punishing all of the DPP force. He couldn't. Kauffman would remove him. In fact, now, Kauffman could send him to a labor camp.

"Sir, we've searched and haven't found anything but chunks of concrete and a few scraps of paper, nothing resembling intelligence worthy papers. It was well mined . . . for total destruction. There must have been several hundred pounds of C4 explosives or something equivalent. There might be a deep part of the bunker accessible after a team with excavating equipment works on it for a month. It's massively destroyed."

"So the only intelligence acquired was whatever Rinehart got during his interrogation of the target?"

"Yes, sir . . . uh, and the three-ring binder belonging to the conspirator. Manager Rinehart showed it to me immediately upon coming down from the blast area."

"Rinehart retrieved a notebook?"

"Sir, yes sir. That's affirmative."

Steinhoff puffed angrily. "Very well, Sergeant."

"Sir, thank you, sir."

"Vid-link, off," Steinhoff said, his voice tailing away as he drifted in thought.

Steinhoff hated the idea of calling Kauffman to give him the bad news. Kauffman would not like reporting to Durand that the DPP had failed. Depending on the information in the notebook, he thought he might be able to survive Kauffman's fury. *What could I have done differently?* He pulled on his chin. Perhaps he could have sent Rinehart in with an incapacitating dart, but even after being hit the target could have triggered an explosive. If the crazy conspirator was determined to kill himself there wasn't much anyone could have done. There was nerve gas, which could have done the job, provided someone could have dispersed it into the ventilation system, and provided the conspirator had not connected his explosives with a dead-man switch carried on his body. There were simply too many questionable approaches.

Chairman Durand could cause problems for Director Kauffman, although the Durand favored Kauffman. At least that was the rumor. It suddenly seemed clear to Steinhoff, he had to see what was in the notebook.

Chapter 7

Eight hours after the William's father blew away the top of a mountain, a v-tran carrying William approached the entrance of his SAC condominium housing area in Fairfax, Virginia. He looked at the time on his watch. "Damn," he whispered to himself. "Fifteen after nine." He didn't want to get home so late and miss seeing the kids before their bedtime. The v-tran had made good time from the airport, but it couldn't account for the plane arriving back in Washington behind schedule. The flight crew executed the individual responsibilities methodically and without error but with a complete lack of any urgency to leave on time. They were just doing their assigned SAC job.

The v-tran whisked past the entry, not paying any attention to the electronic keypad standing guard. William sent his usual disappointment at the same dead skeletal evergreens he'd been looking at for at least three years.

When the SAC moved his family into their government allocated home, the government construction people had just planted the shrubs. The only money that existed was in the form of coupons, which never reached between the reward days. William had always wondered how a payday could be considered a reward day, if a person earned the pay it by providing a service or product. Since people only had coupons for survival, the ornamental plants soon died. He wondered if coupons were a component of the SAC's control. The dead shrubs symbolized State America. He wondered about the condition of the country away from the controlled cities.

The v-tran rolled into his housing area and to an abrupt stop in his driveway. The DPP protector sitting the front passenger seat barked. "Okay, Rinehart, get out. We don't have all night."

William sprang from the v-tran, glad for their impatience to leave in a hurry, which eliminated any further encounter and opportunity for the DPP to detect his concealed items. The v-tran burst backward into the street and sped away, leaving him standing nakedly in front of his small home. He now faced more unknown about his family's future. He looked around at the other government condominiums on his street and thought how well they had been getting by, doing better than a large percentage of the country. William looked at his street with a new eye, at one-story houses on each side of him. The same cookie cutter pressed every house into form, a design consisting of lapped tan plastic siding, two aluminum windows facing the street, and a tiny porch. They were individual structures classified as condominiums. In the oldest section of the housing area, four units had been constructed with two homes physically attached to each other. Regardless, they were all Spartan buildings with thin four-inch walls and aluminum windows that leaked like a sieve. Lynn was always complaining about them in the winter. His condominium was better than most of the SAC housing and better than a lot of the rundown homes in the city. Lynn didn't have to travel far to reach an SAC store, the only place they could buy food or home goods. Besides the bus pickup area, the SAC only allowed them to drive to the market. How was it going to change now that he had failed to collect the undergrounder for the SAC?

He walked toward his front porch, feeling the items under his coat. The package came to mind and then his dad's warnings. God, his family was living in a prison-cooperative. *I'm questioning the SAC. Wrong thoughts, wrong mind, bad thoughts, no bad mind of any kind!* There was that damn voice again, warning him, scaring him, keeping him timid and obedient. He had to fight that voice.

With all that he knew and feared, he didn't know how he would face Lynn. With the way the trip worried her before he left, he couldn't possibly tell her about his new fear, and absolutely couldn't tell her about the blank pages from his father. She was tough but she had a limit to what she could endure from the government. He could only guess how scared she might become if he told her what he had stuffed inside his shirt and who gave it to him.

The chronicle pages under his shirt felt like bugs crawling over his skin. He had been lucky the DPP didn't have him scanned when they walked through the airport. Perhaps it was because he was traveling with a section of the DPP operations group. No one paid him any attention, and hadn't even talked to him. The lethal pages of his father's chronicle were safe for now, along with the transmitter in his pocket, which had miraculously accompanied him all the way home. It didn't make sense for

131

the government to use scanners any longer since terrorists virtually didn't exist, much less have access to flying on an SAC operated plane. *What about the underground?* No one could fly without SAC permission. Come to think of it, the only people walking around were DPP.

At his front door, William glanced down the street again. The limbs the trees along the street glistened like pieces of glass under the moonlight playing peek-a-boo with the clouds. He wondered if they had gotten some rain. On the opposite side of the street and two houses down, the moonlight revealed the glistening skin of a vehicle and its shape immediately warned him that it wasn't an ordinary car. *It's a v-tran.* It sat there silent and motionless, waiting and listening, and watching, watching him like death's soul-collector, merely waiting for the appointed time to act, confirming some of his earlier nervous speculation and his father's awareness. He cast a quick glance at it. He saw at least one man, a head on the driver's side turned in his direction, staring intently through the window. Then he saw the third man. The third man meant it was definitely SACI; at least that was the rumor. The DPP usually had two protectors. Rumors alleged the third SACI man operated a microwave scanner. It had to be the SACI. *I'm being watched.* There was something stark and chilling about being the object of the SAC microscope. He thought of the two children who were taken only days ago. *It has begun.* The clock was ticking.

Bradford Dailey popped into his thoughts, a man who moved throughout his office building collecting trash. Bradford made his rounds possessing a vacant stare, never talking or looking anyone in the face. William remembered talking to him shortly after arriving. The SAC accused, Bradford, a statistical analyst, of divulging secrets to a foreign agent. Curiously, there weren't any secrets to divulge, unless knowing how many different railcars carried corn, soybeans, or oats was a secret. The man merely scheduled the efficient and timely shipping of commodities. A rumor made its way around telling how the SACI used him for a warning to keep everyone walking a straight line. After the Bradford Daily incident, everyone kept their head down and buried in their work. This surveillance had to be part of the intimidation.

He turned the doorknob and pushed open the door, suddenly feeling a blanket of warmth, carrying the smell of home. Lynn walked over to him from the kitchen. Seeing her and the sympathy on her face began melting his tension. She had on her favorite old sweater, now with threadbare elbows; the one with a single red rose on the front, his birthday gift to her back when they were in college. She threw her arms around him and he squeezed her to his chest as they kissed. To William their embrace seemed more like recognition of him living through an ordeal than an expression of their love for each other.

Lynn backed away with her eyes on him. "Hi honey." She smiled warmly with sympathy in her eyes. "Did you have a good trip?"

"Hi back." It was good to hear her voice with its pleasant musical lilt, temporarily purging his gut-wrenching contemplations. He started toward the kitchen. Realizing he still had the radio in his coat, he quickly, with a slight of hand, moved it to a pocket in his trousers, stopped and threw his coat over the corner of the sofa.

"What are you doing?" she asked following him into the kitchen.

William turned to her and placed his finger on his lips, urging her silence. "The house might be bugged with vid-cams and microphones," he whispered.

Lynn froze, the look of horror distorting her face. It was a look he had never seen. Her fear sent a pain to his heart. It was as if all her hope and trust had suddenly been destroyed. She sent a hand to cover her tragic mouth. Again, he held his finger over his lips and whispered, "Please. Vidcams."

She took her hand from her mouth as her eyes softened a little. "What is happening?" Her face lost its color as her eyes grew large.

He smiled at her sympathetically, feeling powerless. "You okay?"

"I think so." Her breast heaved a little as she tried to catch her breath. She gazed at him seemingly dumbstruck before she noticed her hand was shaking. She rubbed her hands together. Lynn lunged across the kitchen toward him, her eyes watering, holding out her arms. "Hold me. I'm scared."

He gazed at her soft blue eyes above her freckled cheeks, took her in his arms, and wrapped her tight to him. Her lips found his as he closed his eyes swallowed by the gossamer moment. As they parted, he held her in his eyes. "I love you so much," he whispered in her ear. He nuzzled his face into her neck, sinking into her wonderful scent and kissed her ear. It was a miracle to have such tenderness amidst their chaotic crazy world, a cold and careless world beyond the walls of their tiny home, which now may have violators watching.

She pulled away, hanging in his arms. "You need a shave and . . . what's in your—"

He cut her off with a frown, whispering, "Shush. I'll tell you all about it."

"What?" she persisted. She didn't move and then she reached for his neck, pushing open his collar a little. "I see you still have on the cross."

"You gave it to me to wear didn't you? It stayed around my neck."

"Thanks for keeping it on."

He nodded. "Honey, did you notice what is parked across the street?"

"No," she whispered. Her eyes grew heavy with worry. "What is it?"

"Where are the kids?"

"In bed," she replied, distracted and irritated.

"I missed all of you, terribly."

"The vehicle . . . it's not a v-tran, is it?" she whispered.

They moved down the short hall running from the kitchen to the bedroom. He sat on the edge of the bed and looked up at her rigid face, which told him of the coming barrage of questions. He patted the bed for her to sit and when she shook her head, he went to her. He placed his finger to his lips again, and inched his mouth near her ear. He whispered, "Honey, I love you, and I will protect you. Please whisper. They can listen through walls . . . and I believe there may be bugs in the house."

She nodded. "Who is it?"

He kissed her neck and wrapped his arms around her, squeezing her tight.

She whispered in his ear, "I can feel you shaking."

"I'm sorry. I think it's the SACI."

"My God . . . William . . . what's happened?" she whispered, her eyes glistening with tears.

"The assignment."

She frowned and as she dropped her eyes, she noticed his shirt. She reached to feel the visible lump at William's waist.

He held out a hand, stopping her. He mouthed the words, "No one must know."

Her fearful face told him of her confusion and dread.

His voice rose. "We may have some strange events in coming days. I could use a drink."

He sat down at the table, glanced around the kitchen, and suddenly popped from his chair, going to the counter next to the refrigerator. He pushed the play button on their small disk music player, filling the kitchen with instrumental music, an SAC military march given him at work, one Lynn detested. He turned it up.

She curled her nose as she frowned. "Please, not that. That's too loud, you'll wake the kids. What are you doing?"

He adjusted the sound level and in a normal voice he replied, "I feel good being back."

Lynn stepped over to him. He leaned into her ear. "They sent me on an assignment to capture an undergrounder they suspected of having vital SAC information. I couldn't tell you anything when I left home because I didn't know anything."

"What on earth!" She stood there in a daze. "Why send a manager like you?"

"I had no choice. You know that." He turned, opened the refrigerator, and took out a blue can labeled, cola, in black. He popped the tab, and took a sip. "That tastes good after not having anything since before getting on the plane."

She stood inches from him, feeding on his eyes, begging for answers. "And now they're watching our house."

He grimaced and whispered, "Honey, they're listening."

Lynn's voice rose again as her brow came down. "You're a manager, for God sake. Why?" Her eyes wouldn't leave him. A moment of silence disappeared. Tears filled her eyes and spilled down her cheeks. "Oh dear God, what's happened?" Her head slumped. She backed away, leaning on the counter, sobbing quietly. "They send all of us to one of those labor camps." She wiped her hand across her cheeks.

"Don't cry, honey." He didn't know what to tell her, but he had to tell her about his father. He couldn't lie. It was no use to try. It was all too common, at least in rumors, what could happen when the SACI started watching a family. Then, what his father told him came back to him. "By the way, I don't want you and the children going to the SAC spa for executive wives. I'd like you to postpone it, even if you already made plans. I want you around the house in case I have to go on another trip."

"You can't be serious. The reservation administrator just called today. It's all set up. We're to go next week. The kids and I were kind of looking forward to it. We're lucky to go."

"You'll just have to cancel it. Tell them you want special permission to visit your mom in Boston."

"That won't work. They'll say I don't have authorization to travel there. Why?"

He sat his drink down, pulled her to him, and stared down into her glistening eyes.

She shook her head, pressing her lips into a line. He wanted to cry along with her, wishing it hadn't happened. He remembered his father's warning, and the chronicle.

"Just a second." He went to the cabinets on the opposite side of the kitchen, pulled open the drawer Lynn used for her favorite cookbook enclosed in a three-ring binder, and keeping his body turned toward the counter, slowly slid the blank chronicle pages from his shirt. He flipped to the back of the cookbook and inserted the pages. "Scrap paper for cooking notes," he announced causally. Still facing the counter, he removed his dad's history book, slid it under the binder, and placed both in the drawer. As smoothly and unobtrusively as he could, he snatched the radio from his trousers and pushed it under the binder. As he turned around, he saw another question coming, foretold by Lynn's raised eyebrow, but she said nothing. He gave a jaunty jerk of his head, trying to move past the moment of tension.

Lynn ran a fist across her cheek, catching a tear, leaving a glistening smear. "Please sit down, dear," she said plainly. "You look horrible."

William grabbed his drink and slumped onto a dinette chair. He gazed blankly at the squares on the tile floor. "It doesn't seem possible," he muttered. Nothing his father told him seemed possible, but his heart told him he had been a fool. The acid of that recognition washed away the blind myth he had created in his hopeful mind, the fantasy that by virtue of his position the SAC might spare them from any of the mass arrests and subsequent labor camps. Strangely, a second ago, even Lynn realized they could go to a labor camp. He wondered if she had heard stories about what happened to attractive women like her in labor camps, what the camp administrators would do once the saw her. He wondered if the SAC had watched them for years, as his father had guessed. They had chased after his father for years. William thought of all his years of hard work, and how he had worked with unquestioned loyalty for so many years, trying to assimilate into their control regime, trying to believe their propaganda and doctrine, wanting to belong, sacrificing his integrity—and his soul. Now he knew the source of his recent awakening, real observations and not illusionary speculation.

Even though his gut said they were real, he would confirm the events his father told him to check. He thought of opening his father's book; it made him feel connected with his father. He had to read the history for himself and chisel the history into the granite of his brain. And later, somehow, he had to read his father's chronicle and learn the secret. He hoped he could read it after the SAC debriefed him—if he was still alive after their interrogation. He also had to get the chronicle in the hands of the underground. He smiled. *Apparently, the underground really existed. I have a shortwave radio to prove it.* God, what was going to happen to his family?

"This seems like a horrible dream," Lynn murmured. She walked over to him, draped her hand on his shoulder, her eyes again spilling her fear in droplets down her cheek.

He took her hand and pulled her lower. She smelled her divine delicate scent of strawberries and thought of how he was going to shatter that bit of pleasure with the next bit of bizarre news. Just then, he realized what he had done; he had searched for privacy to talk with his Lynn. It had been automatic for years, like eating and breathing. Now as a precipice lay before him, waiting to snatch the richness of his life, he awoke to a moment of simple delight and of new horror. "I'm scared for us," he whispered, cupping his hand around his mouth.

"What I don't understand is their checking on you and here you are—a manager. I know they can arrest anyone at any time but you have worked for them for years." She became still, and then she whispered, "Why haven't they arrested me for buying the flower bulbs? That poor woman down the street. She was only trying to buy a little extra food."

"It might have something to do with my trip. And now . . . I know things . . . things they are worried about." His words floated like a haunting breath. "Lean close," he whispered. He was barely able to believe how they were talking in their own home.

Finally, he had reached the time. He couldn't bring himself to tell her what he had smuggled under his shirt or its origin, and his plan to verify his father's warning, but he had to tell her about his father. There was the implant warning, too. How would he tell her about that? Warnings from his father . . . yes, his actual father.

She leaned near his ear. "What else do you know? What haven't you told me? The black v-tran outside is after something special."

He placed his lips on her ear, feeling her deliciously warm and soft skin. Her breath touched his neck, vibrating his hair, giving him wonderful chills. He had to pull himself back from softness, from tenderness, and tighten every fiber inside. "Honey, I met my father."

Lynn stiffened and started to lean backward as if trying to process everything in one sickening burst. She caught herself on the top of a chair, pulled it under her, and slowly sat. She took William's hand and squeezed it, her eyes wide with surprise and then she frowned.

He pulled her hand to his lips, kissed it, ran it over his cheek, and then pulled her near. He spoke softly into her ear. "They sent me to bring him back alive. I was their tool, their trick. I was their fool. They knew he was my father. They manipulated the son to prey upon a father's emotions. The SAC is depraved. They didn't tell me who it was, only that it was a conspirator against the SAC. Apparently, they wanted information he had—and they wanted it badly. He knew they would brainwash him if he surrendered and that he would probably die. He knew he could place us in danger."

"How could that be?"

"Brutal people could torture one of us in front of him, trying to get him to talk. If they failed to get the information by brainwashing, they could even take one of the kids and torture them to make him talk."

She gasped, staring at him, and started to back away. He held on to her, feeling her stiffen.

"Honey," he continued, "he knew what was ahead of him if the DPP or the SACI took him. He blew himself up with explosives. It was instantaneous. He was ready to die. He was horribly sick with lung cancer, spitting up blood, and coughing horribly. The SAC would have killed him during their interrogation. I know it. He knew it. He swore to me that he left mom and us kids alone so he could protect us from the government. He was terribly sorry for what had happened. I think I forgave him the instant he told me to run, just before he let go of the switch."

Lynn began to cry. He pulled her to his lap and wound his arms around her, feeling her chest heaving as her head found his shoulder. Even though she was crying, he needed her leaning against him. He needed to shelter her.

"I think he was a good man. The political upheaval shaking the country many years ago entangled him, back when the SAC grabbed power. Now I have to tell the SACI what I was told, everything he told me." He wanted to tell Lynn that he needed to do some investigation on his own to settle his remaining doubts, but he still couldn't tell her. It would scare her down to her bones, overloading her with more worry than she should have to endure.

"Honey," Lynn started, her voice scratchy as she whispered. "What did you hide in my kitchen drawer?"

"My father gave me a transmitter to contact underground people for help. It might help us get to safety—away from the SAC."

Lynn's eyes froze on him, enormous and white, but she didn't say a word. He could see her mind filling with dread. She had reached her threshold for breaking down.

"Away from the vid-cams?" she asked.

"Yes. I think so."

"Hi, Dad," Stefan said, walking into the kitchen, rubbing his eyes, his sister Marie just behind him, her hair disheveled from her sleep. "I got my 3D video game working again just after you left for your trip."

Lynn quickly wiped her eyes and turned away from Stefan.

"That's great." William stood. "Come here and give me a hug."

As Stefan leaned against him, William bent over a little to hug Stefan, noticing how tall his son had grown. William pressed him tight. "How did you fix your game?" he asked, amused.

"I've been meaning to talk to you about him," Lynn said, rolling her eyes. "I told him not to mess with it and he didn't listen . . . but . . ."

"I don't know, I just did it."

Lynn beamed proudly. "He did it on his own."

"I think we need to see if we can get him into another school—somewhere," William said with a little laugh, knowing it was out of the question.

"Where would we find a new school?" Lynn groaned. "There's no place for him. There are no schools like that."

"Dad, how about some chess tomorrow night? Remember, I'm ahead ten games to eight."

William turned off the music. "Okay, chess tomorrow. Give me another hug and get back to bed." As he hugged Stefan again, he flashed on hugging his own father. He looked at Marie. "Now, my little sweetie."

"Hi, Daddy," Marie murmured, sounding half-asleep, grabbing his waist to hug him before Stefan could get out of the way.

He pulled Marie next to him and picked her up, wrapping her in his arms, pressing her to his chest as he hoped her future would be better. "What's this?" he asked, looking down at the small doll dressed in a blue nightgown, dangling from one hand. He hugged her again and kissed her cheek.

"Oh . . . yeah, Marie made up a song on the old computer and it's really good," Lynn said.

Marie sent her sleepy eyes at William. "Daddy, I'll play it for you tomorrow."

"Honey, I can't wait to hear it." He grinned, showing his amazement. "For now, you two need to get back to bed."

"Goodnight, Daddy," Marie said softly and drifted off toward bed with Stefan on her heels.

"Lynn, what are we going to do with these kids? I know they're not going to get taught the subjects they deserve at their school."

Lynn nodded and sighed. "We could do more work at home."

"Without books?"

He frowned. "I know, I know. We are better off than most people are. We're probably in the top one-half percent. It could be higher." He glanced off and then turned quickly. "Did you do any sketching while I was gone?"

"I did a small landscape. I think it's pretty good."

"I'd like to see it."

"Honey," Lynn began, "what are you going to do about this trip?"

"I'll make my report tomorrow. It's only Wednesday. Maybe by Friday I'll be able to forget all this business and get back to my normal job."

Later, lying in bed, William's reflections swirled in his mind. How many people were like him with wrong-thoughts and how many had the SACI mentally processed? He knew of at least one person, Douglas Crane. Last year, standing at the water cooler filling his cup, Crane let words slip out in a faint whisper, expressing that he didn't think the SAC should tell people where they had to work. At that moment, the hair on the back of William's neck stood up like tiny nails. William had anguished over reporting the comment, which was the obligation of every manager like him or any average citizen-comrade, but despite it happening in an office speckled with overhead vid-cams, he was certain the vid-cams had not heard the violation. William decided to do nothing. He felt good about not reporting the man, although he'd given an oath to do so during the SAC training and indoctrination program for managers. If a com-link or vid-cam, the ubiquitous microphones and video cameras hidden in every office, had picked up the violation, and if he hadn't reported it, the authorities would have sent him to SACI for processing, along with Crane. He was absurdly lucky. Perhaps the SAC had seen it and heard it, and were now watching him for possible underground connections. It was maddening, the SAC information and misinformation, the stories of conspiracies, and how the SAC thwarted them with informants and electronic spying. He felt a spark of guilt for not reporting the man. Wrong thoughts. After all—the SAC provided everything. They only want obedience. That's slavery. No, not even slavery. Slaves were valued property. People in the SAC had no value. Keep fighting the programming. *I have to fight the indoctrination.*

From now on, he and Lynn would be on the SAC stage, performing roles of normal people, if such an animal existed. He had to act as if he were oblivious to the importance of finding his father. He had to find any information he could on what happened, and eventually, when it was safe, he had to read his father's chronicle. Whatever the SAC attributed to his father, they would declare propaganda, and from now on, he had to act as if he didn't believe anything his father, the conspirator, might have said. Maybe they could keep their condominium and avoid the SAC demoting them to one of those dingy apartment complexes where they assigned engineers and record administrators, or worse yet, to the horrible mass housing centers used for laborers. *The short wave. Can I find a way out for Lynn and the kids?*

Down deep in his gut William had a feeling the SAC would investigate the encounter on the mountain with their usual microscopic thoroughness, which meant time could be short for him to study the history as his father had urged. He swallowed hard, suddenly thinking of the SACI taking him from Lynn and the kids and working on his brain. Somehow he had to check the information his father had passed on to him, peel away the golden-tongued veneer of SAC propaganda, try to learn how life had become so scary, how surveillance and control took over, and how they became a controlled form of life. On top of his plight, he had to protect his family against what he feared was true. How in the hell was he going to shield them until they were free? The only thing that kept popping into his analysis was the little radio for connecting to the underground—if they still existed. He had to start thinking with guts.

Late Wednesday evening, mere hours after the DPP disaster on the mountain, Karl Steinhoff walked into his house and slammed the door behind him. The status report on Rinehart arriving home that he had gotten an hour ago still infuriated him. The mission failure under his management could cost him his position or even worse, and Rinehart still breathing seemed to add to his fury.

"What's wrong, honey?" his wife called from her vid-net room at the rear of the house.

"Nothing for you to worry about."

"Okay, just thought I'd ask. Have a drink. It will relax you."

"That's what I'm doing," Karl replied, marching over to a cabinet in the corner of the living room. He poured a glass of Vodka, turned on the gas in the fireplace, and sat in his favorite chair. He sipped his drink, staring blankly at the reaching and curling, flames in the fireplace as they created a cozy yellow glow in the room. Shadowy figures danced across the ceiling. Slowly he began to feel warmth on his face.

"I'm going to bed," his wife said from another room. "You want to look in on the kids?"

"No. They could care less about me."

"Maybe you should give them some of your time."

"No point starting now. Goodnight."

The hours after his wife had meandered off to the bedroom to watch more vid-net before falling asleep seemed ideal for him to think about his problems. Not needing the sleep, he hated going to bed early, even during the workweek. With all the political scenarios rampant in his brain, schemes about grabbing power and worries about merely holding what he had, he frequently found it difficult to sleep. The mission failure chewed at his guts like hungry wolf. He was in trouble and didn't know how to handle it.

He leaned back, reclining in his oversized stuffed chair, propping up his feet, fighting a nonstop analysis about the failure at the mountain. He sipped his vodka, savoring its clarity and smoothness, a quality he enjoyed in his premium bottle, the kind obtainable by only people in the upper SAC stratosphere. From a drawer in a small table at arm's reach he removed one of his special cigars and a packet of matches. He held the cigar up to smell the rare tobacco, as if it were a trophy, a visual symbol of his promising life.

The vid-link unit on the wall in his study located just off the living room chimed softly. He grabbed his drink, walked over to his office, and sat at his desk facing the screen. The screen flickered, but stayed dark and gray. Without a picture, it had to be a surveillance or special operation announcement.

"Section Head Steinhoff," a man said.

"Yes, this is Steinhoff."

"This is SACI Street Unit 251, Captain Colbert, reporting."

"I didn't expect any reports this evening, Captain Colbert," Steinhoff replied, disgust in his tone.

"Sir, sorry, but I was given orders to call your vid-link with status on Citizen-Comrade Rinehart before we rotated our observation teams. Director Kauffman gave us precise orders to keep you informed."

"Yes, very good. What do you have to report, Captain?"

"My report is on something irregular, sir. Rinehart arrived at his home an hour ago and entered the structure."

"That's not significant."

"The manner of the conversation taking place inside the home isn't what we qualify as normal. Their conversation has been highly irregular, above and below our listening instrument's sensitivity. He and his wife are visible on our kitchen video and have been repeatedly conversing directly into each other's ears as if they suspect they are being monitored."

"There's no way they could know," Steinhoff barked. "Perhaps they are avoiding their children."

"Sorry, sir, they seem to know something. I believe their children have gone into their bedrooms."

"Very well, I'll talk with Manager Rinehart tomorrow."

"Thanks for doing your duty, Captain."

"Goodnight, sir."

"Wait a minute."

"Sir."

"What happened to my DPP unit that was carrying out surveillance?"

"Sir, I was ordered to take control and they were relieved."

"Captain, Director Kauffman has authorized me to work with your people on special surveillance requirements. I want your people to pick up the wife for interrogation in the next couple days . . . nothing heavy . . . a good scare will do. Also make certain she is on the list to visit our special spa."

"Yes, sir, we will arrange something. Shall I check on the spa list, sir?"

"I submitted a request. Make certain her and the children are scheduled."

"Very good, sir."

Steinhoff clenched his teeth for a moment, and then his jaw eased. "Vid-link, off," Steinhoff muttered. He sat back and took the last of his drink in a large gulp.

Rinehart's behavior was interesting indeed. Why would they try concealing their conversation? They were obviously hiding something from the SAC and concealing information vital to the security of the State. Such an act was easily grounds for a first level interrogation. He grinned. Rinehart's report would be interesting. He could exercise his influence and power to make certain Director Kauffman sent Rinehart to visit Doctor Conrad Beucher for a brain scan to confirm the truth and determine if Rinehart was holding back anything. He thought he might observe some of the interrogation himself, especially if Doctor Beucher employed his extreme techniques. It would be fitting amusement in payment for Rinehart's fiasco at the mountain. Seeing Rinehart wince in pain was something he'd imagined for years. Perhaps now, Kauffman would finally share the conspirator's secret with him. *Wait a minute . . . how did Rinehart know to conceal his conversation?*

"Vid-link on."

"Vid-link, ready," the computer voice replied.

"Call, Director Kauffman, personal residence."

Steinhoff sat erect as he stared at the vid-link screen and waited for Kauffman to appear. The vid-link chimed three times without a response, and then a monotone recording came on telling him to leave a message.

"Director Kauffman, this is Karl Steinhoff. Manager Rinehart has returned from the mission. The protector engaged in the operation at the mountain reported Rinehart spent quite some time interviewing the conspirator The field operations people reported the conspirator blew himself up as well as the top of the mountain. Twenty men were killed in the blast. I'd suggest Rinehart be interrogated tomorrow while the information is fresh in his brain. Obviously, the information you were seeking from the conspirator may now be locked inside Rinehart's head. I just got an update from your SACI observation team outside Rinehart's house and there are indications Rinehart suspects we are monitoring his house. Furthermore, on the topic of the mountain operation, I assume full responsibility for its failure. Even though it can be impossible to prevent a man from suicide, if he has taken certain measures, I was in charge of the operation and responsible for its failure. I would be glad to resign my position if you so wish. Awaiting your instructions. Vid-link, off."

Steinhoff suddenly realized he should have notified the director as soon as he got the call from the field about the blast. It had been seven or eight hours and he hadn't reported the failure and death of the target. He fought a sinking feeling in his gut.

Chapter 8

When Thursday morning arrived and William groped for the alarm clock, despite the unknown he was about to face at the SAC, he was glad it had come. The clock had ended his bizarre dream, which had him twisting and rolling all night and had caused Lynn to wake him twice. He immediately began thinking of making his report to Steinhoff and Director Kauffman. Because of the high profile nature of the mission, he figured they would want a verbal description before he typed a complete electronic report.

He shaved, showered, and slipped out of the house on his usual schedule without saying anything to Lynn who was starting to get up so she could ready the kids for school.

The isolation, as if a nameless entity, within the collection of fellow citizen-comrades riding the SAC bus, helped William to focus his thoughts. By the time he had arrived in downtown Washington and walked toward SAC Building Three, he had gone over all the subtleties of maintaining a confident appearance, reminders on how to sit, how to react, how to move his eyes, and how to talk. He carried his father's notebook under his arm, and as he crossed from the SAC bus drop-off area over to his building. The third of the SAC government buildings echoed the seemingly impenetrable monolithic nature of Building One and Building Two, so much so that the only way they could be distinguished was by a sign near their entrance. Building Three's front two corners slashed upward toward the sky at the same oblique angle, meeting the other two edges in a point at the top, the pinnacle of a four-sided pyramid. The gray granite planes were more than walls and unadorned sheets cutting into the sky, they were part of the defensive protection of the SAC. It was a SAC prideful fact that it had used the design for bomb blast dispersion. He had seen it in a training film when he had first started working there. The SAC designer analyzed and configured the angled walls using a computer program so they would deflect a bomb's pressure wave, if an anti-SAC radical exploded a bomb in close proximity.

William cast a cautious eye down the street toward Building One, the SAC headquarters building, thinking of the bomb hidden below the road, wondering how the SACI would react to his disclosure. His nerves jangled with electricity unlike anything he'd ever felt before. *You have to stay calm.* He would soon face men who could erase his existence without a second thought, and who would probably look at him as a criminal against the State, despite him supporting their operation. He was nothing more than a bug to them, now with a temporary minuscule value, a remote control bug, a low form of life they could program.

William entered the building, slid his badge in the reader, and looked at the lobby security man for his reaction, partially expecting an instant arrest by security. The security man, another bug of the system programmed he saw daily, the one whose shirt always seemed ready to pop the buttons, signaled William to move forward. William walked on. The man then gave him a second look, frowned, and quickly checked his notepad.

"Wait a minute," the security man said. "You are to report directly to Room 200."

"Thank you. Is that room off the east hall?"

"Yes, sir."

"Thanks."

William walked down a hall he had not visited before. Regardless, it was of the same dreary design, with the same overhead LED light panels, the same boring gray paint on the walls, and the ubiquitous composite tile floor. He passed people looking as bored and lethargic as the workers in his office area. After a minute, he came to Room 200. *You have to be strong.* He remembered his father advising him not to hold anything back. He touched the stainless steel doorknob, hesitated, and took a deep breath, gathering calm and courage. It was all new for him. Perhaps he could have value to them long as they wanted what he knew.

He opened the door as if it were an ordinary staff meeting. He stepped in with his chin up, consciously holding a composed facial expression, and closed the door with a masterful slight thud. Turning back around, he immediately looked straight at Karl Steinhoff, who popped from his chair and approached the door with a pompous nauseating smile, as if they were old friends.

Steinhoff extended a hand. "How you doing, Manager Rinehart?" Steinhoff's eyes dropped to the book under William's arm.

William took his hand and shook it, knowing he was the fly walking onto the proverbial spider's web. "I'm fine, just fine." William knew he had one thing in his favor, knowing about Steinhoff, knowing he was a calculating and despicable human being, out to stick a knife in his back, which he might not be able to avoid, except for what he held in his brain.

"William," Steinhoff said, turning toward the large rectangular table, "Director Kauffman and Director Fournier have taken time from their schedules to listen to your account of what happened on the mountain."

William nodded to the directors. He stood midway along the wood table's length. An empty chair waited next to where Steinhoff had stood. A coffee carafe with cups sat at one end of the meeting table. He found it funny that they had coffee in a meeting where they would likely verbally disembowel him. Regardless of that and knowing how they operated, it was probably good coffee, something his family had never tasted. On the opposite side of the table from him, he faced Director Leon Fournier and Director Helmut Kauffman. Seeing those two men with their somber faces confirmed the seriousness of his situation and confirmed his father's caution. People didn't threaten to use bombs and get away with it, or merely hide one for future use.

Steinhoff gestured toward an empty chair on the side of the table toward the door, in the center of the table. "Please sit here," Steinhoff said and then pulled back a chair at the end of the table for himself on the same side as William. As William sat, Steinhoff slowly eased himself down, his eyes seemingly eating William's every movement. He draped one leg over the other and folded his fingers on his lap with a ritualistic flair.

William told himself to relax. He breathed deeply and as slowly as he could to avoid detection by the feared head SAC intelligence, Kauffman.

He looked at the faces across from him and slid his father's notebook to the center of the table. He tapped the cover of the book with a forceful finger. "This came from the man at the bunker."

Director Fournier and Director Kauffman regarded the book and then stared expectantly at William.

"Manager Rinehart, you are aware that any information you obtained while on the assignment must not go beyond this room," Kauffman declared. "In fact, conversing with a member of the underground is punishable by ten years in a labor camp and considered treason against the SAC. This you did, although with our direction."

"So, I wasn't supposed to talk to the man to get him to surrender?" William asked.

"Impertinence will likewise place you in trouble," Kauffman added.

"I'm sorry, but you seem intent on locking me up for doing you a service," William replied coolly.

"William," Steinhoff began, "there's coffee here on the table, so help yourself."

"Thank you."

"Manager Rinehart," Fournier said, "Director Kauffman invited me to listen to your revelations just in case they touch on our national security, threats from beyond our border."

Kauffman cleared his throat and then rifled his eyes at William. "Are we to understand this notebook came from the conspirator and it is filled with valuable information and not misdirection?"

"Sir, the book was given to me by the conspirator at the bunker," William replied. He reached down the table for a cup and began pouring himself some coffee. "The man told me it contained his thoughts on

155

Chairman Durand." He sat down and sipped his coffee, quickly noticing the coffee was worlds better than the black acid he drank at home. He set his gaze back on Kauffman, thinking of making his positive impression. "The conspirator never said it contained any information regarding security concerns, however those things were discussed. I haven't read the contents. Gentlemen, I'll be glad to start with a description of the field operation in general and then I could give specifics from my interview with the subject . . . if you're agreeable."

Kauffman waved his finger. "Wait a minute. Hold the window-dressing bullshit. Did you or did you not learn anything about a bomb?"

The room fell silent. Time stood still. William felt a sudden wave of electricity. He sipped his coffee. He looked square at Kauffman, fighting his surprise at the question, holding his calm, confident in knowing he had an answer. He swallowed and took another second sip. He sat the ceramic mug on the table with a little thud. "I did. Yes."

"Tell us anything you know about a bomb," Kauffman said sternly.

"You gentlemen, I assume, are aware of the relationship between me and the conspirator. The man was my father, whom I had not seen since I was about twelve years of age. The man left my family like a coward when I was young."

Kauffman snapped, "Yes, yes . . . so . . ."

"The man told me there was a bomb located in the floor of a sewer near SAC Building One, apparently a short distance from here. The sewer was supposed to be identified as L25 running along K Street."

Fournier turned to Kauffman. "I believe Durand Avenue used to be known as K Street."

"We'll confirm it," Kauffman replied sharply. "Manager Rinehart, where is it located in the sewer floor?"

"It's supposed to be fifty-five paces from the tunnel junction."

"Were there any other references to explosive devices mentioned?" Kauffman asked, his tone heavy as if hiding a threat.

"No, sir. Only the sewer."

"Was anything else mentioned regarding the bomb, such as size or sensors or what would trigger the thing if someone would try to disarm it?" Kauffman persisted, leaning forward on his elbows, staring with his piercing eyes.

"The bomb is supposed to be around one thousand pounds of fertilizer. That's all I was told. I wasn't told anything about triggers or anything." The pressure of their interest in the bomb and his freely given answer made William wonder about his chances of staying above the maelstrom of persecution.

Fournier's brow arched. "Hmm . . . and that's all?"

William met his eyes. "I was told nothing about triggers or any details." William sipped his coffee again.

"Did the man say why the bomb was never used?" Kauffman asked.

Steinhoff leaned forward, awaiting the answer.

William glanced at Steinhoff, wondering what devious things were churning in his brain. William continued, "The man said the members of the group responsible for placing it there had died. No one was left to detonate it."

Kauffman looked at Steinhoff and then at Fournier.

"Uh . . . Manager Rinehart," Steinhoff began, "my operations leader, who is now dead, reported you were talking for well over fifteen minutes with the conspirator. Why did it take so long to extract your father from the bunker?"

"It's quite simple. I hadn't seen this man since he abandoned our family when I was a kid, so I had little leverage. Surprisingly, he was alone and well armed. He seemed prepared to use his weapons in a desperate suicide if provoked, and my orders told me to bring him back alive so you could interrogate him. I was trying to coax him, not irritate him. I was trying to fulfill my assignment as made by you."

"It seems you failed." Steinhoff snapped.

"When one of the operations team blew himself apart trying to blow a hole in the bunker, the target became very anxious and extremely agitated. I didn't want to push him, not knowing the fragile state of his mind. The only way I could get him to leave the bunker was with him wearing his vest of explosives for protection. He was afraid of being shot. Then outside, his mind must have snapped. He screamed at me."

William noticed Kauffman flashing a frown at Steinhoff for an instant.

"Manager Rinehart," Kauffman said in a deliberate manner, squinting slightly, "what did you talk about during those fifteen minutes or more with your previous father? Surely there must have been something of substance."

William tried to gather himself without appearing threatened. He nursed a small sip of coffee, savoring the rare taste. Kauffman's penetrating question was like mental landmine and he needed to anticipate his moves in advance to avoid exploding himself. *Relax, relax.* If he looked threatened, it would tell them he had something to hide. Telling the truth had to be nearly foolproof. But how much truth?

"Initially we touched on our family," William said. "I attacked him severely for leaving our family, leaving my mother to raise us. Then he demanded some time to tell me about the circumstances behind his leaving home. He seemed to be trying to apologize and explained some of the history placing him in danger, but I wouldn't allow him to propagandize as long as he wanted on the politics at the beginning of this century. I tried to break it off three or four times but he seemed determined to blow out his own brains right there in the bunker if I didn't listen. He was armed with a high-powered rifle and a handgun the whole time."

"So there weren't any tearful embraces?" Kauffman asked mockingly.

William grinned. "Hardly. I didn't feel like hugging a man who I had hated for so many years. Initially, I thought about strangling the bastard."

Steinhoff sat up. "Manager Rinehart, we want you to prepare a full written report."

"Excuse me, Section Head," Kauffman broke in, his tone once again testing and suspicious. "Did the conspirator mention any names of fellow conspirators? Did he mention the name of any military officers? Did mention any installations?"

William made certain to send his eyes up to the left to indicate he was accessing the factual retrieval portion of his brain and not the creative side. He knew they would be watching his eyes. They were well trained in the psychological mannerisms people manifest during interrogation. "No, sir. I would assume any such references might be contained in his journal lying here on the table."

"Did he mention anything about an underground organization called the FUS?" Fournier asked quickly.

William again felt a precipice before him. "The man said their organization was based on not knowing what anyone else did or even who might be involved. He said he hadn't heard anything from anyone for several years."

"So, this man didn't say anything about the activities of any generals or military?" Kauffman hammered.

"The conspirator said he didn't know what the others were doing, except for the bomb. I couldn't get a sense of how deeply he was involved with it. My written report will cover all this." William realized doubt filled the room like the stench from a carcass, and his body was the cadaver. And—as he guessed, the truth didn't matter. If they suspected you, you were guilty. Besides, it wasn't much bother to eliminate a questionable person. It was only one more dead person to incinerate or bury in a pit.

Kauffman set back in his chair, a finger curled thoughtfully under his lower lip. "Yes, of course," Kauffman replied. "Did you know your father was a political fugitive, a criminal, guilty of crimes against the nascent SAC government? You are aware that you are not to discuss this assignment. It is a crime to disclose or exchange information about SAC activities or information. And depending on the character of the violation you could receive a death sentence."

William nodded.

Kauffman continued, "Well, I have to go to another meeting. We appreciate your helping us this morning with this urgent matter, and I look forward to your full report. Do make it complete, as it will influence how we proceed from this point." Kauffman slid his chair back and stood. He nodded to Fournier and Steinhoff, who also stood.

William rose quickly from his chair, bowing his head a little toward Kauffman. "Thank you, Director Kauffman, and you, Director Fournier, and of course, Section Head Steinhoff," William said.

Kauffman moved around the table, seemingly in no rush to get to the door, and then stopped, first looking down at the table, and then sending his gaze piercingly at William. "Manager Rinehart, did you believe everything your father told you?"

"No! Absolutely not. The man was desperate and appeared tired of life. Besides, conspirators are probably practiced liars. After a few minutes I wondered whether he was insane."

Kauffman continued, "What about the bomb? You believed his information about a bomb, didn't you?"

"Not entirely. I merely took note of it for others to investigate. I found it hard to believe any person or persons could hide such a thing without being discovered. Why would someone want explode a bomb and destroy our state buildings?"

"Why would this man surrender the location of a bomb, after spending years in hiding?" asked Kauffman.

"Maybe because everyone he worked with was dead or because the bomb was too old to be functional," William replied. "I don't know."

"What reason did your father give you for leaving home?" Kauffman asked, watching William closely, never blinking, seemingly ready to decode William's words.

"He said he was swept up in government changes beyond his control, and irrational politics of the time."

"Why the notebook?" Fournier asked. "Why would he write such a thing?"

"He said he wanted people to read it as a warning—for historical purposes," William declared without hesitation, a slight scoffing tone in his words. "He doubted that Chairman Durand saved our country and wrote his own account of our alleged mistakes. I took his gesture as a man's last gasp at having his voice heard by the masses."

Kauffman turned away, raising his eyebrows. He walked through the door ahead of Fournier, while Steinhoff remained inside the room, holding up his hand for William to wait.

Kauffman stopped and moved back to the door. "Manager Rinehart please work the rest of the day on your report so we get the information while it's fresh. I'll advise Director Aldrich of my request so there won't be a problem with your normal duties."

"Yes, sir," William answered, stepping toward the door, not wanting to be cornered by Steinhoff who now followed the directors into the hall. William stopped at the door, waiting for Kauffman and Fournier to walk down the hall.

A few feet away from the conference room, Kauffman paused for Fournier to join him. As Fournier reached Kauffman, Kauffman leaned toward him. "We need everything hiding in Rinehart's brain and I don't give a damn how it's obtained—and I mean everything. I don't believe we have all of what was discussed in that bunker. However, I don't want him killed. Once we lose his brain all opportunity will be lost forever to continue our archeology of that early underground group."

The conversation in the hall chilled William. Fearing the directors noticing he heard them, William backed quickly into the conference room. He looked past the edge of the door and locked eyes with Steinhoff who turned, checking on him.

Fournier tilted his head a little toward Kauffman. "He's all yours. I don't think I need to be involved in this one."

Kauffman nodded extending his hand. "I think you're right, but I wanted to keep you in the loop."

Fournier shook his hand. "Thank you, comrade." Kauffman and Fournier continued down the hall.

William stepped into the hall. Steinhoff extended his arm in William's path, glaring at him. "Manager Rinehart, put all your effort into your report and omit no detail however small and seemingly inconsequential. Your report will reflect on both of us. However, your failure to secure the live removal of the conspirator will weigh heavily on your future. SAC intelligence advised me that it will monitor you and your family the rest of your life, provided of course, that you and your family aren't sent to labor camp. In case you haven't heard, some are in Alaska."

William nodded. "I recognized the importance of this situation and I planned to prepare a very complete report. I will cooperate one hundred percent. It is my duty to serve Chairman Durand."

Steinhoff sneered. "You better."

William's head dropped a little. "I understand. Shall I hold the notebook as a reference for my report?"

"No, I'll take it to the crypto department for analysis."

"If that's all, I have to get to my office and start the report."

"You're free to go. We'll be watching."

William turned and walked toward his section of the building, thinking they were already watching.

Karl Steinhoff watched William walk away, irritated. He felt his hate for Rinehart boiling in his gut, until he remembered he needed to catch Director Kauffman. He walked rapidly down the hall following Kauffman. He wanted to show an example of his forward thinking, hoping to mitigate the damage of the failed mountain mission.

"Director Kauffman, may I have just a minute," Steinhoff said, his elevated voice bouncing off the barren walls.

Kauffman turned to Fournier. "Please excuse me. I have to talk with Karl."

"Have a good day, comrade," Fournier replied and continued down the hall.

"Excuse me, sir, for delaying you," Steinhoff said. "I believe Rinehart's holding back information. Perhaps we should lock him up before he talks to his wife."

"You delayed me from my meeting to tell me that?"

Steinhoff froze, his eyes wide with surprise.

"Very well. Now that you're here, Karl, I did mean to talk to you."

Steinhoff looked him in the eye. He had to or Kauffman would see him weak and incapable. "Yes, sir." Steinhoff's stomach fluttered.

Kauffman's face seemed to harden into tight sinews punctuated with dead eyes. "I've thought about the incident on the mountain and have concluded, given the circumstances, you probably couldn't have altered the outcome, but never fail me again. And—never again wait eight hours to make a report."

Steinhoff swallowed hard. "Yes, sir. I won't. Shall I resign?"

"No!" Kauffman paused. "Oh, yes, make certain you get some information if you have Rinehart interrogated further, but he is not to be harmed mentally. Also, remember, wives usually know something."

"Yes, sir." With a sense of relief, Steinhoff watched Kauffman march away. *Someday, someday , I'll get his job and his power. Someday I will get it.* He noticed a bead of perspiration on his forehead and quickly wiped it away with the back of his hand. He wondered if Kauffman had seen it. Clearing his throat, he started walking in the direction from which he had come. He notice his legs felt a little unsteady. He laughed to himself.

William walked the length of the hall before he convinced himself to take a deep breath. Upon reaching his office area of the building, he went to the men's room near his desk. He leaned over the sink and ran water into his hands, which he brought to his face. He let the water cool his face and try to wash away his tension from the meeting. As he raised his head, he gazed into the mirror. *Compose yourself before turning from the water.* He couldn't act either troubled or relieved. The vid-cams always watched. Hell, he thought, they probably watched a person in the toilet defecating during a daily nature cycle. Actually, up until recently, they hadn't concerned him too much. He had gone about his daily profession, trying simply to hold his SAC job, but now it was as if everything he had heard and seen, had at last, sensitized him to the constant surveillance and the SAC's indiscriminate abuse and treatment of people like waste for disposal. Maybe his father had bequeathed him some of his new awareness, and maybe it had just taken his father's kick in the ass to confirm what he had been toying with in his own mind for too long.

Kauffman, a person William found more threatening and dark than Steinhoff, scared him, and surprised him with the relatively tranquil manner in which Kauffman absorbed the information on the bomb. It appeared as if Kauffman were expecting the information about the bomb and possibly military involvement. It certainly appeared the bomb was part of the reason they wanted his father.

He hated to think of it, but with all their interest in his father, they would definitely be interrogating him again and he hated to think of it, but his family could be on the list for any of their persuasion techniques. William doubted if Kauffman would be satisfied with the verbal report in the conference room and with his forthcoming written report. How long it would take them to inject him with a drug to guarantee truth recall and extraction? For that matter, how long did he have before they would scan his brain? He was probably a candidate for all their toys, the electrodes on his skull, sensory collectors capable of picking up his brain's reactions to suggestions, everything in their depraved minds. He had to move on, to stop dwelling on it and letting his imagination run wild.

Shortly before lunch, after working three straight hours on his report, William thought of his father urging him to do research. Taking a pause from his work, he keyed a code into his computer giving him access to a database for old documents, indexes of businesses and occupations. He wasn't certain why he did it, except he wanted to see history, see what he could of the past, see what the SAC was trying to conceal and slowly wiping from history. He ran his fingers quickly over the keys as information flashed on his display, trying not to leave anything showing long enough that the overhead vid-cams could clearly identify it. Despite having access permission for the database, he didn't have any reason for looking at it. In a minute he found an old listing, dated 2030, containing various stores, pharmacies, hardware, bookstores, and farms. He would like to see a farm. He wondered if he could drive into the country more than a mile or two before the SACI stopped him. What would the countryside look like? Few people from the cities ever saw what had become of it. They didn't allow anyone to see it. He thought of his bus, with its covered windows.

Several farms were located on the way to Alexandria and the listing for a bookstore triggered a thought. The notation in the file gave a date the SAC closed or took over the commercial establishment. A chill washed over him as he looked down the list. The bookstore appeared closed. It was as if he had looked at the obituaries for individual cells that once made up a thriving economic organism.

Thursday night William pulled into his garage under the intimidating eyes sitting in a black v-tran across the street from his home. How long would it take them to remove his SAC car? Suddenly he thought of Lynn and acting strong for her. He thought of her waiting at the door. He expected she would hit him with fear-filled questions the instant he walked in the house. He feared the news about the briefing would deeply trouble her. He wasn't going to tell her what could happen to him, although she might guess it on her own.

When he opened the door from the garage on his way into the kitchen, Stefan and Marie confronted him.

"Dad, where's mom?" Stefan whined.

"She's not home?" William snapped. "You've been here alone?"

"We used the secret outside key to get in."

"She didn't leave a note?"

"We looked," Marie blurted, starting to cry.

"Marie, don't cry," William said softly. "She'll be coming any moment." Lynn's rare behavior scared William, and he immediately suspected the SAC. He kept concern from his face. "She probably took the bus to the market and missed the returning bus. Don't worry. Go do your homework and then you can play. Okay?"

"Yeah, okay," Stefan grumbled.

William poured a glass of water and sat at the kitchen table troubled by Lynn's radical departure from her usual rock-solid routine. A chilly vision of a black v-tran taking her kept trying to get into his head but he repeatedly beat it back, blocking it out. She didn't have a com-link. Few people did and those were the upper SAC executives like Steinhoff. Lynn was the one who knew a couple of the neighbors, but he didn't know who, and undoubtedly the neighbors would run from any involvement.

Suddenly, a low guttural sound rumbled outside, the kind of noise that came from a big vehicle. Quickly, he went to the door leading out to the garage, hit the button for the garage door opener, and ran up the door.

Just then, Lynn stepped out of a v-tran parked in the driveway and walked rapidly into the garage, her face milky-white as if she'd been scared to death. As she got close, her red eyes cried out to William for comfort and safety. He hit the control to lower the door.

"Honey what's going on?" he asked.

She shook her head, and when he tried to take her hand, she flailed both hands at him. She walked into the house, sobbing, her shoulders hanging as if carrying the weight of all their lives. William stared at the v-tran as it sat unmoving, seemingly taunting them with its evil power, until the descending garage door shut them outside of his home. Anger burned in his veins like never before. He wanted to kill them. They had touched Lynn, maybe not physically, but mentally, and for her, a simple mother and caregiver to children, there action was an extreme violation of her life. William thought of his father. The SAC had just demonstrated their control, planting fear, trying to manipulate their minds, proving everything served the SAC, and reinforcing the lesson that sanctuary didn't even exist in one's own mind.

Lynn stood against the kitchen counter, huddled with her elbows to her chest, clutching her mouth with both hands, her eyes fixed blankly on the floor. She fought back sniffles, her breast shuddering, stopping, and then starting.

"Mom," Stefan said in a sympathetic tone.

"Mommy, where were you?" Marie muttered. "Why are you crying?"

"Kids, Mom doesn't feel good. Could you go in the living room for a bit so I can talk to Daddy?"

"What's wrong with Mommy?" Marie begged with a sad face.

"Please kids, Mommy and I need to talk. Mommy's okay. She just doesn't feel good right now."

Marie and Stefan meandered reluctantly out of the kitchen, with Marie looking back at her mom with heavy eyes and a downturned mouth. Lynn didn't move. The moment the kids were gone, she wiped her eyes and slowly swallowed her sobs. She raised her chin with an angry and chilling cast to her eyes.

"Honey, what happened?" William asked.

As if hit by a spark of electricity Lynn stared at William. She placed her finger across her lips indicating he wasn't to talk. She went to a drawer, took out a pad of paper and a pen, and scribbled a note for him.

He nodded at her. He mouthed the words, "Back yard."

She nodded and followed him out the backdoor, which led to the rear lawn, and into the sharp cool air. The light from the kitchen window bathed Lynn's face, painting glistening tears on her cheeks like flakes of glass. William hugged her tight, deciding not to push her for answers, allowing her time to let release the tension and pain she had bundled inside her. She shook against him, and then her mouth found his ear.

"I was interrogated by the SACI," she whispered. "They asked me about your conversation with your father. They wanted to know what you said when you came home. They want me to report everything you say and everything you do. They'll take our children away if I don't cooperate. They will send me to a hard labor camp. What can we do?"

"Honey, you have to tell them what you know, if they pick you up again, except you can't mention those papers I brought home or the transmitter. Those things may be our only salvation. Can you be hard?"

"Those bastards aren't getting my children. Of course I can do it."

"I forgot how strong you are. You're as tough as my mother used to be when my father left home."

"I'm not very strong with those people."

"I think you'll do fine in a battle," William whispered. "Where did they take you, honey?"

"Downtown . . . to some stark, almost empty, building in downtown Fairfax. The windows had been closed off on the inside. It reminded me of a prison. They shined this horrible bright light into my face. They scared me. You can't do anything against them. They could have done anything to me. I've never hated anything like that in my life."

They were escalating the pressure on him and his family. He kissed her on the forehead and then he devoured her mouth. Her kiss told him more than a reflection of their passion, it affirmed her love, and that they would weather the storm together. He hated the idea of her and the kids being involved. It had now gone beyond the vid-cam spying on them. It was as if the SAC had spread them out naked under its microscopic eyes.

When Saturday morning arrived, William held his anxiety in check by staying preoccupied by household activities. Lynn had lost the frown lines above each eye, which had distorted her face for hours after her experience with the SACI. William figured she was blocking the scary implications out of her mind as best she could, just as he did. William had breathed a small sigh of relief after turning in his report to Steinhoff just before noon on Friday morning. At the time, he was tempted to ask Steinhoff why the SACI had picked up Lynn but decided better of provoking more questions. He wanted to tell them to stay away from her but couldn't. Every time he saw them in his mind, taking her and interrogating her, fury built to the point he wanted to do something crazy, anything, tell them all to go to hell, or God forbid—shoot them. But, he had no gun. No one did. It felt good to visualize doing something, taking an action, any action, even if it would have been a foolish gesture. For the present, he had to play their game.

Lynn, sounding a little distracted, ordered William to sit down for breakfast and drink some coffee. He poured a cup and sat down at the table. The coffee, with the usual coarse grounds contained by poor filters, didn't taste anything like the nectar he had had during his interrogation. He sat his coffee down, watching Lynn finish preparing eggs on the range, moving silently as if avoiding him and thinking of their trouble. Stefan and Marie continued playing as usual until the last minute before coming to breakfast.

William picked up his coffee, took a sip. He hoped they could stay detached for as long as possible. She deserved her tranquility. After a moment, she dropped sausage links and scrambled powdered eggs on all their plates, and upon going to the sink to rinse a dish she suddenly stopped and stared out the kitchen window.

"What is it," William asked.

"A really red cardinal, a really pretty one," Lynn replied. Then, as if flipping a switch, she turned. "Stefan and Marie, come to the table."

"Nice, I haven't seen one for a long time." William replied. "It's getting late in the season for them . . . I think."

Lynn sat down at the table, sighed and picked up her fork, running her eyes past the children as they took their places at the table. She turned to William, twisting her mouth a little. "You should have seen all the nasty grease oozing from the sausage in the pan. It's the cheap stuff again . . . more fat than meat, but it's all they had at the SAC market. It wasn't marked low-grade either. The quality of the food is going downhill again, ever since they announced moving more troops into the war. They're ignoring the needs of millions of people."

"Honey, there are quality standards in notebooks for workers to follow," William replied. "The government administrator in charge had to know the meat was no better than cat food. The pork production has been right on target, and I know for a fact there are plenty of workers on the beef and pork farms. The SAC meat packing plants were operating at seventy-five percent, which I believe is . . . uh, plenty of capacity. There's no damn excuse." He looked at the kids. "I'm sorry kids, Dad, said a bad thing. I forgot that I shouldn't curse." Suddenly he remembered the SAC microphone and vid-cam likely hidden somewhere in his house. *So what!* They had bigger charges against him than derogatory comments about the State's food quality. *How about conspiracy or withholding information vital to State security?*

"Okay, Daddy, just don't do it again," Marie said with a funny wrinkle of her nose.

William laughed. "Okay, sweetie." He looked at Lynn and they grinned at each other. He thought Lynn's mouth was tight and fighting the smile. "Was the price the same?"

"No," Lynn said. "It was actually a lower price than the last time."

"Maybe they didn't have enough meat," Stefan said.

"That's possible," William replied. "It's possible the production manager gave them a waver on the inspection requirements so they could make their quota. Numbers are more important than quality. There's always the possibility that all the numbers are false, that nothing is as they say."

"Mom, Stefan wouldn't let me watch the vid-net kid's competition cleanup teams," Marie muttered. "I was watching before breakfast and he turned off the vid-net."

"It's all wrong," Stefan snapped. "You don't want to think about doing that. Those kids are robots."

"Stefan's right, Marie, those kids have to memorize all sorts of strange SAC poetry to stay on the program," Lynn said partially distracted.

Marie pouted and looked down at her plate.

Stefan's observation surprised William. Lynn nodded to him acknowledging Stefan's observation and then the table fell silent for a moment. From the blankness in Lynn's eyes, William could see the SAC problem was chewing at her insides. It had shaken her more than anything he'd ever seen. She glanced at the drawer where he hid the blank pages his father gave him, and then she looked down at her coffee.

He slid into his own memories of home, seeing the time at home before his father had left. The idea of protection popped into his mind and his father's warning. Since the horrible time on top of the mountain and the death of his father, one tortuous dream after another had filled his nights, all of them involving him trying to get his family to safety, him trying to find a way to read the mysterious chronicle, or him trying to convince the SAC that he wasn't dangerous.

Even though he had undergone his own awakening, albeit tardy by many years and still underway, his father had helped him see more clearly. He needed to start reading his father's book right away. Thinking about the book brought to mind more of what his father had said. He also hungered to see what the country was like. For years, travel had been limited to employment commuting by bus or to the SAC market. The SAC had graced him and assigned him a car, but it was likely more of a logistics solution for the SAC than any privilege for him. Lynn had strayed from an apparent allowed path to the market one time and attracted the DPP, who stopped and accused her of belonging to an anarchist group. After enjoying spreading terror and causing Lynn to break into tears with two kids in the car, they allowed her to continue.

What was freedom? He hungered to see open country, something other than his assigned parking lot to catch his assigned bus for work going from Fairfax to the Washington SAC office. He did have enough fuel. Maybe he would take a drive to Alexandria. What could the SACI do to him? Make him turn around. Actually, they were demonically unpredictable and could incarcerate him. He had to use the radio before he did anything stupid—and that would be a moron's folly. Maybe he could go Sunday.

"William, we should talk about . . . the . . . the future." Lynn's voice came out edgy and nervous. She took a bite of food.

"What future?" Stefan asked.

"Never mind," William replied with an amused twist to his mouth. "Your mom and I have things to discuss."

Lynn rolled her eyes. "How did your report go over with those people?"

"I haven't heard anything from anyone since I turned it in. There wasn't much to tell . . . really . . . other than what I had already reported."

"Maybe you'll get a promotion," Lynn answered, her tone a little louder as if for a nearby invisible microphone.

Her face told William she wasn't serious. He frowned and shook his head almost imperceptibly.

"We can hope." She looked down at her plate.

William could see she was struggling to contain her boiling concern. She had her own way of handling trouble and like storm waters building behind dam, her dread would spill over eventually. As he looked at her, he could hear his father's words in his brain, making him fear for Lynn and the kid's safety. He couldn't remember ever fearing much of what went on in his little chunk of the world, and in particular the SAC. *Wrong thoughts, wrong mind, bad thoughts, no bad mind of any kind!*

Chatter from the kids drifted into the distance as he rolled names and events over in his mind, some of the bits and pieces his father had thrown at him in a blur. He stared blankly across the kitchen at the wall, unconsciously probing his plate with his fork. He looked down, barely remembering eating everything. "Do we have any peanut butter left?" he asked.

Lynn rolled her eyes at him. "You and your peanut butter. I think it's all gone."

"I thought I'd have a little with some jam for a little dessert."

"Your usual."

"Yes. I know I'm strange."

"Dad, you're not strange," Stefan said. "I like it, too." He turned to his mother. "Mom, I'm done. May I be excused?"

"I'm done, but I can't eat all my meat," Marie added, looking at her plate as if it were a challenge she had barely overcome.

Lynn frowned a little. "Yes, okay. Set your plates on the counter."

The children erupted from the table and disappeared from the kitchen.

"As for you, peanut butter freak, I'll buy you a new jar when I go shopping, if they have any."

"Thanks, honey." William blew her a kiss.

She gave him a perfunctory smile and poked at her food.

He leaned back, his right hand stretched out toward the table, holding his coffee. He watched Lynn's face and the tightness in her mouth. It had become permanent in the last few days. She desperately needed to talk to him away from SAC spying eyes and ears.

"Okay," she said, motioning with her eyes. She got up from the table, sliding her plate onto the counter at the sink as she started toward their small bathroom a few feet away from the kitchen. William slid his plate on the counter and followed her.

In the bathroom, when Lynn faced him, William's brain locked momentarily as he saw her face pleading to him with her painful silence, begging for an answer to the prison of uncertainty holding them. He took her in his arms and whispered, "Have faith and keep hoping." He looked up, studying the ceiling. Lynn backed away and examined the walls where they met the floor. As William looked, he envisioned finding an intrusive listening device or a worm-size camera somewhere. He placed two towels over the wall heat vent down at the floor, climbed up on the toilet and pulled down the fan cover so he could search for anything possibly looking down through fan's louvered grille. "I . . . I'm not . . ." He looked down at Lynn and motioned with his eyes that he saw something. He whispered, "Hand me two washcloths."

"Not my good ones," Lynn whispered, dismissing him with a frustrated hand. She opened a cabinet door to the area under the sink and removed two wrinkled and frayed cloths. "Here, you can use my old ones."

He laughed to himself, amused at how she prized such a simple bit of the ordinary. He took the washcloths, spread them carefully on the top side of the grille, and then replaced it in the ceiling. "I think we're okay now," he whispered, climbing down. "As long as we whisper we might be okay. I don't see any place a camera could be hidden except in the vent and it's covered. But we still have to whisper."

With wrinkles in her brow and her mouth drawn, Lynn begged, "Honey, what are we going to do?"

"I turned in my report Friday and didn't get any word by the end of the day. I told them the truth and I gave them the notebook my father gave me."

"What about those—"

"Shush," he interrupted. He shook his head.

"Sorry."

He leaned into her ear. "They will stay where they are until this thing runs its course. You should forget about them. They're blank, anyway."

She frowned at him and grinned as if he were joking. "What?"

"My father made notes on the history of the country, the events that destructively brought us to where we are. He made them with old-fashioned invisible ink."

Her face became still as she studied him. Incredulous, she grinned. "Was he crazy?"

William placed a finger to his lips. "No. I think he was a patriot of sorts. There were freedoms back then, which we don't have now, and I don't think there was any government control."

"Why did he have to give you—"

"He said it was to save our lives."

"Oh, God." Lynn's muffled voice cracked with her stress. She took a piece of toilet paper and dabbed her nose with it.

He pulled her up to him, wrapping her tight to his chest, pushing his face into her hair, smelling her intoxicating scent, feeling her warm skin against his lips, feeling her breathe heavily against him. He kissed her neck and whispered, "You remember our first apartment . . . kissing nonstop on the beat-up old sofa, no money, eating popcorn on weekends, and watching that small flat-screen television, the one back before the vid-screens came out?"

Lynn nuzzled her chin into his neck. "They were some of our best days. I'd go back there and exchange them for now in a heartbeat."

Her breath gave him a tingle, as it did almost every time. "I love you, honey."

"And I love you." She raised her head, her brow wrinkled with a question. "What's going on? What aren't you telling me?"

"There's more but I don't want you worrying about it now. For now, you shouldn't go to the SAC spa."

"You know we have to do what they tell us?" Her whispered voice was stark, cold. "With these vid-cams, it's as if we are on a theater stage every minute, acting out a pretend life. We are their marionettes. The government controls the food, which is poor at its best. The government tells us where we can go. If the kids get sick, it's impossible to find a doctor. All we can do is go to the government pharmacy and get pills, which may be nothing more than a sugar pill. My God, the government is even controlling our minds by telling us what we can say and think and what we can't. What kind of life is this? Really, it's not. It's scarcely existing!"

Lynn's words slammed into William's brain. Never before had he made such a stark association, even standing before his father hearing about the political upheaval. It ripped at his heart, hearing his wife cry out so, that the SAC was depriving her and the children of their life, something bestowed to all people on earth by God and not the SAC. They were slaves. And—his wife must have felt it before he did. "We must keep doing everything we've been doing," he said, collecting himself. "We need to act normal in front of the vid-cams."

Lynn grimaced. "What about going to the SAC spa? Isn't it expected?"

"Yes and no. They invite only selected managers, at least that has been the rumor. But, you must not go. My father said they did things to people there."

"What? What do you mean? For God sake, what?"

"Take it easy, honey."

"What on earth could they possibly do? I'll just tell them I'm leaving, if I don't like what's going on."

"They . . . I'm sorry . . . they insert things into people's bodies to control them."

"You're making this up." Then her mouth dropped. "You're serious. My God. They wouldn't do it to a manager or his family . . . would they? That is depravity and enslavement. Humans are not cattle."

"I want you to know absolutely nothing about what's going on or what I do. If I read something or go somewhere, I don't want you to know anything about it. You should be safe if you're in the dark, at least until the minute I have to tell you."

"Tell me you're not going to do something crazy."

He bit his lower lip. "I have to know where we're going, the trouble I'm in, if there's real danger for you and the kids, and if there is—what I can do about it." He flashed on his father making the same sacrifice. "I have to do it for you and the kids. I'm not a hero but I can't let my family suffer. Honey, to the government we have no value except if we can work for them. We could be sent to one of the big government farms or a labor camp. People die at the labor camps . . . on purpose."

Lynn covered her mouth and mumbled through her fingers, "God help us."

William hugged her tight and kissed her on the ear. "Smile before you go out and talk to the kids. We must be actors now." He opened the bathroom door, went over to the counter, poured a cup of coffee, and Lynn began clearing dishes. He stood there for a moment watching Lynn, overpowered by the prospect of their lives teetering on the edge of a cliff. His gazed off blankly. He didn't have the energy to move, as if he were fighting a battle inside his brain, fighting to take some sort of action, but he was uncertain about what it was he should do next. The SAC obstructed every direction he might look for a solution with its infinite universe of controls and surveillance.

He almost forgot the metal detector needed for checking the kids. He had to find a source somewhere; but even talking about such a device brought great risk. The SACI would not only ask why he needed such strange electronics, they'd arrest him. He laughed hollowly under his breath thinking of his reply. *I want to see what the hell you bastards have inserted into my children.* It suddenly occurred to him that his thinking had changed enormously since the SAC had abused him by making him try to capture his father. When they threatened his wife, his thinking became completely devoid of doubt, except he wanted to read the history for himself—and he desperately wanted to see what was out in the country.

The moment he turned in his report with all the information his father had disclosed, as near as he could remember it anyway, the all-powerful guardians of the SAC, three of the directors, would be evaluating what sort of risk he represented to their immoral control. Without question, they'd be watching him, fearing he'd divulge their troubling history to the public, spreading infectious ideas against the SAC, perpetrating wrong-speech and sedition. From the SAC's self-preservation point of view, it was easy to understand their actions.

The circumstances had come full-circle in an incredibly strange way. He was walking his father's footsteps, becoming a victim of events like his father, although probably because of his father. An epiphany came to him or maybe it was just simple logic. If he were to save his family, he'd have to do it before the SAC discovered what he was doing, before they took him in for the hard interrogation, before the brainwashing. Yes, that was something he didn't want to think about, because most assuredly it was a death sentence. Another thing bothered him about Kauffman's people arresting him, something more horrible than the SAC brainwashing him, and that was the SAC torturing his family in front of him. He had to prevent that at all costs. Thanks to his father for that warning.

Awakening from his trance, he felt a mellow softness inside, missing his family, missing the close interaction, playing together like friends as much as siblings and parents. He sat down at the table, clutched his coffee cup in both hands, and finding it still warm, he leaned back sipping it. "Why don't we play some game today?" His tone sounded far away in his own ears, as if it were a wish.

From the living room Stefan blurted, "I was going over to Carl's today to play his war game."

"Honey, I was going to take Marie to the SAC shop to see if it has any good shoes," Lynn said. "She needs a pair for cold weather. Her feet are really growing."

William rolled his eyes. "Okay, I guess I'll just have to go back to North Carolina."

Stefan yelled, "Dad, you're not going anywhere. We won't let you."

"So I guess I'll watch world soccer on the vid-net until you get back." He stopped. "I might go—"

Lynn looked at him suspiciously, her face motionless and suddenly stormy.

"Well . . . maybe . . . I'll go do some work in the garage." He could see Lynn knew what he meant.

"Is that wise?" Lynn asked, her face telling him she knew.

"I'm virtually under house-arrest, so if they want to stop me they will. I talked to an underground conspirator."

She nodded with a blank dejected expression holding her face.

Her dread was justified, he thought. They had already declared their intentions on his family by scaring the hell out of Lynn, hauling her off to one of their local interrogation offices, and threatening to take his children. He couldn't sit back and do nothing. He'd done that for all his adult life. The SAC feared something devastating, something bigger than the bomb he had disclosed and they wouldn't allow him to live, truly live—until he died or they got their information. The SAC destroyed his life—but not that of his precious ones. He needed information to save them. How strange it was—how important basic information could be. That was why the SAC controlled all arteries of the information blood. Information carried life just like red blood cells.

Lynn glared at him, her lips pressed angrily together, giving him one of those looks that told him, she knew he was up to something and she didn't like it one bit.

After Lynn left the house with Marie and Stefan disappeared to a friend's to play, William took a small torch from a kitchen drawer, checked it for producing a beam of light, and continued into the garage. He opened the hood of his car and searched for an object described to him in a rumor, probing with the light in the dark crevices around the engine, trying to locate a small black rectangular box. There it was. He found it attached to the wall separating the instrument panel from the engine compartment, just to the left of the electric brake actuation module. The markings on its surface clearly identified it as SAC and declared it was a crime to remove it. He found no wires entering or leaving it the device. He reached to remove the box with a screwdriver, planning to force it from the attachment and abruptly stopped. The intrusion of his life suddenly angered him unlike it never had before. His mind exploded with indignation. To hell with them. Why should he care if they track him? What was he going to tarnish if he took a drive into the real world? He closed up the car with a burst of satisfaction.

Now, the radio awaited him as a duty or a debt to both his father as well as his Lynn and his kids. He marveled at the idea of using a simple radio for communicating with an underground resource. It seemed the only genuine chance for obtaining freedom. Using the radio scared him. He doubted his ability to follow the proper procedure, and the possibility that the SAC might detect the signal. If they did, they would crash in their door and brutally destroy his family. Where did the men who plunged into battle and saved their comrades get their courage? It couldn't have been the offspring of logic. Perhaps it was born from some sort of hope—or faith—in God.

Later, Saturday night, after everyone went to bed, William turned out the kitchen light, crept over to the drawer and retrieved his book. He felt his way along the counter to the wall and then to the bathroom door. With the book in hand he felt an electric hunger running through him, barely restraining his hand from turning on the light until he had closed the door, preventing any watching vid-cam from seeing his light. He glanced at the fan overhead and the vent at the floor confirming that they were both still covered. He opened the book to the title page and moved his fingers over the paper, as if validating the book was real.

He started reading the section covering the beginning of the 1980s. He read ravenously, page after page, piling up events in his brain like bricks of knowledge, building a foundation. As he read all the events, their causes, and how in many cases, people sought the false god of serving the incapable of the masses by sacrificing the ideal self-reliance, the country's evolution started making sense. All manner of special interest group manipulated the political and social graft of the system, each one seeking to further their cause without concern for the country, as if the country's blood could be extracted forever without the country's body dying. After four hours and tears in the corners of his eyes, he stopped reading. The churning events documented in the book had raised his fear higher than he would have expected, and confirmed his fire of the urgency to get his family out from under the SAC.

Sitting on the toilet lid, he ran his hand over the cover of the book lying on his legs, as if it were the obituary for a beloved family member. He cried, pouring out his remorse for what he had done, for what he had not done, and for his lack of action against a monster. He thought of his time at home when he was a little boy, and he wept over the possibility his own son and daughter could die as prisoners of the State, working at a hard labor camp or in a gruesome smoke-filled factory.

William left the bathroom at half past three in the morning. He went, again in the dark, to the kitchen drawer where he hid the transmitter. He carefully eased it from the drawer to his trousers without turning from the counter and drawer. From next drawer over he gathered a note pad and pencil and slid them inside his shirt. He then returned to the bathroom where examined the transmitter and the code on its back. He drafted a short note using the code of dots and dashes his father had given him. Nervously, he double-checked his code, determined not to send a radio signal up into the SAC atmosphere for any more seconds than absolutely necessary. He checked to see that the radio's power switch was off and plugged it into the wall. He sucked in a breath, turned on the radio, and touched the send button, sending out his sequence of dots and dashes. Immediately after the last bit of code, he snapped off the radio. He felt heart pounding in his chest. *Is anyone actually listening?* Had he wasted his time? He had no way of knowing if anyone out beyond his home had received the signal. *Maybe they were all dead by this time.*

Now, how would he dispose of the radio? He couldn't crush it with a hammer in the garage. The SACI could pick up the noise with their listening devices. He had to find a way to dispatch the hand-size device. Wait. He could quietly bury it in the backyard. The rear lawn was tiny but it had real earth for digging a hole. When Lynn had planted her flowers in the summer, and had planted the illegal flower bulbs from the woman down the street, she had penetrated the fertile soil without exerting massive strength to do it. He retrieved his battery-powered torch from the counter in the kitchen, located Lynn's garden shovel in the garage, and slipped out the backdoor of the garage onto the chilly lawn, which the city lights bathed in a soft powdery glow as they reflected off the low blanket of clouds.

The shovel cut easily into the soft soil where the summer flowers had been and where their spent stalks still poked from the earth. He worked quickly, prying open the soil, making a pocket at the tip of the shovel, winding the cord around the radio, and placing it down into the earth. At last, he felt a bit of relief as he pushed soil over the transmitter, set the tip of shovel on top the radio, and then lunged with all his weight, shearing through the radio. The earth conveniently muffled the crunching noise released by the radio's death. He stamped down the earth on the two sides of the hole he had cut, concealing the signs of his digging. The act he had just completed suddenly struck him as his family's single biggest hope.

Chapter 9

Sunday afternoon the com-link lying on the glass-top coffee table at the side of the hot tub chimed. Karl Steinhoff scowled at the intruding linkage to the SAC organization. *Not on a Sunday.* He kissed the lips of a well-sculpted blonde woman reclining in his arms, allowing the com-link to ring. His wife, with special dispensation because of his position, had gone to New York visiting family, leaving an opportunity for him to get together with his current mistress, Brigitte, for a couple days. He gulped the remaining olive from his cocktail glass before setting it at the side of the tub. Brigitte frowned at him with pouty lips.

"Stay put, sweetie, this won't take long," he said, giving her a quick kiss. He climbed out of the tub, grabbing his bathrobe from the nearby chair, wrapping it around him as he glanced up at the glass ceiling of the sunroom. He gathered himself into his stern mental toughness and then picked up his com-link.

"Steinhoff." He stared angrily at the table as held the device to his ear.

A voice, distant and unnatural came from the com-link. "Section Head Steinhoff, sir, this is Sergeant Kindell on the surveillance team at Manager Rinehart's home."

"Wait a minute sergeant." Steinhoff pressed the com-link tight to his ear. "Okay, go ahead."

"Sir, we're following Rinehart. He has exited his housing area and is driving toward the highway going south. He's leaving his allowed travel area. According to his file, he's never gone this way before. Director Kauffman ordered us to update you if anything strange happened. Sorry to bother you on a Sunday, sir. We were ordered to follow your direction on this case. Shall we request a drone or shall we arrest him for traveling without authorization? We could just follow him."

"Yes, you were correct to contact me with your surveillance status. It sounds as if you have followed your orders. Don't arrest him. Continue with your surveillance, Sergeant. I don't think we should use a drone in this situation. Do whatever you have to and stay on his ass. I want you to learn where he's going, what he's doing, and if meets with anyone. I'll be leaving for the tracking center in a few minutes to monitor his activity personally. He may not know his vehicle has a tracking bug in it. Nevertheless, don't lose him."

"Very good, sir. Oh . . . yeah, our records show that his car has two tracking units, a standard unit added to all cars and a second one we use on special vehicles."

"Which unit is sending?"

"Sir, the special one. The secondary is alive but operating in slave mode."

"Is that normal?"

"It is if a special unit has been installed."

"Keep your eye on him."

"Yes, sir, Kindell out."

Steinhoff turned off his com-link, laid it on the table, and then sent a long look at Brigitte, who was gazing back at him seductively, smiling like a prize up for collection. He found her amusing and teasing expression tempting, but neither the enticement in her eyes nor the thought of her promising caresses could overpower his excitement for accumulating lethal information on Rinehart. And she certainly couldn't wash away his fear of failing Kauffman again. He had to leave her alone and awaiting his return. She was safe. She had passed all the security he could throw at her, including twenty-four hour a day monitoring. She was harmless, a simple creature only interested in living a little better than other women like her, females who hadn't gotten much education or training, and fought like hell avoiding a government farm or factory.

"You probably heard the bad news," he said, tying to sound disappointed. "I have to run over to our monitoring center. You can stay and soak for a while, watch a movie, have another cocktail, whatever you like. Just don't get too drunk to do some serious exercise later on."

"Honey, I'll be right here, ready and waiting," Brigitte replied. "I'll probably find a movie."

"Give me a kiss before I leave." He knelt down and gave her a hand, helping her from the water, letting his eyes feast upon her glistening figure, a shape that began eliciting a battle in his brain.

She grabbed her robe and pulled it closed as she leaned into him for a kiss. He slid his hands under her robe, finding her butt with each hand, pulling her toward him, mashing their bodies together as their mouths consumed each other.

Steinhoff rushed into the monitoring center located at the sub-level one of Building Two. He flashed his identification badge for the security man.

"Thank you, sir," the guard said.

Steinhoff nodded and walked slowly into the SAC surveillance room. He had been there four times before and each time the dimly lighted room filled with rows of people staring at desktop vid-screens in a dramatic manner excited and invigorated him.

He paused a few feet inside the door, giving his eyes time to adjust to the low light. He looked at the duty roster lying on a table for the observers, running his finger down the page until he identified the tasking station covering Rinehart. He walked over to a man watching a large vid-screen. The vid-screen, which was partitioned into four view-windows, showed four different targets. One of the four views showed a dot on a map. Steinhoff watched quietly as the observer typed information on his keyboard, controlling the views appearing on his screen. The idea of observing Rinehart and possibly recording an act of sedition or an act supporting wrong-thinking amused Steinhoff, as if he were watching an animal navigating a trap, one in which he had the lever to spring it closed.

The man at the observer station noticed Steinhoff out of the corner of his eye and sat rigidly upright in his chair as if someone jerked his puppet strings. "Sir, how can I help you?"

"You're following Manager Rinehart?"

"Yes, sir."

"Where did he go? What's he doing?"

"Sir, he's driving outside his allowed area. All I have for him is his location on the map." The man sent his attention back to the display.

"We need to catch this man in his criminal activity."

"Yes, sir. We can do that . . . using . . . as long as we have a surveillance unit."

Steinhoff clasped his hands behind his back and watched silently for a few minutes. He shuffled his feet and pulled on his chin. "Where is he going?" Steinhoff snapped.

"Sir, Rinehart is definitely heading toward Alexandria, Virginia. That's all I can tell you at this moment."

"Thank you. That's what I wanted to know." He wanted more information. He needed it. Rinehart was doing something strange. Why on earth would Rinehart go to Alexandria? According to Rinehart's dossier, this excursion was totally out of the normal course of events for the man, especially a manager with a family, and he didn't have authorization. He reminded himself to not openly show his satisfaction with Rinehart traveling into the world of criminality—and ultimately into interrogation by Doctor Beucher. "I'll get a coffee and be back."

"Very good, sir."

As Steinhoff stepped out of the monitoring room, he encountered Director Kauffman walking quickly toward him.

"I see you beat me here, Karl," Kauffman said, his eyes dancing fiercely.

"Yes sir, thanks to your insightful orders your surveillance crew called me with an update."

"I thought you might like to administer this case with my people. Your units are good but not equipped like mine. And it's good experience for you. I might add . . . of course your units don't require the same equipment . . . for their normal surveillance operations."

"Thank you, sir; I appreciate your renewed confidence."

"I'm not certain it's entirely renewed—yet," Kauffman said with a turned down brow and a slight squint. "Where is our man going?"

"Sir, he appears to be on his way to Alexandria, perhaps he's meeting with someone from the underground."

"I doubt if he would be so visible if he were."

Chapter 10

It was nearly three p.m. Sunday and the sun sent shafts of gold through holes in the clouds, white clouds that partially filled a brilliant blue sky. William had long since breached the boundary the SAC allowed him to drive from home with his government issued car, and he now headed toward Alexandria on Virginia State road 236. A v-tran began following him the minute he turned out of his housing area, shadowing him like a black specter about to swoop down at any time. But it hadn't. It was clear they didn't need a tracking device if they were going to follow with a v-tran. For now, with only three or four cars traveling the highway, the v-tran driver appeared satisfied to keep a lot of distance, maintaining a position barely within sight. The cars he saw were undoubtedly authorized SAC vehicles.

Out the windshield of his car, he saw a gray band stretching out before him, segmented like a worm with regular occurring separations in the aging concrete road. He drove down the highway, faintly remembering traveling on it somewhere around his first year of college or possibly before.

It knifed across hills and meadows, separating the overgrowth on each side like an incision into the body of the land. Weeds encroached up to the edge of the crumbling and cracked horizontal stone band. The road told him of its years, jarring his car as his tires crossed some of the larger scars in the surface.

He had finally pierced the SAC barrier. He now satisfied his hunger, needing to let his eyes touch the countryside, let his mind absorb images of the open land away from their prison condominium housing area. He had to see it. He needed to confirm what he had heard over the years and had not been able to see from the SAC bus with its cloaked windows. It was inexplicable, like being afraid, and yet needing to look in a coffin at a deceased human. He had heard a dead and disheveled country existed beyond the SAC restrictions, beyond what it allowed him to see. He hoped to see freedom and feared he would be horrified if he saw it, because of what it would mean—but he needed to verify that the country was dead and that the SAC had destroyed it. He needed to see the dead country one last time for himself, with his own eyes—just in case the SACI arrested him.

The only people who ever crossed such country and saw what it was like were the poor souls heading for a labor camp. No one ever returned from those. Was that the reason no one ever returned from the labor camps and government farms, because they had seen the country? Perhaps the people at the camps had seen the real country, had seen the truth, that it was desolate and sick and in failing health. The SAC didn't want the returning people to inform the masses. But what about those small cities spread across the nation? Had the SAC moved people to the massive city centers for total control? It seemed they had done just that—needing to hide their secret of the deteriorating land. But he was jumping ahead of himself. He hadn't seen it yet.

Going back to his moment of decision and the way his mind was struggling; he could have been in a dream. He had swallowed hard when he left home, knowing Lynn's fear and knowing he was taking a big risk. He remembered hoping the radio signal he had sent had reached an underground savior, so if something happened to him his family would have a chance for safety, which he had nearly concluded was beyond his reach, especially with all the eyes trained on him. Down deep, something told him he could handle the SAC's questions about his little trip in the car. After all, didn't they need him? They needed what was in his brain, just as his father. If they didn't need him, they would have already sent him to a labor camp—to die.

Perhaps the v-tran was curious about where he was going, suspecting him of meeting members of the underground, and that was why they hadn't stopped him. If it would follow on the highway, he wondered if it would continue tracking him once he reached a tangle of streets in the city. Since it would be fruitless for him to try escaping their imprisoning observation, he might as well do what he had planned.

Looking at the pastoral setting enticed a speculative thought about moving to the country, and its real feasibility. Of course it wasn't.

Now that he was several miles out from the city, other than avoiding cracks and chuckholes in the road, he started fulfilling his objective, taking in the rural panorama. It was as if he were looking a picture album covering years gone by. The amount of open space stunned him, made him hunger for having such a world. The landscape on his left and right side of the road declared its struggle in the artifacts still fighting nature's elements. People had cut some fields to below the knees and others remained fallow with spikes of tall, rust color weeds. Fields of stumbling-over cornstalks occupied a farm with workers moving slowly across the field for some purpose. He saw perhaps ten people in one field, all wearing gray SAC work clothing, bending over and picking up something in a harvested field of corn. They invoked his thought of work-camp laborers. He got a chill. He turned his head from the road, quickly looking for the administration facility, and caught a glimpse of an old farmhouse with several weathered out buildings. He saw no guards with guns.

He saw what he had hoped to see, country. He had wondered if he would see a real free farm, one operated directly by a farmer. He now realized that was a stupid thought. Of course, nobody owned property of any kind. It all belonged to the SAC. Everyone who worked, worked for the SAC. Farther down the road, the houses were equally scattered and the space between them showed signs of harvested crops, although a few still had the same mature brown cornstalks standing in the fields. It was similar to the countryside he had seen in North Carolina driving from the airport to the mountain bunker. Here, every house he saw from the highway had a symptom of death, something lifeless about its appearance. It either missed its protective skin, or its shingles, or the occupant had boarded over the windows, as if the lives contained within had resigned themselves to a slow death. Most of the houses stood with a collapsed out-building nearby and surrounding yards with a decade's overgrowth of weeds and scrub trees. He felt as if someone had reached inside his chest and torn away his heart, as if he had looked upon a deceased person in the coffin. He wanted to cry out, to beg someone to tell him that he was seeing an exception, and not the rule. How could the countryside be allowed to deteriorate to such a condition?

The rolling land looked plagued, as if sores had burst and expelled putrescent piles of refuse. The neglect filled his vision in the distance and in the foreground, a tragedy of man. Heaps of discarded chunks of lives and discarded property had accumulated over years. Obviously, waste removal had not existed for the countryside. The SAC probably only used it in the cities to prevent disease. He spotted another rarity, although it was now an affliction appearing on every farm he passed, idle rusting autos. People had parked the autos alongside the barns and outbuildings and on some properties, they had retired large trucks. The SAC had prohibited large trucks many years back. He couldn't determine if these parked trucks were in working order as he passed by on the highway, but the surrounding weeds seemed a strong argument they were dead metallic creatures. He had seen two trucks a few years ago on his commute to the bus pick-up area but the SAC eventually swept them away with its cloaking hand, so now you rarely saw a truck in the city. He guessed the government had to use them somewhere at some time, perhaps at night.

His eyes froze for a moment on a distant farm field, darted back to the highway in front of him, and back to the field. A real tractor rolled through the field with a farmer driving the tractor down through his corn, harvesting it. The sight elated him, and then as he thought of his father's years, it sent his heart plunging. The existence of part of his world appearing tranquil, uncontrolled, and perhaps nostalgic, raised momentary hope that there might be life away from the SAC, but then he grounded his observation in the reality of his world; the farmer was no doubt the indentured servant of the State, and probably barely surviving. He had seen data while he was making his own reports for the upper level SAC executives and the data indicated life was quite severe on farms. He turned his head, trying to snatch another glimpse, trying to see if the farmer had on the telltale gray SAC work garb. He couldn't distinguish the color; he'd driven too far.

Seeing the trucks, the tractor, and a farmer made him struck him with a question about the SAC food supply, and how it might exist on perilously thin ice, only supported by slave labor. How much of the crops were diverted into the black market? The SAC had severe penalties for black-market trading in commodities, such as beef and chickens. In his job, he had seen how all the grain had to go through various SAC commodity-clearing facilities scattered across the country. He had seen reports on people who had been assigned to tenant farms. *Even that's slavery.* The tenant could never relocate and they were held to strict quotas regardless of the weather. Tenants treated like trash to be discarded, died on their farms.

If only he could take his family into the country to live and survive, perhaps do a little bartering, good hard labor for food. To do it, he would have to go somewhere with a forest so they could cut wood for heat. Then he remembered, the SAC had made it illegal to cut firewood about fifteen years ago, to stop people from cutting down all the trees, to avoid using coupons for SAC utilities. The SAC controlled all the electrical power and gas. What a dream.

Out through the windshield and the side window, the patches of the blue sky seemed more brilliant, bigger. In places where the land was less rolling, he could see unencumbered from north to south, unaltered by the jagged outline of sky-piercing concrete buildings. He could breathe, really breathe, without a cautious catch in his diaphragm because of the SAC watching. He was in open space that the SAC hadn't totally strangled by its control technology. He'd forgotten what the open land was like. The open land was freedom. Tears welled in his eyes as he looked across the pastoral country and saw the country's ravaged carcass. As much as the sight of the country's sickness saddened him, he appreciated seeing it, and was glad he had breached the SAC regulation. He was viewing the cadaver of a once vibrant body. Suddenly, he felt a spark of rage against those who had stolen a country and freedom from its people, against the SAC.

He came to a sign indicating there was an exit one mile ahead for a crossroad. He recognized it from the SAC database as one associated with businesses. He took the ramp off the highway and came to a stop. He looked in the direction from which he came, wondering if he should return home. He didn't see the v-tran. Checking the road before him, he remembered the data. The computer he had seen listed stores farther east and included a book shop, although he had no doubt about it being either closed or closely watched. He told himself he hadn't come for another book; his father's was just fine. However, he was exceptionally curious about the existence of any stores, stores not held by the SAC. A voice on the edge of his brain whispered the SAC controlled and operated everything. There were no more free businesses—but he had to see.

He drove north on Callahan Drive toward King Street, one of the streets he'd found in the database, and then southeast down King Street, covering a mile, repeatedly checking his mirror for the v-tran. There they were. He saw them again. They were still lurking behind him, their headlights like two eyes staring at him in his mirror. He decided not try running from them or hiding from them. If they wanted to stop him, so be it.

He checked his instrument panel, looking at the number of miles he had remaining for his supply of hydrogen fuel. It was fine, plenty to get home. Suddenly he realized he almost certainly would not find fuel anywhere around the area.

As drove east down King Street, he traced his eyes across the buildings lining the street. It was another example of business-murder by the SAC, killing a once thriving business area. It was a depressing statement of past and present. The buildings gave a brutal contrast between the effects of a socialistic disease and the vibrant freedom-nurtured businesses of his father's time. The decaying remains of the SACs attack on man's self-respect and man's spirit, stabbed his eyes. An infection of discarded paper and cans cluttered the street. Random weeds reached out from cracks in the sidewalks, businesses possessed cracked and missing windows, and dark filled buildings instead of light and life. It was as if people stopped taking care of everything, stopped moving forward, and focused solely on surviving, holding on by their fingernails. People didn't seem to exist. *What kind of thoughts are these? Mine! SAC, get out of my head.*

He checked his rearview mirror. The v-tran followed several car lengths behind him. Why were they allowing him to continue?

He drove on. There were no other cars traveling on the once vibrant commercial artery with two lanes going in each direction. The atmosphere hung with an unnatural feeling, eerie, as if he were rolling over a gigantic lifeless carcass. A complete concrete building stood void of windows and doors like a bleached skull exposed to the sun. He passed block after block of abandoned buildings, their broken windows like open sores, their boarded up doors like feeble bandages left on the wound after the patient had died. Peeling and running paint on storefronts and signs were like tears remaining from cries and protestations over restrictions and controls. Derelict signs for long-ago fashions in contemporary furniture whispered the existence of prior vitality, decades in the past. The signs above the shops for Fargo Carpets, Fleetwood Jewelry, Mancini Plumbing and Heating, Sander's Pizzeria, Wolf Mortgage and Loan, all testified to the once free spirit of the army of entrepreneurs in a free country. Old Town Theater went past on his left, the marquee a yellowish white where big black letters once alerted movie watchers about the film shown inside. A church, not a big one, but sizeable, stood dispirited nearby. The former owners had barricaded the door with two large boards. Still displayed on the church sign out by the street, were the words, "In God We Trust." A painted window sign at a jewelry shop spoke of its fine chronometers and the shop next door advertised gourmet chocolates. Three boarded-up hotels displayed advertising signs declaring foreclosure and offering a reduced sale price. He wondered how many cities across the country had streets such as this. Decades in the past, this decay must have portended the death of the country. Strangely, not long ago, William probably would have gazed upon the decomposing flesh with impervious detachment, but now it stabbed him in the heart.

At last, a reassuring indication of commercial life came down the road toward him. A truck lumbered like a large animal across the wasteland, rolling on eighteen wheels, its brown cargo body a tarpaulin covered mystery. When it passed him, the SAC letters on the driver's door smothered his mistaken hope.

He stopped for a traffic light, operating as if for a flow of ghost vehicles. He noticed the v-tran had slowed to a crawl quite some distance behind him. Upon starting again, on the right side of the street, a man and woman walked slowly down the sidewalk, their attention seemingly locked on the sidewalk below their feet. Their dress was dirty gray SAC trousers with the distinguishing dark gray stripe down the side of the leg and their gray coats appeared to whip like tissue paper in the chilly breeze. They looked like laborers, possibly from a nearby manufacturing facility. He watched them in his mirror until they walked into an SAC market, a small building displaying the letters "SAC" that had been sloppily painted over the name of the original owner, Carino and Son, which was still visible above the storefront. As was typical for SAC stores the windows displayed no signs and the interior functioned under dreary lighting conditions. He had gone with Lynn twice to their SAC market and agreed whole heartedly with her that they were depressing places to buy groceries and that the store staff were like cantankerous street police.

Farther down the street, he passed man wearing the same government clothes, but this person stood motionless on the sidewalk with his shoulders hunched over and his hands plunged into his pockets. The man stared fixedly at a picture of Durand pasted on the side of an old brick building, a dilapidated structure whose second story windows were boarded shut. A snarling dog emerged from an opening between the buildings and ran at the man. Another building blocked William's view before he could see what happened and he turned back to his driving. *What a horrible existence.*

Old homes now lined the road in front of him as the area transitioned from business to residential. However, they matched the run-down character of the previous business district, with roofs patched haphazardly with non-matching shingles, and holes showing the underneath vulnerable wood skeleton of some homes. Metal bars protected many of the structures, covering windows and doors, but he saw no people.

Far off in the distance, he saw a faint sparkle of the sun off the Potomac River, which an angry gray cloud quickly erased. He passed an area of vacant lots strung along the road as if a disease had obliterated them leaving only earth. Then came more surviving buildings, structures with the same illness, with the same scars he had already seen, peeling paint, street trash collecting at the base of their foundations, and weeds erupting from cracks in the concrete, nature seemingly reclaiming its property. Out of the corner of his eye, on the right, he saw a dreary sign atop a one-story concrete block building, a sign for a little bookshop, Bunches of Books. He slowed as he drove past. The tiny windows showed no life. At the next intersecting street, he turned around and drove back to the shop. He glanced on down the street and saw the v-tran coming slowly in his direction. He wheeled into the small parking area behind the bookshop and as he reached to turn off the car, he stopped, watching for the v-tran. When it didn't appear after a few moments, he got out. *They'll stop me at any minute!*

He looked around the area for vid-cams, up on old telephone poles, on the sides and roof of the shop, trying to pick out any shape not belonging to the structure. He didn't see anything surveilling the parking area or anything watching at King Street covering the corner of the shop. He didn't see any people. It was possible the v-tran was allowing him to walk across their spider web where he'd get stuck.

An indescribable urge took his hand and made it open the car door. He walked to the rear door, an all-metal customer door that the owner obviously employed for security. He found it locked. He glanced down. From the amount of dirt, leaves, and odd paper trash collected against the threshold of the door, it appeared no one had opened the door for a long time. It was another death at the hands of the people who had formed State America. He thought about walking to a front window to determine if the owner had left any books behind, and then the futility of such a gesture strangled the idea.

He walked back to his car, pulled out of the parking area, and turned toward home, satisfied he had answered his question and had confirmed another horror of his country. He resigned himself to fight for his family at any cost on his own head. After traveling two or three miles west, back toward the interstate highway, he once again saw the v-tran following him, maintaining the same position until he drove up to the entrance of his housing area at about four o'clock. As he rolled slowly into his housing area, the following v-tran stopped on the street behind him. He couldn't quite see all the way to his house, but he suspected another v-tran was waiting across from his house.

Despite the possible dire consequences, he had been a free bird and seen what he feared.

As he suspected, when he reached home, trouble sat blocking his driveway, waiting on him. A v-tran waited for its next victim. They had to be SACI. He pulled alongside the curb, just short of the driveway leading to his garage. He pushed the garage door opener button on the center console of his car, and as the door rose, he stuck his head out the window. Two men dressed in gray tunic jackets and matching gray trousers got out of the v-tran and walked toward him. William looked back toward the housing area entrance and didn't see the other v-tran.

"What can I do for you gentlemen?" William asked, yelling a little out his window, his stomached tightening by the second.

One of the protectors approached his side of the car as the second man looked in the passenger door window. The SACI man, easily identified by the unique cropped haircut, slowly moved next to his car door, staring ominously at him, his unmoving eyes alert and large. The man pushed his chin forward seemingly inviting a challenge of his authority. William sat extremely still, dropping his smile, looking plain-faced at the man, lowering his eyes slightly in a submissive posture.

"Where have you been, citizen-comrade?"

"I made a small trip into the country. I'm allowed to drive my car. I'm a manager and I work for Director Aldrich of the SAC." William felt is heart pounding again as a tingle ran though him from adrenaline going into his blood.

"You didn't get authorization for your trip. You are not allowed to travel where you went. You are not allowed out of your five-mile zone. You drove out into the country, which is forbidden. That is a crime subject to imprisonment. You also stopped at a bookstore, which is also a violation."

"Protector, the bookstore was closed."

"The fact that you stopped shows intention to obtain illegal printed documents. It shows intention to violate the positive thinking regulations."

"I wasn't seeking anything. I was merely curious whether the shop was open and had any books, books authorized by the SAC."

The protector grinned at William and then at his partner. "That's a lie. And that's another violation of the wrong-thinking rules."

"I meant no disrespect, protector. It was just my awkward way of telling my intent. I drove down to Alexandria to blow off a little steam after having an argument with my pain-in-the-ass wife. I saw a v-tran following me. When it didn't stop me, I thought I was allowed to continue."

The protector on the left side of the car, turned his head, listening to the com-link in his ear, and then gave a head signal to the other man. "Okay for now. We may still arrest you. No more driving. Only drive to your bus for work or your assigned market."

"How can I contact you if we have an emergency or something and need to use the car?"

"Just walk across the street to our v-tran."

"Oh . . . okay. Are you monitoring our street for something?"

The protector twisted his mouth mockingly. "Yes. We're monitoring you."

"Why?"

"You tell me."

"I haven't done anything wrong?" William said, holding up a pleading hand.

"Then why are you worried?"

"I'm not. May I continue?"

"Please do."

"Thank you, protector," William replied with a respectful tone.

They walked slowly back to their v-tran, mumbling something to each other before they got in. They then pulled across the street, stopped, and stared at William.

William drove into his garage, shut off his engine, and sat there for a moment trying to collect himself. He started to get out and stopped, thinking how desperately he wanted to get his family to another life. He had reported everything to the SAC . . . well nearly everything. Obviously, they suspected he knew something more. He wrote everything about the bomb in his report, where it was located, right down to the number of steps.

What else could he have told them? Of course, he had omitted the information about the implants for brain control.

The inside door between the garage and kitchen opened, revealing Lynn silhouetted by the kitchen light, looking at him fearfully, her hand moving to clasp her mouth, and then, after a moment, her eyes softened, becoming sympathetic. "What on earth are you doing? Oh William, heaven help us."

He climbed out of the car and met her at the door with a quick kiss, not wanting to allow the violators to intrude as voyeurs into their personal relationship, wanting to close off the SAC world as soon as possible. "We have a black v-tran across the street—again."

She sighed with a painful breath. "They were sitting in the drive for over an hour. Were you talking to them just now?"

"Yes. They say they are watching me."

"Oh my God," she gasped.

"Let's go inside. Don't worry about it. I made my report. I told them everything." *That never makes a difference.* He reached for the garage door control and pressed it.

"I don't want to know where you've been. So don't bother telling me. Supper's ready."

"Good," he said as he sent an anxious glance at the bottom of the v-tran disappearing behind the bottom of the garage door. He followed Lynn from the back hall into the kitchen, went to the sink, washed his hands, and sat down for evening dinner. When William looked at Lynn, she avoided his eyes, and plowed her fork into her pasta. She only spoke when she asked for a piece of bread. The silence and testy aura around the table found Stefan's observation, although his reaction was limited to a frowning glance at his dad and a questioning gaze at his mother. Marie went about her diner as usual and upon finishing quickly requested her freedom to go play. Stefan followed a few moments later.

William tortured himself trying to configure his explanation and his effort to soothe Lynn's broken nerves.

Chapter 11

Monday morning on the bus going to work William couldn't quit thinking about the history he had read last night, whether the radio had worked, what Steinhoff would say about his trip, and even more immediate, how he was going check his kids for implants.

He walked from the elevated bus drop-off and over to the stairs, marching as usual with the others like himself, but feeling different. This morning he found himself studying people, their reactions, and his surroundings, as if he were detached from his usual SAC world, as if he were off in the distance looking back at himself. At the ground level, he remembered hearing of a man who could get things, items not approved by the SAC, such as scanners. He considered it for only a moment before acknowledging to himself that he had no other choice, regardless of not knowing how much he could trust the man. He had to find a casual approach to meet the man without arousing too much attention from the vid-cams.

Upon emerging from the stairwell of the parking garage along with other SAC-brain-conditioned workers, entering the bleak concrete foyer, William recalled something his father had said. Looking with new objectivity, he noticed people standing in front of a large SAC vid-screen, which hung on the wall just before the garage exit to the street. The mere fact the people were standing there wasn't unique. People were watching a screen displaying a picture of Chairman Durand on a daily basis in numerous locations around the SAC office buildings. However, whenever William had listened, they invariably had the same commentator making remarks in a boring monotone. This cluster of people exhibited a different eerie behavior. Looking with his new eyes, the people seemed to have lifeless faces like mindless mannequins, as if they were under some sort of trance. It must have happened before and he had blindly rushed past. His father's words flashed through his brain.

Standing at the rear of the group, he tapped an older man on the shoulder, an average looking chap with thick glasses and shaggy gray hair. The man didn't move or acknowledge William's intrusion. He moved around the man and like the others. The man's face was fixed and unexpressive. After the picture of Durand disappeared from the screen, every man and woman continued toward their destination as if someone had flipped a switch in their brains. The hair on the back of William's neck stood up. How many people walked through their lives thinking they were living normally, living freely, living with full consciousness, knowing they existed as slaves purely at the distorted discretion of the State?

He continued walking toward his daily prison with the stream of automatons, fellow slaves. His delinquent revelation that they were all mesmerized disgusted him. For the first time he observed the curious way people moved. The SAC employees walking with him plodded along with dreary lifeless faces, with their eyes cast miserably at the pavement, as if their life had no hope or pleasure. No one was engaged in any friendly chitchat. There was no spark . . . no life. He looked up at his building across the street, no longer awed by its massive structure, not that he had ever liked it. It was almost scary the way the hideous monolithic granite reached skyward, more like an ancient tomb than a happy place to work. He had never considered such a thing in all his years working there. It was wrong-thought . . . what he was thinking. *Wrong thoughts, wrong mind, bad thoughts, no bad mind of any kind!*

William came to the street and stood at the curb. Light rain fell, spreading a shine on the concrete. It chilled the air. Now he noticed that even the flow of traffic seemed listless. No one was in a hurry, although in the past he had seen a v-tran speed down the street. Was it because people had no reason to hurry?

He crossed the street, sprinkles of the cold rain dropping on his bare head, bringing his thoughts back to his own problem. Somehow, he had to get a scanner for his kids.

Within minutes of reaching his desk, William cleared his brain of family concerns and lost himself in the collage of tedious details demanded by his normal job, coordinating messages on the computer with the different areas of responsibility, authorizing a request for additional workers at the northern steel mill, relocating lives without their permission, an act repugnant to his father, and an act William had almost always carried out with automatic and thoughtless efficiency. Now, that act made his fingers hesitate above the computer's virtual keys.

After an hour his mind drifted to the words he had read last night, words in the history book, words that confirmed the rights for freedom had existed for people decades in the past, and that one of those freedoms would have prevented him from ordering the movement of people without their agreement. The book had begun to feed his soul with its truth. He hoped he would be able read all eight hundred pages, as he was certain his father had done.

Another thirty minutes of mundane methodical tasks went past and he had caught up with his work. Lunchtime approached and it seemed a good opportunity for contacting Nick in the cafeteria about a scanner. He had greeted Nick only casually at the water fountain and coffee area. It was perhaps Nick's unusual behavior, not like a normal SAC employee, that William felt he might be safe to approach.

At twelve-noon, with his usual speed and blank detachment, William walked to his assigned cafeteria, this time looking for Nick. The cafeteria was a large windowless space with a ten-foot ceiling and rows of overhead translucent panels that made the room sterile and somewhere he never lingered eating his lunch. The security people had placed vid-cams at the ceiling, covering every conceivable angle where a camera could record a potential wrong-thinker.

William had seen Nick in the cafeteria several times. Nick carried himself quietly with what William thought was an introverted character, but he was obviously smart since he serviced equipment in the building. As William thought about Nick, had to acknowledge the man was one of the stranger people he'd met working there. Curiously, people had whispered Nick could get things, and if you needed information, you needed to see Nick.

William had to find a casual way to move; he couldn't move about the cafeteria overtly trying to find Nick, appearing to have a plan for a specific conversation. If he did, he would attract the attention of vid-cam monitors. You didn't just bounce up to a chap and strike a boisterous conversation. Any irregular behavior caused heads to pop up in unison like a family of rabbits disturbed from eating in a clover patch.

William followed his usual pattern, moving through the food dispensing line at the counter, picking up a small carton of milk, an artificial tuna fish sandwich, and a cup of soup. After having his lunch card punched, he looked over the room of tables with their attached stools, holding his tray of food, his body jangly with electric indecision. Nick Freeman sat alone in the far corner of the room. He made his way around two tables, walking with his head turning left and right, acting as if he didn't see anyone familiar, slowly approaching the table where Nick sat. He sat opposite Nick and he didn't say a word, keeping his eyes on his tray. He poured his milk into a glass.

"Nick, how are you doing?" William whispered without raising his head.

Nick slowly looked up from his soup, a frown of surprise making him squint, his spoon hovering above the bowl. "What?"

"I'm William from Department 57. My desk is near the copy machine. I said 'hello' to you a week or so back, or maybe it was longer."

Nick nodded slightly. "Okay, I guess." He blinked several times as if he had something in his eye, and pushed the spoon of soup into his mouth.

"Can I ask you a question about electricity?"

Nick directed his eyes at William without moving his head. "Sure, no problem," he replied slowly sounding interested but with a tired character to his words. "What . . . what do you want know?"

William whispered, "What do you know about metal detectors?"

"I don't know anything about those things. I think they're against the law anyway." He lowered his head. "I have to go back to work now." He moved his shoulders and started to stand.

"Don't go. Please help me . . . for my family."

"You're with the SACI."

"I'm not. You know I'm not with the SACI. Please."

"You need to be very careful asking about such things. You get sent to hard labor camps for that sort of thing." He stared at the table, keeping his face oriented toward the table. "You want one?" His voice was low, but clear, and precise, as if he had suddenly become a different person.

"Is there a store where I could buy one?"

"There's no place to buy one," Nick whispered.

"Oh. Sorry to bother you." William took a bite of his sandwich.

"But . . ."

"But what?"

A smile started to form at the corner of Nick's mouth until he glanced up at the ceiling across the cafeteria with his eyes. Immediately he looked back down into his soup and murmured, "They're watching, always watching."

It was then William realized Nick was concealing his mouth from the ever-present vid-cam by nearly bowing his head down to his bowl of soup. "Can I buy one anywhere?"

"I can get you a very simple one for a hundred in coupons."

"How do I know it will work after I give you the coupons?"

"You want it to check someone in your family. I know." Nick closed his eyes and then jerked his head strangely.

"What are people looking for?"

Nick frowned, leaned forward a little, and whispered, "The implants, Rinehart, the implants. Where in the hell you been? A lot of people have them. You can tell. It's easy, too. The people stare at the big pictures of Durand. The tracker version is stuck in people's backs and the mind switch type goes right behind the ear. The mind switch is the nasty one. It does something to their brains—like hypnosis. The one I saw had two little wires coming out of it . . . supposedly the SACI connected it to a nerve bundle. After a person gets one of those nasty buggers, it takes a serious EM field to disable it and I've heard they sometimes rupture. Better left alone I guess, but that's up to folks to figure out on their own. I suppose a delicate hand could cut it out, if you could locate the little devil. "

"What . . ."

"Then there's one that goes in the sinus cavity. It's the newer one, easy to kill, but it too can rupture."

"So you can get a device that actually kills them?"

"I don't cheat people who are trying to save their family. The device I can get has found many devices for many people."

"One more thing. What do you know about the underground?"

"You go too far."

"God almighty, Nick," he whispered.

"God doesn't have anything to do with it."

"I always thought you were sort of off. No offense."

"That's my secret. And you know why."

William drank his milk, and took a bite of his sandwich. "How long does it take?"

"Give me a couple days."

"How am I going to get it out of the building past the detectors?"

"It's not big, about the size of a pack of cigarettes. It's made of very small circuit stuff . . . very small. It's not exceptionally strong and a person has to place it right on the skin, but it'll pick up whatever they buried in the body. On Thursday, you bring a pack of cigarettes with a foil liner, which will be detected by the scanners. You'll have to sign them in. I'll walk past your desk and shake your hand. You have the coupons in your hand when we shake. Leave a drawer open and I'll drop my cigarettes in your drawer, which will contain the scanner, and then I'll take out your pack. When you leave work you'll have a pack of cigarettes to declare when you sign out."

"What if they open my cigarettes coming in or going out?"

"They never check people's cigarettes. Trust me, I've done this before." Nick looked up without raising his head. "We've been talking too long. I've got to go. Finish your lunch before you leave and don't go down the same hall as me."

"Wait. Do you have a device to disable these things?"

"No, but I know a guy."

"This whole thing sounds like a disaster waiting to happen."

Nick began laughing, stood beside the table, and said loudly, "That was a good one." He walked to the trash container, dumped his lunch, and shook his head weirdly while mumbling to himself.

William stared at the last of his lunch, getting the same feeling he had when he was walking up the mountain road toward his father's bunker, fearing a protector would shoot him at any moment. He had just set a tricky and tenuous mechanism in motion, and he could see in his mind's eye, security people stopping him when he tried to leave the building with the electronic device in his pocket. His gut told him that he had made a mistake talking to Nick? Come to think of it, Nick had volunteered much of the information, and confirmed his father's warning. The way Nick accused him of being with the SACI and then quickly disregarded it was problematic. It was too easy. Nick wasn't as naive or stupid as he acted. Now—he wished he hadn't talked to Nick.

Chapter 12

When late Monday afternoon arrived, Karl Steinhoff had just finished reading Manager Rinehart's report on the operation at the mountain bunker for a second time and could scarcely keep himself from issuing an order to have Rinehart arrested. Rinehart had infuriated him with the report's vagaries and smoke. Little of the information would benefit him or the SAC except the small portion about the fertilizer bomb. The little weasel claimed he didn't hear anything about any members of the underground, which was ridiculous. Somehow, while operating within Kauffman's oversight, he was going to squeeze Rinehart for more information.

"Vid-link, on," Steinhoff said sternly.

"Ready."

"Dial William Rinehart's workstation."

Manager Rinehart materialized on Steinhoff's vid-link screen.

"Good afternoon, Section Head Steinhoff. What can I do for you?"

"Manager Rinehart, I've just finished going over your report again and I would like to thank you for your getting it written in a timely fashion, although it is very sparse in details."

"I'm sorry you found it inadequate."

"Didn't your father mention any military generals or any of their subversive activities?"

"Sir, I prefer to reference the man as the conspirator or target, if you please. However, addressing your question, I tried to record to the best of my ability the conspirator's historical references, but he didn't mention any associations with people such as generals. As I recall his expression throughout his proselytizing was rather plain and unemotional. He displayed the most emotion when he referenced my family. And as I mentioned in my report, he didn't know people from other portions of the underground. They were anonymous to each other. Does that help, sir?"

"Is there anything else you can remember about his reference to the bomb?"

"No, sir. I reported every detail."

Steinhoff studied the vid-screen, every movement in Rinehart's face, looking for hints of deception. "Very well. Oh, yes. I don't think you should take any more drives without approval."

"Can you tell me why I'm being monitored?"

"No reason," Steinhoff snapped. "It's just a matter of follow-up after such an operation, especially one failing so miserably with the target killing himself to avoid interrogation. Obviously the man had something to hide from us."

"The SAC doesn't think I could have prevented a crazy man wrapped in explosives from blowing himself apart? The DPP gave me no assistance while I engaged the man inside the bunker. The man had a gun on me the whole time, ready to shoot me dead. He had a dead man's switch connected to his explosives, which would have been problematic at best."

"We don't know for a fact he had a gun on you."

"I'm sorry but it happened. Search the debris at the bunker. You should be able to find a handgun and a rifle."

"Well . . . perhaps Director Kauffman will want more confirmation. No more questions for now. I'm sure we'll be talking again soon."

"Thank you, sir," William replied.

Steinhoff heard an inflection in Rinehart's voice. Did Rinehart's tone carry anger or a resentful inflection? It better not. No matter right now. He would see to it his brain was worked over by Doctor Beucher. "By the way Rinehart, your whole family may be called to make reports to the SAC, including your children." He watched Rinehart's face finally show concern. "Vid-link, off," Steinhoff snapped.

As the vid-link went blank, Steinhoff immersed himself in the momentary pleasure of torturing Rinehart. He still didn't understand all the background, the information Kauffman was holding secret. He hated being outside the information circle. Perhaps he could learn more from Director Kauffman if he kept digging.

"Vid-link, on."

"Ready."

"Dial, Director Kauffman."

The vid-link screen came alive with Kauffman staring into the screen as if caught off balance. "Ah, Section Head Steinhoff."

"Director, I was curious if you had read Manager Rinehart's report."

221

Kauffman sighed tiredly, moved some papers on his desk, and folded his arms on his chest as he looked into the vid-cam. "Yes, I have." He glanced down in thought, his brow lowering as he then looked up. "It's all plausible, but it lacks meat in with the potatoes. I can't believe he wasn't told more in relation to the bomb we found in the sewer, or something about military personnel certainly involved in its placement. We know there were military people at the early stage of the underground. A few were prosecuted and terminated."

"If I may ask, what were you looking for?" Steinhoff probed.

Kauffman grinned and laughed under his breath. "Karl, I have to give you credit for being persistent." Kauffman glanced down and off to the side. "You're still looking for more secrets. We need to know about any military officers who may have been in contact with the father. It would help us complete our picture of the structure of any underground organization and the possibility of a continuing threat."

"We can still introduce him to Doctor Beucher."

Kauffman chuckled. "Yes we can. In due time. In due time. Is that all? "

"Yes, sorry for bothering you, sir."

"That's okay, Karl. Have a good afternoon."

"Vid-link, off," Steinhoff said, realizing that Kauffman had looked down to his right on his question, the sign of creative thought, not factual thought. However, knowing the depth of Kauffman's intelligence background, it was quite possible Kauffman could defeat the normal neuro-lingusitic signs.

After Steinhoff ended the call, the reference to William's children echoed in William's mind, terrorizing him with haunting visions of his kids been scared and threatened. He could see poor little Marie pouring out tears. His impotence and lack of control to protect them infuriated him. He kept his head bend down, avoiding the overhead vid-cams, not wanting to show his disturbed face. He quickly wrote a note to himself to check labor levels in sector four in the northern region, folded it, and then hung it over the top of his desk computer screen, which was an ancient panel screen with a vid-cam. The note covered its built-in vid-cam quite well, but he couldn't leave it there for long. It was possible for Steinhoff to spy on him, watching his facial reactions and William didn't want any more eyes watching him than were already located on the ceiling around the office.

With every tick of the clock, William felt the pressure building on him to complete safety measures for his family. Other than hoping to hear from his meager radio transmission, the metal detector was probably the most important thing right now, and he'd have one soon. The urge to read his father's chronicle was driving him nuts, but he had to wait until they were through with scanning his brain—if ever.

So far, his father's briefing had been spot-on accurate, although understandably shy of innumerable juicy and troubling historical details on political corruption. Perhaps the chronicle pages would explain why Steinhoff and Kauffman were interested in military generals. Were they concerned about something connected with military people who had turned against them? Possibly military people still existed and had a connection with an underground. If the SAC persisted with their questions, he didn't know how he'd satisfy them since he didn't know anything of value other than the blank pages. He grinned on the inside, thinking of his father making blank pages.

He stared at his work on the computer screen, his hands hovering over the virtual keyboard ready to enter data, but he couldn't make them move. Tired of the constant electronic eyes on him, he bent down as if he were reading his monitor. He felt his hands quiver a little. *You have to keep your nerve.* At this point in his war with the SAC, he couldn't lose his head, not if he was to help those who needed him, and keep the monster-government from enslaving them with brain-control devices. He had work to do, saving those at home, reading his book, getting the metal detector and walking out of the SAC building with it, and eventually escaping to another place to live. He sat up straight and checked numbers on his monitor.

The strange words his father mentioned leaked into his brain. *What we frequently want is right under our nose.*

Freedom. Where could they go to find freedom? Could they go out of the country by way of a remote location in the north, crossing into Canada? He had heard Durand's security watched the southern border at Mexico with a sizeable force and employed an electric fence. His father escaped, even though it was only to hide in a remote mountain location, but that was before the vast number of vid-cams. Vid-cams were growing by the minute, feeding their observations into the massive surveillance pipeline where they would eventually feel the SAC eyeball's scrutiny.

What about his father's request? He had promised to visit the infamous sewer where the underground hid the bomb. Maybe he could do it in the future, but keeping his promise looked bleak.

A soft chime rang from the ceiling as the office vid-screens swung down from the ceiling, screens located every twenty feet along the length of the room and likewise across the room. William promptly sent his attention to the closest screen, showing it his most interested and alert facial expression. A woman in a gray tunic coat with short mannish brown hair stood military-straight behind a black podium.

Her voice erupted in a stern monotone. "This is an AFPAK war announcement. The SAC is pleased and proud to announce the volunteer goal of one hundred thousand recruits has been achieved on the heels of a successful operation that struck the Followers of OBL at a fortified location in the southern area of the Badakhshan region in Afghanistan." The screen displayed a heavily bearded Arabic man in a white robe holding a machine gun in the air. "A recently obtained video from the Followers of OBL gave details of a plan to launch an Iranian manufactured nuclear armed missile at State America. The Department of State Protection under Director Fournier has raised the alert level to deal with this threat. Please send letters to support our forces. Please see your office coordinator for free stamped and addressed envelopes."

Now for a new alert. The Department of State America Intelligence has identified the leader of an underground resistance organization. His name is Adolf Bane. All citizen-comrades should study this picture of him stealing precious supplies, which were about to be shipped to our wonderful farm production centers. If any citizen sees this man, they should report to their nearest DPP facility. Remember Adolf Bane seeks to make our life more difficult by stealing from all of us. This ends the announcement. Thanks to Father Durand."

The screens folded up against the ceiling as if they had all been blown by a wind whirling though the office. They left behind a room full of silent bodies, the pulse of which came to life slowly in a stream of faint whispers. An electrical equipment hum replaced the whispers as all the citizen-comrades assumed their correct-thinking again.

William recalled the SAC had talked of fighting this invisible foe for years, the group called, Followers of OBL. He didn't even know who or what OBL stood for. He knew for certain, the same military campaign had been underway in Afghanistan since he'd been at SAC. It never ended despite consistent reports of success. The announcement about an underground surprised him, especially since the SAC had, at one time years ago, denied its existence. The picture on the screen of a man in his fifties with a heavy mustache and dark bushy eyebrows certainly looked like a villain. Normally, before meeting his father and his awakening, he would have accepted what he was told about Adolf Bane, but since his recent revelation, he wondered if the man was real or a hate-target concocted by the SACI psychological intelligence people.

He rested his eyes for a moment, closing them and rubbing them with his fists and then removed the paper he'd placed over the vid-cam on his computer monitor. He went back to his scheduling and personnel quotas, looking more thoroughly at the background of the people, trying not to send families away from their current homes, something he had never worried about of before.

The sun had hovered behind clouds all day and as William pulled into his garage after work Monday evening, it was as if the dark of the garage were transitioning the cold gray day into night. William climbed out and stood for a moment at the back of the car merely staring at the SACI v-tran sitting across the street. He saw no movement. Something had rebelled within him, pushing him to let the v-tran know he could watch them too. It was risky, but he felt good standing his ground. Perhaps the stress had finally nudged him over a milestone of calm. *When are they going to come for me?*

He said nothing to Lynn as he walked into the kitchen and saw her standing at the refrigerator, her head directed toward her purpose and showing no sign of turning at him with a cordial greeting. He wanted to say something soothing, but thought she might start crying, and seeing her pain would penetrate what thin barrier he had formed to fight their peril. He needed his strength for her. He could see intensity in her eyes and could see the anxiety chewing away inside her. In the living room he asked the children how their school was going, hoping Lynn would join the conversation, but she remained silent and in the kitchen preparing dinner.

Later, at dinner, as Lynn placed the ladle for retrieving spaghetti sauce on the table, she caught William's attention with a long penetrating look that was neither angry nor accusative. The brief connection told William they would talk after dinner. He desperately wanted to help ease her mind about everything but he didn't think he could say much to help her. He couldn't brush away her fears.

They began eating and after a few moments, William realized the children were being unusually quiet, which solidified the atmosphere as if molten glass had formed into a fragile piece of art. Regardless, he couldn't let these valuable hours together pass tainted by awkward circumstances or bruised feelings. He wondered how many more dinners they would have together, time merely to sit in their own home, enjoying something to eat in their cozy kitchen. He felt an urgency descend upon him, a sudden need to absorb every wonderful moment possible with his family.

William wrapped pasta around his fork and looked over to the children. He ran his eyes up and around the ceiling, uncertain anything was there, but it was a logical location for one of the ever-present vid-cams. For now, it didn't matter if "they" were watching, although the idea left a bitter taste in his mouth. He hated the idea of the SAC violating his home. Lynn popped up, went to the cooktop and returned with a bowl of steaming mixed vegetables.

"I'm not eating those," Stefan declared.

William smiled on the inside, but held a straight face. "Someday you might be glad you had them to eat. We are fortunate to get them."

Stefan scrunched his mouth and stopped. "Hey, Dad, is there something going on at your work?"

"Why?"

"Because I was called out of class today and had to go to the office. I had to talk to some official person . . . I don't know who . . . a man who didn't like kids. He asked me . . . I don't know . . . a bunch of questions. The jerk frowned at everything I told him, as if he didn't believe anything I told him. His breath smelled bad, too."

William nodded his understanding, flashing his eyes at Lynn for an instant. "What was the man asking?"

"He asked if anyone had bought any books recently. He asked if I knew books had to be approved. Oh, yeah, and he asked me if you ever talked about office work at home. There was a bunch of other crazy stuff, too."

Lynn rested her fork on the table and stared at Stefan, he mouth drawn into a stern line. Her eyes narrowed. "Those people are going too far." She stopped, turned, ran her eyes over the kitchen, and then sighed. "Too far! That's all. Just too far."

"Listen, I went up to the door of a bookstore the other day, but it was closed. They knew where I was. They followed me. The SACI said nothing."

"The man asked if you guys argue much. They asked if you buy anything over the quota . . . that sort of stuff."

William reached under the table and placed his hand on Lynn's leg to warn her not to get so upset in front of the children. This was something he rarely did and he wasn't quite certain how she'd react, whether she would accept his sympathy or continue expressing her defiance. Curiously, she didn't acknowledge his concern, and chose not to regard him.

Stefan continued, "This guy also asked if someone was sick in our family. He said I was required to report anything that looked wrong around our house. I thought it sounded like spying to me and it kind of made me angry."

William tried to laugh sarcastically as he sent his eyes up at a furnace vent near the ceiling, thinking of a vid-cam looking down upon them. "Stefan, it sounds like one of those periodic security evaluations they run on employees. I haven't had one for a long time. I guess it was time."

Lynn shuffled her eyes from Stefan to William and smirked.

"I wish they wouldn't bother me," Stefan replied. "I had to answer all those questions and then I got a bunch of questions from kids in my class."

"Both you and Marie must always answer their questions as best you can. It might be unpleasant but you can do it. Okay? Can you do that for me and your mom?"

"Sure, Dad," Stefan replied.

Marie nodded meekly. "Okay, if you say."

The SACI obviously made Stefan feel as if he had done something wrong. He remembered how nasty kids could be when he was in school. The SACI carried out unscrupulous activities on the powerless population, and enlisting children into spying on their parents fell at the bottom of the slime—just like Steinhoff. That type of intimidation was widespread, part of the sickness of the system.

William swallowed the last bite from his dinner, wrestling with the problem of what to tell Lynn and what not to tell her. If he didn't fill her in on most everything she would chew at him relentlessly until he capitulated with a white flag. Unquestionably, she had the strength to handle fearful questions, but her knowing too much would endanger her. Answering her worry-filled questions and seeing her cry when he confessed the rotten truth tortured him. He was certain the best way to protect her was for her not to know much of anything. That way if the SACI ever questioned her again, she wouldn't have to avoid the truth and risk penalty of imprisonment for lying to the State or endure some manner of torture, although the SACI wouldn't let innocence block their path to snatching information from an unimportant number on the population census roster.

Stefan's problem was another obstacle. They were probing about his dad's late night reading, which William could explain as an intestinal bug causing gas after meals, and the frequent visits to the bathroom late at night, but how did they know? If he blocked the vents, how did they know someone was in the bathroom? Somehow, the SACI was watching and possibly listening. William's mind saw the sick SACI scaring his innocent children. *I hate the bastards, hate them, hate them. Leave my wife and children along!*

Late in the evening, after Lynn had run the kids off to bed, William expected Lynn to hit him with her questions, but instead she went quietly to bed, not saying a word, averting her eyes from him. He knew the intimidation of the children and the v-tran's presence outside the house stricken her with horrible questions, and he didn't have the answers. He decided not to breach her emotional fortress, knowing that she would soon be scratching at him about their situation.

Their situation had certainly changed for the worse. The unfolding events seemed written on some cosmic scroll, events beyond his control, which despite his effort to build safety in their lives, was whirling him and his family into a perilous political maelstrom, just as it had his father. How could one man or the underground threaten such a powerful organization as the SAC? What was it they really feared from him or his father?

William closed the bedroom door so Lynn wouldn't have to fight the light leaking in from William's reading in the living room. After a while, he turned off the lights and slipped into the bathroom to read the last five chapters of his father's history book. The chapters went quickly and when he finally closed the book, his father was again in his head, and he was thankful for his own awakening. It was all bittersweet, sweet knowing what was going on and not being in the dark. But, he felt sad and disappointed knowing a controlling government was uprooting his world just as it had his father's. He felt more fearful than ever for his family.

His fear brought back a troubling question. Should he destroy the history book? That question wrenched his gut. He couldn't destroy such important history, such a precious piece of his nation's past. No. He would hide the book in the furnace cold-air return. Perhaps he was assuming too much but that location sounded good. He walked quietly to the furnace located between the bathroom and the garage, just off the kitchen. With SACI eyeballs watching, he couldn't possibly hide anything. He turned off all the lights, opened the louvered door to the furnace as softly as possible, and began removing the front cover of the furnace, trying to avoid scraping any metal. One of the spring clips holding the cover released a small protesting screech. He slid the book inside, locating it off to the right in the cold air section, replaced the furnace cover, and inched the door closed. If anyone was listening, they probably knew something was going on but there was no way to determine just what.

Suddenly he wondered if the vid-cams might have the capability of seeing in infrared. It was too late now. He went to the sink, carefully found a glass, and ran a glass of water.

Minutes later, he slid into bed beside Lynn and suddenly thought of the much-needed scanner. If Nick knew about scanners maybe he'd know something about escaping the vid-cams, escaping a life in which the SAC herded them like cattle—and facing random slaughter. His throat tightened for a moment. Since coming home from the mountain, he had had some sort of nightmare every night.

Chapter 13

From the minute the SAC ordered him to victimize his own father, nearly every moment moved William across the game board of a hideous contest, toward the endpoint when a member of the SACI would say those infamous words, "You're under arrest." Tuesday morning at work, he sat at his desk with a cup of coffee. It was still early and he was thinking about a v-tran following his SAC bus to work. It was a demoralizing game, a damn sick game of intimidation, and a game of threats. The SACI watched him leave home, watched him walk to Building Three from the bus drop-off, and watched him enter the building, not leaving one inch of his travel unmonitored. As he sipped his coffee, he surrendered to the urge to look at all the others, the other similar rabbits. He glanced around the office, taking care not to look like he was interested in anything particular. Examining the faces of his fellow workers, he wondered how they felt about their life. It was highly possible that the SAC had brainwashed various portions of the population and that those groups of people accepted life under the SAC as the quintessential way to live. Of course, he couldn't ask anyone how they felt. No one could. Down deep, he wanted to laugh and tell the SAC they weren't fooling anyone. Then again, they probably weren't trying to hide their goons or their threats. He wondered if the hands on the clock were moving him closer to their special brain treatment. *Paranoia. You're becoming unhinged.*

He pressed a key on his computer, starting about his normal duties, blocking out what danger might and what might not come his way. The computer failed to come to life. It was a malfunction rarely seen in the office and it sent an electric wave through his nerves. Through all his years, he had experienced only one problem before. Beads of perspiration sprouted on his forehead. The SAC could accuse him of purposefully destroying State property or being incompetent. He fumbled in his desk for a procedure manual and then called technical support. Twenty minutes later a man with a brown beard, looking to be in his fifties walked up to his desk, staring at William through dark-rimmed glasses. William looked plainly at the man waiting for a comment. The lean man with a friendly round-face and balding hairline started to smile and then stopped. William wondered if he was working up to a sharp rebuke for breaking the computer. The man set a small metal toolbox down on the floor with a thud.

"I understand you have a slight computer malfunction," said the man, his voice sounding a little amused, even though his face didn't show it.

"Yes, that's correct. I'm William Rinehart."

"Yep, I know," he replied, his speech almost lazy, but confident. "Your name's on the wall right over there. You're a manager."

William laughed. "Sorry."

"Okay, if I'm going to have a look, I suppose you should get up out of the chair."

"Okay." William popped from the chair and moved behind the man.

"You may not know it, but you're actually running from a micro-server which continuously communicates with the central hub array. By the way you are running one of our oldest display panels." He removed a flat book-shaped object from the bookshelf located above the back portion of William's desk, and placed it flat on the desk in front of him, covering the virtual keyboard.

"A micro-server, that's interesting," William muttered. "I'd like to understand how it all works."

"By the way, I'm Russell Wood. Been here for years. Anyway, the central data archive for the whole affair is a bunch of computers connected together in such a way they never all go down at one time. They have more servers and storage devices than you have people in this room, for that matter, three or four rooms, and . . ." He paused and began in a whisper like someone's breath, "And they all use the last molecular CPUs Intel developed before the company was taken over by the State and two of their key scientists fled to Brazil." He voice got louder. "The main hub is located in Building One. Most of the failures are like yours and in this little local computer. Look at it. You wouldn't believe something smaller than a few sheets of paper and no thicker than a thin pad of paper could do such things. This little baby connects to a remote server, which is the distributor unit, and it sends your work to any of the available massive number-crunching machines running thousands of parallel processors. The unit you have here is pretty old. We have very few parts for this dinosaur. Most people like you have a unit that came out after this one and is thinner than this."

"So you've seen a lot of changes?" William asked.

"Lean down here so I can talk without yelling."

There wasn't much noise. William leaned slowly toward the man.

235

Russell turned to him with his face deathly solemn. He looked William in the eyes. He mouthed the words, "You need an implant tracker killer?" Russell paused and then spoke in a normal voice, "I'm gonna have to get inside this machine and service the exchange board."

"What did you say?" William asked softly, dipping his head down a little, barely moving his mouth.

Russell laid a small flashlight on the desk, pulled the computer toward the middle of the desk, and began removing the tiny screws. "Lean down here so you can hear me better."

William stepped over to Russell's left, bending down, feeling the man's breath, and smelling his perspiration.

"I saw you talking to Nick Freeman," Russell whispered. "Big damn mistake." Russell looked up for a second and then back down. "Keep your face tilted toward the floor so the vid-cams can't read your lips."

William moved away from Russell, stepping toward the opening of his cubicle. He stood there shaking with electric nerves.

Russell frowned at him and lowered his left hand, pointing stiffly at a spot on the floor next to him. He wiggled his finger, gesturing for William to come back beside him.

"Look, you ass," Russell whispered. "Lean over the edge of the desk like you're interested. Where are your guts for God sake? I'm trying to help."

"I don't understand." William reluctantly inched over to the desk, more worried the vid-cams would detect his odd behavior while talking to this man.

"Sure you do," Russell continued. "You broke the law by asking about a scanner. I read your lips the other day there in the cafeteria, and if I read your lips the vid-cams did too."

William froze, not certain who or what he was facing, suddenly trying to calculate his next move to avoid a possible SACI trap. "I . . . don't know anything." His first guess was the SACI had sent the man acting as a member of the underground, so they could catch Nick . . . as well as him. In his corrupted world where reality didn't exist without the SAC twisting it, who and what could he believe? Nick seemed as much on the level as this guy.

Russell lowered his nose nearly into the computer and then he whispered, "Don't bother with that crap. We know about Freeman and his scanners, except we don't know what he's doing. He may be working for the SACI and fishing for people searching for the underground."

William turned and stepped back from Russell again. "I have to go to a meeting," William said, sounding like a mewling pathetic coward. He heard his own voice and hated it.

"Manager Rinehart," Russell said in a cold voice. "Could you please hold my light for me while I work on your computer? I need your help."

William took the light, and directed it into the computer housing as Russell began turning a screwdriver.

"That's better," Russell said with a groan, as if he were angry. He whispered, "Look asshole, you think I'm SACI. If you want help, you're gonna have to trust me. Don't move if you want help."

"Whose help?"

"Listen, Rinehart, if you take anything from Freeman, don't try to exit this building with it. We're pretty certain he's working for the SACI."

"How do I know you're not with the SACI?"

Russell grinned diabolically and laughed. "Damn interesting pickle isn't it? There's no guarantee either way, except for trust. Think about it. Why would I risk talking to you at your desk? Freeman won't be able to help whoever it is you're trying to help?"

"Shit," William blurted with a breath.

"Besides, he didn't mention the nanobots, did he?"

William stared at Russell, his mouth gapping.

"Manager Rinehart, please stop moving the light."

"What are you talking about? Dammit! Stop this game."

"Some implants release nanobots from the sinus cavity and some merely trigger hormones. The nano-biologicals travel to the brain and start causing problems and sometimes irreversible damage. Freeman's device just locates the implants placed in children's backs and some younger adults. I have a device that can solve both problems. The SACI activates these devices at different times after they have implanted them, whenever they want to experiment with their human guinea pigs or spark a demonstration. The trick is to kill the nanobot before it's activated."

"What do these nanobots do, exactly?"

Russell curled his lip. "We don't know much about them, but the others cause a massive release of endorphins and other hormones. We also know both kinds can kill the subject. Some poor bastards stare and stare at signs after they are implanted. Ever see people just staring at signs?"

"Do they do implants at the SAC spa?"

"That's one of the few places we're certain about. We've been watching the place for a several years." Russell stopped and leaned back, running his hand over his head as if he were resting. "How do you know about the spa?"

"Someone told me. I can't say who." William suddenly realized he knew something valuable.

Russell looked at him as if William were trying to sell him a rotten piece of SAC meat, and then he scratched the back of his neck. "Manager Rinehart, this is a real tough one. Give me a minute to rest my eyes."

William knocked some papers on the floor and stooped to pick them up. "Why were you watching me in the cafeteria?" he whispered.

"Actually we were watching both of you."

"What?"

"You have a radio transmitter, don't you?"

"No."

"Yes, you do. You used it."

"The SACI could have detected it, too. Still doesn't prove who you are."

"You used an old radio protocol. We figured out your location, tracked it to you, and then we connected it with someone we've been trying to locate for a long time, someone with your last name, someone a lot older than you."

"Still—the SACI could have done the same thing."

"Okay, don't believe me. It's your neck."

"I can't believe you. It's too dangerous."

"You're in a sticky mess and you've got to get them off your ass. You have to believe someone. It might as well be me. Figure it out. How do I know things?"

"They're . . . they're watching my house twenty-four hours a day."

239

"Regardless, when Freeman comes to make his drop, don't take it. Have your desk cleared off and locked so there won't be any place for him to drop off the device. Stand and walk away, leaving him holding it. Stay away until he leaves. If he approaches you anywhere, tell him your position doesn't allow you to talk with him."

William wanted to believe this man was telling the truth, but couldn't. It was too incredible that someone like Russell would come to him after all the years he'd been working there. The radio. It had to be the radio. Nevertheless, his advice was sensible—regardless of his association. William started to smile, remembered the vid-cams, and blurted loudly, "Do you know how to fix my computer or don't you? I've got a lot of work to do."

Russell rolled his eyes. "Excuse me, sir." Russell then whispered, "We have to end this now. Go get a drink of water and don't come back for several minutes, so I can leave. We'll be in contact outside the office, three flashes with a light. Only three flashes will be us. Never say my or anyone else's name. I need to talk with you again. For God sake, stay alive."

William walked to a water cooler in the far corner of the expansive room, filled a paper cup with water and slowly sipped it, letting his eyes reach out into the distance over the cubicles of automatons, all of them following the rules out of constant fear. The more he thought about Nick Freeman and his directions, trying to leave the building with a device, the more it did sound like a potential trap. If not a trap, it was at least an exceedingly risky adventure. Now he faced the dilemma of trusting another total stranger—but one who had disclosed information about the nanobots. It could be part of their obfuscation, another path they were pushing him down within the SACI labyrinth of deception. While he felt queasy about Russell, the man sounded logical. Still, Russell could be part of an elaborate web woven by the SACI.

Tuesday evening seemed like the previous day. Arriving home from work, William rolled his car onto his driveway and stopped. He studied the men sitting in the v-tran across the street from his home, not with a challenging belligerent inspection, but with a look of acknowledgement that he knew their purpose of intimidation. Three men sat in the vehicle, although he could only see the silhouette of the third man in the back. They didn't move. He continued into the garage and as the door closed behind him, he laughed under his breath at the waiting game.

"I see we still have the guard dogs across the street," William said walking into the kitchen, where Lynn stood next to the sink, rinsing a glass in stream of water.

She didn't reply.

"The v-tran is still parked across the street," he repeated.

"Yes, I know," Lynn said sharply. She stepped to the refrigerator, reached for the handle and stopped. She turned and folded her arms.

William took a glass from the cabinet and poured a glass of water. "I'm sorry," he said softly. He pulled a chair back from the kitchen table and sat, waiting for Lynn to release with her frustration.

Stefan walked into the kitchen and sat across from William. "Mom, can I have an apple? I'm hungry."

Lynn walked silently over to the stove. "No. Dinner's about ready . . . besides we don't have many apples left."

"Dad," Stefan began, "why do we have a v-tran with three men sitting across the street every day? It's creepy."

"Yeah, they're probably doing something," William muttered.

Lynn turned her head quickly to William. In a quick glance, she threw him a frozen stare. He'd seen the same expression over the last few days. The threat hovering over them like a storm cloud was raining havoc down on his family's emotions and he didn't know what more could do at that moment. Lynn returned to the sink, her hands moving quickly, staying busy with scraping a carrot, her attention riveted on her task. William ran his hand over Stefan's head, ruffling Stefan's hair a little. "They might be doing a study of traffic or energy use . . . I don't really know."

"If you ask me, something's going on," Stefan said.

Lynn snapped around, sending another blistering stare for an instant before going back to her work. William knew she was silently crying for answers. "After dinner, honey," he said, "we probably should talk."

Lynn nodded silently.

William watched his children during dinner, frequently drifting back to thoughts of the time when he was with his father. He studied his children's mannerisms, the little quirks making each of them unique and precious, marveling on the inside at how wonderful it was having such a blessing, little nuggets of joy that would continue through the years after him. His father must have felt the same thing. Suddenly, sharp regret pierced him as he wondered if his children would be slaves to State America under Durand or Bruner. He laughed sadly to himself at the irony of the question, at being slaves, since he had never perceived the subtleties of his world as being remotely controlling. He had merely accepted it as the way things were.

An hour after dinner William sat in the living room watching vid-net screen and the propaganda version of world events, the SAC version of news, which they presented with an economy of monotone words. Lynn came in and sat beside him, took his hand, and squeezed it, not say a word.

After a moment she leaned close, kissed his ear, and then whispered, "The v-tran across the street scares me terribly. How are we going to survive?"

He kissed her on the neck, hating the things he would undoubtedly have to tell her over the few next days. "Nothing has happened at work so we might be fine," he whispered. "I may investigate the possibility of moving south to the mountains where my father was hiding or maybe to the northwest. They can track our car and we wouldn't get far walking. So I don't know—"

"How far west?"

"I don't know, honey. It may not be possible. Things have to move slowly and very carefully or the SAC will kill all of us."

"You don't mean it."

"They will eliminate me and then who knows what they'll do to you and the kids." He wanted to tell her about the device, but knew she wouldn't understand what he was trying to do or the risk he was taking. He kissed her quickly on the lips and stood. "I have some reading so I better get at it." The urge to tell her more about what was taking place burned inside him like an underground smoldering vein of coal, but he couldn't tell her about their fire just yet.

Wednesday, William battled his nerves as he tiptoed through another day of guessing and waiting. He had tried to keep busy all morning and at lunchtime, he walked down the hall toward the cafeteria, trying not to hear conversations around him, trying not to do anything suspicious, and trying to keep his eyes on the floor. A security man approached and stopped William, ordering William to follow him to a room at the front of the building.

William walked into the sterile, gray room and crossed the asphalt tile floor toward a conference table where Steinhoff sat. The room was about the same as the last conference room they ordered him to visit. It had a long table bordered with chairs. However, he hadn't encountered anything like the large glass panel occupying one wall. When he realized he couldn't see through it he knew its purpose, observation. Three corners of the room had a vid-cam. William smelled an odor bringing to mind a solvent or a pine scented cleaning agent with a biting acidic overtone. From the use of the cleaning agent, he guessed another person had spent time in the room and not under convivial conditions.

William expected Steinhoff to start applying pressure. On the far side of the table with Steinhoff sat a man with brown hair and massive shoulders. A second man with average build and a gleaming hairless head, sat at the end of the table staring with piercing narrow eyes. Both men accompanying Steinhoff were dressed alike in gray SACI suits. William saw them as Steinhoff's resource of brainless muscle.

It seemed he was in for another game of wits. *What do they want today? Breathe normally.* He couldn't permit his nervousness to constrict his diaphragm and influence his voice. Facing such creatures from the dark crevices of human depravity, beings who exulted in the misery of others, he had to control his body language. They would be watching all of his biological signals to uncover any deception and his level of fear. For a split second he thought of God, and asking for help. He thought of the cross Lynn had given him, and saw her face in his mind's eye for an instant.

"Please have a seat, Manager Rinehart," Steinhoff said, the corner of his mouth curling with a disingenuous smile.

Steinhoff's face warned William that he was providing some sort of sadistic amusement for the section leader. He wanted to leap across the room and choke the miserable life out of Steinhoff. He took in a measured breath, pulled back a chair, and sat on the side of the table toward the door, opposite Steinhoff and the one man.

Electricity ran through William as the evaluation process commenced with penetrating laser-gazes shot across the table from the three men. He folded his fingers and rested his hands on the table. "What can I do for you, Section Head?" William asked with an even voice. He released a long breath and looked Steinhoff square in the eyes. For some reason he suddenly remembered the time they were competing against each other, when Steinhoff wasn't anything special, certainly not intellectually. Steinhoff didn't scare him back then, but now he had to respect Steinhoff's power, which could easily kill.

"Manager Rinehart," Steinhoff began, "these two men are with the TMD group under Director Kauffman. One of our best, Doctor Conrad Beucher, has trained them and in fact, they work for him. They've come here to participate in the observation of your testimony about the operation on the mountain."

"If I may inquire, what is the TMD?" William asked plainly. "I don't think I've heard of it.

Steinhoff smirked. "Oh, that's quite possible. Regardless, many people have received treatment at the facility. Surely someone with a position such as yours would have heard about it."

The man sitting at the end of the table with a dead face added, "We are with the Thought Mentoring Department. We do just what the title says. We help people with their thoughts and recall, their memories, in an effort to reformulate accurate and complete histories of events."

William nodded slightly. "Sounds interesting. How do you accomplish such a thing?"

The man with the big upper body sitting next to Steinhoff tilted his head to the side and nodded. "Information on our technology is confidential."

William folded his fingers on the table. "Okay, gentlemen, what can I do for you?"

"We like to see that kind of attitude," the big man replied. "By the way I'm Citizen-Comrade Hans Webber and this other gentleman is Citizen-Comrade Neal Johnson. Our job is to get answers and report to Citizen-Comrade Doctor Beucher. If you tell us what we need to know— you and your family will have a wonderful life."

"I don't understand," William protested. "I made my report. I gave you the man's notebook."

"We want to know everything about the bomb," Neal said, sitting back with his arms folded on his chest, his face dead still, the skin at the beginning of his baldhead wrinkling in horizontal rows.

William tried to remain a rock. He spoke slowly, "I reported everything, where it was located, its size, and its composition." He paused. "Have you found the bomb?"

Hans pointed a sharp finger at William. "We ask the questions."

"If you have, then you know I've told the truth." William glanced at Steinhoff, who looked pleased with himself.

Neal tilted his head and looked up, squinting at William. "How many people worked with your father? Who gave him directions? How did they exchange information? How many more bombs are there? Who were his military connections?"

"The man told me—" William began.

Neal snapped, interrupting, "Make certain it's the truth, because you are being watched every minute of the day and so is your family."

"He . . . he said his information came from the newspapers years ago. I reported all this."

"What else?"

"He mentioned notes were sent to him in cigarettes and he also used a radio for messages. He chattered some about politics in the late 1990s, about political parties and such, which sort of went right through my head. I assumed all of it was in his notebook. It was all a blur of complaints and accusations. That's about it. That's all . . . nothing about bombs other than the one I reported."

"We'll tell you when we've reached the end," Neal snapped bitterly, leaning forward in his chair, his chin jutting forward like a weapon. "We will tell you when you can go, when you can see your family, when you can take a piss." He stopped for a moment as if searching for words and then found William's face. "Do you understand this? Look at me and answer me. I want to see your eyes."

William confirmed to himself what he had expected to happen, that the countdown clock had finally struck the zero hour, and the SACI

247

persecution process had begun in earnest. They would undoubtedly attack his mental state. "Yes, sir, I understand completely and I will cooperate completely."

"We want to know names of the people who helped the conspirator," Neal barked.

"I was never told any names, other than what I included in my report."

Hans hit the top of the table lightly with a fist. "Bullshit, he must have mentioned military people. You've just forgotten—or you're hiding it."

"I'm not hiding anything. He never mentioned any names."

"You have to be hiding his contacts," Steinhoff said. "People don't survive on a mountain without support."

"I'm not hiding anything."

Steinhoff squinted menacingly. "We should gather your family and interrogate all of them, including little Marie. How would you like that?"

"They know nothing. I know nothing about any military connections. How can I tell you something that I was never told?"

Neal nodded to Hans, who cleared his throat and wagged his finger at William. "If you have information and don't tell us, and then we learn of it later, your life will become hell. Manager Rinehart, you're free to go if Section Head Steinhoff is agreeable."

Steinhoff sneered, laughing under his breath. "Yes, that's fine." Steinhoff smiled maliciously.

"Am I free to go?" William asked softly.

"You know, Rinehart, our patience is at an end," Steinhoff said. "The director and I are understanding men, but when someone doesn't cooperate we have no recourse but to use extreme measures to secure the information." Steinhoff gave a sneering laugh. "Yeah, you can go."

William nodded and pushed himself up from his chair. He nodded at Steinhoff, who merely stared at him as if he were a bug. He walked from the room with his chin raised, although the adrenaline running through him left his nerves feeling jittery as if he had run a mile. He went to his cafeteria for a cup of coffee and solid food. A big clamp seemed to squeeze his head. Despite the short encounter, it had mentally drained him. He would see those men again. He had to follow his father's advice. The likelihood he would be around to give advice to his son and daughter as they grew older was growing increasingly unlikely, even if he did divulge everything, including the chronicle. So why do it? The promise.

At the coffee station, he poured a cup and stood in a daze, his mind drifting back to the question haunting him. Why was the SAC so interested in all the details surrounding his father? Based on their reaction and their less than enthusiastic response the bomb was obviously only one facet of their probing. Perhaps they were more worried about a military connection. They had hit that topic more than once. Perhaps they had reason to fear an underground, one that still existed, and maybe there was a real man named Adolf Bane. Would any of his reports ever satisfy them?

Later that evening, after dinner, exhausted from the stress of his encounter with Steinhoff, William fell asleep on the floor in front of the vid-net. However, before he had time to dream anything bad, Marie crawled over to him and pulled on his nose. He rolled over onto his knees, and as she giggled, he chased her into the kitchen. He grabbed her, squeezing and showering her with kisses on her rosy cheeks. After enduring another pull on his nose, he released her to scamper back to her only doll and her scraps of cloth on the floor in the corner of the living room.

William poured a glass of water, stood at the sink drinking, and looked at his reflection in the kitchen window. Beyond the glass, evening's paintbrush had already colored the background black. Suddenly, something struck the house. He stared out the window. He was certain he had heard something strike the back of the house, something hard like a stone. As he looked out the window, a small light flashed on and off at the end of his property. He didn't move. He thought of Nick and then of Russell. It had to be Russell Wood. The light came in three flashes, a pause, and then three more flashes. His gut wrenched with his decision to take a chance. His logic raced over his options.

"I'm going out back for some air, honey," William said, thinking Lynn was in the living room.

Just then, she came out from the bathroom off the kitchen. "You're doing what?" she replied, speaking over the rumbling sound of their troubled washing machine.

He pressed a finger to his lips for her to lower her voice.

She frowned and shook her head angrily.

Her face told him she was scared. He mouthed the words with his hand cupped around his lips, "It will be okay." He walked out the rear door as quietly as he could, out under a chilly, star-speckled night ornamented with a lustrous moon. He walked slowly toward the location of the light at the back of the lawn, the damp coolness of the grass going through his shoes. A dark shadow engulfed the bushes at the property edge except for where the moonlight struck the uppermost leaves. The bushes rustled and then he heard branches scratch across the surface of fabric.

"Stop where you are," a man's voice demanded in a whisper.

It wasn't any voice William recognized with certainty. It could have been Russell Wood but he didn't know. It could have been an SACI trap. "I'm, William Rinehart. What do you want?"

"Too much light. A drone could see you with infrared."

The bushes rustled again. He felt something hit his leg and drop on his foot. A small dark object lay next to his shoe. He picked up a small box, which fit the palm of his hand.

"What is this?" William whispered. He didn't hear a sound. "Anyone there?" There was no reply. He went back to the house, pausing just outside the door, looking out at the sheltering blackness, trying to make sense of what was going on and whether he had placed the family in irrevocable danger, although it seemed that question was irrelevant since this afternoon.

In the tiny hall by the kitchen, William turned toward the corner, blocking vid-cam eyes from view, and opened the box. Inside the cardboard box was black rectangular object. On the upper left corner of the object, which was about three inches wide by four inches long, his eyes seized upon the white label with the word, "scanner." The device for checking his family was at his fingertips. It had a small panel covering the location of its batteries. A meter and two control buttons were on its top. He found a piece of paper stuffed in a slot in the box. He slid the paper out far enough that he could see the paper contained the instructions for the detector and electromagnetic disruptor. He felt a wave of elation mixed with anxiety. He hoped it worked as he was told, disabling the hideous electronic implants once they were found. *How can I use this device without being seen?*

William went into the toilet off the kitchen, his nocturnal reading room with the towels covering the vents and ceiling fan. "Stefan, will you please come here."

Just then, a chime came from the vid-screen in the living room. "Please standby for an important SAC announcement," a woman said with a clinical voice. "Reports are just in for the fall crop production and under Chairman Durand's fine administration the SAC can report the grain and poultry quotas have been surpassed by two percent, therefore every family will be getting a free turkey or chicken for the fall feast day. And a new report has just come in on the second United Afghanistan Victory battalion. It has experienced losses in the Kandahar area, in Afghanistan and near the Pakistan border. Chairman Durand is asking everyone to participate in a peace rally scheduled for Saturday on the vid-net. Lastly, the SAC has identified the man in this picture shown here as, Adolf Bane, leader of the underground resistance trying to destroy Chairman Durand's hard work. Our wonderful DPP stopped Bane's people from destroying one of our critical electrical power plants, which if taken from the system, would have cut power to millions of citizens. All citizen-comrades are asked to make a report if they see this man. Peace to Chairman Durand, our Father."

"Did you hear what they said, Dad," Stefan asked.

"Yeah, Stefan, I heard it. Please come."

"I'm playing, Dad."

"Now—please come now."

"Okay," Stefan replied grudgingly.

Stefan stepped into the door of the bathroom and stared with a frown at his dad, as if William had lost his senses.

"What does—" Stefan began.

William clasped his hand over his son's mouth and then held a finger to his own lips. "Shush," he whispered.

Stefan nodded with an instantly mature face, more aware and knowing than William expected. A burst of pride ran through him. His son was growing up.

William removed the black device from the box and held it up for Stefan to see. "Turn around and lift your shirt," William whispered into Stefan's ear. "I'm going to check you for something that may have been stuck under your skin when you were a baby. This will not hurt in any way."

Stefan flashed a look of disbelief for a second and then raised his shirt up to his shoulders.

William pushed the on and off button at the top of the device. A small red light came on. He moved the device over Stefan's back and around his neck, hoping the signal didn't activate. He repeated his motion, with the same result. It seemed the State had not violated Stefan's body. Then he wondered if the device really worked.

"You're okay, son," he whispered.

Stefan looked at him and whispered, "The government?"

William sighed, thinking to spare his son the anguish, but he could not lie. He nodded.

Stefan nodded silently and walked slowly back to the living room, his smile replaced with the seemingly new look of early maturity.

"Marie, please come to the kitchen, honey," William said.

Lynn emerged from the bedroom, following Marie into the kitchen where she nearly gasped when she saw William stooped down in the bathroom, holding the electrical device.

Marie bounced over to him. "Daddy, what does that thing do?" Marie blurted.

"Nothing really, honey," William said softly. When she got close, he pulled her into his arms and whispered, "We're going to play a game and you can't say a word or you lose, and then you'll miss out on the surprise."

Marie whispered, "What surprise?"

"You must be quiet while I wave this thing around you. I'm searching for an invisible fairy."

"What's a fairy?"

"You have to whisper honey." His daughter had never heard of fairies. What else from the wonders of childhood would she miss because of their life? "I want to run this box over your back. It will locate areas we should wash better. Good idea. Right?"

"I guess," Marie muttered. "But I washed really well."

"I know you do, sweetie."

Lynn stepped into the bathroom and pulled the door closed. "Honey, let me hold up your shirt," Lynn whispered, kneeling down. She lifted Marie's shirt up above Marie's shoulders.

William moved the device over Marie's back. A second red light came on and went off. He moved the box more slowly across the shoulder area, and just below the base of Marie's neck, it came on again. His heart sank. He looked at Lynn and she glared back. Lynn looked as if she might burst into tears. William swallowed a lump in his throat as he turned off the scanner, and then pressed the button for turning on the electromagnetic disruptor. He held the device for a few moments over the spot on Marie's back and then turned off the disruptor. Again, he passed the device over Marie's back, hoping not to see the warning light. It didn't turn on. He sighed and nodded to Lynn. Lynn opened the bathroom door.

"Okay, honey, you are perfectly clean," William said. "Give me a big kiss, please."

"Thanks, Daddy," Marie replied before she gave him a kiss and pranced back through the kitchen.

Lynn closed the bathroom door and looked at William expectantly. "What does it do?"

"It's a scanner for locating implanted electronic devices used by the SAC for tracking."

"Oh my God." She closed her eyes for a moment and then snapped back to him. "Stefan's clean?"

William nodded.

"When did it happen?"

"I was told it happened when she was born. They weren't doing it when Stefan was born."

Lynn whispered with sharp words, "That's absolutely perverted . . . an abomination for God sake. How did . . . you . . ."

He placed the scanner back in its box, and pushed it into his shirt before motioning for Lynn to open the bathroom door. He whispered into Lynn's ear. "I don't want to tell you anything that you would ever have to hide from the SACI."

Lynn clasped her mouth with a hand, letting her eyes to slide closed, and then she nodded as if conceding a part of her spirit to their new peril.

"Honey, I'm taking the trash out to the garage," William announced, grabbing the container from under the bathroom sink, slipping into the dark garage where he slid the scanner box under the wooden steps leading into the house.

Later in the evening, lying in bed waiting for Lynn to finish in the bathroom, William thought of what he had done for Marie. He drifted back to the time when he was a kid at home with a father, mother, and sister. He had been so unaware of what was going on, innocent, and so centered on his own little world. He was young and protected by his mom and dad. Some of the things his father had told him about the richness of life in his father's youth came back to him. Those times seemed too soft, too easy, and too incredibly comfortable to have ever happened, like a dream existence in a child's fantasy book. When he was young his family had burned tree leaves in the fall for fun and cooked a sweet called marshmallows on the end of a stick held in the flames, and they cooked a hot dog on a stick. William remembered playing with toy cars made of plastic, unlike the metal one's his father played with in the dirt. The food from his father's time even sounded tastier, coming from small family owned bakeries and butcher shops, the smells capturing your nose the instant you crossed the threshold into a shop with wooden floors. Suddenly, he remembered something called a root beer float, something else lingering in his brain connected with his Mom, a drink she liked and had mentioned one time, and how great it was on a hot lazy summer day. He would have to research the composition of a root beer float someday. His mom loved to talk about those old times with fireflies lighting the evening and mourning doves cooing at sunset.

He remembered how his family gathered at his great grandmother's house for fried chicken and the famous apple pie made with apples collected from the backyard. Another fragment popped out of his memory about his grandfather, Ted, whom William had never met. According to his father, Ted was a skilled tradesman in a manufacturing plant that created parts for the big cars and worked hard to help pay for his father to go to college. That once gentle life had been smothered somewhere in the past, and it was a mystery he hoped his father's chronicle would help him understand, although change was impossible now. Despite that, he still had to know what happened. It was killing him not to read the chronicle.

Lynn turned out the light and slipped under the covers smelling wonderful as she curled next to him, deliciously warm. She draped an arm across him, moving her head next to his chest, breathing against him, her rhythmic movement trusting him, believing in him, drawing from his strength. How many more times would he feel her lying next to him? It was as if the impending tribulation had formed ripples in a sea of spiritual energy, ripples that he could almost sense by pushing his finger into the air.

Into her ear he whispered, "I was questioned today by two men from the SACI, the ones who do the brainwashing." He felt her stiffen. "I don't want you involved. Your job is to take care of the kids. Okay?"

She whispered into his neck, "Yes. But—"

"Stop," William interrupted. "This will kill us if we let it. If you don't know anything, there won't be anything for you to worry about divulging or feeling guilty about. Part of their method is to scare us and control us, to make me feel guilty, to make me become psychotic, to make me fear what they might do to you and the children. I don't want to worry about losing you guys or seeing you harmed. I will tell everything I know. It's possible they could split us up. You may have to take the kids somewhere safe to live, without me. Also, if they take you to the SAC spa, they may try implanting electronic devices into you and the kids. I don't know how, but that's what I've learned."

"That's pure insanity."

He kissed her. "I know you'll do what is necessary to make certain our kids get a chance to grow up. Right?"

She nodded into the hollow of his throat. "It's as if a sickness has come over us, making our lives so dreary and scary," she whispered.

He closed his eyes and kissed her, holding his lips on her skin for a long memory- building moment, and then he embraced her, capturing her, melting into one body. He felt her shudder, silently crying in his arms. "Never trust any of them."

As he gazed through the dark, he remembered his new connection to an existence outside SAC, Russell. *Could Russell get his family to safety?*

Chapter 14

As William walked out the back door to the garage to get in his car Thursday morning, leaving for his bus pickup depot, he began rumbling over scenarios involving his planned aborted exchange with Nick Freeman. At one point, he had hoped for the day but now he dreaded it. As the v-tran followed William's car on his way to catch his bus, he asked himself how he would avoid Nick and whether he should. *Russell is real.*

After driving a mile, he realized something new. The sight of the black vehicle lurking behind him like a ghost no longer scared him, no longer made his pulse race, and no longer made him wonder if they'd arrest him. He possessed a strange calm, as if he were reconciled to his destiny.

After arriving at work and he was walking across the street to his SAC building, he noticed two men standing in the open blatantly watching him, and another man near the parking area exit leaning against a light pole holding eyes on him. He laughed to himself at their effort to intimidate him. *Tick tick tick.*

It then struck him, that if Nick Freeman was indeed a part of their game, it didn't make sense for the SACI to arrest him trying to leave the building with a scanner, especially if they wanted to discover more conspirators, the conspiratorial leaders of the invisible underground group directing him. Nevertheless, he didn't want to take the chance with Nick.

William got a cup of coffee and settled in at his desk, studying the usual numbers of people working in his facility and on the various labor facilities. An hour after starting he heard someone humming obnoxiously, approaching from behind him, exhibiting the kind of personal excess that no one in the office would ever venture. He turned around and caught a glimpse of Nick Freeman shuffling down the aisle. He quickly locked his desk and sprang to his feet, briskly escaping up the aisle, following Russell's directions. William stopped next to the door for the floor's security person, where he turned to check on Nick. Freeman's confused face slowly morphed into an expression of anger. Freeman stood beside William's desk staring at him.

"Do you have a problem, Manager Rinehart?" the rotund security man asked, leaning back in his chair so he could see around the doorjamb.

William stepped back, out of the way, looking toward his desk. "I didn't like the man standing near my desk. I believe he needs to be removed so he won't see my sensitive work."

The security man came to the door, stared at Nick Freeman for a moment, frowned as if wrongly disturbed, and waved his hand for Freeman to leave. Nick nodded casually and departed the office by the route he had come.

"Happy?" the man grumbled.

William nodded. "Yes, sir. Thank you."

At nearly midday, Helmut Kauffman sat at his desk, checking his Thursday morning correspondence on his computer. He read and then erased a message from Chairman Durand, which was time-dated, eleven o'clock Thursday morning. At first, he took it as an intrusion into his management skills but as he let it soak in his brain, mentally walking in the Chairman's shoes, he understood Durand's need for rapid resolution of their problem. A potentially lethal cancer could spread, if there was a grain of truth to the old intelligence report. Durand may have been up in years but he knew how to protect his government.

"Vid-link, on," Kauffman said, thinking it was time to kick some ass.

"Ready."

"Call, Section Head Steinhoff."

In a moment, he looked at Karl Steinhoff.

"Director, what can I do for you?" Steinhoff asked from his office, quickly sitting more erect.

Kauffman kept an unexpressive face as he laughed a little on the inside, and told himself Steinhoff's reaction was because his own power. It drew respect. Power attracted favors and obedience. "Karl, Chairman Durand needs us to end our problem. He wants it solved. I've given you a few days, thinking Rinehart might be more forthcoming, but I'm afraid our time is up. Please process Rinehart over to Doctor Beucher in the mentoring department. We need to use our expert at information extraction. Doctor Beucher should be able to obtain the secrets in Rinehart's brain. I want Doctor Beucher to have total freedom to use all the tools in his laboratory to extract everything from Rinehart's brain."

"Immediately?"

"Tomorrow will be fine," Kauffman snapped. "He's not going anywhere."

"What about brain damage? Sometimes . . ."

Kauffman paused. "Do not destroy the brain if there's the possibility for future recall, in case there's a blocked subconscious for some reason. Beucher is very astute in dealing with those little problems, however make it clear he is not to destroy the brain."

Steinhoff nodded. "Yes, sir. The procedure will commence immediately. I will closely monitor Beucher's work. Can you share anything on the type of information you're seeking?"

Kauffman smiled but his face held subtle distrust. "Karl, I'm reassured by your persistence. Thank you." Kauffman looked plainly at Steinhoff, wondering if he should place the whole Rinehart family into a holding facility.

Steinhoff sat forward in his chair. "Sir, one more thing. I've arranged for Rinehart's wife and kids to visit the spa. They were on the list. I just moved their date forward."

"Very good. It will be good to get more control, although there isn't any way they can disappear." Kauffman nodded. "Vid-link, off." Kauffman considered Steinhoff's actions and whether he would ever reach the mental level required for the strategic mind game played by an SAC executive.

Lynn stood in the door connecting the kitchen and garage, clutching her mouth, her chest shuddering with her sobs, as William pulled into the garage Thursday evening. William's heart sank, fearing the SACI had done something awful to make her cry. From the car he saw tracks from tears rolling down Lynn's cheeks glistening in the garage light, suddenly arousing his fear. Stefan peeked around her from behind the edge of the door.

"What's wrong?" William shouted, quickly climbing out of the car. He rushed to her, hungering for an answer that wasn't something disastrous.

"Marie didn't come home from school with Stefan. He says she never got on the bus at school. He says he saw a v-tran parked in front of the school when his bus pulled out."

William hugged Lynn, pressing her head into his shoulder. "We'll figure out something. I can't believe they would hurt her. I can drive to her school. They are probably using her for leverage, maybe as a source of information, but nothing more." He stopped for a moment. "There's no one I can call to get help. I'm sorry but we are on our own. If she's not home soon I'll drive to the school." Rage directed at the SAC gripped him, torturing him with a vision of destroying the SAC buildings in an act of acquiring retribution.

William reached for the garage door control to run the door down.

"Stop," Lynn yelled.

He spun around and saw a black v-tran roll to a stop in the driveway. He walked over and stood a few feet from its front bumper, his anger boiling barely under control. The back-right passenger door opened and Marie dropped to her feet on the driveway.

"Hi sweetie, Mommy's waiting for you," William said, kneeling down to her level.

"Okay," Marie popped and scampered past William on her way to Lynn.

Lynn, standing at the front of their car, scooped up Marie and smothered her with kisses.

"Why are you crying, Mommy?" Marie asked as Lynn eased Marie back to the floor.

Lynn dabbed her eyes with a tissue, swallowing her sobs. "When you didn't come home with Stefan I got very worried."

"I was okay."

"I can see you were, honey."

William walked to the rear of his car and stood. He folded his arms on his chest, sending his eyes out like a warning to the v-tran, connecting angrily with the driver sitting behind the darken windshield. He couldn't see the driver's face but he imagined a sour grin looking back at him. He wanted to walk over to the driver's window, wait for it to descend slowly and then slam his fist into the man's face, but he couldn't do anything. They knew it, and they knew he knew it. Even yelling would have been wrong with the kids nearby. Yelling at the v-tran would only have scared Marie, who seemed unconcerned about the whole affair, and it would have most likely gotten him immediately arrested. For now, he had to swallow the poison of diffusing the tension. He turned toward the back of the garage and walked slowly back to Lynn and Marie.

"Sweetie, it looks like you got a special ride home," William said.

"I missed part of my art class," Marie said with a painful tone. "We were going to finish our bird pictures with real water color paint."

William nodded. "Let's go inside and get you some dinner." He decided to let the emotions cool before he'd try asking Marie any questions about her visit with the men in the v-tran.

It seemed like only a few minutes had passed, before William was placing the plates on the dinner table with Marie behind him setting the knives, forks, and spoons on paper napkins. After they sat down and began eating he began probing into what was going on in Stefan and Marie's world, pushing questions at them, provoking thinking-answers instead childish joking, asking them about what they wanted to do when they grew up, asking what school classes they liked best, and asking about their favorite things in school, things he'd never taken the time to delve into before—when time seemed infinite. Each little detail pierced a hole in him as he realized the little treasures he had pushed into the background, and what the SAC obedience had and could cost him. The State wanted him to trade the reward of knowing his children with their wondrous thinking and creative energy for its existence. The State could take his children at its will. The SAC had extracted the price from him with their programming, and it had to end.

Dinner ended with Lynn serving a desert of butterscotch pudding with a cookie and serving William a stern look as she sat down to eat. "Marie, what did those men want at school?" Lynn asked.

"They wanted to know if someone was sick and who was going to the bathroom late every night, and they asked why people were whispering all the time."

Lynn frowned and blurted, "It's none of their damn business!"

"Mommy, what did you say?" Marie puffed.

"Well . . ."

"Marie, honey, Mommy is upset about those men," William said. "They didn't tell her about keeping you late after school." How did they know someone was in the bathroom late at night and they were whispering? They had to be looking through the walls with some device, infrared or microwave. He'd heard of infrared. It all was a violation of their lives, but they were powerless to stop it.

"I'm sorry, honey," Lynn said. "If you're done with your pudding why don't you go jump in the tub for a bath so you're ready for bed?"

After dinner when the long shadows of dusk had turned completely black under the moonless night, leaving only a faint glow of city lights rising above the horizon to tease the sky, Lynn went into the living room where William was sitting and signaled him with her eyes to follow her back to the kitchen. She leaned up to his ear and whispered, "There's a light flashing out back. I heard something like a stone hit the back of the house a moment ago. When I looked out the window I saw three flashes."

William went to the sink and ran a glass of water. He placed the glass to his lips, drinking slowly, searching through the window and out into the dark, looking for the light Lynn had seen at the back of their property. Just then, he heard something hit the back of the house. A moment later, he saw a light.

Lynn whispered, "Is it friendly?"

He nodded. "Honey, keep the kids out of the kitchen."

Lynn looked over her shoulder to check on the kids. Stefan had his head bent over his homework and she heard Marie singing in the bathroom as water ran into the tub.

William walked over to the door leading into the garage, flipped off the kitchen light, and slipped out into the garage. He then exited through the rear door out of the garage, leading out to the backyard. He crossed the lawn, going to the back, listening for a voice, hearing nothing, and seeing nothing move. "Who's there?" William whispered as he reached the darkness at the end of the yard.

"Rinehart, did the scanner work okay?" a man whispered.

"Dammit, who's there?"

"Don't be an idiot. Russell Wood. Don't talk above a whisper or we'll both be dead."

Russell emerged slightly from the blackness of the bushes.

"Are you under some sort of cover?" William asked, sounding relieved. "My eyes are still adjusting to the dark."

"Yes. It's to conceal my body heat from the infrared eyes in any drone flying around." Russell extended his hand. "Move over here into the bushes so we're not detected. The bushes will help."

William took three steps into the blackness of the bushes and shook Russell's hand. "Yeah," he whispered. "I found an implant in my daughter's back. Thanks. By the way . . ." William stopped, paralyzed by what he suddenly remembered. "Wait a minute. Just wait one damn minute."

"What the hell's wrong with you?" Russell snapped, raising his whisper dangerously loud.

"Do know a Rachel York in Leesburg, Virginia?" William asked, his tone cautious and testing.

"What? You . . ." Russell stammered.

"I'm going," William replied abruptly, turning quickly, a sinking feeling in the pit of his stomach for falling into an SACI trap.

"Wait, for God sakes. She . . . uh, wait a minute . . . uh, she runs a clothing shop . . . for babies."

William breathed a sigh of relief and turned back to Russell. "Thank, God, you're real."

"Damn right, I'm real. Where did you get that old exchange code? I almost didn't remember the reply. You've been thinking I was from the SACI, haven't you? You didn't believe me even after I gave you the scanner. "

"So what. I'm not a stupid ass."

"Okay, okay, where did you get the code?"

"My father gave it to me."

"Holy shit. You might be able to help us."

"I can't tell you how much better I feel about talking to you. And that reminds me of what I was going to ask you."

"Shoot," Russell replied.

"Would it be possible for my wife and kids to escape to the mountains somewhere?"

Russell's head moved to the left and right as he ran his eyes quickly around the perimeter of the yard. "Why the mountains?" Russell asked in a testing tone.

"It just came to mind as a good place. The SAC sent me . . . uh, to help capture a conspirator down in the mountains of North Carolina. I didn't want to go, but I had to. It was the shock of my life . . . horrible. I never knew who they were after."

"Was the person on the mountain your father? Was he hiding there?"

"Yeah," William said, swallowing hard, hearing a strange hunger in Russell's voice. "He was hiding out in an old military bunker."

"I'm sorry for what you had to do."

"I didn't know who the SAC was trying to capture until I got there. They wanted him bad—and they wanted him alive. They must have known I hadn't seen him since I was about twelve. I hated his guts. But I never knew the truth about him."

"William, I'm here to talk about your father. Where is he? Are they brainwashing him? He might have valuable information for our cause."

"My father's dead. He blew himself up before the SAC could get to him. And I can tell you, the SACI wants whatever was in his head and they want it damn bad. They sent his own son to make him surrender. What a horrible thing they made me do." He stopped.

"He's not dead," Russell said in a grave tone. "He can't be dead. He was a great patriot."

"Well, he is. Perhaps he's finally finding some peace in the hereafter. And regardless of you knowing a code word, which the SACI could have obtained, I'm still a little uncertain about you."

"You're all alone—and against them. You don't know whom to trust. I know that."

"That may be so, but I'm not exactly stupid," William said, biting the words.

"So? Are you going to take a chance on me or not? You took the scanner. You're standing here now talking to me. You must feel something's right. Make up your damn mind. Just being here is very risky for me. They have all sorts of surveillance electronics, infrared scopes, sensitive microphones, and all that kind of equipment. I had to walk a mile to get here unseen. They could catch me in the next five minutes. Hopefully these bushes will give cover from any infrared scanners."

"Yeah, I guess I don't have much choice."

"What can you tell us about your father?"

"While I was talking with him, before we reconciled, he briefed me on some historical events related to the beginning of the SAC. He called the beginning of the political turmoil and our current oppressive government, the precursor, and he swore he could help save my family. He wrote a bunch of history down, called it his chronicle. He was going to use his shortwave radio to get his chronicle to someone in the underground before he died. He had cancer or something horrible. He was coughing up blood while I was talking with him. He knew he wouldn't live long even without being brainwashed."

Russell looked around. "We wanted him badly, and we wanted him alive. He was a pioneer and a patriot. Did he mention any other people who could be contacted?"

"No," William whispered. "What's this about him being a patriot?"

"Your father was part of the first underground attempting to save the country from becoming a totalitarian state."

"He gave me his notebook, which I gave to the SACI."

"Shit. There could have been some connections in it—and clues."

"Clues to what?" William whispered.

"To our history," Russell replied, distracted, still warily looking around the yard.

"The notebook I gave the SACI didn't contain his chronicle. It was bullshit he concocted to hide the real information. It was a decoy."

"What?"

"Don't worry, I have his real chronicle and it will never be revealed if I'm taken, because I haven't read it yet. He didn't want me to read it until after I had faced their brain scan. He wanted me to read it after I went through all their interrogation and brainwashing. I just want my family taken to safety as soon as possible. Once I've done that, and I've read my father's final words, you'll get the chronicle. I swear it."

Russell inched closer. "Rinehart, why in the hell are you interested in trying to leave utopia?"

"You don't have to be sarcastic."

"Sorry."

"I've had to survive the best I could for my family. You know this isn't life. This is slavery or worse. Once my family is safe, it will be easier for me to deal with the hell that comes my way. My father said Durand's replacement would take the country further into hell. I know now that I will probably pay a price for my lack of integrity and courage. After talking with my father, I also know I still have a chance for a reckoning."

"What makes you think you need to get your family out now?"

"Any minute the SACI is going to take me in for brainwashing. They've already interrogated my wife and son, and just today, they approached and questioned my little daughter. My family is safe. They could be tortured in front of me to make me say anything the SAC thought it needed."

"How do you know you are going to be arrested?"

"The interrogation meeting this morning. They want more of what's in my head, information about my father. They may kill me. I told them about the bomb, but they're after more."

"What?" Russell burst, nearly raising his voice again as he pushed his face closer to William. "What's that about a bomb?"

"My father told me the location of a big fuel and fertilizer bomb. He knew the SACI would torture me to find it—and strangely, my father didn't seem too disturbed. He told me not to hold anything from them."

"They must think you know more than you're telling. Look, there has been a legend floating around in the FUS for years."

"The what?"

"It stands for, Free the US . . . it means the damn underground, man. Damn, Rinehart, don't you know anything?"

"Sorry, but they don't send announcements around within SAC about subversive activities. It's risky to know much about that shit. I'm supposed to report it. I'm not supposed to think about it. In fact, they've repeatedly said the underground was a myth until recently when they announced the name of a man they wanted to arrest, an Adolf Bane. So what's this legend of yours?"

"I heard about that announcement, too. Adolf Bane's bullshit. He doesn't exist. They made him up. They want the masses to have a villain to hate. Now—back to your father. There has been a story, legend if you will, telling of a man who knew how to destroy the SAC. Maybe that bomb was the solution." He stopped. "Ah shit. I knew the story was too good to be true. Most people didn't really believe it anyway. The SAC bastards are like a flesh eating bacteria, consuming people like food. I don't know how your father could have heard the intelligence, but from what we know, your father was right about Durand's replacement, Bruner. There is a plan we've heard of, a plan in which they won't need vid-cams. Every person will have at least one implant for control by the SAC. People will become, in a sense, human robots. Plus they will control all births."

"Why hasn't this FUS been able to bring down the SAC?"

"You're talking about toppling a whole country with enormous resources as well as an unparalleled surveillance and control structure. Hell, they have vid-cams nearly everywhere. They have helicopters and drones flying with infrared to track vehicles and they can track people with the implants. We can't make a large enough strike. You need to cut off the head of the monster in one stroke of the sword. Otherwise it's suicide."

"Look, Russell, can you contact my wife and get her and the kids into hiding when the SACI take me? If you can get my family to safety, I promise to get you the chronicle and all I can remember . . . everything my father told me."

"Sure, I can do that for you and—for your father's years of service, for holding on so long and keeping the fire of freedom burning."

"I had thought once, that if my wife could go visit my mother in Carlisle, Pennsylvania, then the underground might have an opportunity to extract her and my kids, but travel is impossible—for any reason. There must be a way!"

"Yeah, we should be able to arrange something. I don't know what . . . but . . . yeah, something." Russell was silent for a moment. "Damn, I'd like to read your father's notes. Okay, how are we going to get the chronicle if you die during their interrogation? I hate to mention it, but it does happen."

William wrenched his forehead in his hand, thinking of his burying the radio. "I'll bury instructions for finding the chronicle two meters east of the last stone paver coming from the kitchen door. I'll protect it in something and place it in an empty soup can."

"That sounds reasonable. Thanks for that. I hope, for both of us, we don't have to resort to using it."

William nodded slightly. "If I remember any other information I'll try to get it to you."

"You know—if they take you in and run you through their brain scanning process, you may betray me, your wife, your kids, even your mother. And after they release you, if they release you, they'll watch you the rest of your life. If your wife escapes through our system, you won't be able to see her again without placing her in serious danger."

"If I have any brain remaining after they work on me, I'd never knowingly betray my wife. I'd rather die. I'd die to save my family." He cast his eyes to the ground. "That's what happened to my father. He fled to save my mom and us kids. I hated him all my life, but I never knew why he left. Thank God we talked before he died."

"We have observers watching the SACI building and we'll have one watch your house. If your wife needs something in a hurry, have her run the garage door up and back down, go to the front door, step out for a moment, close the door and reopen it for a few seconds, then turn on the entrance light at the front door. After she completes those steps, have her go out and look at the light on the porch for a moment before closing the door again. Doing those steps shouldn't raise too many suspicions, and if it does, she could easily excuse it. If you think of any information beneficial to our cause you'll pass it to us, won't you?"

"Absolutely," William said. He heard a noise and snapped his head in its direction, in unison with Russell. Tingles ran up William's neck.

"Just a bird," Russell whispered. "No worry. I have spotters down the street. I have to go. Take care of yourself. Try to stay alive."

William shook Russell's hand and watched him disappear into the blackness.

Returning from the back lawn, William went to the kitchen drawer where he had placed the pages containing his father's chronicle. He had a sudden urge to read them, panicked he wouldn't get the chance if he waited. Standing there beside the drawer, he stopped with his hand on the drawer, reminding himself to have patience and faith. There was that concept again, faith. *Mom had faith.* If he read those pages and the SACI tortured him, he would spew his guts. He'd certainly betray anything of significant value to his family, to the underground, and maybe shatter any chance of revolution. He had to wait and hope he would have the mental faculties to read his father's notes after the SACI was finished with him. From what he had already heard from his father, he suspected it contained a secret hidden for decades.

Someone pounded on the front door. Marie ran screaming into the kitchen with Stefan following, their faces stricken with fear.

"My word, who could that be?" Lynn asked, with a hand over her heart.

William answered her calmly. "I have no idea. Everyone stay here while I get the door."

Three strikes fell against the door as if a person were trying to knock the door down.

"I'm coming," William yelled, reaching for the lock. He opened the door. Two men in the typical gray of the SACI stood ominously stiff, glaring at him.

"Are you William Rinehart?" the man in front asked sternly, his tone deep and his words resonating, as if they came from a man twice his size. William met the man eyeball-to-eyeball. The man with dark bushy eyebrows and a heavy beard seemed nervous as if expecting violence. A

275

second, taller and thinner man, stood behind the first, looking plain faced and bored.

"Yes," William replied easily. "What's this about?"

"May we come in?"

"Why?"

"We need to search your home."

"Why? What for?"

The man stepped through the door, pushing William out of the way with a hand on his chest. The second man followed two steps behind the first. They immediately began looking around the living room and after a few moments, they gravitated toward the bedrooms, their heads in constant motion searching for something.

"Identify yourselves or I'll call my SAC director."

"We don't have to, but for your information we work for the SACI," the bearded man said.

"Why are you at my home? Could you give me your names?"

The men split up, each entering a different bedroom, leaving William standing in the hall.

"We don't have to tell you anything. My rank is captain and I have orders." The man opened the closet and fumbled with hanging clothes for a moment.

William heard the other man open and close a closet.

The bearded man swung around. "You have an attic?"

"No."

"You have a basement or crawlspace?"

"No, this place is on a concrete slab. What are you looking for?"

"Dean, let's check the garage," the bearded man said.

The two men started toward the kitchen, nearly pushing William into the wall to get past. As they entered the kitchen, Lynn stood next to sink, her arms wrapped protectively around Stefan and Marie. William exchanged silent glances with Lynn. William could see she was being strong for the children, but her strength had to be paper-thin. The men went out into the garage, looked around, and returned to the kitchen with blank faces. One of the men looked into the bathroom, glanced at the ceiling, and then stared at the vent near the floor. He turned to the kitchen, frowning as if he had a question, but said nothing.

"Why are you here?" William asked.

"Don't ask that question again. That's all you need to know."

The two men walked arrogantly toward the front door, surveying the house as if reluctant to leave for fear they had missed their treasure. William followed a few feet behind and then standing in the doorway, watched them get into their v-tran and drive toward the entrance of the housing area, leaving another v-tran ready to pounce from across the street.

William walked over to Lynn and the kids, who were huddled together and waiting in the kitchen. He wrapped his arms around them, wishing that their troubles were over. He a question formed on the edge of his thinking. Was the search somehow connected to Russell's visit? It was possible they were still trying to catch bigger fish using him for bait.

"What did they want?" Lynn whispered, her words catching in her throat, sounding as if she would cry.

"I don't know." Of course, he knew. It was everything. It was their way of elevating the pressure, playing with his mind.

"Honey, what are we going to do?" Lynn whispered.

"We keep doing what we have been doing. That's all we can do "

"How can they just barge into our home and search with no identification or charge or without our permission?" She paused and then, to avoid the children hearing, she whispered into his ear. "We are only animals under their control, nothing more than cattle."

His father's history book surfaced in his mind, and the important events that he had read. She was right. The book had touched on similar trespasses of people's lives.

Later, after the house was quiet and Lynn was asleep, William fulfilled his promise to Russell and slipped out the backdoor, burying instructions on how to recover the chronicle. Machinations of the SACI and his father's legacy swirled confusingly in his mind, along with vaporous objectives for his approaching tribulation. The SACI would be coming for him soon.

Chapter 15

Friday morning William walked into the kitchen for breakfast and immediately saw Lynn's eyes shadowed and gray, looking bruised from worry. She rinsed a dish in the sink, retrieved milk from the refrigerator, poured a cup of coffee, dumped in a spoon of sugar, and after adding a little milk, she stirred it while looking fixedly ahead, clanging the spoon as if she were trying to break the cup.

William sat and assembled a bowl of cereal. He could see Lynn was weakening under the strain. They were in uncharted territory and his stomach knotted with anguish with what he had decided during his sleepless night lying in bed. The words he must assemble and pass over his lips lay moaning in his mind, pleading they should be replaced with gossamer pleasantries. He watched her sip her coffee across from him, afraid to think how many more times he would do it. What he was going to do, he had to do. He had to say goodbye. It was the worst thing he had ever contemplated, and he had to do it before the kids came into the kitchen for breakfast, and before they would race to the school bus. He remembered his father's confession on the mountain and of his father's terrible pain when he had performed the same heart-searing duty. He waited for Lynn to take another sip, studying her lips and the warm moisture lingering on them from the coffee, making them even more luscious, torturing him with the thought he may not taste them many more times. The ghostly distance in her eyes betrayed her emotions that she knew the SACI could take him at any moment.

"Honey," he began softly, "if I don't come home some evening from work, I want you take care of the kids for both of us. I wish there was a way for you to go to your mom's but SAC travel restrictions—"

She gasped. Tears pooled in the corner of her eyes. Her breast shuddered.

"Honey," he whispered, his eyes glancing upward without moving his head.

She stared at him almost warily, as if he were stabbing a knife into her heart. "No."

"You must. You have to save our children. I love you more than anything and I know how hard it will be, but the kids need a chance to walk in the woods totally free someday."

She sobbed into her hands, looking at him, spilling her pain.

He got up and sat next to her. He leaned into her ear and whispered, "If you leave for safety leave me a signal. Turn a glass open-end up in the cupboard on top the plates if you're okay and turn one open-end down on the plate if you and the kids are in trouble and need help." It wasn't as if he could help them if they were in trouble, but at least maybe he'd know about them.

He took her hand and led her into the bathroom so they talk without fear of having their lips read. He made her promise to go through the garage-door-signaling maneuver to make contact with Russell's people to obtain their help to escape or avoid arrest. Of course, he promised to meet her and the kids once he was free from the SAC and its mind-destroying section, the SACI, but it was a lie, and he could see by the stiff line of her lips that Lynn knew it was a lie. She understood he was trying to make it easy for her. He kissed her, absorbing her soft moist lips and her breath on his face, her gentle perfume drifting to him, tearing at his heart. He remembered just then, the scent she wore was her prize, a little luxury. She had bought it by saving coupons from the food budget, long, long ago, when they felt free, back when the market carried some luxury items. She shuddered against his chest as he held her. The word, God, popped into his brain. He prayed Russell was indeed as reliable as he seemed. He pulled himself away and looked at her and at her searching his face. He felt her pouring her love into the moment that seemed a formation of a crystal that would release light in future years. He went to the door. She took his hand and squeezed it. He nodded silently as he pursed his lips and then he went out into the garage. He stood next to the car for a moment absorbing the image of her standing in the doorway. "I love you," he said.

"I love you too," Lynn replied, covering her mouth with an anxious hand.

The garage door went up as William held his gaze on Lynn. Suddenly, Lynn's eyes screamed out in pain, forcing William to turn around. A black v-tran sat waiting in the driveway ready to pounce on him, its engine running, throbbing with a low guttural sound like an animal preparing to swallow his life.

Lynn shook her head, as if it wasn't happening, crying into her hand.

William stood motionless as two men, a smallish mustached man and a man of average build showing a scar on his left cheek, climbed out of the v-tran, and walked toward him. Their horrid gray uniforms and their deadly plain faces declared their intention. William guessed these agents might be upper-level intelligence agents. Their clothes, unlike the gorillas that marched through his home, weren't crumpled swatches of cheap fabric, and their shoes were shined brilliant black. *This is it!*

"Manager Rinehart, you are required to come with us," the slightly smaller man said with an emotionless tone.

"Why? I haven't done anything."

"You are to come with us to SACI headquarters."

"Am I under arrest?"

"Yes."

William nodded and walked to the v-tran where the scarred man opened a door for him. He caught a fleeting glimpse of Lynn standing at the door with a hand clasping her mouth before the v-tran moved down the street.

Within moments, William saw his neighborhood slipping out of sigh. The moment had arrived in an almost surreal manner, unlike what he had pictured in his mind. It seemed as if the SACI agents were conveying him off into the distance with an unearthly coach, headed toward an awaiting hell on earth. The v-tran with its shaded windows lumbered unrushed across the city, down the highway, and into Washington, as if it were conveying something no more urgent than a corpse. As he watched the road slide past him, road that he hadn't heretofore been allowed to see. The main traffic appeared to be the morning's slave workforce carried in the numerous SAC worker buses. How hopelessly morbid the buses looked from the outside.

When they passed SAC Building Three and approached SAC Building Two, the home of SACI, William's expectation was confirmed. He was, indeed, about to face something he could scarcely grasp. He had a mental image of his future hours, an image fed by horrible rumors, stories of torture with electrical devices aimed at destroying a person's memory, possibly wiping away their brain until the hand of death eased their pain.

The SACI agents pulled up to a metal door in the rear of Building Two and escorted William through double doors, down a hall to an elevator where they dropped down two floors below street level. A man in gray tunic coat opened a door a few yards ahead. When they reached the man, William found the letters on the badge on left side of the man's chest, identifying him as CC Behr 503, faintly puzzling.

"Take him to Room 100," Behr directed.

"I figured that," snapped one of the men behind William.

They walked down the hall as if they had practiced the formation and movements, stopping at Room 100, where a burly man held the door open. William had seen him before. It was Hans, his inquisitor from the conference room interrogation. A second man aided Hans, the one with strange eyes and baldhead. William gazed into the room, mesmerized.

"How do you like our truth extraction room?" Hans chirped as the escorting agents backed away. "I'm sorry, I meant to say, the truth mentoring room." The man with the piercing eyes laughed hideously, stopped, and guffawed stupidly again.

Standing with his hands to his sides, seeing the tools of mental rape, William was naked and impotent. He thought of the people who had stood where he was and considered himself lucky for holding more significance than some poor laborer in need of a mind treatment. He did have some mysterious value.

"Over there," Hans directed, pointing to the left side of the room. "Neal, please get the patient's clothing from supply."

William gathered picture of the bizarre looking room, trying not to speculate on the function of the devices, but failing at blanking the horrible thoughts. Two large chairs located in the center of the room gave him a chill as he imagined the sickness using them for afflicting pain. The room reminded him of a hospital operating room, although no operating table existed. Except for the area occupied by a blackened rectangular window to the left of entry door, three and four-foot high stacks of black electronic control units covered the walls. Their red and green-lighted digital displays with lighted control knobs, and numerous toggle switches, confirmed the frightening thoroughness of the distorted minds that used the room.

One stack of four electronic control units caught William's eye. Each of the units had a separate identification. The top unit was labeled alpha, the next one down was called beta, and then came theta and delta. The terms meant nothing to William except that they were Greek words. The overhead fluorescent lights hammered the room in stark white clinical light. Bundles of cables crisscrossed the floor like a gigantic spider web. A large white mechanical arm with wires extended down from the ceiling. At its bottom, two horizontal arms extended from it. One arm reached over two or three feet above the white chair and the other arm stretched over above the black chair. They looked like something used by a dentist or surgeon, except that a clear plastic helmet hung down from each arm directly above each chair. Each of the chairs had straps for restraining a subject's chest, arms, and legs. *This is hell's workshop.* William had little doubt he would be sitting in one of the chairs before long.

Hans laughed under his breath, grinning grotesquely. "I think I'll give you a little tour until the doctor gets here. It's one of my small privileges . . . letting our patients know the special attention coming their way." He pointed at an object in the room. "Over there we have our special chair with its electronic hat for checking brain signals when we question a subject. Likewise, you might find it interesting that we can actually insert specific signals back into a person's brain. When the doctor does that, he can trigger all kinds of interesting emotions. We can scan the brain and determine if the subject has seen something or heard something. It seems the brain tells all, whether the person wants it to or not." He looked at William and flashed his eyebrows, showing the same unbalanced diabolical grin. "And over here," Hans continued, pointing to the right side of the room, "is another chair we call the dental chair. This has to be my favorite." He stopped and glanced around for a moment. "Doctor Conrad Beucher is the man who has been developing techniques for what he calls the mentoring of truth. He should be here in a few minutes. He'll be your guide on our little trip to return you to the SAC family, Father Durand's family. It's our duty to make well all those citizens who become sick and go astray." Hans arched his brow and squinted strangely. "I want you to know. I'm your friend. I want to help you come back to the family as easily as possible." He cocked his head a little. "However, some subjects do not return to the family as easily as others, but . . . uh, we really do our best." He laughed.

William's eyes traveled from the electronic horror to Hans, and down to the floor. He was almost certain Hans possessed a demented mind, and should have received psychological therapy at the hands of Doctor Beucher. Then, at the edge of his mind was his father. *Father would have certainly died in this place.*

As he waited, William told himself, he had to be strong for his family. He stood there with his hands hanging impotently at his sides. His body shook. *I have to stay live, no matter what.*

Neal and another man returned to the room with a plastic basket holding items looking like clothes and towels. The man following Neal spoke with an authoritarian tone. "Neal, why don't you place those things over by the generator and then you can go back to your office. I think Hans and I will do fine.

"Very good, Doctor Beucher," Neal replied.

"Ah, who do we have today?" Beucher asked in a small affected voice as he walked up to William, running his eyes from William's head down to his feet, as if measuring William for a suit of clothes.

William, with a stealthy gaze, tried to connect the doctor's diminutive nasally voice with his hideous electronic toys. Beucher seemed more like a creature than like a human, moving his eyes with jittery excitement, as if savoring the coming moment when he would take a thrill from extracting life from his victim. William found his appearance creepy, possibly because the doctor displayed an unusual combination of bodily features. Deep fissures cut down his round face at the corners of his mouth, making his teeth pronounced. Above his smallish nose, his effeminate eyes lay deeply under a bushy brow of gray and black hair, which made his eyes look as if they were in a shadow. William couldn't help thinking of the man as another gruesome organism from the dark abyss that was the SAC.

Beucher sent his attention to something off in the distance and then glanced down his nose at William for a moment, a haughty curl distorting his upper lip, and then he walked over to a desk. He looked fixedly at his film-computer. He picked up the paper-thin pad, held it splayed like book, probing the screen with his finger, whisking through the screen content with the dexterity of a surgeon.

"Yes, yes, now I see. It's Manager Rinehart, the carrier of information which has aroused the interest of Father Durand." Beucher turned back to William with one eyebrow raised. He frowned, making a mocking expression. "I think your face has suddenly lost its color. Yes, I see beads of sweat forming on your forehead. It's about time. It's statistically a normal reaction. Now, back to the information locked inside that brain of yours. Perhaps your memory of the exchange with your father has improved. Would you like to make a new and complete deposition of all you know?"

William dropped his eyes to the floor, bewildered in his sudden search for words. The perspiration on his forehead wasn't the only thing brought by his introduction to Beucher's special room. His stomach churned. "I reported all the important facts . . . all . . . everything I could remember."

"Oh, but you haven't, because if you had you wouldn't be here. I've been given the responsibility by the SAC to return you to Durand's family. The people, to whom I report, have told me there's more information locked in your brain."

"I've reported everything. I served the SAC to the best of my abilities."

"Take a seat in the left chair, the white chair. It's our vision chair." Beucher pointed to the chair dismissively as his eyes went back to his computer screen for a second. "Some people might think we use instruments of torture or hang people by their thumbs or push sharp things under the fingernails, but that's foolishness. We don't have to go to such hard labor. It's much easier than all that. You see, the brain is where pain is recognized and computed, as well as a person's senses of logic and reality. Our device, in all modesty, my device . . . it talks to your brain. I can tell your brain whatever I want. I can make you see an elephant when there isn't one. I can also make you see a snake large enough to swallow you whole. I can make you feel needles all over your body. So with our little introduction out of the way, please have a seat in the white chair."

Hans nudged William toward the chair, moving him sideways and backwards until his legs hit the chair. William sat in the chair, nervously placing his hands on his thighs, looking forward as his anxiety stuck him with needles. He tried to think of what he might say. His thoughts scrambled over each other trying to escape as a worthy coherent piece of information. Nothing new formed in his brain. After a moment, he gave up and merely looked impotently at Beucher. Beucher would probably discover what he wanted regardless of what he did. He heard Hans doing something behind him. His muscles tensed, preparing his body.

Beucher snapped around from his computer, checking William. "Just relax and tell us whatever you can remember from your conversation with your father. Take your time. We have lots of time, lots of time."

William gestured with one hand as if making an appeal. "First, you must know my father left our family when I was twelve. I had no love for the man. I think one of the first things he mentioned was about the SAC killing my sister for knowing about a plan to implant people with electronic devices. We talked about my mother living in a facility for seniors. Then he demanded to talk about the cause of the terrible state of our country—as he saw it. He began to ramble about political parties back in the 1990s, his work for the Justice Department, and then he made comments on government corruption. He went on and on about the people giving up their freedom for a utopian promise made by government people."

"That's all?" Beucher asked with a skeptical squint.

"Yes, as near as I can remember. The other information about the bomb and its location was in my report. I reported everything."

"Did he mention names of people he worked with?"

"Only one. I think I stated the information correctly in my report."

"What do you think should be done with people who plot against the State?"

William stopped himself from bursting out too quickly, but there were questions in his mind now. They were new. "I believe they should be investigated."

"Anything else?"

Again, he slowed himself, trying not to answer quickly. He scratched his neck and sent his eyes to the upper left so the man could see he wasn't accessing his creative part of his brain and therefore lying. "If the facts substantiate violations of the law they should be prosecuted." He tried to relax, to breathe, and clear his mind.

"Did your father have a conspiracy plot to attack the State?"

William struggled. "I don't know."

"He told you about a bomb, didn't he?" Beucher asked harshly.

"Yes."

"He was carrying out a conspiracy, wasn't he?"

William stared blankly. They were going to force him to agree. He knew it. "I guess."

"There's no guessing. Give me the truth."

"All I can tell you is what he told me about the bomb. I can't tell you what was in his brain."

"Hans, lower the mind-scan helmet," Beucher said and went over to a vid-link on a desk at the corner of the room. He reached down and pressed a key. "Citizen-Comrade Monroe, please come to Room 100."

The helmet slowly descended to William's head. Hans stood beside William, centering the helmet above William's head.

Chapter 16

It wasn't long before a woman with brown hair, cut to perhaps two inches, entered Room 100. William caught a glimpse of the identification tag pinned on the left side of her chest, identifying her as, CC Monroe 351. He had to think for a second. Finally, he made his jittering brain recognize the letters. They were, CC, which stood for the common SAC government category, citizen-comrade. Where was his brain? He had known that. It was a label meant to collect all workers into a family, another of the SAC's psychological attempts to build collective thinking. The uniform, the same a gray coarse-thread fabric Hans wore, that all the agents wore, made her small face, cold and fierce.

"Monroe, see to the patient's straps," Beucher said. "And then prepare the instruments for the second chair."

Monroe nodded. "Yes, sir." She began strapping William's ankles tight against the lower portion of the chair.

"Hold your head still," Hans ordered, pressing a control, lowering the cap over William's head.

The metal electrodes of a helmet startled William with their icy touch. He felt the electrodes contacting his head from front to back. Hans ran a strap under his chin, attached the ends together, and tightened the helmet over his head. Some of the electrodes pushed against William's scalp and some didn't, and some of them simply hurt, feeling as if they would cut into his skin. "This thing hurts," William said.

"This isn't a hat shop," Hans snapped as he went about his duties.

After Monroe strapped William's legs in place and wrapped the heavy plastic strap over it his wrists, she applied a strap around his chest, never once looking up or hesitating in her machine-like manner. William wondered how many human beings the woman had strapped down with the same the procedure.

"Now, Manager Rinehart . . . no, wait," Beucher said. "We can't use your name any longer." He twitched his mouth as he thought for a moment. "What about Mr. Rinehart? No. That won't work either. How about Citizen-Comrade Rinehart? No, no, no." He paused, looking at his computer lying on the desk, and turned back with a depraved grin. "We will call you patient, Ninety-nine. And please don't mistake your number for the total number of people we have processed. We are way beyond that figure . . . well past ten thousand." He paused in a moment of thought. "Okay, Ninety-nine, we will ask you questions and you will have your brain scanned. While the scanning is taking place, we will see your brain's involuntary reaction on our display. We will know what you know without you answering. You may just sit there and relax. We're not going to adjust your brain in this chair today. We are merely going to probe for the truth. Perhaps I'll use one of my newer achievements, a device that allows me to see images as you see them. Even though it's still in development and has a few minor bugs, it's quite interesting, and productive."

William clenched his teeth, feeling his jaw muscles tightening in anticipation of an electrical shock, or some sort of impulse about to shoot through his brain. A switch clicked behind him, sounding like it came from where Hans sat at a control panel. The helmet enclosing his head tickled as if ants were crawling over his scalp. He shook his head.

"Stay still, Ninety-nine. I'm going to ask you questions and you will answer with the truth. It will go easier for you if you tell the truth. I know Hans likes me to use the other chair, but you're a smart person and won't let that happen. Monroe, are you ready on the second chair?"

"Yes, sir."

"Good." Beucher sat at his desk and looked down at his computer, sliding his finger over its virtual keys and controls displayed the screen. "Patient, Ninety-nine, don't think that because I'm looking at my computer that I can't see your reactions. I have a live picture of you on my display. So, your first question. Did you talk with your father in a bunker?"

"Yes, you know I did," William replied calmly.

"Good. Did you talk about his conspiracy?"

"I don't know what he was doing?" William stiffened, thinking his answer was too vague. He turned his head but the chest strap holding him prevented him from seeing anyone other than Beucher. Not knowing what Hans was doing was like standing on a scaffold with a black hood over his head and rope around his neck, waiting for the floor to drop away from under him.

Beucher walked over to an electronic control panel. "Did this man identify any people from his group?" Beucher continued with a clinical voice as he looked at the panel.

William took a deep breath, trying to relax the muscles in his arm, easing his grip on the arm of his imprisoning chair. "He didn't mention anyone from any group. The man said the groups were unknown to each other for security reasons."

Beucher concentrated on his display. "My display is showing me a jagged green line. It indicates you had a problem answering my question, Ninety-nine. If you're lying, your treatment can get, shall we say, more stressful. I don't want to make it painful if I can avoid it. When a patient is tortured it can make their memory unreliable and we don't want those issues. Do we?"

William recalled the woman his father had mentioned. No, it was a code word. It wasn't in the binder he had reported. There were the blank pages. No. He couldn't mention blank pages. He had to remember the woman, the code word, merely as a woman's name. Beucher was right. His memory suffered from some sort mixing of words, events, and people. Sitting in Beucher's torture room had unknowingly stressed him, making his heart race. He felt a growing pressure in his head. "There was one person, but I'm not certain about the name. It might be Rachel Lee somewhere in Virginia." He turned his head a little trying to see Beucher's reaction. Suddenly, a light flashed before his eyes, but his eyes were on the Beucher. He closed his eyes, trying to understand what he had experienced, knowing Beucher manipulated him, and expecting pain to attack him at any moment. A tingle ran over him. He felt something was coming at him, an oppressive pressure, and then the scent of flowers flooded his nose. There couldn't have been flowers anywhere. It had to be the machine.

"So you were told about a woman named, Rachel?"

"Yes, yes," William struggled, his words swirling in his mind as he grabbed for them, as if he were chasing leaves swirling in the wind, catching only a fleeting glimpse of a leaf's shape or the light penetrating it. He breathed rapidly as his heart began pounding. *It's in my mind.* Slowly, as if on a cold draft leaking through a window, he felt a sense of sadness and despair. He thought he might cry. Tears came to his eyes. His thoughts froze, leaving him staring blankly with watery eyes. He moved his tongue around inside a dry mouth. The next moment a cool sensation refreshed him, moving over him like circulated air. His tears became chilled lines down his cheeks. His breathing slowed.

"Interesting isn't it?" Beucher snipped with a dark smile. "It does seem you were told about a woman called Rachel. What about her?"

"I think she was someone in the conspirator's movement. That's all I can pull together."

Beucher turned to him. "What was the bomb and what were the plans to attack the SAC?"

"I reported all I was told about a bomb. It was a fuel and fertilizer bomb . . . big and placed in a sewer near Building One. There isn't anything else I can tell you. I can't remember the number of steps to reach it. I think I knew but . . . I'm sorry."

"Who were the military men involved with the conspirator?"

"I . . . I don't remember. He never mentioned any."

"You didn't mention any in your report. Why?"

"I don't know. There weren't any to report."

Beucher nodded to Hans. "Matrix the delta and theta phases please."

William's thinking suddenly froze. He squeezed the arms of the chair, his hands feeling as if they wanted to vibrate with nervous energy, as if electricity ran through him, driving him to uncontrolled agitation. He let go of the chair and then he clenched his fists. His head quivered like a tuning fork, causing the helmet vibrate on his scalp.

Beucher stared at the display, rubbing a finger across his upper lip, and then he turned. "What you said appears to be true, according to our mind mapping." Beucher sighed as if he had been working strenuously. "What do you know about the conspirator's connections with military officers? Did he mention any names, or ranks, or branches of the military?"

Still immersed in the nervous agitation, William gasped for air. His heart hammered in his chest. His vision began growing narrow. *I'm alone, all alone. I'm away from everyone.* His father. He'd said it would be like this. He released his fists and clenched them again. He closed his eyes, trying to hang on to his awareness, fighting with all his strength against the jangling, itchy, and unsettling wave of electricity running through his body. He held his teeth tight together. Again a wave of depression engulfed him, drawing sadness to the forefront of his mind. He had no will to live.

Beucher pointed to Hans and nodded.

Suddenly, William's senses were free. His body experienced nothing from Beucher's machines. He felt totally at ease, air freely flowing with his deep, hungry breaths.

Beucher's forehead wrinkled as he pressed his mouth into a tight line. "Answer my questions completely." His voice came out in a bored mechanical monotone.

"What were they?" William asked, swallowing hard. "I want to answer them."

"Military officers. Were there any mentioned?"

William fought through his memories, but couldn't remember anything with his labored thinking. "The man . . . I don't think . . . he didn't mention any names or contacts." William gasped, trying to catch his breath.

"Your scan looks questionable, although it's partially clear. Perhaps we can move on for now. Did you share any information with your wife . . . something you shouldn't have?"

William closed his eyes. "I told her I met my father. I told my wife he explained his reason for leaving home was because of political turmoil and because of his work with the Justice Department."

"Monroe, are we ready for the dental chair?"

Monroe nodded.

Beucher turned back to the display and studied William's brain signals. "I'm very surprised, Ninety-nine." He hesitated, thinking for a moment. "It looks like we need to do some additional study. We are going to initiate a corrective phase in our mentoring treatment." He hesitated. "I think you know about the rules for reading books. You must understand— you are not permitted to read books forbidden by Chairman Durand. You were wrong. You broke the rules and you must acknowledge it before we can let you go. We cannot allow a member of our society to circumvent the State's judgment on what is appropriate for its citizen-comrades. The State must watch out for its citizens and prevent them from harming themselves. Citizens are not allowed to use electronic scanners for locating implants. Citizen-Comrade Freeman said you were interested in such a device and you agreed to buy one. Our scan found thoughts in your mind about a book you read. Our scan finds everything, so you might as well explain everything."

"I did not buy a scanner from Freeman," William said determinedly, struggling to swallow. "The man is a liar. My father gave me a book to read. It was old." Suddenly, William needed to rub his throat but couldn't.

"Was the book an authorized version?"

"I don't think so."

"You kept it and read the book anyway. A true believer in Father Durand would have turned it over to authorities."

"I didn't think it would hurt if I read it."

Beucher laughed. "Turn it off, Hans."

Instantly, William's throat muscles relaxed, allowing him to swallow without struggling. Whatever they were doing to him stopped. He pulled in a deep replenishing breath, realizing how good it was to breathe freely. *Oh God, they're putting me in the torture chair.* Beucher's treatment exhausted him and he faced more. How could he handle more of their twisted inhumanity? *I'm tired.* His fatigue hung on him like a mind-numbing weight, making his muscles feel like he couldn't possibly move them. So far, his time under their control had only been a few minutes.

Beucher stepped in front of William, glaring at him, shoving his face mere inches from him, as if taunting him. William could smell his breath, a minor abuse compared to what they were doing to his brain.

"Patient, Ninety-nine, you had what we call, intent. You broke rules. Your intent is as much a violation as the act itself. Your thinking was wrong and we must correct your thinking process. That is why we are moving you to the black chair. It is my job to make you a better member of Father Durand's family. You are guilty. You drove to a bookshop, a clear demonstration of your intent to do something against the rules. The SACI agents followed you. Your violation was blatant and abusive to Father Durand. Your father's book is subversive and contains conspiratorial words. It is a violation." Beucher backed away. "Hans, unhook our guest and move him to the black chair. Ready, Monroe?"

"Yes, sir, all the monitors are up and functioning."

Hans unstrapped and lifted the helmet from William's head, released the straps around William's chest, legs, and arms, and then glared at him. "Well, get out of the chair."

William started to stand, wobbling as he transferred weight to his feet.

Hans grabbed William under the left arm and helped him stand. "Now, go to the other chair. I'm not going to carry you. You must walk on your own."

William lifted his left leg and when he put weight on the muscles, they were rubber. The room spun before his eyes as he started collapsing to the floor. Abruptly, he felt Hans's strangling grip at his arm, holding him up, and tugging him toward the second chair. Hans slammed the palm of his hand into William's chest, sending him falling backward, falling as if weightless until he landed in the black dental chair.

"Next time I'm going to let you crack your head on the floor," Hans snapped and then glared contemptuously at him as if he were a piece of dirt.

William labored to grab hold of mental clarity. *They are going to kill me. I have to stay alive.*

"Patient, Ninety-nine, I see you have a few residual effects from our mentoring," Beucher taunted, the sound of prideful satisfaction in his tone. "Never mind them they'll soon pass. We're going to replace them with something else. We are going to mold your mind, so you can walk with Father Durand's family."

"I didn't do . . ." William struggled. He heard himself slurring his words as his eyes slid closed. He fought to reopen them and to lift the veil of his mental fog. Beucher's horrible mind device had caused his distorted speech. He knew it.

"Oh, but you did," Beucher replied. "Monroe?"

"May I be of further assistance?" Monroe asked.

"Monroe, I understand you want to do more," Beucher said, grinning. "You will, but in due time." Beucher backed away from the instrument panel, leaning around in front of William. "Hans will you please strap Ninety-nine into the black chair . . . so he doesn't fall out and get hurt. An accident would hinder his rehabilitation."

"Yes, sir." Hans attached the straps around William, duplicating the same fixturing procedure used on the first chair, and then he lowered the second helmet, guiding it over William's head. "Hold still, or else," Hans grumbled.

William, through his lingering mental haze, thought he felt something different about the second helmet. He didn't know what it was but in addition to the button-sized electrodes, he detected ridges of interconnecting metal bands running from front to back.

"Ninety-nine, did you wonder why he have two chairs, and why one was white and one was black?" Beucher asked with a teasing inflection in his voice. "By having two chairs, the patient, such as you, quickly learns that when they are moved to the second chair, the black one, they are going to experience some form of pain. It works well to increase the results of our treatment . . . our productivity, shall we say. It's sort of a psychological color-coding for people. Maybe in the black chair you'll realize and accept how you broke rules. We must teach you that cooperating doesn't mean betraying your honor. You will learn there are many paths to truth in the world and you are to take the one the SAC requires."

Beucher's words entered William's ears sounding muffled, but understandable. *Lynn and the kids . . . remember them . . . fight for them.*

"By the way, Ninety-nine, the SAC has arranged for your family to visit the exclusive SAC spa while you're here with us." Beucher nodded to himself. He regarded William, elevating his bushy eyebrows. "We know your wife has broken some sort of regulation, although I haven't heard what it is . . . in addition to the illegal purchase of flower bulbs. Nevertheless, the DPP and the SACI will find more law infringements. They are very creative. Perhaps after she's been at the spa and had a chance to sample SAC's nurturing, we'll bring her here for a little more questioning. Maybe she can remember something you've forgotten." He looked down at the floor, thinking for a moment, and then at William. "Ninety-nine, did she know you tried to obtain a scanner?"

William thought of Beucher torturing Lynn. He gnashed his teeth, concentrating on getting control. He battled to associate words about Lynn being tortured. He wanted to plead for them to exempt his wife from his interrogation and punishment. "She . . . she doesn't know anything."

"Was that a grimace or a smile I just saw? With that face, you must be happy you are being rehabilitated. You don't need to thank me." Beucher glanced at Hans, who was standing behind the black dental chair, and then at Monroe, as if they were his audience. "I forgot to mention that there could be aftereffects from the first chair. You're probably curious about being off balance right now." He laughed grotesquely. "We also induce a sort of mental anesthetic with our mind scanner. I'm quite proud of it."

"Please leave my wife out of my conflict with the SAC," William groaned. "I . . . didn't do anything terribly wrong. My wife is totally innocent."

Beucher looked at Monroe. "Monroe, get ready with level number one, please."

Monroe nodded.

"Yes you did, Ninety-nine," Beucher sneered. "You owe everything to our Father and the SAC. You live by the grace of the State. The State gives you everything and only asks for your obedience in return. You depend on the SAC." Beucher nodded at the Monroe. "Level one, zone A, please, Monroe."

Just then, a small vid-link chimed as it slowly rose from out of a slot in Beucher's desk.

"Monroe, hold up on that for a moment," Beucher snapped, frowning angrily. Beucher walked over to his desk, shaking his head, grumbling something inaudible, and then dropped onto his chair. He glared at the vid-link. "What is it?" he snapped before any image appeared on the twelve-inch square screen.

"Excuse me, Doctor Beucher," Steinhoff said, his eyes growing narrow for a moment.

"Sorry, sir," Beucher replied. "I meant no disrespect. I was preoccupied with initiating the next phase of the patient's treatment. My concentration was elsewhere. How may I help you? I am at your service."

"I'm sorry to interrupt your work, but I wanted to ask if you would be interested in having Rinehart's wife and children at your disposal. She's scheduled to go to the spa in a day or two with her kids, but I can arrange for you to get her today, within the hour, if you like. You could use her and then send her home later today. Regardless, she can't miss the scheduled visit to the spa. Everything they perform has been scheduled."

"I could make use of her today. I definitely could . . . and the children. Yes, yes, I agree, she must still be sent to the spa. Thank you. Please proceed. When can I expect them?"

"I took the liberty of anticipating your interest. They should be there at any minute."

"We'll let them watch this last portion of the mentoring process. Is that all?"

"That's all for now," Steinhoff replied, sounding irritated. "Vid-link, off."

Beucher's vid-link started to drop back into his desk and before it had disappeared, Beucher had popped from the chair and taken two steps toward William.

The doctor faced William with a sarcastic smirk. "We have a special treat for you and for your wife . . . oh, and your precious children. They are going to watch from our little observation booth behind the glass over there." Beucher turned toward a window.

Agent Neal opened the door to the office area and observation booth, and held up his hand. "Doctor, we have visitors for patient, Ninety-nine."

Beucher nodded and mumbled, "I'm very impressed with Section Head Steinhoff's forward thinking." Beucher motioned for Neal to bring the visitors into the treatment laboratory. "Here she is now. Bring them out here to me."

The door next to the observation window opened. Agent Neal pushed Lynn Rinehart through the door, sending her forward in a lunging step, nearly causing her fall. The children burst from the door, trying to stay at Lynn's side.

"Mom, are you okay?" Stefan asked when he reached his mother with Marie next to him.

"Yes, Stefan, please be quiet for now."

"Come over here," Beucher said. "Come here where you can see your husband's face clearly and he can see yours. Bring the children."

Neal nudged Lynn again.

Lynn frowned, reaching down, groping for Stefan's hand. "Take your sister's hand," Lynn said, urgency in her voice, pleading. She took half steps forward, moving slowly toward Beucher, her eyes dashing from the doctor to William and to the doctor as she pulled Stefan and Marie along with her. Tears spilled down Lynn's cheeks. "William," she murmured from under her free hand that covered her mouth.

"What are they doing to Dad?" Stefan asked, looking up at his mom.

"Daddy, what are you doing?" Marie asked sorrowfully and then she began whimpering. She plunged into Lynn's leg, hiding her face.

Beucher studied Lynn. "This man you call your husband, we call Ninety-nine." Beucher pointed to William. "Wife of patient Ninety-nine, tell your husband that he needs to confess the truth so he can come home to you, so we don't have to place you in the same chair and have him watch you. Maybe we could have you and Ninety-nine watch your children occupying these chairs simultaneously. We have done it before."

"No!" William cried out. "She's innocent. They are innocent. She doesn't know anything."

"William, please tell them everything you know," Lynn murmured, barely loud enough to be heard."

"I have. I swear that I have. Please let her go home with our children."

"They are going to watch," Beucher snapped. "Section Head Steinhoff thought it was a good idea and I agree."

"Please leave my family alone," William barked.

"Perhaps she will remember what you have forgotten—once she's seen you under our mentoring procedure. Neal, take them back to the observation room, and make certain the children watch the proceedings."

Neal grabbed Lynn by the back of her blouse and pulled her backwards until she turned and walked back through the door with Stefan and Marie in tow."

Tears rolled from William's eyes. "I've told you everything. She knows nothing. Please don't use my children."

"Monroe, please continue."

Suddenly the muscles in William's neck and back pulled tight as a wire, a wire connected to a take-up spindle, a spindle that slowly turned like a torture rack from the Middle Ages. A wave of electricity ran through him, burning, tingling, and biting at his nerves. He groaned from the muscle-ripping body contractions. He closed his eyes trying to endure the pain. He had to be strong Lynn. She was watching. The kids. He didn't know how long he could endure Beucher's torture, but he knew he had to fight with everything he had.

Beucher smiled with childlike amusement. "You must obey Father Durand's rules and those of his SAC." He wiggled his mouth as he thought for a moment. "Notice how this phase in your correction does nothing to influence or diminish your memory, which we want to keep, just in case there's a little something you might recall . . . after more persuasion. "Level one, zone A, off."

William's muscles relaxed. The pain disappeared. Exhausted, he breathed rapidly, trying to satisfy his body.

"Monroe, set level one on zone B."

"Yes, sir," Monroe replied, reaching for a control knob. Monroe turned a large black knob counterclockwise, sending a needle on a gauge to zero. Then she turned a second control knob under a dial labeled zone B. She stopped when the needle on a gauge pointed to level one.

William's stomach churned. Pressure grew and moved upward in a wave, pushing on something in his chest, sickening him as it pushed gas into his esophagus. The bloating gas nauseated him. Then gut-ripping contractions brought tears to his eyes. He needed to double over to endure the pain but the restraints held him. Without any feeling or pressure warning, he defecated in his undergarment. The waste ran with disgusting warmth down his legs. Tears of dehumanization pooled in his eyes. Again, he desperately wanted to grab his stomach to contain the pain. He remembered his father's words. In addition to the pain, they wanted him to experience the removal of dignity. Surviving was his objective, and if staying alive meant getting down on the floor and crawling in his own excrement, he would do it. *Lynn's watching. Oh God, why does she have to watch?*

"Beucher held up his hand to Monroe, his fingers spread. "Level one, zone B, off."

William felt the pain dissipate except for the lingering strain in muscles. He struggled to swallow as the fluid had left his throat.

"This is where you learn how difficult you want this to be. The sooner you cooperate the sooner you can go."

"I want to help," William muttered. "I have been helping."

Beucher went over and sat at his desk, checking his computer for a few moments before he turned with an evaluating gaze. He sniffed the air and nodded. "I think you'll have to agree it's quite remarkable what we can do with various stimuli to your brain. You have just done what everyone does, on that control setting. You are no better than a floor sweeper or a manure shoveler." Beucher turned toward the observation window. He picked up a com-link from his desk and placed it to his ear. "Neal, has she been encouraged to contribute all information regarding the conspirator?" Beucher asked.

Neal nodded to Beucher through the window. "She says she's sick and lightheaded. She says she doesn't know anything."

"Let her watch the whole procedure," Beucher said, "and then take them home so she can wrestle with her conscience. Tell her how children hold up when they are in my chairs." Beucher dropped the com-link on his desk and walked over to William. "It seems your wife doesn't have much stomach for your performance."

"Please let her go," William shouted, fighting dryness in his throat. "For pity's sake she is innocent . . . and knows . . . knows nothing. I've not told her anything." William's mind screamed hatred at the sadistic and demented doctor, his mind feeling it would burst from the violent loathing, a blinding evil cry for vengeance never before experienced.

"Time will tell." He paused, looking in his thoughts, and then he nodded as if agreeing with himself. "My instruments will tell us if it's true."

William waited for the next violation of his nervous system. It looked as if there wasn't anything he could say to influence Beucher. *This man is inhuman.* As if a whimsical spark, a sudden fury from the abuse provoked William to envision grabbing the bastard by the throat and squeezing him until his eyeballs popped out and rolled across the floor. The straps reminded him of what he couldn't do. William took a deep breath, feeling better, but with some lightheadedness. He had to forget about revenge against Beucker.

He tried to remember what he knew about brainwashing, testing himself to stay alert, demanding that he keep his logic working. He did remember something about brain washing. Where had he learned it? Wait. His father had mentioned something. Yes. A key in brainwashing was gaining control of the subject. They would try to make him completely dependent upon the controller. They would try breaking his normal behaviors. *God, how clinical that sounds.* Something else bothered him. Now he remembered. In addition to his father, he had read something about brain washing in college, before the State destroyed many of the books. It was his psychology class. The word, underground, popped up at the edge of his thinking, and then brainwashing. Were there more elements? Damn, his thoughts were erratic. That was all he could steal from the dark tired corners of his brain.

"Now, let's go back to the incident where you visited the bookstore," Beucher began. His tone was low and deliberate. "What you did was wrong. Wasn't it?"

William swallowed hard. "I didn't do anything. I knew my car probably contained a tracking device. I saw people following me. They let me go where I went. I just stopped to see if it was open. It was closed."

"But you knew reading your father's book was wrong, and you knew driving outside your allowed area with an SAC car was a violation."

"I didn't think it would hurt anything to read my father's book," William replied, his eyes getting heavy, hanging nearly shut. "It was a very old book."

"Why did you violate your driving area? Were you contacting the underground?"

"I . . . I'm sorry. No, I wasn't looking for the underground."

"What were you looking for? And you had better tell me this second or you'll feel more pain than you can imagine in your wildest dream."

"I . . . I wanted to . . . I wanted to see if the country still existed."

"What do you mean?"

"I wanted to see if the country was a prison, with guards, with no trees, with vid-cams, without . . . life."

"Did you find what you expected?"

"I don't know. But I'm sorry."

"Of course you are. There are places we do not allow citizen-comrades to go because they can destroy a citizen's will to live. We can't have that if we are to progress as a society, as a State."

"I'm sorry."

"What if the bookshop had been in business? Would you have gone in?"

"I don't know . . . no. I was scared."

"But you were not scared enough to throw away your father's book."

"It was an old book." William coughed.

"Level one, zone C," Beucher said to Monroe. She smiled. Beucher's eyebrows arched. He nodded as he studied William, a childlike look of amusement hold his face.

Pain shot into William's stomach. He locked his teeth together to fight it. *It's coming again.* He tried to grip tight to the little bit of toughness he had in his brain, seemingly where his courage was stored, the new courage that had passed to William from his father in those final moments on the mountain.

Beucher nodded more vigorously. "We know you were reading the book in your bathroom at home. If you're innocent, why did you cover the ceiling vent in your bathroom? Were you afraid of being seen reading an illegal book?" Beucher paused. "Monroe, level two on the same zone. Wait, add delta phasing to it."

Nausea again consumed William and took over his mind. Pain grew by the second, building until he couldn't contain the volcano rising from deep inside his body. He vomited his stomach contents out and down his chest, splashing over his strapped-down legs, tears rolling down his cheeks, tears not from a loss of dignity, but from the shear, wrenching strain on his body. Again, a convulsion in the abdominal area gripped him, squeezing like a giant hand, sending more contents up and out. The convulsion relaxed for a moment, and then the process repeated until his stomach wrenched without producing any vomitus.

Beucher looked on with a superior knowing smile. "Monroe, off."

"Now, Ninety-nine, are you still innocent?"

"I . . . I don't know," William replied, barely able to utter the words. "No . . . no."

"Well, perhaps we have a little progress," Beucher said arrogantly. "But you gave in too quickly. How do we know you aren't pretending?" He stared at William. "What did you mean when you told your wife that the kids need a chance to walk in the woods totally free someday?"

"I might have been thinking of getting a new SAC house near a wooded area."

Beucher laughed. "That's pretty sad. Not even a good lie. Monroe, go to zone F without the delta, and use ramping amplitude."

"Yes, sir."

Slowly the muscles in William's face began tingling, stretching as if weights were pulling on the skin. His mouth gaped open with the onset of a sharp pressure just above his brow and below his eyes. Fluid drained from his nose, over his upper lip, and down to his chin, mixing with saliva oozing from the corner of his mouth. He wanted to close his eyes but he couldn't control the muscles. The piercing pain held him at the precipice of passing out.

Beucher gazed at William, studying him, right elbow cupped in his left hand as he pulled thoughtfully on his chin, his face barely a foot away from William. Beucher nodded. "Monroe, you can shut down. Hans, remove the helmet and straps, and please take Ninety-nine to his quarters. I think we need to enhance his treatment tomorrow." Beucher covered his nose. "You really smell. Please avail yourself of the small shower in your little room. Oh, yes, remember this tonight when you reflect on today, the sooner you accept the truth, the sooner you will be free to go. All Father Durand wants is for everyone to become a member of the SAC Family." Beucher stepped over to his desk and picked up his con-link. "Neal, arrange for the woman and children to be taken home straightaway," Beucher said.

Nearly limp, Beucher's torture had nearly drained William's body of energy. He barely understood what was happening around him. The electrical signals sent through the helmet had wrenched his muscles to the point he was uncertain if he could walk. He heard Beucher say they were taking Lynn home; at least he thought he did. *Good, good.* The clinical room around him dissolved in and out of focus, as if he walked in and out of fog, but he was breathing again, freely. He was alive, still alive. Maybe he could endure their torture. *Maybe I can do it Dad!*

"Hans, take him to the holding room for a quick rinse with soap. No point in stinking up the whole place. No, wait. Let him clean his own mess."

"Yes, sir. Should I give him a clean coverall suit for tomorrow?"

"Yes, this time," Beucher replied and pompously puckered his mouth as he squinted. "Your progress tomorrow will determine whether you get a clean uniform for tomorrow night. Don't think for one second that we're finished with your wife and kids. If you don't show more progress she'll be in the chair and you'll be watching her spew her guts. Think about it. And children don't do well in my chairs. They scream and scream."

"Can I go home tomorrow?" William asked feebly.

Beucher turned to Hans and rolled his eyes. "Hans don't be too harsh with him tonight. It's his first day. He still doesn't understand his responsibility."

Hans laughed under his breath. "Yes, sir."

William knew then that he wasn't going home anytime soon. He was their amusement. *They're going to make me beg.*

Chapter 17

Steinhoff opened the door to Room 100, barely able to contain his eagerness to hear Beucher's report on Rinehart's torture and surrender. It was nearly noon on Friday. Seeing Beucher sitting at his desk staring at his computer, he paused with the doorknob in his hand, and then pushed the door farther open with a sudden authoritarian thrust.

"Section Head Steinhoff, I'm sorry I didn't hear you at the door." Beucher stood quickly, clasping his hands at his waist. "Welcome."

"How's your new patient?"

"We call him, Ninety-nine. He had a bit of a rough day, but I'd say he's making progress. Thank you for sending his wife and brats to watch. That was a bonus for the treatment."

Steinhoff walked over to Beucher, thinking he might hear some interesting revelations. "Thank you. I had hoped it might accelerate your progress. Do you think you will be able to gather all the information that is important to our directors? This is highly significant and has a lot of visibility."

Beucher's eyes rose under his brow as he cleared his throat. "I will extract all viable and beneficial information contained in the subject's cranium. The SAC has no need to worry about the complete processing of this patient. I have every confidence that my past successful experiences will be once again confirmed and repeated."

"You need not be so defensive."

"I'm sorry if I sounded defensive. It is just that I've been doing this for—"

"Very good, Citizen-Comrade Beucher," Steinhoff said plainly, holding back his irritation. "When you are certain you have extracted all that he can remember, everything mind you, I think we can wipe him clean."

"Section Head, could you please call me Doctor Beucher or perhaps Comrade Doctor?" Beucher asked hesitantly.

"I've called you by the same title before," Steinhoff replied, fighting the urge to curse and warn the man he should show more respect.

"Yes, but I don't think it's appropriate around my staff. You can understand such issues."

Steinhoff uttered, sighing, "Very well, Doctor Beucher."

Beucher lowered his head slightly as if thanking Steinhoff. "Thank you so much, sir. Now, regarding the wiping question. You know he'll likely die?"

"Do they all die?"

"Nearly all, yes, within a short time."

"Okay, let's see how he does. Make certain you have everything before you do it. You probably should check with me before you do it." He looked across the room and then at the black chair. "Yes, make certain to check with me before wipe it clean."

"As you wish, Section Head Steinhoff."

"Did having his wife and children watching have any impact?"

"Yes, but not as much as when we set the little beggars in the chairs and make daddy watch them squirm in pain. That helps a patient retrieve the smallest and most vague memories, and it saves time."

"What about quality of the recall?" Steinhoff asked.

"No change in quality."

"Amazing."

"Children are a very instrumental tool, if you can control them sufficiently."

Steinhoff shook his head slightly, turned, and walked down the hall. He wondered how long a man like Rinehart would hold out under Doctor Beucher's mentoring. Rinehart didn't seem to be an exceptional physical specimen. In fact, William Rinehart was a typical soft office clone, looking just like everyone else who worked in an office for years. There was, however, something about Rinehart's face. He hated Rinehart's smug little face. He hated how Rinehart still showed the same persistent look of intelligent awareness as he did when they first bumped into each other when they started working for SAC. Perhaps that look irritated him more than anything did. Regardless, he would sip his whisky long after Reinhart's last treatment by—Doctor Beucher.

Chapter 18

It was late Friday afternoon when Russell Wood arrived at his apartment after leaving his work at SAC Building Three. He descended to his basement room, cockroach haven as he called it, thirsting for a good drink, trying to appear normal to any SACI people who were tracking him. He had found his room in a crumbling, nearly condemned, apartment building in southwest Washington. N-regs occupied the building like the cockroaches, but they needed it. They were poor people, and as far as the SAC was concerned, the lowest form of human life in State America. And because of their living one mouthful of food from starvation, the SAC had never registered them on any population listing after Durand took control. They lived below the level the SAC considered an underground force. They were largely uneducated, unhealthy, and were more trouble to the SAC to collect for labor camps, than they were worth. Occasionally the SAC carried out mass arrests, which often turned into mass executions in old buildings. The n-regs never surrendered to an arrest despite their lack of weapons. They existed purely on a black-market level.

Russell's room was nothing more than a stopover that he paid for with cans of food that he would purchase with his coupons. The building was free of vid-cams, as far as he knew. Despite him finding it barely tolerable for sleeping during the week, he was making a difference for the cause. Russell liked the n-regs, liked talking with them. They were simple people merely trying to exist. But living there was his job for the underground. He had to do it for appearances. He had struck a good relationship with the poor unfortunate souls who lived there, paying them generously for protection of the beat-up motorcycle that he used to get to the downtown SAC building and to his underground meetings. At least his basement room wasn't like a sewer, where some of the n-regs lived.

He had hid and lived in a sewer, starting at a young age. As far as he was concerned when it came to survival, sewers were indispensible. He had called a sewer home more years than he could remember. One simple reason had caused it. The SAC had screwed up the country when he was very young. The SAC hammered the memory of that day in his brain, the day his normal life stopped. It was the day his family had fled a small city near Alexandria, Virginia, for the mountains north of the Shenandoah National Park. On occasion when he thought back to his youth, he marveled how he had lived. He had wondered how many people had been educated in a sewer like him when they were growing up. His dad and mom had caused it, deciding to fight with the underground rather than trying to hide forever in the forest. He respected them for what they did.

Russell walked up the stairs, through a first floor hall to an empty room where he parked his motorcycle. He rolled it out the exit door, immediately checking the area around him for the SACI or the DPP. He jumped on his bike and rode toward downtown where he spent thirty minutes going from one parking garage to another where he rolled his motorcycle into a waiting panel truck and then climbed into a waiting beat-up car.

Several minutes later, he and his driver were traveling across the Route 29 bridge, headed south to Route 50, and then west. As usual, he breathed easier when they arrived at the abandoned and overgrown sewage treatment facility north of Fairfax, Virginia, and he had descended into its maze.

"It's about time," a woman said, stepping out into the sewer tunnel from an opening in the sewer's wall of red brick, the brick barely distinguishable from the covering of dirt, vegetation, and randomly attached trash.

"Claudia, the last thing I need is crap from you," Russell snapped with an amused smirk. "I was worried I had someone on my ass at one point when I was still on my bike."

Claudia met him a few feet from the door, now smiling warmly. "Give me hug, you old sewer rat. I missed you."

Russell wrapped his arms around the only woman he had ever loved since being a sewer rat and the only woman who had ever said she loved him. He kissed her, wishing they had time to live—simply live somewhere out in the country. He would settle for less. He could absorb happiness from the smallest amount time alone with her. The most levelheaded woman he had ever known, she had broken his heart when she turned down his proposition of marriage. Nevertheless, he couldn't stay angry with her when she said she'd marry him when they could live free, when the country was free. She was right. "It's really good to see you, honey. I'm glad to see you haven't been taking crazy risks."

"You've been careful haven't you?"

He raised his eyebrows and then dropped his eyes.

"Your body language is telling me that you've been bad."

"Well, what about you?"

"That's sort of why I'm here, Bobby," Claudia whispered.

"You shouldn't use my real name, honey. I love you for doing it. I love you, sweetie. You feel so good." Russell couldn't remember the last time he'd heard his real name. It was probably the last time he saw her. "I could stand here squeezing you forever."

She kissed him and whispered, "I love you, too, Bobby Garland."

"I love you, Brenda Collins." He looked into her beaming eyes and stroked his fingers through her short hair just above her left ear. "When are you going back to long hair?"

"You know it's part of my cover," she replied backing away a little.

"What's this meeting all about?"

"You'll hear soon enough. I haven't heard."

He didn't see any hint in her face, but he felt a twinge of hope for what they might discuss. He started walking with her toward the door. "What's going on?"

"Let's get in there. They're waiting on you."

It was the same room he had been in before, austere, with its unpainted concrete walls, and low ceiling speckled with simple incandescent light bulbs. He had thought more than once that it was a good thing he didn't suffer from claustrophobia because the ceiling was barely eight feet. Russell couldn't count the number of times he'd been in the room, and had never heard the history of its original use. The early undergrounders sectioned off the room, arranging sleeping bunks in three rows of four, all of them maintained with military discipline neatness. They had set up a kitchen in the other section, which was about half of the room. He had eaten many meals there. Two rows of six-foot long tables, accompanied by folding chairs, occupied an area near the propane-gas cooking stove.

The odor of food cooked in a skillet lingered in the air and added a sign of living and a touch of normalcy to the room. Russell found the smell of grease lingering in the air, a treat, like a tiny piece of the real world. Someone must have come across meat worthy of gracing a plate or possibly eggs from real chickens, which were easier to conceal in the woods. It made him instantly hungry.

Other than a place for the meetings, he had pictured the place as an underground tavern, only this place had no booze, and was as serious as a coronary attack. No one was ever animated and there wasn't much humor heard in the sewer.

Russell surveyed the people sitting at the tables, counting fifteen, which was a good number for a meeting. They all looked somber, anxiously anticipating the announcements that would come from the men standing in front of the group. A man of medium height, dressed in khaki colored clothes and military boots with a short-cropped head of salt and pepper hair was talking to one of the men sitting in a chair next to the group's table. The man stepped toward Russell the moment he noticed Russell.

"Ah, Bob, it's good to see you," the broad-shouldered man said, his voice booming as if he were giving orders to troops. He extended his hand, smiling. "I'm sorry, it's Russell, isn't it?"

Russell shook his hand, feeling muscles that did more than type on a computer. "Yes, Major Thorton, but it's okay here."

"I'm an old soldier and not one of those CIA types." Major Thorton smiled, moving his eyebrows upward on a worn and wrinkled face, and then he winked.

"Nice to see you, sir. It's been a while. Too long."

"That it has." Thorton patted Russell on the shoulder. "I'm glad we have young guys like you carrying the load for us old-timers."

"I'm not that young any longer."

"You're not pushing seventy either," Major Thorton replied.

"How's General Wilcox?" Russell asked.

"Fine, still cracking the whip and kicking asses."

"Why the meeting, sir?"

"Well, from what I hear it's your fault." He grinned at Russell. "I guess we better get going—now that you're here." Thorton walked to the front by the stove. He stopped next to the two other men dressed in military khaki clothes, whose dress showed no rank. He stood chest-out with his feet spread.

Russell sat beside Claudia who had saved him a chair, joining the group of men and women sitting at the tables in front of Major Thorton. Claudia patted his leg. He loved it.

"Thanks for coming today," Thorton began. "I think most of you know Captain Barkley to my right and on his right, Captain Sever." He glanced at the floor and then with a stone face at the people before him. "Something has happened. I'd like to say remarkable, but time will tell." He glanced at Russell and then at the group. "A potential source of valuable intelligence may be available to us. In addition, lives are at risk, as always, and I believe we are obligated to consider them for rescue. You notice I said consider them for rescue. As you know our war with SAC is far bigger than the lives of individual patriots, but where their contribution to our victory is obvious or someone has paid the ultimate price we must consider rescue if we can. It is just such a situation facing us. Russell, would you tell us about the people you have contacted and then I'd like Claudia to add a little spice to our cake."

Russell stood in front of his chair, cleared his throat, and turned toward the people behind him. "Major, I guess I'll start with our first observation."

"Go ahead."

Russell cleared his throat again. "We've been tracking a mole, a person working undercover for the SACI. We had guessed they were using this guy as a tool to draw out people who they suspected of belonging to any sort of resistance or underground. It's also possible the SACI could be using him as a tool to sucker in discontented souls. Anyway, a few days back our people monitored a shortwave radio signal. Some of the earliest patriots had used the same signal and a very old protocol. We tracked it to a man named William Rinehart, who is an SAC manager living in Fairfax. Later, when I saw this manager talking with the mole in the cafeteria in SAC Building Three, we took action to make contact. We needed to find out how he got the protocol and to see if it was a trap. I cautiously contacted him at his cubicle at Building Three. To his credit, he was very suspicious of me. After I demonstrated our help and after we did some checking, we learned he was the son of one of our long lost people. In fact, he's the son of the longest surviving member to be in hiding, Henry Rinehart, the attorney from the Department of Justice. I later learned from William, that the bastard SAC sent him, Henry Rinehart's own son, to capture Henry, the father." Russell stopped as his throat got thick and his eyes watered.

"Sadly, Henry destroyed himself. According to William, his father was dying from lung cancer when he met him at a mountain bunker during the SAC raid. Luckily, I think William had been contemplating escaping from the SAC world. The reason we must consider this encounter opportunistic is, astonishingly, he hadn't yet been programmed as an SAC mindless robot. If he had, I'd be dead. Instead, I was able to talk with him three times, once at his desk in my initial contact, where I warned him about the mole, and two more times behind his home. The good news is, before paying the ultimate price, his father gave William some writings. William said his father called them his chronicle. We must get these writings. William knew he was headed for brainwashing at any minute, and I must tell you all, the acorn fell close to the tree because he has the same courage as his father. It's a subtle kind of courage, I think spawned from trying to protect his family, but it's boiling below the surface like a volcano getting ready to blow. Knowing what the SAC might do to his brain, he promised to get me the chronicle—and he begged me to get his family to safety. Unfortunately, he was right, because the SACI took him away in one of their damn v-trans Friday morning, and our observation people haven't seen him since. Also an SACI v-tran took William's wife and kids to Building Two today, we assume to apply additional leverage on William during their mental torture. One our people reported the SACI dropped them off back home this afternoon. It is quite possible the SACI could torture his wife in front of William." Russell stopped, his gaze unfocused, his mouth pulled tight. He flashed his eyebrows as if awaking from a desperate thought. "Well, that's about it, Major." Russell sat down and sighed from the load lifted from his shoulders.

Claudia took his hand and squeezed it. She whispered, "Good work."

"We will now hear another element of this new development," Thorton said. "Claudia, could you fill us in on your intelligence?"

Claudia stood, stepped forward two steps and turned, facing her fellow undergrounders. "My assignment has been at the SAC spa, the facility they have been using for development of their implant procedures," she said, her voice cracking a little. "Excuse me, but they are brutal heartless bastards the way they have been doing it to children." Tears pooled in her eyes.

"It's okay, Claudia," Thorton said.

Russell handed her a handkerchief.

She dabbed her eyes. "A day ago I saw the name Rinehart on the spa schedule and it was highlighted with a notation for manager level spouse. It listed the wife as Lynn, and two children, Stefan and Marie. When I heard Russell's news something clicked."

The major coughed. "Clearly the SACI is preparing these poor souls so they can exert maximum leverage and control on this family. We suspect they are searching for the same information we have been scratching to find for years. Regardless, we're going to do something we've not done in a long time, if ever. We're going to extract the wife and kids from the spa with Claudia and Dirk's help. Of course, this will cost us Claudia's valuable undercover position at the spa, but this is more important. Besides, there's not much more we can learn about their device implantation program. William may have shared information with his wife. Of course, Claudia and Dirk will create their own extraction plan since it's their backyard, and they will be given whatever equipment and transportation they need. Claudia, please check with logistics for whatever you need. I mean it, anything you need. And if anybody down there gives you a hard time, refer them to me."

"Major, I'd like to be part of the extraction mission," Russell said. "Once William is brain-scanned he'll use my cover name and my position with the SAC will be lost."

"I understand, Russell. I really do, but you are too valuable in the city, even if you have to operate on the periphery, trying to get intelligence from workers. If you hadn't been in that building, we wouldn't be in the loop on William Rinehart and would have missed news on the development of SAC's massive surveillance center in their building. You all know that if we don't stop the surveillance center—the hangman's noose will strangle the country to the point no movement will go unmonitored. They have the video camera manufacturing plant going three shifts and seven days a week. They have been replacing vid-cams as fast as we can remove them. They have escalated their pressure on civilians, arresting innocent people in the proximity of the vid-cams we've taken, requiring the population to report any removals or destruction of the vid-cams. If unchecked, vid-cams will be on every square mile of this country or worse. That is why another audacious operation to take care of that growing problem is being evaluated." He looked at everyone at the tables with a slow evaluating gaze. "Good luck everyone. Keep the faith. Our forefather's fought for our freedom to form this country. It's our time to follow the in the footsteps of those original patriots."

Chapter 19

Hot water poured over William, standing in the tiny shower that was part of his SACI cell, trying to assess what had happened to him, waiting for clarity to return to his head. He had no idea of the time, only that it was after his first experience with Doctor Beucher's torture room. He was amazed he was still alive. Having picked him up so early in the day, they could have tortured him for hours. Lynn and the kids had watched. He remembered that. He would do anything to prevent Lynn and the kids from watching Beucher torture him again. Just then, he remembered walking down a long hallway to this cell. He hit a gap in the next bit of his memory. He must have passed out on the floor when they pushed him through the door. He had no way to determine the time of day with the building being devoid of windows like a stone mausoleum. He had a fuzzy memory of Hans and Neal removing his clothes and checking them for anything that he could use for an escape or suicide.

When he later awoke on the floor and saw he had access to a shower, he used all his energy to move his body where he hoped hot water would remove his pain. It seemed they had played one of their games and used a hot shower as a reward. He closed his eyes and stood leaning against the shower wall, allowing the hot water pour over his head and wash down over him, slowly carrying away his aches and pains just as he thought. It was wonderful. His head was slowly clearing. *Reward and punishment.* God, how stupid he was. There would be more of the same torture, all intended to bore into his brain like a gnawing bug. The black chair. He didn't remember much after Beucher moved him to the black chair, except pain, such horrible pain. It was incredible that humans could treat other humans with such vile mechanisms.

William tilted his head back and allowed the restorative water pour down his face, and even though it wasn't very hot, it felt great. A few times in the days, weeks, and even months preceding this moment he had envisioned the SACI holding him prisoner in relation to him fracturing the behavioral rules for correct thinking. However, he had never dreamed of facing such brain manipulation devices. How could he? Only demented souls conceived of machines for destroying a human's mind, the single element that made a human more than an animal. As the warm water trickled down over his body, he tried to think, to analyze, and keep his mind actively working. He didn't know if he had the strength to endure more torture and survive. Nevertheless, here he was. He was alive. *They're not done yet!*

After a few more minutes, he stepped from the shower still weary, pulled on a gray suit, a one-piece uniform with a zipper running up the front, and then he sat on his cot. He heard footsteps outside his cell. They were faint but he guessed they were from a hard-soled boot. Metal clinked inside the lock of his cell door, resonating as if within something massively heavy, a dungeon door of iron. It was a key. The door opened slowly, seemingly fighting its considerable inertia. After a few degrees of arc, open only a few inches, a burly hand placed a plate of food on the floor just inside the room. The hand retracted as if it were part of a remote controlled device. He took three tired steps to the plate and limply stooped, his arm dropping to pick it up as if his muscles were stretched bands of rubber with no memory to return to their normal position. He wasn't certain if he could keep anything down but the beans, a piece of some sort of composition meat, and a slice of hard bread, looked good. Back on his cot, he looked at the food as imperative, as a key element in his survival, thinking he had to keep up his energy. As he bit into the dried-out crusty bread, he tried to think of any additional information he could give Beucher in the hope they'd reduce his torture, but then remembered it may not be enough for people who were more intent on making an example of him or in the case of Steinhoff, only interested in revenge.

He wondered about the time. It had to be early evening, past the usual time he'd be driving into the garage at home. At least the SACI allowed Lynn to go home again. It had to be the time when she would start checking out the front window for him, although she probably realized she wouldn't see him pulling into the driveway today, especially after seeing Beucher torturing him. He prayed she would use the signal with the front door to escape and very soon. He didn't know how he'd hold up if she were tortured in front of his eyes. He wouldn't. He prayed she would be strong. If only Russell could act now to help her and the kids escape.

A thought materialize in the distance on the edge of his thinking and then he focused on it. It was about Lynn. What was it? Yes. They let her go home. Why would they do that?

William heard metal rubbing against metal. *Wait.* Was he imagining it? He wasn't certain he could trust his senses. Nearly holding his breath, he listened. Another heavy metal door clanged closed, and it was not far away. A vibration came from his wall as if something or someone had bumped into it. Was there a person in the next holding cell? He moved over to the wall and placed his ear to it. Deep sobs penetrated the wall into his ear, the sound of pain, a person's outpouring of pain. He pulled away from the wall, appreciating more his survival of his first encounter with Beucher's chamber of horrors.

Back on his cot, he took a bite of bread. He pushed his fork into the lump on his tray that looked like meat, forcing what he'd heard in the next cell from his mind, concentrating on his food, holding it up on his fork, wondering if it was real meat. The smell was an unappetizing oily odor. A voice in his head told him to close his eyes and eat it. He had eaten food that bad before. He bit into it. It tasted like scrap oil mixed with grain products. *I have to eat it for survival.* He swallowed it, fighting back a sensation that he was going to gag. *I've already puked for the day thank you.* He finished the rest of his plate. If they took him tomorrow, he would need all his strength.

What else could he tell these people to show his support of the SAC? In the morning, he'd tell them he wanted to visit the sewer to celebrate identification of the bomb and saving part of the city from destruction. Perhaps he could mention something about his father not having any contacts for the last few years. He'd tell them everything and hold back nothing . . . except the blank pages. Wait, why should he do that? After all, they were blank.

He set the plate on the floor by the door, went back to his bed, and gazed blankly around his cell. He had never thought of it, a human didn't need much. There wasn't much to his cell, a small sink, a small toilet, and a cot pushed into the corner of the room. The room was about four feet longer than his cot and maybe ten feet across. The absence of windows didn't bother him. The one thing that surprised him was the shower. It put him in mind of an old-style phone booth he'd seen when he was a kid. Obviously many of their victims suffered the same bodily release as he had. He dropped down on the narrow bed, a thin pad spread over a wire mesh, and he rolled over onto his side. He curled up with his knees nearly to his chest. There was a single light on the ceiling and no switch to shut it off. He wondered if it would ever go out so it wasn't shooting into his eye, so he could sleep. He closed his eyes against the light and quickly dropped off to sleep.

The next morning Hans swung open the cell door, and stood ominously in the doorway, his face full of contempt. He waved his hand and barked, "Okay, move your ass."

William pushed himself up on his elbows, paused for a moment, and then he sat on the edge of the bed. His stomach and back muscles were tight piano wires. His lingering fatigue fought him as he tried to move. He got his legs under him and stood, but as he took a step, he swayed off balance. He caught himself with his hands on his knees.

"What day is today?" William whispered. He thought it must have been Saturday. That day made sense. It would have been his day away from work, but all that was bizarrely distant and alien, like a dream.

"Come on, move your ass," Hans snarled. The burly laboratory helper grabbed William's arm, jerked him from the cell, and gave him a push down the hall, sending him stumbling, falling to the floor. William landed on his hands.

"Get your ass up, you clumsy piece of shit."

William got to his knees and slowly up to his feet, fearing another blow from Hans.

In what seemed a blink of time, William stood in Beucher's electrical brain manipulation room, trying not to look at the electrical instruments, trying not to anticipate how they would torture him.

"Good morning, Ninety-nine," Beucher said in a phony cheerful tone, walking into the room with Monroe following a few feet behind.

"I remembered a couple things," William said, his speech slow and labored. "I asked the conspirator if he had any contacts and he mentioned the name of a woman, Rachel, but it doesn't make sense since he said he hadn't gotten any communications for quite some time. Also, I've thought about this a little bit, and I'd really like to go down into the sewer someday and see where the bomb was hidden, the bomb that I helped to locate and save Chairman Durand. I helped save people's lives. I should get some credit for doing that. I've always been a loyal employee of the SAC."

"That is interesting, Ninety-nine," Beucher replied, offering a tight flashing smile. "Maybe we could allow your request after you've completed your mentoring. Maybe you're starting to understand that we are trying to help you, help you realize how wrong you were, and see the distortion of your thinking process."

William closed his eyes with heavy resignation. From Beucher's tone, he knew he hadn't deterred them from hooking him up again to the hat with the electrodes. Beucher loved his toy for sending invisible signals into brains like William's, taking away his control, stealing his mental images, and possibly rendering him at some point a human-cabbage. Beucher seemed determined to secure his playtime. Lynn and the kids could survive, if Russell helped.

William traced Beucher's movements and he recorded every word in his brain, as he fearfully waited for Beucher to issue the specific command to unleash the electronics. In a few moments, the doctor began the process, the same as the previous day. They placed William in the white chair and threw questions at him like a hideous auditory hammer. Beucher played with the levels on the mind-searching instrument and after what seemed an hour to William, Beucher went to his desk and looked at his computer. William a candle flame of hope lighted in his mind as he thought he had held up better than the previous day.

Beucher returned from his momentary study, ordering Monroe to change the brain processing level, moving it to what he called level two with theta overlapping delta signals. The room blurred before William's eyes and then returned. His thoughts danced from one word to another not landing long enough to form a complete thought. The light from above became an opaque glow. Then Beucher's voice disappeared into what sounded like a tunnel, seemingly echoing in his ears from off in the distance. William felt his mouth was moving but he didn't know why. His eyelids slid closed. With all his concentration, he fought to open them. Once open again, he could only hold them there for a moment before they slid down as if drawn by massive weights. Slowly, darkly, plunging despair engulfed him, despair the SAC found his family, as if they had told him they were dead. Tears drained from his eyes and his chest shuddered. He wanted everything to end. Rampaging rhythmic repeating tones mixed with words replaced his despair, sweeping through his mind.

William didn't know how long, but he eventually pushed open his tired eyes, and saw he was in the black chair. Hands were attaching a helmet on his head. He tensed himself, awaiting Beucher sending signals, which would wrench his body. The words, "Durand the Father" repeated in his head and then the phrase, "You're guilty of wrong-thoughts."

"I see you're back with us," Beucher sneered. "As you can see we've fitted you with a special piece of clothing, actually more appropriately called a collection suit. We do have our standards for hygiene and mentoring room cleanliness. After all we have to work here day after day."

William looked down at the provision they had made for their depravity. They had dressed him in a full body enclosure, a cocoon formed from clear plastic pants with a plastic shirt that attached to the top of the pants with a zipper. Seeing it, he feared the level of their planned abuse. They must have prepared him while he was delusional or passed out. Beucher's helpers had cinched the pants around his ankles, apparently to prevent leakage of his potential defecation.

"Monroe, please go to level three for zone C," Beucher said in a purposeful cold tone. "I think we can achieve more progress on Ninety-nine."

"Yes, sir," Monroe replied. "Any variations?"

Beucher snorted a laugh to himself and then declined her proposal with a slight shaking of his head.

Instantly, the muscles in the middle of William's back knotted, pulling tight. Then radiating pain gripped his back, stealing his breath. A spear of nauseating pain shot from his back and to a spot just above his stomach. He screamed explosively. Then the pain stopped.

"Ninety-nine, do you freely confess to obtaining an illegal book and a device to scan for electronic implants?" Beucher barked.

"I got a book from my father and I read it," William struggled, his rapid breathing distorting his words.

"What about the scanner?" Beucher demanded, inches from his face. "You acquired one didn't you?"

"Yes."

"You also used it, didn't you?"

"Yes . . . I . . . I used one." William didn't know why he hesitated. It was as if his thinking wasn't his own. He knew he shouldn't hesitate. Indecision on his part would make them suspicious.

Beucher shook his head, squinting at William. "During a preliminary search last night a scanner was found in your home, in your garage, under some steps." He stared at William. "Level three, zone D." Beucher studied him coldly.

William tensed himself for pain after hearing Beucher's command, but he didn't feel any and tried to see what Beucher was doing. Was Beucher zapping him with a different type of signal?

"You know, in a few years we'll be using a more far-reaching technology to mentor the population. It will be as simple as having people line up for an inoculation for the flu virus or something else equally creative that we'll declare as necessary. A few nano-modifiers injected into the body will do wonders. Of course, we will still have to do occasional thought-mentoring in this facility, but for the most part the nano-modifiers will provide a well-conditioned population." Beucher paused, rubbing his chin with a bony finger, studying William's face. "You need to realize how wrong you were. You need to realize we're trying to help you. It is perfectly okay for you to say you were wrong. It's part of personal growth. Now, tell me how you made a mistake. You can do that much for yourself. Take a first step toward getting out of here." Beucher glanced at an instrument panel and then stared at him, waiting for a response.

"I was wrong," William replied weakly.

"You are guilty of social treason. Aren't you?"

"I . . . I don't think . . ."

"Not good enough." Beucher connected eyes with Monroe.

There it was, William thought, the churning in his bowels. His stomach wrenched with waves of pain, moving from the left to the right, and then back again. He felt it dissipate a little, but then suddenly, horrible pain hit his lower stomach and like a dam breaking, he lost his bowel contents. The disgusting warmth found its path around his thighs, bringing him the demoralizing realization that he had passed waste over himself. The degradation brought tears to his eyes. The fowl stench escaped, passing the neck of his cocoon-garment, seeping up to his nose. He sobbed.

Beucher's eyebrows arched as he looked with a cold detached gaze. "All you need to do is understand your mistake. Answer our questions clearly and honestly." He then yawned. "It's quite simple, Ninety-nine."

William swallowed hard, unable to think what he should say.

"Level four, same zone," Beucher snapped. "No, wait. Make it zone C and go to amplitude two." Beucher studied William as if he were a specimen under a microscope.

A muscular cramp shot through William's upper torso, emanating from the middle of his back in between his shoulders. It penetrated deeply, as if it were knifing straight through him, piercing him with a strange nauseating pain, locking his muscles. He could barely breathe. He desperately needed to bend over to stretch his back muscles but the straps held him fast. He breathed with short puffs. His vision narrowed, leaving only a small circle through which he could focus. After a moment his head floated. He closed his eyes. Blackness filled his vision and he lost consciousness.

When William opened his eyes, he sat slumped in the black chair without any restraints. He sat up and rubbed the sore muscles in his neck through the layer of plastic, slowly looking around. It felt good merely breathing in long deep breaths without pain. The easy air tasted precious. He felt as if he had been running miles and could collapse at any moment.

"Okay, Hans, buckle him in again. He's not going to thank us for stopping."

While Hans quickly replaced the restraints, William struggled to put words together, fighting an uncooperative sluggish memory, knowing he had to say something, but unable to do it. Moments ran by as he felt Hans doing something. His mind slogged through mental mud.

"Wait, wait, thank you . . . wait," William said, struggling as he felt a tingling sensation suddenly run over his scalp. His stomach wrenched. Quickly the pressure pushed upward from his stomach in a sudden convulsing wave, but nothing came up. He groaned and exhaled. "I was . . . wrong. I was wrong on everything. I love Father Durand."

"I see we're making a tiny bit of progress," Beucher said. "It's your lesson for today. When you acknowledge and appreciate us going easy on you, you'll do better. Won't you?"

The muscles in William's neck drew his head backward and then his stomach tightened with biting, burning pain. The cycle repeated until he passed out. When he woke, he was unrestrained again. "Thank you," he murmured weakly, and then words as automatic as breathing came out of his mouth. "SAC loves us. SAC gives life."

"Very good," Beucher replied. "Hans you may walk Ninety-nine back to his cell. See to it he has a bar of soap for his shower. Turn on only the cold water for the shower today, please. We need more progress for a hot shower."

"Yes, sir." Hans grabbed William by his upper arm and pulled him from the chair.

William, his feet spread apart, swayed momentarily. He rubbed his forehead, fighting to hold his eyes open.

"By the way," Beucher said in a grave tone. "Ninety-nine, don't try talking to your neighbor. We are watching you every minute and it would be severe for you if you did. Hans, take him to his cell."

When Hans pushed William into the cell, something clicked in William's tired foggy brain. Perhaps it was the parallel between him and his father, a totalitarian state forcing both of them into isolation, making them endure torture, although his father's torment was years of isolation and loss of family. William leaned on the opening of the shower, his eyes watery and blurred. His ears still rang with the song from Beucher's device. He lost his stream of thought. He battled to form something from a muddled mess of words. After a moment, he stopped trying and stared blankly, tiredly, and acceptingly at the shower floor.

Several minutes later, a man opened the door and set a tray with bread and soup on the floor. He was hungry, but afraid to eat, uncertain whether he could eat without collapsing to the floor, uncertain he could hold the food down. He had another thought and then it was gone. *What was it? Drugs. They could drug me.* Three thoughts. He was getting better. He still needed the food and he had to shower.

He forced himself into the cold shower, quickly lathering with the soap to wash away the stench. Out of the shower and shivering, he climbed into his clean uniform as quickly as he could. He felt more lucid even though his head ached. What was it his father had said? Dam, what was it? What? Yes. They would make him betray his family with their torture. They were controlling him, destroying his self-esteem, and breaking him down, part of the reason they made Lynn watch his torture. They were making him endure the shit in his pants so he'd understand who was in control with the power to destroy his self-image. He didn't know if it was working, but he didn't need pride, and he didn't care about self-image. He cared about his family and wondered how long it would take Beucher to take away his caring for them—or his memory of them. He'd cut their names into his flesh to prevent that from happening.

He began eating. *How long will they keep me? Maybe I should try to keep count of the days.* Keeping a count of the days could cause a problem if they found out and didn't like it. He would do it for the sake of not losing connection with the outside world. What could they do to him that they hadn't done? He stooped down next to his small sink and pressed his ear against the wall. He listened for a moment and then scratched two lines on the wall. This was only the second day.

Something else hit him. Dammit. He searched his last moments, trying to make associations, trying to retrieve what he started assembling in his mind. There it was. The SACI had invaded his home. How else could the SACI have found the scanner? Of course, they could say it wasn't truly his home, since everything belonged to the State.

Chapter 20

It was nearly half-passed eleven on Saturday morning when Lynn looked out the front window toward the entrance of their housing development, the fifth time she'd looked this morning, always with a lump in her throat. She prayed to see William's smile at the door, hoped the evil people had satisfied their demented hunger. She was still exhausted from crying last night, lying alone in bed thinking of William, knowing he was in the hands of the worst humans on the face of the earth. The pain on William's face as the sadistic man tortured him had replayed like a movie in her mind all night. She would never forget that image—and the monsters responsible. Never.

Every time she looked out the window and failed to see William, her heart sank further into confusion about what to do to protect the children. Was it time to follow the procedure? Was it time to raise and lower the garage door, trying to get help from the enigmatic underground? She didn't know whether she should risk going through with the steps to signal someone out there in the world. How could someone even exist below the sensitivity of all the vid-cams and the SAC paranoid security? She feared her time to act might run out if she didn't do something soon. The SACI had arrested her yesterday before she could do anything. The black v-tran was no longer across the street. It didn't have to be there. She was powerless. They could torture her and she'd never see the children again. They could torture the children.

Just as Lynn walked back to the kitchen, she heard a car outside. She quickly whirled around, her chest throbbing as she rushed to the window. Feverishly she groped at the drapes, hope holding her breath prisoner in her lungs, waiting to see William coming home. In the driveway she saw one of those horrible v-trans. Would the SACI take her to watch William's torture again? She saw her children in the back seat. Two of those men were in the front seat. She froze, tingling bumps growing on her arms, and then she ran to the front door. She opened the door and immediately faced a gray-uniformed man whose stern cold face challenged her.

"Why do you have my children?" Lynn blurted. "They were playing down the street at one of our neighbors. They weren't causing any problems."

"Mrs. Rinehart, I'm with the SAC travel service, here for your trip to the SAC recreation center here in Fairfax. Don't be alarmed. This is a gift to some of the special managerial families. Your husband qualifies for this privilege. You're to think of it as a reward for the family and for William going on his special assignment to the south."

Suddenly, William's warning shouted in her brain like an earsplitting alarm. She didn't have any idea what to do first. She understood that her actions had to be normal and had to avoid arousing the suspicion of any wrongdoing. How could she leave William? "I can't leave home. My

341

husband is expected home soon," she said, shaking her head at the man, worry wrinkling her forehead.

"The SAC has assigned him to another project. It will take him several days, so you can see, you're totally free to enjoy this SAC luxury." The man spoke with a bland mechanical tone.

His eyes appeared to Lynn as those of a person tired of a repetitive task. "My husband was being interrogated yesterday. I saw him. He's not on a special project."

"That was a misunderstanding. This trip was scheduled before his interrogation. He's already reassigned. Never mind those complications. He's fine."

She frowned unable to make sense of what the man was explaining and then she realized it had to be a lie. It had to be. *He's not fine. He's being brainwashed, you SAC clone.*

"You'll likely be back home before your husband."

Why were they taking her away with the children when they had just employed her as a beneficial blunt instrument in the practice of brainwashing William? It had to be part of their game. If she did go, they could still return her to watch the demons torture William at any time . . . if they still interrogated him. A voice in her head told her there were no other options.

She nodded her compliance. "Very well, let me close up the house and get some clothes for the children."

"Okay, but don't take too long. Please come directly to our vehicle."

Lynn went straight to the kitchen cabinet. Confused, she turned one glass open-end down on top of a plate and then placed a second glass beside the first, open-end up. She stopped for a moment, frantically thinking. She wondered if anyone from the underground, or whatever it was, would be watching the house. She remembered the signal. It was desperate but she had to try it. After collecting clothes, she went to the garage, opened the door and immediately closed it. Then at the front door, she opened it, stepped out, returned, closed the door and reopened it for a moment, before closing it again. She then turned on the front porch light, went outside and stood looking at the light for a moment before going back into the house, completing all the steps she was told. *Please, God, let someone be watching.*

Lynn climbed into the v-tran uncertain how to act, feeling herself trembling. She smiled at her children, thinking she had to make them feel at ease.

"Where are we going, Mom?" Marie asked.

"Yeah, Mom, what's going on?" Stefan blurted.

"We're being given a few days entertainment at a fancy spa."

"A what?" Stefan asked.

"It's a place where they have games for you guys and warm massages for adults, that sort of thing."

"I'd rather stay home," Stefan added. "Where's Dad?"

"Not me," Marie said.

"Dad's busy at work, honey."

Lynn suddenly wondered if the men would ask her about her opening the doors. She would simply tell them she was preparing the house. She looked at the small overnight bag of clothes for her and the kids, questioning whether she'd brought enough and the right things to wear. After the men backed out of the drive and started down the street without a single question, she breathed a sigh of relief.

The v-tran ambled along with the kids looking straight ahead at the translucent panel separating the front seat from the second row of seats. Lynn couldn't see anything in front of the panel. She figured it was part of the same procedure that William experienced everyday on his bus ride to work. The side windows were also cloaked with what looked like a movable plastic sheet. Stefan reached to lift the plastic sheet on the left hand window to look beyond the v-tran.

The protector in the front passenger seat barked, "Boy, don't do that. It's not allowed."

Stefan snatched his hand back and after a moment whispered to his mom, "Why can't I look out?"

"I don't know, honey," Lynn replied, knowing that telling him more could scare him.

As the vehicle jostled along, Lynn found diversion from her looming despair for William by reflecting on her duty to safeguard the children. She looked at Stefan and Marie, fearing their future lives under the SAC, and she couldn't believe she hadn't seen the whole canvas before, instead of looking only at their small isolated piece of the society. Her children were so innocent, like all children their age, occupied with the bits of the world sparking their growing souls, sparking their brains, and sparking them toward a future life-interest. Then a voice in her head shouted, no person could select their future now; the SAC restricted everything.

Going back to her childhood, at her children's ages, she spent too much time playing pretend, impersonating fashion models, singers, being a mother to her favorite doll. However, back then, some people said such roll-playing was good for children. It didn't hurt her. When had her dreams, her surroundings, and her country plunge down the abyss beyond anyone's reach? She had gone to parks, to a lake once or twice, and she even recalled going to a protest rally with her parents. *I was in the fourth or fifth grade.* Her grade school had too many children in her classes, as far as she was concerned. The kids seemed to be sitting on top of each other. Her parents had made a big fuss about paying the teachers; it seemed there wasn't enough money to pay teachers what they wanted. Then it came to her, a problem connected with the state or city unable to pay its bills. Just then, a memory fragment materialized into a complete pattern; it dealt with the government arresting a history teacher for teaching something they didn't like. He was talking about something called the Constitution. She remembered that word because it reminded her of her grandfather who had talked about something by that title, and anything her grandpa talked about fascinated her.

Her grandma popped into her mind. One of the first stories she'd heard grandpa tell was one that drew a scolding from grandma Ellie. It was the story of the horrible terrorist poison gas attack somewhere south of Virginia on the east coast. She couldn't remember why grandma scolded grandpa.

Those were wonderful years when she visited with her grandparents in eastern Pennsylvania. They always had a big garden, and canned their own pickles and beets. Their sweet corn was wonderful. Such life was long gone. She watched her children staring blankly at the panel creating the v-tran's imprisoning rear seat.

She hoped God was watching them and William. She remembered going to a country church with her grandparents. Even William's mom had gone to church when they were first married. After William joined the SAC, they told him he couldn't go any longer, not if he wanted to keep his job. *God help us.*

About three quarters of an hour later, somewhere north of Fairfax, Lynn felt and heard the vehicle slowing. The rear window coverings rolled up into their enclosures allowing Lynn and the kids to see outside the vehicle. Lynn assumed their purpose was to allow them to see the entrance of the spa and in doing so, feel a false sense of comfort and lower their emotional guard. They drove through a gate identified by a prestigious looking sign with raised gold letters reading, SAC Management Retreat. The hair went up on the back of Lynn's neck. She thought of what William had told her. The v-tran followed the winding drive through dense woods, stopping under a portico, ready to dispatch them onto a green carpet leading into the entrance of the three-story, red brick building. The low rectangular structure with long narrow windows distributed along the length of the front appeared more like a medical facility than a spa for massages and recreation for unwinding.

A woman marched up to Lynn in an official manner, carrying herself with a rigid posture in the comportment of a soldier meeting a high-ranking officer. Lynn immediately thought of her as a DPP protector. The woman stood before her in her crisp, gray suit coat and precisely creased pants, more a protector than a hostess at a relaxation center. Lynn stepped onto the carpet, glancing at the woman's black, business-style shoes with short heels, and after a cursory glance at the woman's brown, short-cut hair, she stiffened herself. She looked for her kids. Her heart throbbed in her breast as she felt a surge of excitement in her nerves. She tried to calm herself, knowing she'd have to use her brains and courage if they were going to get through this situation safely.

The woman smiled for a fleeting moment as if it were a boring task she had to check off a list and then she gestured toward the door. "Come this way Mrs. Rinehart, everything is ready for you and your children. We hope you'll enjoy your time refreshing your spirit. My name is Claudia Winter. I'm assigned as your restoration coordinator. My responsibility is to make certain you enjoy your stay in our SAC facility."

"Thank you," Lynn replied and turned to the kids. "Stefan and Marie come along and stay close—please."

"Mrs. Rinehart, don't be concerned for the children. They are perfectly safe here. You'll see. In fact, there are many activities they'll do in our children's areas while you're engaged elsewhere."

Lynn glanced at Stefan and Marie, who had moved close to her. "I will take care of them as I always do, and they know how they are to behave."

"Very well, Mrs. Rinehart," Claudia replied, raising her brow. "Please, come this way."

Lynn and the kids followed Claudia to the green, double-door entrance. "Can you tell me our departure time?" Lynn asked. "My husband doesn't know where we are."

"I'm sure he will be informed. You are scheduled for departure on next Friday."

Lynn replied abruptly, "I'm very sorry, but that's impossible. We better cancel this visit and reschedule." She stopped, began turning toward the v-tran, and saw it had already driven away. She spun around and glared at Claudia. "Please call us another car."

"I'm sorry, the next transportation isn't scheduled for two hours," Claudia said sharply, and then she frowned. After a second, her mouth softened and her frown melted. "All our drivers run on a tight and very fixed schedule." Claudia's tone softened to a gentle persuasive manner. "I'm sorry. Please come in and let us show you the enjoyable activities we have for you and your children. Perhaps seeing what we have will help you relax. After all, you are here for that purpose. You need not feel uncomfortable."

Lynn sighed. "Okay, I guess it won't hurt." No sooner than she spoke, she thought of William's warning. Perhaps it was ill founded. Regardless, if she let her guard down the children could fall in harm's way and she wasn't going to let that happen. She would keep the kids close to her, and when it came to her own safety, she'd make certain not to lose control.

Claudia took them down a hall adorned only with a light green carpet and doors spaced along its length every fifteen or so feet. They turned down a second hall where Claudia stopped and opened a door. "This is your suite," Claudia said pleasantly. They stepped in. "You have three small bedrooms and a small area for talking or reading. It has nice upholstered chairs, a coffee table, and a gas fireplace with fake logs. But it will make it cozy if you like."

"It's nice Lynn," replied, nodding as she looked around.

"Please follow me to the registration room."

Claudia escorted her and the kids down another hall to the room labeled the registration room. Inside, two desks sat several feet apart with a two chairs in front of each one.

Claudia gestured with an open hand as if offering peace. "May we have the children sit over at the desk with Counselor Stagg while you meet with our other counselor?"

"I suppose that would be okay."

Counselor Stagg smiled warmly at the children and waved her hand from them to approach. "I would like to tell you about our games."

Stefan and Marie walked over to the other desk and sat in front of Counselor Stagg, who ran a hand through her reddish hair, reached into the desk and then handed the children each a lollipop.

Lynn sat down in front of Counselor Hazel and Claudia left the room. Hazel, opened a folder, and changed the order of a few papers, which gave Lynn a chance to overhear part of the discussion her children were having on swimming in the indoor pool, game activities, and movies.

Hazel, a sandy-blonde woman with razor-thin eyebrows and a small voice, began to describe the first day's schedule, which included a massage and skin treatment. When Lynn looked to check on her children, a woman had started escorting her children away. "Wait, where—" Lynn began just as the children disappeared past the door. She pushed her chair back and stood, consternation painting her face white. "Wait, I need to know where my children are at all times. Tell me where they're going."

"They'll be fine," Hazel purred. "You needn't worry."

"I'm sorry if I sound angry, but my children are never free to wander about. If I can't monitor them, we'll have to leave. We have special rules in our home." She noticed she had raised her voice and was breathing more rapidly and it seemed her words had little impact. She wanted to scream for her children and run out the front door.

"That's quite understandable, Mrs. Rinehart," Hazel replied calmly. "Please be assured they are safe. I'll take you to the youth activity section. You'll see where they are and that they're very safe. Then maybe you can relax."

Lynn walked along with Hazel, trying to control her anxiety and her civility, submitting to a tour of the building, walking down four connecting halls, all of which looked rather innocuous. As they moved through the hall, Lynn tried to take the opportunity to look for irregular activities, but every door was closed. When they reached the activity room where Stefan and Marie were engaged, she found they were perfectly safe and occupied with a three-dimensional video game making them interact with a game console and a wall-size vid-screen. When she saw them safe and happy, the tension ran out of her like liquid draining down through her body. It seemed she had built her fear on false assumptions. She hoped she had made a mistake. She allowed Hazel to take her to a treatment room for a massage. Hazel opened the door and extended her hand palm up as if presenting the person inside. "Mrs. Rinehart this is where you can relax."

Lynn entered the massage suite as Hazel disappeared down the hall. The scent of flowers immediately engulfed Lynn. The room was the most wonderful space she had seen. Indirect lights illuminated four intersecting arches composing the ceiling. Vanilla and lavender colors warmed the walls, and around the edge of the room potted plants filled in four areas on the floor. Several of the plants nearly reached well above eight feet but were short by at least three feet from reaching the ceiling. Lynn loved the humid essence of the plants.

"Welcome, Mrs. Rinehart, I'm Sylvia, your massage therapist."

"Hello," Lynn replied, an uncertain tone tainting her tone.

The young woman in a white medical uniform, seemed very pleasant, but Lynn heard William's warning in her head, and his words again chilled her with the thought the SAC had her and the children trapped.

"Please slip out of your clothes over there in our changing booth and put on the massage robe. It's cozy so you won't get cold."

Lynn looked toward the corner of the room at a door decorated with a painted twining vine speckled with lavender colored flowers. "I've never . . . I don't want . . . do I have to do this?"

"I'll be using ointment which may stain your clothes. You'll really like it. Everyone's like you, a little self-conscious at first."

"Can't I just pull things down or up as you work on one location or another?"

Sylvia smiled. "The door will be locked and no one else will be coming in until we're done. So you needn't feel uneasy."

"If I have to," Lynn replied grudgingly.

Lynn disrobed and took her position, lying half-naked on a heated massage table, at which point Sylvia placed a drink on a stool at the head of the table.

"Here, try this. It's delicious. You'll like it. It's a strawberry daiquiri."

Lynn sipped it and grinned. "It's really good. Real strawberries?"

"Oh, yes. Isn't it good? I've not had one for a long time. We're not allowed."

After the sweet drink, Lynn relaxed, yielding to the young woman's soothing muscle-manipulating hands and the dreamy smell of the lotion. Even though she released a few grunts as Sylvia completed her procedure, Lynn never dreamed anything could be so warm, relaxing, and refreshing. It was as if everything up to that time melted away by the minute. With Sylvia's hands kneading her neck muscles, Lynn's eyes slid closed. She caught herself, seemingly at the precipice of her foggy mind with terpsichorean shadows and forced herself to stay awake. Again, her eyes slid closed.

Lynn slept on the massage table, dreaming and finding herself hiding, seemingly in a dark building, listening for footsteps, searching the dark for movement, fearful she couldn't get back to her children. They were gone, somehow separated from her, and she had to get out of the building to find them. Someone was looking for her, trying to lock her up in a windowless cell. The sound of grinding stone on a concrete floor filled the background, over which the faint noise of approaching footsteps threatened her. Lynn thought she heard a voice.

"Mrs. Rinehart," Sylvia said. "Mrs. Rinehart, wake up."

Lynn pushed open her eyes and realized she was looking at the floor of the massage room. She jerked a little. "I guess I fell asleep." The voice ripping her away from her dream startled her.

"Yes, you did, but everyone does the first time. It's time for you to retire to your room with your children in preparation for dinner, which will be in about an hour."

"How long was I asleep?" Lynn asked absentmindedly, rubbing an itch on her nose.

"Maybe thirty minutes, maybe a little more."

"Why didn't you wake me?"

"We have orders not to," Sylvia replied apologetically. "We should probably go."

Lynn walked into her suite and found Stefan and Marie watching a children's program on the vid-net. They were safely back, but she still had to be vigilant against the uncertainty ahead. They had a long time to go before getting back home and she didn't see any way out of completing the schedule without drawing trouble down upon them. Falling asleep disgusted her and she swore it would not happen again. "Did you guys have a good time?"

Stefan reluctantly pulled his gaze from the program. "I guess, but this place is sort of weird."

Lynn smiled at Stefan and Marie as she thought they both had heavy looking eyes and that they must have enjoyed their new adventure. "Other than this minor headache," Lynn said, "that just came over me, I think we've done well. I miss your father."

"Me, too."

Marie looked sadly her mom. "I miss, Dad, too."

Stefan yawned. "Mom, I wouldn't mind going home tomorrow."

Lynn rubbed her forehead. "I agree, but they want us to go by their schedule." She paused for a moment, retreating into thoughts of caution, repeating the warnings in her mind. "Do either of you feel any pains anywhere? Were you both wide awake all afternoon?"

"Yeah," Stefan replied, "we were playing that big game for a long time and then we had something to drink." Stefan frowned. "I felt a little sleepy from playing the game and might have closed my eyes for a little while, but I was awake."

"I just wanted to check on your safety," Lynn said, still fuming with herself for falling asleep during her massage. "Were you together?"

"Yeah, we were." Stefan rolled his eyes.

Following dinner, Lynn decided she and the kids would watch a vid-net program in their room on Durand's effort to save endangered wolves, instead of joining other guests in a large theater room.

She couldn't help worrying terribly about William undergoing the psychological manipulation and the brutal physical torture. She struggled with another puzzle. Why had the SAC sequestered her and the kids at the spa while they tortured William? She had no contacts for information and the SAC surely knew they didn't interact with their neighbors, except for the kids playing down the street. The black blanket of control dropped over them, made her feel utterly alone and cut off from what had been their life.

Later, after convincing Stefan and Marie they should get some sleep for tomorrow, coaxing them into bed, leaving the door cracked, allowing her to hear them, Lynn laid down in her room. However, like the previous night at home, she missed William's solid presence, his body moving on the bed beside her and even the odd noises he made sleeping, and the security he had always given her, although they both knew it was an illusion. She hovered on the verge of crying, wondering what would become of their family. Her own family had been as benign and ordinary as a glass of water, exhibiting little color or turbulence, going about their daily routine year after year until she went off to college. It was then the world slapped her in the face, when she'd decided to study economics, when a man named Durand began altering the nation's economy, when he destroyed her dream for a career. However, if it hadn't been for her job as a part-time office assistant in the engineering department she never would have met William. What a hunk he was then, all consumed with structures, design, and forces, and what not.

At the time, William completely immersed himself in school, and like her, devoted little attention to the politics that was taking place in the country and the government. And then he saw the government as a safe haven to earn a living. Even as she told him it was a good idea, she remembered feeling sad that he wasn't using his engineering education.

Lynn could see herself back during the early months of William's job with SAC, wishing for the old times, the simple glass of water from the well on her grandparent's farm, the simple summertime band concerts, and the pancake suppers she had gone to with her parents. Sure, there was an evolution taking place then, but it seemed so distant and then it rushed up to them like a snarling wolf and consumed them before they knew how to react.

She looked at the red display of the small clock sitting on the side-table and envisioned William in the SAC building. The clock warned her that it was one-thirty in the morning and time she should try to let go and fall asleep. Her tension slowly drained and her breathing shallowed. She had nearly drifted off when she heard a whisper in the dark. Lynn's eyes shot open. She immediately thought the children had climbed out of bed. A spot of light washed across the suite's wall. She quickly sat up, her heart jumping into her throat.

Another whisper came to her. "Lynn Rinehart, I'm a friend."

It was a woman's voice, but she didn't have any friends at this place. "Who's there?" she whispered. Lynn slid her legs over the side of the bed, wondering who would say they were a friend. She quickly threw on her robe from a nearby chair and wrapped it around her. She stood holding her hands up, clenched into defensive balls of flesh. "Please, what do you want?" Lynn asked harshly in a low voice.

A face, partially in silhouette and partially painted in the ghostly light from the open door, moved into the bedroom. Lynn felt the air move.

Someone approached her in the dark. *It's a woman.* A shadowed figure stopped just out of her reach.

"Don't be afraid, we're here to take you and your children away to safety," the woman whispered.

As the woman inched closer, the face shocked Lynn. "You," Lynn blurted. It was Claudia, approaching her, smiling sympathetically.

"I acted gruffly as part of my cover," Claudia replied. "We must move quickly. The security alarms have been disengaged, but we don't have much time. We know your husband's been taken by the SACI. You want to find safety for you and your children, don't you? It was your husband's wish."

"Did William tell you?"

"Not me, but he told another member of our network."

"We have to go now," a man whispered from the doorway. "Get your children, now. Or don't, for God sakes. But make up your mind or we're all dead."

Claudia burst, "This is Dirk, my colleague."

"Yes, yes, we'll go," Lynn replied, new strength in her words. "But how?" She went to the closet and groped for the small travel bag.

"Never mind gathering personal things," Dirk urged. "We only have minutes. So move as fast as you can."

A minute later, Lynn and the children scurried behind Claudia and Dirk, rushing silently down halls toward an objective Lynn could only hope was safety. They stopped at a door marked by a red glowing exit sign and a second sign specifying the door for service and deliveries. The cold air rushing in when Dirk opened the door gave Lynn another morsel of hope as if it were invisible food.

Dirk surveyed the area outside the building and motioned for everyone to move quickly and follow him. Once outside the rear entrance, Claudia took position behind Lynn and the children. Lynn carried Marie and kept Stefan in front of her as they rushed along following Dirk across a glistening lawn under the gentle glow of a silver half-moon in a clear sky. The cold air hung deadly still as if the night were holding its breath for them.

As their escape consumed mere seconds, Lynn felt as if her life were flashing by out of control, seemingly just beyond her grasp. She sensed it might be their only real chance. First, it was William, and now she was plunging with the children into unknown peril. Her heart pounded as her lungs fought to keep up. Perspiration on her forehead reminded her of her fear and spontaneous judgment to leave with people unknown to her. A question flashed across her mind. The flashing moments pressed against her. The question begged for an answer. Had she made the right decision? The recurring voice filled her heart with panic, stealing her breath as they raced through the surreal night. What would happen to them now? *God help this be right.*

Quickly, silently, Lynn and her children followed Dirk across the last few yards of the dew-laden lawn where they disappeared into thick trees and brush. Claudia continued guarding the rear, walking behind her and the kids. Lynn strained to hear Dirk's guidance and warning about the path. She assumed they were going to some sort of transportation. She hoped she hadn't misplaced trust in the strangers. She marveled that William arranged their escape. But, why were they being helped?

Suddenly, Lynn felt depressing doubt in Claudia and Dirk's ability to elude the massive SAC organization's monstrous network of vid-cams. She stopped. "Wait, the children and I shouldn't be involved in this sort of thing. The SAC will catch us. They always catch everyone. The children are innocent. Surely the SAC will understand."

Claudia blurted in a whisper, "What are you doing?"

Lynn turned to Claudia. "Kids wait."

Dirk stopped, walked back, and stood next to Stefan. "We can't do this," Dirk snapped angrily. "We don't have time for this."

Claudia got into Lynn's face. "Look, Mrs. Rinehart, you and your children will never be safe and be never free. Your husband is probably going to be brainwashed very soon. He wanted you safe. He asked for help to get you free. That is what we are doing."

"I saw them brainwashing him yesterday," Lynn said, starting to sob.

Claudia spoke quickly with urgency in her tone, "Then you know. If they've started their process, they could come for you and the children at any time. They will torture you in front of him or they will torture the children in front of both of you. If they send you to a camp, your children will most likely be sent to a different place. With your fine looks, the camp controllers will have you move in with them. If you get common-labor, you could be forced to work in wet and freezing conditions. Your clothes and shoes will never dry out, the rations may be short and you'll never gain back your energy. If you get sick, they may not give you any medical treatment. After all, they have more bodies to replace you. You will die! You must come with us. You must believe me. They even torture children. We can save you! People who go to the camps never return, never."

"I don't know . . . but," Lynn said, her throat constricted.

"Let us get you to the truck before you do something you'll regret. It's just up here a few more yards. Please. Trust us. We have to hurry."

"But the SAC catches everyone," Lynn said, whining, nearly sobbing. "They always catch you."

"Dammit, no they don't," Claudia snapped in an angry whisper. "They didn't catch William's father for twenty-six years."

Lynn looked at her children, a lump lodged in her throat. "Okay," she groaned reluctantly, walking again, pushing Marie on the shoulder to get her to move.

The panicked race resumed through the blackness of the trees and brush, only broken by a rare shaft of moonlight spearing to the ground. Lynn rushed cautious steps, staying close behind the kids, walking up to a small panel truck before she realized it was there. Lynn had seen the type of truck once before under the operation of an SAC food delivery team in the city.

"Dirk, we have to scan them right now," Claudia urged, sounding out of breath, kneeling down to look at Marie. "We can't risk being tracked."

"What's that?" Marie whimpered.

"Scan us for what?" Lynn asked, confusion and fear in her tone.

"It's very likely they may have implanted one of their electronic devices into one of you," Claudia continued, reaching for Lynn to draw her close to the vehicle. "Please, Mrs. Rinehart, let Dirk scan you and your children. We can't go until we do the scan. It's for your own good and for our safety. Please."

"William scanned the children a few days ago."

"We know, but it has to be done again," Dirk replied sternly.

"Okay, do me first so the children can see."

"Dirk, do it!" Claudia snapped.

Dirk opened the driver's door and removed a small box with wires. "Just stand still, Mrs. Rinehart," he said. He passed the device all over her body. No signal light erupted. He then passed it around Lynn's head. A red light blinked on. Again, he moved it slowly past Lynn's forehead. "I'm sorry Mrs. Rinehart, but it looks like they've inserted one of the little nasties in your sinus cavity."

"Oh God," Lynn gasped, grabbing her mouth in horror. "How?"

"Take it easy, dear," Claudia whispered, patting her on the shoulder. "You're in luck, honey; we have a new electronic implant killer for just such a bug."

Dirk opened the passenger door. "You'll have to sit inside the truck so I can kill the little devil," he said sympathetically. "Before I do that, let me check the children and then we'll all get into the truck."

"Do the kids, please," Lynn replied, panicked.

Dirk waved the sensor slowly over Stefan's back, immediately finding an implanted device between Stefan's shoulders, and then he repeated his scan on Marie, finding the same result. "Okay, one job complete. Everyone get in the truck. We'll kill these bugs and get our asses out of here."

Lynn and the children sat in the back seat of the truck. Dirk sat on the front passenger side, plugged a wire into a power outlet, and turned back to Lynn just as Claudia started the truck. "Okay, Mrs. Rinehart, lean forward so I can disable the device in your head."

"What are—" Lynn began.

Dirk broke in, "Don't worry, I've done this before. It's safe." He held the humming bug killer device against Lynn's forehead. "Hold still for me for a few seconds. We want to make certain we get it." He moved the device away and ran the scanner past Lynn's head again. "See, no light. You're okay, and you didn't die."

"What?" Lynn burst.

"I'm joking, dear," Dirk replied. "Now, the boy."

Stefan turned around on the seat, allowing Dirk to slide the device slowly over his back. Dirk duplicated the procedure with Marie, who giggled when the cold bug-killer touched her skin. "Done!" Dirk barked. "Claudia, take us out of here fast."

Still fearing capture, Lynn watched the dark path from which they came, and as the vehicle moved, she saw Claudia quickly pull an optical apparatus down over her eyes, something looking like swimmer's goggles or tiny binoculars that made Claudia look like a big bug with black protruding eyes.

"What on earth do you have over your eyes?" Lynn burst.

"Night vision glasses," Claudia snapped. "We can't turn on lights. This truck is also covered with an insulator where heat is generated so a satellite can't track our infrared heat signature. The truck also has a device that cools the exhaust before it exits into the air. We only travel at night. That's why the SAC won't find us."

They drove through the woods for several minutes, bouncing along the dark heavily treed road, which was barely wide enough for the truck to fit between the trees in some locations. Abruptly, Claudia jerked the steering wheel, turning onto a paved road. She tramped down on the accelerator, driving with the night vision glasses, and traveling faster than Lynn had ever gone, at least since she was young. Lynn envisioned them shooting through the dark toward an unknown impact. As she tried to see what was flashing past the windows the single lane road seemed to burrow through the night. Lynn could only see a black sky and the occasional shafts of moonlight. She thought of their peril. "You weren't joking about me dying back there were you?" Lynn asked.

"The devices like the one you have inside you can rupture if they overheat in the fluctuating magnetic field," Dirk answered softly. "Correct. I wasn't joking."

"What do they do to my head?"

"We're not certain about everything," Claudia said, "but one of their models releases nano-bots, which are nearly invisible molecule-size mechanical units. We think the little mechanisms go to various locations of the brain. We're certain that another version causes the release of specific hormones and body-controlling compounds. The SAC sends out a signal that activates them. We have observed and are relatively certain the devices have made people stare at outdoor SAC display boards showing Durand's face, have made people go into a rage of anger, and have caused people to sink into an instantaneous sobbing despair. They also provide the SAC with a method for tracking a person. The ones in your children were just for tracking."

"Who on earth gave them justification to treat people like animals?" Lynn asked.

Dirk shook his head. "The people did, years ago when you and I were babies—maybe even before that. There was a time, back in the early 1900s, in what was called the USSR, that millions of people were killed for something as small as gathering leftover hay on a collective farm."

Lynn patted Dirk's shoulder. "Thank you for saving us? I fear running away is not going to be easy."

"Freedom isn't easy," Claudia said firmly.

"Oh . . . yeah, why are you helping us? What about my husband?"

Dirk looked at Claudia just as she slowed for a tight curve in the road. "This road isn't much fun, especially in the dark with night vision glasses," Claudia said agitatedly.

Stefan blurted, "Mom, I hear a helicopter."

"Good ears, son," Dirk said. "We'll be fine for a few miles under these trees. They can't see us unless they use a spotlight and the trees should give us enough cover. I'm surprised they're not using night-vision equipped drones. We would have to park under trees if they did."

Claudia barked, "This road is a bear." She hit the brake, slowing, and then she accelerated, making the vehicle lurch forward. "Lynn, we believe your husband has vital information." Claudia lowered head and tilted it to one side for a moment. "The information was passed on from a man many of us thought was dead or never existed. This man had become a folk hero of sorts, a real patriot. At one time, we believed the SAC created him as a propaganda trick, one of many false stories used to get the underground going in circles. But now we know the man was real."

"You mean William's father?"

"My grandfather," Stefan murmured.

"Yes, son, your grandfather," Dirk replied.

Lynn began to cry. "William is being brainwashed horribly. They made me watch."

"What do you mean, Mom?" Stefan asked. "You mean that guy we saw."

"I'll tell you later."

"Mrs. Rinehart—" Claudia started.

"Please call me, Lynn."

"Lynn," Claudia continued, "we're doing all we can. But you must know he's in the SACI building and that's not good. We cannot get in there. No one can."

"I know," Lynn whispered. "But it was horrible, what they were doing to him. They hooked him up to their brain machine."

"Then you know what the place is like," Claudia continued. "We don't have any of our people in there. But—if he's anything like his father, he'll keep his sanity. You should know— he really did ask us to save you."

"Dad, did that?" Stefan asked.

"What did dad do?" Marie asked in a whisper.

"Yes, son," Dirk replied. "He's a good man in his soul."

"Lynn," Claudia began, "coming with us was your only decision. I don't mean to scare your children but they should hear everything about their world. If they had shipped you and the children off to a labor camp, they would have treated you like animals. Before they ship you to your camp, you must remove all your clothes, and discard all your belongings, nice shoes, nice coats, rings, watches, belts, toothpaste, leaving you without possessions and vulnerable. They shout at you, rush you along into trucks or train cars, which have little or no ventilation, where they distribute underwear and coveralls. Women do not get anything for support of their breasts. From what we know about the children, which isn't much, they treat them horribly. I tell you this because you need to know. The world needs to know."

"Thank you," Lynn replied evenly as she digested Claudia's lesson.

"Mom, where are we going?" Stefan asked.

"Yeah," Marie whispered. "Where are we going?"

"Kids, don't bother with that now," Lynn answered warmly.

"Well, we are going into the mountains where we can hide from satellites, vid-cams, and SACI spies, and we can only drive at night."

"What about, Dad?" Stefan burst with panic on the edge of his words.

Claudia cleared her throat. "Maybe he'll join you someday soon."

From the character of Claudia's voice, Lynn knew she had heard truth, and a meaning differing from false, cloaking words of hope. In her heart, she would always keep hope, but her logic told her the odds were not in William's favor. She prayed for a miracle.

"There's a light shooting through the trees up ahead," Dirk said. "Keep the pedal down."

Chapter 21

Helmut Kauffman's office door opened without the intruding visitor knocking. He shot his eyes at the door, considering a serious rebuke for whoever breached his threshold with such disrespect. When the person emerged in full view a shower of self-correction washed away his anger. He had been too quick. No. He hadn't. It wasn't a mental failure to react as long as he hadn't accused someone of breaching respect erroneously. He raised his eyebrows to show energetic interest and sprang from his chair.

"Chairman, what can I do for you?" Kauffman asked as he analyzed Durand's furrowed brow.

"I'm sorry to bother you, but I was in this part of the building this morning and thought I'd stop by," Chairman Durand said walking stiffly toward one of the chairs in front of Kauffman's desk.

"Please sit, sir. It's nice of you to stop by. We don't get a chance to talk much, face to face. Sir, is there anything I can do for you? You look troubled, if I may say."

Durand placed a hand on the back of a chair, rubbed it back and forth, moved in front of it, and eased himself down, releasing a small sigh when he came to rest. "Back's bothering me again . . . getting old." He smoothed a wrinkle in his trousers and picked off a piece of lint.

"You look great, sir." Kauffman sat and folded his hands, resting them on his desk.

Durand's attention fixed on Kauffman, "Well, knowing what your particular talent and business is, I suppose you've guessed why I'm here."

"I have a couple guesses," Kauffman said with a ripple of his eyebrows, smiling a little.

"Helmut, I'm still concerned about this conspirator's son, and what he may have buried in the remote memories of his brain, what he may somehow tell a member of the underground . . . if they would ever get their hands on him. I would suppose you have that contingency covered. Besides that, I'm afraid Beucher will destroy any memory the man has. Once his memory is gone, this resource will be worthless, absolutely gone. We wouldn't even be able to use him as a double agent, and our opportunity for that control would have been wasted."

"Sir, he may not know anything beyond what he's reported, and in fact that's my gut feeling. However, I agree with you—totally. He's a resource we should exploit to the maximum. There's no urgency for us to wipe his brain. I must confess, sometimes I wonder about Citizen-Comrade Beucher's methods and his objectives, or perhaps I should say, his exuberance for his job."

Durand pulled on the mottled skin hanging under his chin and nodded. "Yes, but he does get results. How long has the man been in the mentoring program?"

"A little over twenty days."

"That long?" Durand said, shaking his head.

"Yes, he was brought in on a Friday about four weeks ago. In fact his wife and kids watched him the first day and were taken back home."

"Does the subject still have a viable mental state?"

"Yes, he's still quite resilient. I believe Doctor Beucher is taking his time."

Durand arched his brow. "Maybe we've been lucky."

"Sir, I'll have Beucher terminate his procedure so the man still has enough mental capacity to help us—however we decide to proceed in the future. If we give him some rope, keep our eye on him, we may be able to scoop up more members of the underground. Maybe he'll be useful as bait. My gut tells me the underground would like to talk to him and pick his brains."

"Odd choice of words," Durand countered, grinning.

"Regarding Rinehart's wife . . . I believe I mentioned in my last report to you that she had disappeared and so far we've been unable to locate her and the children. We suspect members of the underground infiltrated our staff at the spa in Fairfax."

"Clearly an unfortunate incident, but Doctor Beucher should be able to overcome such an obstacle. I'm not worried about her. It doesn't make sense that our pigeon would risk telling his wife dangerous information in the presence of their children."

"I agree . . . unless he's an idiot. He seems the opposite and quite intelligent."

"I trust you have the necessary people trying to find the wife." Durand grabbed the arms of the chair and pushed himself to his feet.

Kauffman rose. "I do, sir," he replied, tapping a finger on the desk. He watched Durand's face.

Durand nodded a little as if agreeing with himself on the decision and extended his hand across the desk. "Thanks for your support."

Kauffman took his hand, shaking it gently, feeling its loose soft skin, feeling its lack of strength, feeling its age. "You're very welcome, sir. Oh, by the way. Regarding Doctor Beucher, I have arranged for two well-qualified men to undergo training on Doctor Beucher's methods and equipment. After all the doctor won't live forever and we should have a back-up."

"Excellent step. Has the doctor gone off on any tangents again, not following orders to stop washing when told?"

"No, not for a long time. I believe I scared him into correct SAC thinking the last time he deviated from our request."

"Being prepared for such an eventuality is very prudent."

"Thanks."

Durand pulled on his chin, allowing his eyes to drop before coming back to Kauffman. "You know . . . I'm still concerned about the story we heard from the underground conspirator Beucher brainwashed several years ago. You know that legend. I had expected us to clarify those questions after all these years."

"We will be watching Rinehart until he dies naturally or is executed. If he knows anything or learns anything we'll be on top of it, sir."

Durand turned and walked toward the door. "Very well, I'll check with you later on."

Kauffman noticed the stiffness in Durand's stride as he left the office. He checked the time and knew 7:00 a.m. was too early to catch Beucher, a creature of habit and conformity, particularly regarding his work hours, but he could leave a message.

"Vid-link, on," Kauffman said.

"Ready."

"Get me Doctor Beucher."

Kauffman listened to the vid-link chime on Doctor Beucher's end of the connection until a mechanical voice recited a message that the doctor was not in his office, followed by a brief notice of the office schedule. At last, the vid-link solicited a message.

"Citizen-Comrade Beucher, this is Director Kauffman calling regarding Manager Rinehart. You have another day with him to extract what you can. Chairman Durand and I are concerned about the future viability of his brain if you twist him to the extreme under your mentoring. We don't want him totally cleaned. We don't want him damaged to the point he can't recall anything—just in case. Please make certain to comply with this request. I'll drop by in a day to see how you're doing. Thank you." He sighed. "Vid-link, off."

Chapter 22

The pressure pushing William's bladder shattered his dream, a horrible nightmare in which he repeatedly tried to open the heavy steel door on his father's bunker, trying to flee from Doctor Beucher. He sat up on the edge of his mat and dropped his feet to the floor. His head throbbed. He didn't move. The cell blurred in his eyes. He stared blankly across his tiny space, collecting himself. The cell's air chilled the perspiration on his neck and chest. He loaded weight on his legs attempting to stand. The prison cell turned slowly around him. He closed his eyes for a moment, trying to gather strength, and then he staggered over to his toilet. When he made his way back to the safety of the bed, he reminded himself to confess everything to Doctor Beucher again today, just as he had yesterday.

It was another day after another bad night. Come to think of it, he had not heard a sound from his neighbor last night. *Maybe the person's dead. Stay positive. I can't think those thoughts.* He laughed under his breath at the irony of him trying to control his own thoughts again, controlling them for himself instead of for the SAC. They were his thoughts. The SAC didn't create them in the neurons and synapses of his brain.

Just as he lay back down, a metal object clanged starkly against the cell's steel door and then the door abruptly swung open, revealing a familiar bulky form.

"Excellent timing, Ninety-nine," Hans sneered. "You have an appointment with Doctor Beucher and our thought mentoring program." Hans sent his usual menacing face and then grinned like a schoolboy full of spiteful ideas for torment. "Get your ass up off that bed and get moving. I think today should be a lot of fun. I'm looking forward to it."

William sat up, glancing at his lines on the wall under his sink, counting five marks, five days of holding onto life. Wait a minute; he remembered counting the same number of marks before. Had he forgotten to make marks or had someone changed his count? Was he losing his memory?

"Okay," William said feebly. "I want to tell Doctor Beucher the truth, just like I did yesterday."

William stood at his bed, wobbled for a moment, and walked to the door. He stopped and waited for Hans to move out of the way. *Here goes another day.* William tried not to think of the torture that was ahead of him, as he had yesterday. He focused on living—to the exclusion of everything else. What else was there if he didn't survive? He laughed to himself at the simple irony.

"Come on, get moving," Hans said, grabbing William by the arm and pulling him into the hall.

William stood as Hans had positioned him in the hall, waiting for Hans to close the door. He looked at Hans' hands. Did Hans have on rubber gloves? He thought he had seen them before, but he couldn't remember. He felt something wet swabbed across the back of his neck. When he started to look back, Hans slammed the heel of his hand into William's back. He toppled forward into a sprawled dive at the floor. He landed on his hands for a fraction of a second until his arms weakened.

Hans bent over, grabbed William under the left arm and pulled him up until William rested on his knees. "Now get your ass up the rest of the way."

William struggled to his feet and began walking. He swayed to the left and back left with the first three steps. His stomach began churning as if it knew Hans was taking him toward the torture chamber. Outside Room 100, William's stomach cramped, wrenching him over, making him reach for the wall to hold himself up. The building spun around him. He leaned against the wall, hunching over trying to fight through the pain, trying to collect himself as he had yesterday, but in spite of his battle, he spewed the contents of his stomach across the floor.

"You bastard," Hans yelled. "You did the same thing yesterday. I told you to get your ass in the room."

Hans opened the door and slammed his fist into William's back, sending him flying forward like an untethered marionette. William sprawled on the floor barely catching himself on his forearms. Beucher stood at his desk, an elbow resting in the palm of the other hand, pulling on his upper lip, observing the incident as if it were an experiment in his behavior modification. Hans stomped over to William, pushed his arm under William's left arm, pulled him off the floor, and then pulled him to the white chair.

William slumped into the chair. His muscles quivered in his arms. His dread for what was coming grew by the second. With his strength already waning, he leaned to the side of the chair, clutching its arm to hold himself upright.

"Hans, we're doing the same procedure as yesterday," Beucher pronounced mechanically, sitting at his desk not taking his eyes from his computer screen he held in his hands.

"Yes, sir," Hans replied quickly. "Ninety-nine spewed up out in the hall again."

"Perhaps the food doesn't agree with him," Beucher whispered.

Hans nodded.

"Hans, you swabbed his neck?"

"Yes, sir."

"Hmm, perhaps it's the composition on that swab. It has worked on better than eighty percent of our previous visitors." Beucher turned and looked at William. "Ninety-nine, what are we going to do with you?" Beucher's tone was taunting.

"Doctor, I want to confess all my criminal activity," William said. "I want to go to the sewer that I warned Father Durand about. I want to kiss Durand's picture there. I saved him. I was wrong reading the book. I'm sorry, very sorry. Tell me what you want, and I'll do it. I'm sorry for the scanner . . . all my wrong thoughts. I deserve to visit the sewer. I love him and I saved him from a bomb."

Beucher didn't move, as if he didn't hear a word, his eyes having gone to his computer. He stared at some numbers in a small highlighted box on its display, as if something were critical, and then turned to Hans. "Hans, call someone to take care of that mess in the hall and then take your position on the controls."

"Yes, sir."

"Ninety-nine," Beucher said as if he were pronouncing a prison sentence, "you have concealed a connection with conspirators seeking to inflict destruction upon Chairman Durand's state. You made a mistake, a seditious mistake. You can apologize for your mistake and make this process much easier. We want to help you. Going to the sewer could possibly be a reward."

"I apologized. Just now, I apologized. I'm sorry, truly sorry. I didn't know what I was doing." William didn't think about what he was saying. The words flowed from his mouth smoothly, automatically, spewing onto his tongue from a little voice in his brain. "Wrong thoughts, wrong mind, bad thoughts, no bad mind of any kind."

"That's right Ninety-nine," Beucher said disdainfully. "That was very good. Yes. Hans, did you get hold of the custodial people?"

"Yes, sir, I did."

"Good, then you can get Ninety-nine ready."

"My pleasure, Doctor."

Hans pushed William backward into the white chair and threw the strap around William's chest, attaching it, cinching it tight. William sucked in a breath and then another. In his tired brain, he assembled the foggy proposition that Beucher may have drugged him. He had wondered about it in fleeting thoughts before, but could never hold onto them. He looked at Beucher's face, which now appeared like a grotesque caricature, blurry and warped. He felt someone applying straps to his legs. *My head feels strange. Fight being tired.*

"I received a report about your wife and children," Beucher sneered. "Apparently they didn't like their accommodations at the spa. They disappeared during the night."

Beucher moved inches from William, his warm breath pouring sickeningly over William. How many times had he done that? William hated it. *Someday maybe the SAC will end you! Wrong thoughts—*.

Beucher continued, "You need not worry though. The SACI will find them very soon . . . and bring them here for thought mentoring. Then we'll be correcting the whole family. That sounds amazingly wholesome. Our protectors are quite good at capturing runaways. I've heard they even wager of how many hours it will take to recapture our misguided lost sheep."

"Wait a minute, you told me the same thing before. I know you did. You told me the day after they disappeared. You've been telling me the same thing, day after day." William's eyes slid closed.

"Very good," Beucher replied, laughing under his breath. "This is the first time you realized it."

"Monroe, please lower the mentoring helmet on, Ninety-nine."

"Very good, sir."

"Hans, fix the helmet straps while I check my computer again."

Beucher picked up his computer, adjusted its size, collapsing it down to the dimensions of a book, and stood there as if he were carrying a platter in a restaurant, poking at its screen. "Ninety-nine, did you know anything about your family leaving the spa?" Beucher asked, staring down at his computer, his question coming out like a mere curiosity.

"No, sir," William replied. "I requested help. That's all I know."

"Sir, I think we're ready," Monroe said.

"Thank you. I think this will be a good day for, Ninety-nine. Down into your hidden thoughts we will drill again, somewhere that only you have traveled, the place you go when you're alone at night. We're going to take care of those nasty old wrong thoughts. How can you love our Father as you should with those energy-burning negative mental processes?" He paused. "Level three, delta ramping, Monroe. Thank you."

William tensed himself a little, fighting through the drugs, waiting for an aberration in his mind, a burst of light or some signal aimed at making his thinking stumble or aimed at rendering him unconscious. He waited. Except for blurring vision, he felt lucid. Then it came. Slowly bands of colored light appeared in his mind, an image of his cell door, Beucher's maze of wires, Hans's distorted face, and then Beucher's face. The room spun and faded into a dark blur. He had to close his eyes. He saw a flashing white light, a blinding brilliance, penetrating harshly, as if he had no eyelids. He wanted to claw at it, to get rid of it, but as with previous experiences, the restraints paralyzed his arms.

"Were you aware of your wife's connection with the conspirators?" Beucher asked.

Beucher's voice came at William in a droning hypnotic tone, lingering with an echo in his head, rising and falling, over and over. "I asked a man for help," William yelled frantically.

The hypnotic voice in his head repeated.

"Uh . . . I'm not . . ." William stuttered. "I met a man and asked him to help my wife."

"What else?"

"I didn't know if anything would happen." *SAC loves us. SAC gives life.* Had he said it? "SAC loves us. SAC gives life."

"We're making progress again," Beucher replied, holding up four fingers to Monroe, who nodded. "Just remember what you said and the SAC will love you."

William squeezed his eyes shut, fighting off the strobe light blistering his brain. The light battered his eyes for a minute and then it stopped. He saw a reddish haze. Whispery indistinguishable words fluttered around in his head. The words came from Father Durand, from a robed figure, and then from a uniformed protector of the DPP. He heard three voices at the same time condemning him for betraying the Father of the state. Lynn's face flashed across his mind's eye. A soft monotone voice slid over him, accusing him of placing his family in danger. *Are my kids safe? Home. Something at home. I had to do something.* Then the voices were gone. He fought to hold on to one thought after another, a thought of Stefan and Marie, Lynn, a chronicle, blank papers, and a sewer. They seemed to be his thoughts. A murmur slid underneath his thoughts like background noise. It mentioned Durand and seemingly circled around and around and around on a record.

He opened his eyes for a second. "I feel sick." Nausea crept into his stomach. *This is the white chair.*

"The white chair does have its flaws," Beucher said. "What military people helped your father? Have you told us everything?"

In William's head, a second voice interlaced and joined with the first. It told him the correction process would be easier if he would trust Doctor Beucher, and if he would write down his mistakes. His wife wanted him to cooperate. The words in his mind thrashed him as if he were walking through a thicket where swinging branches slapped him in the face every few steps.

The strobe came on again for what seemed several minutes, although William had no real sense of time. He heard talking in his brain and then the light faded. He had a vision. He stood at the edge of a cliff overlooking a canyon of brown and red stone. His father stood beside him, frowning at him.

His father spoke, "Son you should make it easy on yourself. Tell them you are a member of the underground. Tell them every detail. Confess your love for Father Durand. After all, he provides for you. Ask for a piece of paper and a pen, and write it down. You must write down all the things I told you at the bunker. Tell them about the military members of the underground. Save yourself and love Father Durand."

William stood there, unable to move, his mind frozen—absent of thought. He tried to think of what he wanted to do and couldn't remember what it was from only a moment ago. He couldn't put words together and he couldn't think what to do, as if he were walking through mud and couldn't lift his feet. A brilliant white light blasted his eyes, even while he had his eyes closed. Then everything became black.

"It seems Ninety-nine drifted off, Hans," Beucher said with a grotesque little laugh. Beucher approached, moving his face to within inches of William's as if trying to see through William's skin and into his skull, mesmerized by the plaything before him.

William opened his eyes and only saw a blur. He still sat strapped in the white chair.

"I spoke too soon," Beucher said, jerking back from William. "He is still awake." Beucher glanced to Monroe. "Restart at the fifth step."

A monotone voice started in William's head. It had same speech rhythm and words as before and mentioned confessing his crimes completely if he wanted to live and if he wanted his family to live. His head floated for a moment before he drifted off. Then just as quickly, he awoke. He found he was still sitting in the white chair. His face felt limp and uncontrollable, but not numb. He drooled from the corner of his mouth. Slowly, his head slumped to the right until the chinstrap of the electrical headgear stopped it. The voice in his head became multiple overlapping voices, all saying different warnings. He blacked out.

Hans slapped William, jarring his head from one side to the other, as if it were on a hinge. William screamed, awakened in the middle of a nightmare. His shoulders lifted away from the chair, forcing the restraint strap into his flesh. He thrashed feebly within his restraints to get free from the horror of the light and voices rampaging in his head.

"Would you like to say anything?" Beucher asked.

"I . . . I talked to a man called Russell about my family," William stuttered, keeping his eyes closed. "And I . . . I want to be in Durand's family. I love the SAC." He coughed.

"Ninety-nine you are guilty of social treason . . . wrong-thinking. Ninety-nine, do you think we should allow every citizen to read the books you have read?" Beucher asked softly, tauntingly.

William moved his tongue around in his dry mouth and tried to swallow with his constricted throat.

"Surely you can nod your head," Beucher said.

William moved his lips and tried to open his eyes, but couldn't lift their heavy stone weight. On a feeble breath he replied, "No, we can't allow that." He swallowed. "It . . . it would destroy the SAC. I know that. I . . . want to help."

"Without control, our society would be overtaken by outside harmful forces. Don't you agree?"

The muscles in William's face grew tight distorting his face as he struggled to swallow and answer. He could see Beucher speaking to him but the words penetrating his brain came distorted and muffled. It had to be the machine.

"I'm sorry you're having difficulty," Beucher said mechanically.

"Punish me if you will," William groaned. "The conspirator told me to read his notes. I gave you his book. I kept the blank pages."

"That's good," Beucher replied and pointed a finger at Monroe, who nodded. "We aren't concerned about blank pages, only the ones with print." Beucher paused, thinking for a moment. "By the way your wife and kids have been located, and will soon be sitting in that chair."

William passed out again.

When William opened his eyes, he heard a phrase in his head, 'State America loves us, and Father Durand loves us.' After several repetitions of the programming phrase, Beucher turned it off.

"Let's see if Ninety-nine has learned enough to avoid the black chair today," Beucher said, pompously tilting his head to one side and then the other, as if he were losing his balance.

"Have you given thanks to the SAC for your home?"

"I guess," William said hesitantly. "I worked hard for my home."

"Ah . . . there's a problem. It is not yours. It belongs to the SAC. You don't own anything, not even your clothes."

"Have you ever sought out people known as the underground?"

"No."

"That's a lie. Do you know Father Durand does not allow us to meet in groups?"

"Yes."

"Do you know why?"

"No," William replied. His head ached.

"People meeting in groups engage in wrong-speech. They use wrong-thoughts. They speak against the SAC. Then those people talk to other people. This breeds unhappy citizen-comrades and unrest, which in turn causes workers to perform poorly."

"Did the conspirator on the mountain tell you about the people who coordinated the bombs used by the underground?"

"I . . . no."

"Don't pass out," Beucher barked. "If you do, you'll wish you hadn't. Now tell me about bombs. Your wife told us you know something about the underground."

"I don't know anything about plans or bombs. I reported what I know. It was a damn sewer bomb. I don't want to know anything. I want to forget."

"You better not forget."

"My wife . . . she doesn't know anything . . . she's innocent . . . she loves Durand like I do."

"You're lying, dammit, and you're going into the second chair," Beucher shouted angrily. "Now, even if you ask to sign a confession for your crimes I'm not going to let you do it. Did you know the SAC could take away your wife and children? They do not belong to you. They are presents from Father Durand."

"Punish me so I can prove my loyalty to Durand . . . so I can keep my wife and children." *My oath. What oath?* William's head spun. "Wrong thoughts, wrong mind, bad thoughts, no bad mind of any kind," he murmured.

"Hans, move Ninety-nine to the black chair."

William woke sprawled on the floor of the tiny shower in his cell. His prison guards had dropped him with his legs half in and half out the shower opening. He couldn't remember them moving him to the black chair, although he remembered screaming, or perhaps it was one of his nightmares. They had placed him in a plastic collection suit again, and his cloth prisoner suit felt wet, cold, disgusting, and no doubt soaked with urine. Another smell floated to his nose, the foul contents of his bowels. Despite hating it, the collection suit had done its job. He looked at his legs. They had tied the pants tight around each ankle with cords and he was sitting on a sheet of plastic, which he figured they had used to convey him down the hall, all to avoid soiling their precious torture facility. What demented bastards they were.

It took all his strength, but he peeled off the filthy uniform, wadded it into a ball, and started to throw it outside the shower when he saw a bucket sitting near the shower opening. He compressed the stinking garments into a bundle and pushed it into the bucket. At least he had a way to wash. He stepped back into the shower, readying his mind and body for what was to come when he turned on the cold water. He clenched his teeth against the sudden cold shock. With the chilling water striking him, he ran soap over his body with fleeting strokes and found warmth again as he quickly dried off. He climbed into a clean jumpsuit and sat exhausted on his bed.

With elbows on his knees, he grabbed his head with both hands and sobbed. He didn't know why he was weeping, except he felt lost, felt he had lost hope, and felt he couldn't remember things the way he should. He was losing events and bits of time from one day to the next. He couldn't remember much of what happened in Beucher's room today from the time Hans pushed him into the white chair. There were only bits and pieces that flashed through his brain. Each day it was evaporating away, more and more of his connections to events of his life were going out of his head. He had almost arrived at the point where he didn't care about living, about fighting on, fighting like his father had said, and like he had promised. *Can I make it to the sewer?* He had promised.

His cell door opened and a man sat a metal plate of food and a cup of steaming liquid on the floor, and then slammed the door closed, sending in a burst of cool air from the hall. As William sat there looking at the food, he realized the muscles in his back ached terribly again, and the muscles in his upper arms burned. He wondered if he could lift them to eat. He stood and took a step toward the food. A strained stomach muscle stopped him. It was no doubt from Beucher's black chair. Thank God, he had no recollection of being tortured, except for the after effects on his muscles. He didn't have any idea of whether he had said anything of substance. That was incredibly scary. Soon he would confess to anything they wanted. Maybe he had already. It was a small price to pay for his family being safe. Thank God, he remembered his family. *Say their names. Remember their names! Lynn, Stefan, and Marie.* He'd done it, remembered them. He toppled over on his side on the bed. He closed his eyes. He was thinking he wanted to write down his mistakes like Beucher had asked numerous times. He surrendered to his tired body and mind, and fell asleep.

Sometime later, William didn't know the time, but judging from the temperature of the coffee and food, probably at least an hour, a whispering voice infiltrated his cell like a spider walking across its web. He covered his ears and it disappeared. That meant it wasn't merely in his head. It urged him to accept the fact that he had broken rules. The voice told him that he had failed on his assignment to bring in his father-conspirator. That failure clearly showed Father Durand he was a criminal. The ghostly voice urged him to repent for his wrong thinking by condemning his materialistic wife. He had to confess it to complete his rehabilitation. His wife had betrayed him with another man. She had beaten his children and offered to give them up to the State. He needed to declare his thankfulness to Father Durand to start his healing process. William ate his cold food with the voice repeatedly coming at him. He tried to block the voice from his brain but it was like trying to swat a fly buzzing around just out of reach.

He wondered if he would ever surrender so totally or whether he'd merely die. Would he continue to know the difference between their lies and the true world, and would he continue to shine the white light of reason on everything they said and did?

After swallowing the last fragment of bread, he sat on the floor too tired to rise, leaning against the wall, staring blankly at the asphalt tile on the floor, seeing speckles of dirt sticking up from its smooth surface, noticing their different shapes and color. His arms hung lifeless on his lap. His sore abdominal muscles made his breathing jerky. The voice from the speaker continued.

William opened his eyes to another morning in prison. It was as if he were in a repeating dream, waking and waiting for the moment the cell door would make that horrid sound, the sound of the key turning in the lock, which was followed by the noisy hinge. The waiting, chilled to the bone from fear and the lack of heat in his cell, clawed at his hope for life. Day upon day came the same anxiety about Room 100 and the same question of whether he could endure it again. Fatigue racked his muscles every minute now, and not just after the torture, and his hunger now consumed more of his thoughts. He was certain he wasn't getting enough protein to live long.

The next day, with the same clockwork timing, he was back in Room 100 undergoing Beucher's thought mentoring in the white chair with the strange visions appearing in his mind without his control.

Early in Beucher's procedure, someone knocked on the door. Beucher snapped his wristwatch into view. "It's only a quarter of nine," he snapped. He puffed disgustedly as he turned toward Hans. "Hans, dammit, go see who it is." Beucher turned his attention back to William, studying William's reaction to the mentoring signal.

Hans scarcely stepped from the room before he returned to report, his tightened face showing his surprise. "You are wanted at the door, sir," Hans said hesitantly. "It's the Director."

Beucher's brow came down as he puckered his mouth. "What?" Beucher studied William. "Hans, shut down Ninety-nine while I'm in the hall."

"Yes, sir."

Beucher walked over to the door, hesitated for a moment, and stepped into the hall. Why was the Director here? The Director said he would come by. *Why do they always come when I'm in the middle of a treatment?*

"Citizen-Comrade Beucher, how are you progressing with our prize?" asked Director Kauffman, standing with his hands clasped behind his back and his chin sticking forward authoritatively. Karl Steinhoff stood behind him with a stern evaluative face.

"Comrades, you flatter me with your visit and personal attention," Beucher replied, lowering his head a little as if bowing. "Our patient, Ninety-nine, known to you as William Rinehart, is an interesting case. I'm working with him at this moment."

"Dispense with any embellishments related to your techniques," Kauffman said dryly. "You've had him for about four weeks, give or take. Correct?"

Beucher frowned and looked down at the floor as if he were making a calculation. "This is the fourth week, sir." He then looked at the director. "I have obeyed your directions and I have pushed him toward the unstable region . . . uh, the rigorous levels, for only limited periods."

"Surely by now you have determined whether he has any valuable information beyond what he presented in his report."

"In my process of thought mentoring, punishing him for the book, the scanner, and the trip violations—"

Kauffman interrupted. "The man's minor transgressions are not of interest to me. Did he or did he not say anything related to weapons, military control, or any people in the underground?"

Beucher swallowed hard and shifted his feet. "He did not. He mentioned the names of two, probably inconsequential people, a man called Russell, and a woman called Rachel Lee, and he has repeatedly said he gave us the conspirator's notebook, and all he took out was the blank pages. Of course, he's talking about the notebook from the mountain operation. I believe he's starting to doubt who he is. His self-image might be crumbling by his losing hope. I suggest we reduce his treatment to no more than three times a week and we increase his protein ration so he doesn't go insane. However, I'm perfectly willing to continue pressing for the answers you want."

Kauffman looked down his nose menacingly at Beucher. "Has he ever mentioned Robert Zeilinger or a Simon Tiefenbacher? Surely you'd remember those names, Citizen-Comrade Beucher."

"No . . . no, not those names."

"And you are certain there haven't been any references to names associated with the sewer bomb?" Kauffman continued.

"No, nothing more than what we knew when we began working with him. Director Kauffman, as you know I've been privileged to serve Chairman Durand in my present capacity for several years now. I'm confident we have extracted ninety-five percent of relevant information from the man's brain."

Steinhoff stepped forward, which drew a disdainful gaze from Kauffman. "Is he still sane?" Steinhoff asked. "Have you scanned his brain?"

"Valid questions, Karl," Kauffman added. "Have you corrected his thinking to the point he can no longer remember anything connected with his father?"

Beucher pulled on his chin and swallowed. "Yes, we have scanned his brain several times. I scan his thoughts every time he's in our chair. I'm always looking for his consistency as well as content. He has said several times he wanted to visit the sewer where he saved Durand from the bomb. He's referred to it as a reward for serving Father Durand."

"Was it an honest desire?" Kauffman asked. "Or was it something planted during other conditioning?"

"It appears quite genuine, sir. He hasn't been programmed by anyone else."

"And what of the other scans?"

"Yes, sir, most confirmed he was telling what he believed to be the truth. A couple proved problematic, as there didn't seem to be a real connection in his brain. They either never existed or weren't related to any real experience, which gave me an indication he was losing grip on his reality." Beucher peered down his nose arrogantly. "Uh . . . I . . . I think he's close to the edge."

"In your opinion, could more information be brought out of his subconscious if he were allowed to visit the sewer where the bomb was hidden?" Kauffman asked, his cold, gray eyes fixed on Beucher's face.

"Possibly, but what do you think is still buried in his brain?"

"Names, locations, plans, answers to old legends, the underground, the usual. We need to know if there are more bombs like the one he reported." Kauffman hesitated thoughtfully. "Are you certain he still has his brain—as I requested?"

Beucher jerked his head slightly, more like a nervous twitch than a controlled movement, and then he nodded nervously. "Yes, yes, he should be able to remember that portion of his past. In a few more days, I wouldn't be able to affirm the same, even with the limited use of the severe signal levels. If I'd known . . ."

"You were advised, my good citizen-comrade doctor. If your 'so-called' limited severe levels were a risk, you should have terminated their use as we requested. Perhaps the review board should look into your competency and adherence to directions."

"I . . . I followed your requests."

"Director," Steinhoff began hesitantly, "perhaps using the man's children would bring improved results."

"You mean, torture them in front of him?" Kauffman replied, gravely.

"Yes . . . yes, sir," Steinhoff said. "Doctor Beucher, what do you think?"

Beucher smiled as if his mind were somewhere else. "It has had great success in other cases."

"I think we can save that as our last measure," Kauffman replied, turning dismissively. He took a few steps down the hall, stopping abruptly, turning back with his eyes shooting from under a burning brow, locking onto Beucher. "Let him go home! We'll keep him under close observation, and house arrest. I want his brain intact. Understand? This has the chairman's attention and grave concern. Understand?"

"Very well, sir," Beucher replied, bobbing his head obediently.

Kauffman resumed his walk.

Steinhoff, followed a few feet behind Kauffman. "Sir, I'll initiate an immediate investigation into the names Rinehart mentioned. Perhaps

Doctor Beucher could extract more information before Rinehart is released."

"No!" Kauffman snapped. "I want him out now. You supervise. We can always reinstitute the mentoring process." Kauffman took two steps. "I do like your idea of checking into those names, although I would have thought it had already been investigated."

Steinhoff cleared his throat. "Sorry, sir, I'll assign a person to check back through Beucher's daily reports for threats and names of interest."

Kauffman sighed audibly. "I want you to know everything Rinehart does. If he talks in his sleep, I want you to know what he says, and if it means following him into a sewer, you'll go with him. Agreed?"

"Yes, sir."

"Karl, work with my people to find Rinehart's wife and kids," Kauffman said, his face steel, metallic and cold. "People don't escape from State America. We need the wife and kids for more pressure."

"Yes, sir."

Karl Steinhoff dropped into his office chair, unconcerned about the vid-cam watching him, slouching tiredly, leaning back with his left elbow resting in his right hand, pulling on his lower lip. He hated the thought of Rinehart slipping through his control, even if his control was through his proxy, Doctor Beucher. He glanced at the clock on his desk. It had been an hour since he had gone with Kauffman to see Doctor Beucher. Running through him like molten metal, his hatred burned for Rinehart. If he took the risk of displaying his emotions under the SAC burning vid-cam scrutiny, he could pay the price of negatively influencing his performance record. The SAC functioned because all its executives followed orders for fear of losing their favored positions and their lives. The SAC wanted a homogeneous cold-thinking executive level. *Sometimes I have to be an individual. Too damn bad if they see me pissed.*

He said, "Vid-link, on."

"Ready."

"Doctor Beucher."

In a moment, Beucher appeared on the screen. "Yes, Section Head, what can I do for you?"

"Doctor, I was wondering if you could give William Rinehart one more examination, possibly . . ." Steinhoff started with hesitation in his voice, the kind he knew would draw Beucher's attention. "Uh . . . could you use one of your drugs to cloud Rinehart's vision . . . uh, so that he would think his wife and kids were watching him . . . like that case . . . about a year ago with . . ."

"You're referring to Victor Melbourne," Beucher broke in quickly. "The treatment worked remarkable well. However . . ."

"However what?"

"Patient Ninety-nine, Rinehart has been sent home."

"That is unfortunate." Steinhoff nodded and leaned back in his chair.

"Yes . . ." Beucher said, drawing the single word out as if it were painful.

"Vid-link, off," Steinhoff said, blankly watching Beucher's disappointed face fade to gray on the view screen.

"Vid-link, dial SACI surveillance center."

"Protector Gene Wallace."

"Protector Wallace, this is Section Head Steinhoff. I'm looking for the person in charge of the search operation Director Kauffman initiated, the one directed to locate the family of a Manager Rinehart."

"Yes, sir, that would be Protector Paula Rubin. I'll transfer you."

The vid-screen flashed gray and returned with the image of a shorthaired woman of slight build in the usual SACI uniform. "Protector Rubin," the woman answered sharply. "Section Head Steinhoff, I've been expecting your call. Director Kauffman advised me to help you all I can."

"Protector Rubin, has any progress been made?"

"Sir, we know the wife and children had help from the underground. They apparently have technology to circumvent our infrared scanners. The satellite, helicopter, and drones picked up nothing. At this point, we are doing a sweep of abandoned buildings in cities in a hundred mile radius and we have two groups double-checking vid-cam recordings. I don't think we'll find them unless someone sees them and reports them."

"That's unacceptable," Steinhoff growled, squinting as if all his hatred for Rinehart would burn a hole in his eyes. "Add more people to the search."

"Yes, sir, I'll requisition another hundred people. That will bring us up to two hundred."

"Protector, finding these people is vital."

"Yes, sir."

"Vid-link off," Steinhoff snapped, seething with anger over Rinehart's family slipping through their fingers and for Kauffman releasing Rinehart. Regardless of whether Rinehart's brain had given up all it contained, they should have kept him imprisoned. The director should have allowed Beucher to wipe Rinehart's brain. Of course, Kauffman probably had

393

hopes of enticing the underground into attempting a rescue of Rinehart. If there was a way, Rinehart was going to die.

Chapter 23

Pain seeped from William's body. His legs and lower back felt like he had run nonstop for days and were now nothing but stretched rubber bands. It struck him that his suffering might have been an equitable price for what now awaited him. He mustered the energy and endured the pain with an inner smile, walking up the front steps of his own home. He turned the doorknob and found it unlocked. The unlocked door didn't entirely surprise him but he wondered about the fate of his family. He swung the door open, pausing with a particle of hope, hoping to see a loving face waiting for him. He listened for voices, the voices of his family, and stepped inside still listening for anything. No sound, no laughter, no crying, and no footsteps from happy feet. Then he remembered Beucher's taunting. They had escaped. His greatest desire, except for reading his dad's chronicle, had apparently materialized. Thank God for that.

Turning back to close the door, he caught sight of the black v-tran that had delivered him, now driving out of his housing area at the end of his street. Then, to his right and diagonal from his home, he saw another v-tran perched on the street ready to pounce. He pushed the door closed with a quivering hand and slowly returned his eyes to what remained of his home.

He slowly took in life's trivial components, the sofa, its pillows, the color of the wall, dust gathered on the living room table, and the kitchen in the distance. William's eyes told him this was home, but he couldn't hear his family. They weren't there. He was alone, horribly alone, but if they were safe, it would be adequate. He listened again. No sound from Stefan or Marie. Lynn wasn't coming towards him from the kitchen as she usually did. It wasn't home any longer. It was a hollow lifeless shell. He stood just inside the door. He smelled stale air, air that had been prisoner like him, closed off from life passing through it. The stillness tore at his heart. His home was gone, his life was gone, and so was his family. Had the underground saved them? His eyes filled with tears. He hoped with all his heart and soul they had found safety, even if he never saw them again.

He clasped his forehead in his hand and rubbed his skin, massaging down as deep as he could into the thin flash over his skull, reaching the source of his pain. He sighed as he began dispelling the pain's violation. The sofa retained only one cushion of three and the other two were on the floor. All three had spewed their white fuzzy guts through knife wounds. He dropped onto the cushionless area of the sofa, dropped his elbows on his knees and rested his head in his hands. He cried as a pall of hollowness draped over him. The despair pierced him to the bone, bleeding away his will to continue. Several minutes later, a flash of thought hit him like a sparked flame in his brain.

Time. What day was it? Time had stood still for him, left him disconnected from what he knew. He needed to check the date and the time. The only measure he had for time was one brainwashing session after another, like clock ticks toward mental oblivion. Right now, it looked like the middle of the afternoon. He pushed himself to get off the sofa, moving against his physical pain, moving against the pain in his heart, making his way to the kitchen and further through the violation of his life. The goons of the SAC had desecrated his home, his place of sanctuary, and his personal space precious for his freedom for thinking and breathing. But now he knew better than ever that it had never existed as sanctuary. It had always belonged to the SAC and they had controlled it. He had never provided anything for his family that—they, had not observed or allowed.

The product of their destruction lay everywhere almost as a symbol of his destroyed life and their ownership. From the articles strewn all over, broken dishes in the kitchen, drawers left open, and their contents on the floor, it was clear the SACI went through the house looking for more information, and they would no doubt come again for his brain.

It was as if his life was for nothing, as if he had wasted all his years trying to provide for Lynn and their kids. The parasitic government had sucked life. It used its people like hosts. He grabbed his mouth trying to hold back his crying. He had destroyed his family. Wait a minute. He rubbed his temple with his shaky hand. The SAC had sent him after his father, so he hadn't really destroyed his family. The SAC had done it, just like they had with his father. *Get a grip. My promise!* He had survived. He had to control his depression. It would hold him prisoner and he couldn't let that happen. He had to do something. He felt it, as if a wave welling up inside him, but he couldn't remember. How would he know if Lynn and the kids were safe? He sighed. *SAC loves us. SAC gives life.* Wait a minute. He had to clear his head. Beucher's torture was still twisting his thinking. *Damn those people!*

He sat down on a kitchen chair, breathing deeply and tiredly, rubbing his eyes, trying to remember why he had read his father's book, why he kept hearing the words, 'blank pages' in his brain over and over. Had his father told him that? Wait. *My head . . . still sluggish, still.* What had his father tried to explain? His father's book gave information about changes to the country, its history.

Sitting up, he glanced at the tabletop and realized Stefan's chess set was setting there, although the pieces were scattered across it and on the floor. Then he noticed a torn piece of Stefan's yellow school paper on the floor. Again a hollow feeling grew inside him as he envisioned his little boy, who wasn't so little any longer, although he could easily see in his mind an image of his boy and his daughter when they were small. They were precious images he loved, times when they were so innocent and learning how to play, and their amusing steps as they learned about their small world.

He reached down and picked up the yellow memory of his son. He turned it over and began reading. Was it for him? Was it possibly something the goons from the SACI had left behind? He read it aloud, "Dad, I found your old watch. My old pal Russell and I were playing together when I saw it under the sofa. I hope you can use it. Stefan." He smiled a little. What in the hell was that all about? It was strange for Stefan and he didn't remember a watch. The chess set and Stefan's note bothered him. If he had left it somewhere, the SACI surely would have taken it. The note seemed to be out of place and most curious, but he couldn't deal with trying to make sense of it now. His body craved food and real sleep, which he hadn't gotten for he didn't know how long. He was too tired to eat. And, he needed to get rid of the pain in his head, and added to that, his muscles were still killing him. Moving like a stream of vapor Beucher's voice kept coming and going in his head. He went into the bedroom, dropped onto the bed, and quickly fell asleep.

William woke from his sleep later in the evening, feeling the same tired and achy muscles. Even in his own home, he hadn't slept soundly. His nerves still sparked as if Beucher had sat there tripping them with his electrical stimuli. William seeing and hearing in his mind Hans opening the monolithic cell door. He lay there looking up at the dark ceiling, again feeling alone, and again hoping his family was safe. He reached over and touched Lynn's pillow. The odor of something floral, soft and sweet, floated to him. Part of her was on the pillow. Her wonderful perfume or her night cream was coming from it and it was heavenly. For a brief moment, her lingering essence warmed him, and then as he thought of missing her, a pall came over him, returning tears to his eyes. Numbness filled his brain for a moment, trying to consume him, and then he ran his hand across the place on her pillow where her head would lay night after night. She was wonderful. *They have to be safe.*

Thinking of his family and his hope for them washed away his daze. He wanted answers. He sat up on the edge of the bed, dropped his feet to the cold wood floor, and tried to muster energy to get up. Suddenly, his thought froze on what he had lost—his family, his life, and maybe his mind. Why he should bother going forward? What was he going to do? His head hung as if he couldn't support it any longer and he stared blankly at his feet, no words forming or flowing. He closed his eyes. Abruptly, light flashed before his eyes. He jerked his head back. He opened his eyes. The light washed across his vision again and he closed his eyes, trying to escape the torture. A strobe light flashed in his mind's eye interspersed with flashing images of Beucher's hideous face, images of Hans walking him down a hallway, images of the white chair, the black chair, and words, those hideous threatening words. The words began worming and slithering through his mind. His hands trembled as he sat nearly paralyzed. Eventually the visions stopped. He opened his eyes. His mouth was dry like it had been under Beucher's control. He didn't know how long he had sat on the edge of the bed, but it felt like half and an hour.

A black ant crawled into view, slowly making its way across the floor to some destination under the bed. He raised his bare foot to crush the invader but stopped. He wouldn't do it. He'd give it a chance. He thought of his father.

His father had given him a chance—and his mother. Didn't his father tell him things? Yes, yes, he had. His father had told him things to give him a chance. Chances are what fathers gave their children. He did it, too. Part of it was coming back to his brain, what his father had said. He remembered again, what his father had said on that mountain. Yes, his father had told him the reason why his father had left home, and he had told William about the chronicle—the blank pages. *Tell Beucher. If I don't, he'll put me in the black chair.*

William forced himself up, pushing through the lingering aches in his back and leg muscles, mentally willing himself to walk to the kitchen. It was horribly void of the lives he loved. He couldn't help thinking of his family filling the space—that the SACI had violated. The debris on the floor infuriated him. *Vid-cams. They are watching me.*

He would make coffee. God, coffee sounded good. He hoped there was still food in the house. "Soup," he said, his dry voice sounding foreign, almost like an intruder. He looked for a can of soup, and then looking past the pantry, the family calendar caught his eye. It made him realize he still didn't know the current date or how long the SACI had interrogated him. *I was going to check the date and forgot.*

Startled by a sound behind him, William spun around toward the living room. It erupted again. It was the horribly familiar hum of the vid-net coming to life, entering his home, surprising him and making his heart race. Someone had not turned off the vid-net unit. He walked to the living room, and discovered a new vid-net unit, one much bigger than they had before, and the SAC had mounted it on the wall where the old one had been. He looked around its approximate, three-foot by two-foot frame, and all around the room, and couldn't find anything to control it. There simply wasn't any way to shut it off. It was a perpetual connection to SAC's description of the world.

"Breaking announcement," a female voice began sternly. Simultaneously video of a mountain terrain speckled with moving soldiers and wheeled personnel carriers filled the screen. "News for November eighteen. Our brave forces have advanced against the AFPAK rebels sending them deep into the mountains. These rebels have obtained a nuclear weapon and have promised to destroy State America. SAC operatives have confirmed suspicious shipments reaching Mexico intended for transportation into our country. The military extends its thanks to all citizen-comrades for helping provide the necessary resources to our service people—who keep our homeland safe. The SAC extends his thanks to everyone and gives its reassurance that it will win the Afghanistan-Pakistan,

AFPAK, war at all costs and protect our citizen-comrades. To show our support, next Saturday at twelve noon, there will be a national rally. Every citizen-comrade is urged to attend the rally outside their local office of the DPP. Food coupons will be passed out to those attending. Chairman Durand will be making a special address to the nation." A picture of Chairman Durand filled the vid-net screen. "Long live, Father Durand," the voice added before the screen dissolved to a dead gray color.

William stood motionless, staring at the blank screen, until a click and hum came from the refrigerator in the kitchen as its compressor activated. The noise broke his trance. He rubbed his eyes. What was going on? The left side of his head, just above his left ear began aching with a dull pain. He grabbed his head and squeezed with both hands, feeling chilled. He took a sweater from the closet on his way back to the kitchen, nearly staggering, until he reached the sink, where he poured a glass of water down his dry throat. The water surprised him with how good it tasted, but the pain didn't fade. He sat the glass on the counter, noticing his palms were sweaty. He rubbed his hands together, not able to remember ever having sweaty palms before. What he had experienced seemed connected with a memory. Was he feeling the effect of Beucher's chairs or . . . did he have implant? If he had to guess, Beucher had screwed up his nervous system . . . but he was alive. He had to forget Beucher for now—or he might go mad.

He looked at the kitchen window. The hour had to be late, explaining the twilight. Quite some time had passed since he'd gotten back home, enough to allow him to start recuperating. He wondered if he would ever feel normal again. The clock on the nearby table told him it was 6:45 p.m. They would be just finishing dinner if it were a normal day. *My soup. That sounds so good. Where is it? The cabinet by the window?*

Several minutes later he had heated his soup in Lynn's tiny microwave, had started coffee brewing, and had taken his first taste of tomato soup in a long time. A month or two had passed since Lynn had fixed it with sandwiches for dinner. The soup sparked the inside of his mouth as if bringing it back to life. He raised the spoon to his mouth, thinking he had been given back life when his hand began trembling, spilling the soup. He arrested his shaking hand with his free and curiously steady left hand until the tremor disappeared. *They are animals!*

After three more slowly moved spoons of the tomato nectar, he noticed his headache had almost disappeared. The soup tasted so good. He consumed the soup quickly and then ladled more into his bowl at the stove. From the refrigerator he removed a piece of wheat bread which he then dunked in his soup and savored every bite. The emptiness in his stomach had improved. He poured a cup of coffee and sipped it at the table. The agility of his mind seemed to have improved, although he kept feeling compelled to apologize for something. He had the bizarre thought he needed to thank Beucher for the soup.

What was to become of him? The SACI had made his house a prison and a trap, and it would catch anyone who approached. Beucher had boasted he wasn't free just before the SACI goons came to take him down the hall toward a waiting v-tran. It clearly meant the house was under total surveillance, inside and out, complete observation, beyond anything they had used previously on his family—for years. *I'm sorry. I love Chairman Durand.*

He was apologizing. *Stop brain.* He laid the spoon down and rubbed his head. He looked around the room.

What was he going to do in the presence of all the vid-cams and new microphones, as if he were their bug in the jar? Could he fight the SACI in a game of wits and strategy? *They're probably going to kill me anyway, so they can go to hell!* He raised a spoon of soup and saw his hand shaking again. They did that to him. *I did it for Lynn, Stefan, and Marie.*

As he sat there in an absence of threats and pain coming daily, a voice tiptoed through his mind, telling him that he needed to do something. He couldn't remember what? It was like an itch, a nebulous itch that he needed to do something. There was a reason for him being alive . . . but he didn't believe in destiny. He took another spoonful of soup and gazed around the kitchen wondering about the people watching him. Perhaps he should wave and wish them a good evening.

A clear thought suddenly struck him. Perhaps he should maintain some appearance of mental deterioration. It might benefit him at some point, although he didn't know how or when. An implant could make him act off balance and with all the time he had spent under the SACI's control, there had been many opportunities for them to stick an implant in his head. It could be his excuse to act strange and nonthreatening. However, he must guard against Doctor Beucher's subconscious programming creeping into his decisions.

First things first. The date and time. He looked over at the calendar next to the refrigerator, the location there where Lynn had placed it year after year. The SACI had taken him on a Friday; he thought the twenty-first. Yeah . . . it was the twenty-first, and now it was the eighteenth of November. He had been gone four damn weeks—and he only clearly remembered three days. He remembered, Beucher told him he wasn't permitted to make marks under the sink in his cell. Beucher must have changed his marks to confuse him and they must have given him drugs. They must have.

Emptiness spilled into his brain, trying to swallow him again. He bit the end of his tongue to bring his mind back to the present. *Make the kids proud.* He had to go forward for his family for the memories he still had . . . before they took them away too. How curious and almost funny it was, his fortune of being alive with enough mental faculty to know he was lucky. All because of his father. He loved his father and mother and sister. His family had saved him. He realized his emotions were on a climbing and falling irrationally. *Use your brain.*

Why didn't Beucher keep him until Beucher had completely washed his brain? *Think.* He drifted off blankly as he gazed across the kitchen. *Quit!* He had to focus, to work his mind. The SACI thought they could get more information from him. They needed him. That was it. They needed him to have a brain so he could help and so they could believe him with some measure of confidence. Maybe they were also trying to catch someone from the underground, using him as bait.

It was all so curious, his father's life and now his, and how parallel they'd become, except his father had been strong from the start, while he had been soft, acquiescing to the poisonous vine slowly strangling everyone, closing his eyes to the truth. He wanted to do more for his Lynn, his Stefan, and his Marie, before the SAC took his life, and they surely would—when he was no longer of value. *Dad was tough.*

Gossamer threads of memory came together about his father and the items his father had given him. He had made a promise. The promise connected with blank pages. He sat motionless, staring across the table, hearing only the dull hum of the compressor in the refrigerator and a faint tick of the kitchen clock. He sat like a marble statue, trying to think, trying to repair connections in his mind about his last days at home. He sipped his coffee.

The night he came home from the mountain had been the beginning. He started to slide the chair back to get up, and then hesitated. *Wait you fool.* Fear of the always-present watchers brought him back to his senses, stopping him. *Don't show them you're recovering.*

With devious purpose, he moved his head wildly, rolling his eyes as if he were mentally impaired. He stopped and dropped his head toward the table, letting it sag. As he did, another spark of memory returned to him. It was Lynn's signal. Wait a minute. Something else. The blank pages were his father's chronicle. He had to read it, if it was still in the house.

Mindful of the watching vid-cams, trying not to be obvious with his interest, he rose from his chair, rolling his eyes wildly, and staggered over and opened the cupboard. He shook his head as if he were coming out a seizure. He reached for a glass, taking note of their arrangement. Lynn had placed one open-end down on top of a plate, and one open-end up on the plate. One was to be down if she was in trouble. It had to be a signal that she didn't know. Beucher mentioned the spa. She may have been confused. Maybe she didn't know if it would be trouble or not. He ran a glass of water, holding it with both hands, sipping it while he moved his head irregularly. He began thinking of his next step.

He sat his glass down and began opening the cabinets. He ran his hands over the cabinet doors feeling the surface. He took down a plate. He cocked his head to the side, continuing his mental charade. He stepped to the drawer where he remembered placing his father's legacy. Judging from the guts of his home the SACI had strewn all about the floor, he was hesitant to look for the pages, hesitant to have his hope dashed. He figured the SACI had searched the drawer in the kitchen and probably emptied it. Virtually holding his breath, he pulled open the drawer. His eyes groped for a familiar shape in the random mess. The SACI had destroyed Lynn's neat arrangement. Then he saw it sticking out from under a disarray of small pieces of paper, pencils, and writing pads. He couldn't believe his eyes. *Don't let them know.* Her cookbook was still there. He lifted it from the drawer, keeping his back to the sink, thinking that was the likely position for any SACI vid-cam. He shook his head as if bothered by a fly. "Cake," he groaned. He slowly flipped the pages to the back of the binder. There were the chronicle pages, innocuously blank, sleeping peacefully where he had placed them, waiting to be brought to life. *Leave them in the cookbook.* "No cake," he mumbled. Now he had another problem.

How could he read them without the vid-cams betraying him? Not possible in the open. If he read them, discovered some fantastic secret information vital to the SAC, and the SACI suddenly scooped him up for Beucher's horror chamber, they would learn what his father had protected. William stood there not moving, frozen by anguish, searching his brain for a logical solution to the problem. In his gut, it seemed there was a clock ticking away on his freedom. He had no real way of knowing his remaining time on earth, but if he did anything, it should be sooner rather than later, which meant, he simply had to risk reading his father's chronicle.

William turned toward the sink as if exploring for something to cook. He frowned for the vid-cam audience. In addition to finding a way to read the pages, his first conundrum was finding a way to make the writing visible. In addition, there were two or three hundred pages, not exactly a trivial problem. The only place offering a small amount of concealment and heat to activate the invisible writing was the electric oven. If he could insert them while baking something, perhaps he could make the writing visible.

"I need something else to eat," William muttered, thinking of a potato, and heating the pages. "I haven't had a baked potato for a long time."

With his intention declared for the SACI watchers, he faced a new dilemma. Where could he go to read the pages once he brought them to life?

Chapter 24

Lynn Rinehart sat in a room carved in mountain rock, reading an old romance novel with a tattered paper cover. When Claudia had offered Lynn the book she had flinched, jerking her hand back, thinking of the SAC rule about prohibited, socially corruptive literature, but then Claudia reminded her they were free of the SAC. The paperback, originally published in the late 1980s, according to the book liner, reached a point in its plot that opened tender and tortured thoughts of William, but despite those thoughts the book helped her pass the time. When Lynn read that the main character in the book, a self-made wealthy woman, discovered her recent love was sharing his love with another woman, Lynn closed the book on her lap and gazed around the room, thinking of her love for William. She thought he'd like her mountain accommodations.

From the first moment she had stepped foot into the room, Lynn had found it quite amazing and surprisingly homey with its rough stone, painted walls, and wood furniture. But as she thought of being safe in the cozy room she visualized William in the horrible brainwashing room.

The ghastly thought that she would never see William again haunted Lynn. The way the SACI worked and the torture she'd seen made her hope fragile like a porcelain rose. She wondered if people would ever rise up if they had seen the same brutality that she had seen. That was silly. The SAC controlled everything. If anyone attempted such a thing, the SACI would kill them, ship them off to a labor camp, or drive them insane. The only medicine that helped remove those troubling visions of her William was her children. They helped her climb a mountain of grief. William had tried to save her and the children, and now she had to soldier forward alone with that campaign. She could do it. There was no other choice. *What is William doing at this minute?*

If only she could get some news. She hated being a pest and a burden on those who had saved her and her children, who had brought them to the safety of the old mine in the mountain, but her soul cried out for information about William.

She glanced to see if her children were keeping busy. "Stefan, please finish that page of math before doing your reading, and Marie, I want you to finish reading that chapter we started," Lynn said. "Your education depends on both of you wanting to learn and me helping you. I'm going to go talk with Claudia for a few minutes. Okay?"

"Yeah," Stefan muttered, not looking up.

Marie looked up at Lynn with a quick glance. "Okay, Mom."

Outside their room, Lynn walked along the tunnel, finding herself taking in the rock formations, as she had several times since she had been there, finding the shaft an incredible engineering accomplishment, the creation of a dry hallway through stone, well over eight feet high, and buried safe somewhere inside the Allegany Mountains. Regardless of feeling safe, she still missed the sunlight. She knew she would miss twiddling with the few flowers she planted each spring in her little backyard. Even now, in the beginning of winter, she would have been walking around the house during the day, something William had jokingly described as her inspection of her miniature empire.

Down the shaft twenty yards, in a room apparently dedicated to administration and planning, judging from the charts on the wall and the tables, Lynn found Claudia, Dirk, and three other men to whom she had been introduced, but whose names she'd already forgotten.

Lynn knocked on the doorframe, the outside of the framework used to border the opening in the rock. "May I come in for a minute?" Lynn asked hesitantly in a low voice as she dipped her head apologetically.

"Certainly," Claudia replied with a quick smile. "Come in, come in."

Lynn started to turn toward the door. "I'm sorry . . . if this is a bad time I can . . . I can come back."

"No, no," Claudia replied, waving the fingers of one hand, gesturing for her to come in.

"I'm sorry for asking again, but has there been any word on my husband?" Lynn stepped over near the people who were looking at several pieces of paper spread out on a large table. She glanced at the paper and then quickly away, uncertain whether she was seeing something she shouldn't. "It's been about four weeks."

Claudia looked at her with sympathetic eyes. "Yes, it's been four weeks. We do have a little news. We're pretty certain he's back in your home now, but he's under very heavy surveillance, tighter than before, basically house arrest. While he was gone there was a lot of activity at your home, the con-techs were in an out as if they were having an old fashion house warming."

"Excuse me, but what is a con-tech?"

"Sorry, honey," Claudia began, "they are connect technicians. The people who install all the vid-cams, microphones, and such."

"Oh," Lynn began. She was afraid of the answer but she had to ask. "Do . . . do you think William's okay. I mean . . . in the head? They were torturing him. I saw it. It was horrible." Lynn heard desperation in her own voice but couldn't help it.

Claudia dropped her eyes as her brow wrinkled. She then looked at Lynn. "Honey, we don't know his condition. We can only hope. You can't give up hope." Claudia patted Lynn on the shoulder.

"What about getting him out?"

"Our commander said it was way too risky to try anything except a radio connection. Well, not exactly radio, a type of radio. We can't use ordinary radio."

Lynn frowned. "What do you mean?"

Claudia turned and waved an open hand to a short, round-faced man with button-brown eyes, wearing a dirty white shirt and rolled up sleeves. "This is, Sterling Masters, one of our technical people . . . I should say scientist. Sterling, can you please tell her about the communications . . . the special radio effort."

"I'd be glad to. Okay, Mrs. Rinehart, this is a little complicated, but here goes. We are going to use one of the newest methods of communication to get in touch with your husband. We call it, quickie. Actually it's spelled, QEQIE, which stands for quantum entanglement qubit information exchange. It's communication on a quantum level, uh . . . like on the atomic scale but smaller and stranger."

Lynn's mouth gaped. "What on earth?"

"It's something the SAC people are probably more than ten years away from developing . . . maybe twenty," Sterling added with a prideful grin. "Luckily, we saved a few top scientists from Stanford, Caltech, MIT, and Livermore Labs, such people as Zeilinger and Tiefenbacher, who have worked for years in one of our labs hidden out west. With this technology, the SACI will never detect a signal, let alone resolve any message. They're still using electromagnetic or optical direct-connection principles, which are like beating on drums in a jungle compared to our stuff. They may have their brain scanning tricks, all their drone aircraft, and their network of vid-cams, but they don't have what we have."

Claudia started to grin and stopped. "Thank you, Sterling, you don't have to explain any further."

"What's going on in here," said a man with a rumbling low voice.

Lynn turned around as the other people with her faced the door. A tall man stood just inside the door, dressed wearing what Lynn thought were military clothes, striking an authoritarian military posture, his eyes vibrant with energy. His wrinkled face, close-cut brushed-over hair, and the manner in which his focus touched each person as he worked his attention around the group, told Lynn he was someone special. His khaki colored shirt held no metals and gave no indication of rank, but she was certain he looked like a military officer, and one of high rank. At his waist, the man wore a military web belt with a sidearm in a holster. The belt buckle appeared to be the only indication of military association. In a moment he was motionless it glimmered in a bit of light; she could just make out a

413

shiny brass square with an eagle above a globe. Despite the dress and strong posture, she could see the man, who had mostly gray hair, was approaching his senior years.

Claudia stepped over to the man and shook hands with him, beaming widely. "Lynn, this is Harlan Wilcox, Marine three-star general. General Wilcox, this is Lynn Rinehart, William's wife."

"Oh yes, I know who she is," Wilcox replied with a slight squint and gave a warm smile as he extended his hand. He lowered his head slightly, nodding with a barely perceptible movement as if showing appreciation.

They shook hands and Lynn sensed his eyes sympathetically touching hers. The general's wrinkled hand, spotted, and enormous, captured hers with surprising strength.

Wilcox looked at Lynn somberly. "We appreciate your sacrifice and we share your pain every minute your William is in enemy captivity. And by the way, I'm no longer a three-star. I'm just one of the soldiers."

"Thank you, sir," Lynn said, her eyes glistening with tears. "Excuse me, but you were once a real general?"

Wilcox smiled a little, wrinkling the corners of his eyes, bringing to life in the lines composing his facial canvas, the years and burdens he'd experienced. "Yes, Mrs. Rinehart, I was once a full general with the Marines of this country at the time Durand took over the military. When the bastard fired my boss, four-star Jeff Marshal, the Joint Chief, I resigned and tried to work under the radar screen. I could see the shit was hitting the fan. Excuse my language ma'am. "

"General, was the country always the way it is now?" Lynn asked, her tone soft and heavy.

"Heavens no, we were free to do anything," he replied. He looked off as if seeing a ghost in his mind. "It's ironic that it was our very precious freedom of choice that became the weapon used to build the country's prison of control. We had freedom of the press. It became so tainted by its naive belief in a mother-government that it removed itself from a critical responsibility—that of freedom's guardian. When the holocaust struck, Durand imprisoned the people of the press right along with everyone else. And perhaps some of the press received the worst treatment because the SAC recognized the invisible potential damage they could exercise."

"General, let me know how I can help get my William back from those SAC bastards."

Wilcox nodded and put his arm around her shoulder, hugging her for a moment, and then he looked around the room. "I see Sterling's helping. Brilliant man. We have great hope for communicating with William and finding an escape for him. By the way, did William ever tell you anything his father shared with him?"

"I'm sorry, but I think he was trying to protect me and the kids by keeping us out of the trouble. If we didn't know anything, there was a chance we wouldn't be bothered. He hid some writings by his father."

"We know about those. Thanks for letting me check. By the way the SACI would have tortured you and your children—even if you were innocent." He looked at his watch. "I have to run, but I'll be kept informed on every step and I'll help wherever I can." Wilcox walked out and joined two military-uniformed men in the shaft outside. They spoke briefly and walked down the hall.

Claudia laid her hand softly on Lynn's shoulder. "Lynn, one of our agents placed a watch in your bedroom at your home, and when the time is right, we'll signal William. The watch is a transceiver using QUQIE."

"Oh, so he'll be able to communicate back—if he can get away from the vid-cams."

"Precisely," Claudia replied, sounding cautious.

"One more question, if I may."

"Sure."

Lynn took a big breath. "Why did you risk so much in getting me and the kids to safety?"

"I see you're pretty logical," Claudia said. A little grin formed. She swallowed hard and then her eyes filled with tears. "You are a human worth saving." Claudia took Lynn's hand. "Besides, we can use more helpers, and your husband can help our cause. Perhaps a colder reason would be that we wanted to keep you out of the evil hands of the SAC. If we have you, then the SACI can't grab you and torture you in front of William's eyes, making him say something the brainwashing may have missed. It's a long shot but a possibility . . . and he may have vital information for our freedom cause."

"Thank you for being honest," Lynn said plainly, nodding slightly and then she walked slowly out into the passageway, returning to her room.

"Lynn, are you all right?"

Lynn stopped, turning to see Claudia coming after her. "I have to be all right. I don't have a choice."

"I hate to see you so depressed. You must know that we all care about you and the kids. You are part of our family, the freedom family." Claudia took Lynn's hand, looking sadly into her eyes.

Lynn hugged Claudia, doing it quickly, so she wouldn't break down crying. "You know, you're my new friend. I don't have any others."

"We are all your friends now, but I hope you and I can be friends for a long time."

Lynn backed away a little, glanced at the floor and back at Claudia. "You know that stuff you told me when we were escaping, the stuff about the labor camps. I had never heard that before. If William had ever heard that, he must have decided not to scare me by telling me. Was that really the truth?"

"It was . . . but I only told you part of the story. Only a few people have escaped to tell us their story of the labor camps. That's how we know. Once arrested, prisoners are interrogated under horrible conditions. They are kept in rooms so small they cannot lie down and the light is never turned off. They make prisoners kneel on their knees for hours while their SACI judgment administrator demands a confession with the promise of leniency. From the interrogation center, the SAC loads hundreds of prisoners into special railcars. In the summer, prisoners going south die from the heat. If you're a female and you look nice they will use you for pleasure. If a woman refuses she will likely die. Camps are places for SAC free labor.

"My God, what horror," Lynn said, her eyes glistening with tears.

Chapter 25

William stood against the kitchen counter, trying to analyze how he could convert blank chronicle pages into a journal of visible words. A dull ache and then a squeezing sensation struck his head, disrupting his attempt to focus his thoughts. Jittering images, fragments from Beucher's room flashed in his mind. He stood motionless until the episode passed. A moment later he gathered a deep breath, thankful the pain had left him so quickly. He was curious if it was part of a recurring pattern of torment.

He pushed his ailment to the distance as best as he could and thought about converting the invisible writing on the pages to observable writing. Using an iron for clothes or using the oven appeared his only options. The oven would provide the fastest method for the bulk heat processing of the pages. It also provided a way of avoiding the spying SACI eyes.

He opened the drawer, removing the cookbook, leaning close to the counter, trying to block the view of any vid-cam. He bent over slightly and slid the blank pages under his sweater. "Maybe I'll have a baked potato," he mumbled, closing the cookbook. He moved over to the refrigerator, took out two potatoes, noticing they felt too mushy for cooking and eating. From a lower cabinet he removed a cookie sheet. At the oven, he bent over, removed the pages from his shirt, and held them under the cookie sheet and out of sight. He placed the cookie sheet on the oven shelf, and maneuvered the pages onto the top of the tray. He placed the potatoes on the oven self to the side of the tray. *I have to keep the heat down to be safe.* He set the heat as low as he could, laughing under his breath, thinking the rotten potatoes would bake into a horrible mess. After removing the potatoes, he planned he would complain in front of the vid-cams that they were rotten.

Fearing the possibility of the paper overheating even at the lowest setting, William crouched in front of the oven. After five minutes, he opened the oven door, eagerly looking for writing on the blank pages. Not seeing anything, he closed the door and waited for three minutes. Again, he looked in the oven. Dark marks had appeared on some areas of the top page. He continued peering into the partially open oven until at last, the writing on the top page was completely visible. He couldn't believe that he was finally going to read his father's chronicle. His father's secret. The SAC and underground both hungered feverishly for the information contained on the pages, as if it possessed the secret of the ages. The SAC clawed for it because they feared people might learn about the country before the SAC had imprisoned all the people, mentally and physically, although the director's persistence about military connections raised another possibility. As for the underground, their interest was perhaps a little more nebulous, however its potential contribution to the historical record would be valuable to them since its author was one of their early soldiers.

He stuffed the pages under his sweater before moving the potatoes from the rack to the cookie tray. He closed the oven, placed the pan on the counter, and poked a fork into one of the potatoes.

"Not done. Dammit, they're rotten. To hell with it." He hit his fist on the counter, wondering about his acting. *Now, where am I going to read the chronicle?*

Total concealment from a vid-cam was problematic at best, but that's what he had to invent. How could he create total darkness, something that infrared spies might detect but would block his activity? Suddenly, an old memory connected to the filament of his thought, taking him back to his childhood. Without saying more about food for the benefit of the hidden observers, he went to the linen closet, removed two blankets, and took them to the bedroom. He studied the light as he placed them on his bed, adding to the blankets already there. He stood beside the bed, assessing the light, considering how dark he could make the room. At the moment, only the light from the hall illuminated bedroom, but if he shut the door he could make the room black and fine for reading—if he read under the blankets. He kicked the door closed and found he had nearly total darkness. With the room dark, he quickly removed the chronicle pages from his sweater and placed them under the blanket to wait for his hunger eyes and mind.

Back in the kitchen, he felt new energy from knowing he was finally going to bed to read his father's description of what his country had once been. He fought back his amusement as he considered an image of a grown man reading under a blanket with a torch. He hoped he had enough batteries to keep a torch burning long enough to allow him to read under the blanket, all night if needed. For the challenge ahead he would need a good jolt of coffee, as insurance he would stay awake.

He found the instant coffee, made a large cup, and fought his anxiety to gulp it down. The taste of his coffee was grossly inferior to the coffee he had in the conference room during his inquisition. He guessed the coffee Lynn had bought was the same chemical soup he drank at work, which was rumored a synthetic concoction of malt mixed with caffeine. Since the SAC didn't trade outside the country, they didn't import coffee, although he had heard of efforts to grow coffee somewhere in Texas. The conference room coffee was real, and if he were to guess, the SAC had procured it from the black-market smuggling gangs in Mexico.

William took his coffee into the empty living room and sat in his favorite chair, sipping the coffee as he glanced around the room, thinking of his family, missing their talking, missing their little squabbles, and missing their opinions on what was going on around them, and maybe most of all—he missed their happy voices. Damn, he missed them. His gut told him that Russell had fulfilled the agreement. The hollow feeling resurging inside made him want to pound his fist down on a table, a wall, or the arm of the sofa, but he had to maintain his deception of imbalance. He had to fight the depression almost as if he were still connected to Beucher's machine. He may have been alone, but it was proper now—since he had declared war against the SAC.

Just then, on the wall opposite where he sat, the vid-screen flickered in concert crackling emerging from its speaker.

"Important announcement," a man said in a mechanical sonorous tone. "Negotiations have broken down with Iran and Pakistan on the prohibition of biological agents for armed conflict. Chairman Durand has ordered the expanded production of anti-viral and anti-bacterial serums, as well as other preventive medicines, enough for every citizen to receive a nasal inoculation of each. He has also ordered an upgrade of all our early warning scanning systems. Volunteers are being encouraged to help with our effort in the AFPAK military theater of conflict. New enlistees will be given an additional year's coupons, which have no time limit and can be used by their family."

A black and white picture of Durand filled the screen, the camera angle of the photograph shooting upward, accentuating his stern jaw. "This is Chairman Durand and I am very proud of the citizen-comrades of State America. We all should look forward to a time of peace and tranquility in the very near future. In the meantime we must be steadfast with our war effort."

The picture on the screen changed to one of Durand standing in front of a government building with the SA flag waving in the background and Durand staring off into a distant sunset.

A woman's voice broke from the speakers. "Long live, Father Durand."

William found the voice a lie with its unemotional tone and quite incongruous with the visionary image on the screen.

The screen went blank and thankfully silent as far as William was concerned. He stared at the blank screen, thinking how sick he was of the SAC bulletins. The SAC violated his life again, the private space in which he breathed and existed. He set his coffee down and went to the vid-screen, looking for a power cord, lifting the screen out from the wall enough to peer behind it for its electrical connection. A big cord emerged from the wall and went into the back of the vid-screen. He pushed his arm as far as he could behind the screen, trying to grab the wire. The attachment bracket holding the screen to the wall broke away from back of the vid-net unit, allowing extra wire to uncoil from the wall as the whole screen tumbled on the corner of a small table. The corner of the table pierced the display screen, taking its horrid life. William stood back breathing heavily, looking at it hanging lifelessly by its umbilical wire running from the wall. Instead of his habitual fear, he felt a sense of satisfaction for exacting revenge upon those who had parasitically sucked upon his life.

"Aw . . . damn, now I won't have any vid-net," William groaned, as he silently laughed to himself. "I'm tired. I'm going to bed." He suspected someone knew he had broken the screen but he was far from caring. He rubbed a sudden ache in his forehead as he went to the kitchen. It was then, in the kitchen, something coalesced in his brain, the announcement of nasal injections for the citizens. Had the SAC made a phony excuse so it could implant a large portion of the population with their control devices? He laughed at himself and his newly activated suspicious mind.

He stopped. Why had he gone to the kitchen? He stood there pushing his brain, cursing his apparent loss of short-term memory. Something for bed. The torch. Where was it stored? He had a distant feeble memory of placing the torch somewhere, but the recall was foggy. One of the kitchen drawers stuck in his mind. The second drawer he pulled open held the family's emergency torch and four batteries. He wrapped them in a towel before turning away from the counter and flipping off the light.

At the bedroom, with the all the lights off in the rest of the house, he felt good about the level of darkness in the bedroom and the prevention of any vid-cam snooping. He closed the bedroom door, flipped off the light, and began probing his way to the bed. Nervous excitement played with his breathing, something he hadn't experienced in years. He took off his clothes, leaving only his shorts on, crawled into bed, pulled the covers up over his head, and began organizing himself, preparing to read by the light of the torch like a sneaking twelve-year-old child.

The only way the SACI could detect him was with installed infrared cams, and even then, the blankets would provide an insulating layer spreading the heat. The torch and papers wouldn't give off much heat, which he hoped would confound any infrared.

Something popped into his thinking connected with the SACI seeing him. Beucher had said they knew he was reading in his bathroom, which could mean only one thing. Obviously, they had been looking through the walls with some sort of infrared or radar system. He didn't know if radar could do such a thing. With the bed aligned parallel to the front of the house and the road outside, he figured he'd turn on his side, making certain he directed his back toward the front of the house, using his body to block an image of the torch and the papers.

Now under the covers, William turned on the torch and directed it at the wrinkled pages containing his father's chronicle. He was thankful for another chance to get to know his father. He had no doubt his father had poured his heart and soul into his writing. Not only were his father's thoughts important to feed his own soul, he desperately hungered feed his mind the causes of destruction of the country, hungered to know what happened to his father, and hungered to know his father's big secret. After twenty some years, why was his father such a severe threat to the SAC, and apparently so valuable to the underground?

As he turned to get comfortable, he smelled Lynn. It was her pillow, pulling on his heart, bringing an image of her to his mind. He took a deep breath. He wanted to reach out and touch her . . . to embrace her. He wanted to feel her lying beside him. *For you, honey.*

He turned back to his father's pages. As he looked at them for the first time, he realized they were slightly smaller than the old eight by eleven inch paper, and his father had written the text by hand. His father had completed the writing with extraordinary precision, straight and neat, with no sign of an elderly person's shaky hand.

Again, he felt an electric tingle as he read the title at the top of the first page. The significance of what he had in his possession immediately struck him. On the pages, his father had written an account of the past, valued history that the SAC hadn't cleansed. The value of the pages of history made their preservation paramount by any means possible. He had to hide them for Russell. He began reading.

Chronicle of a Disappearing Country

To the reader of this chronicle, I attest I have set down the events as accurately as I can remember, and that I make no apology for my opinions. On the contrary, it is because of the absence of vociferously expressed commonsense opinions, a lack of education, and the lack of courage by the people of this country, that this country has been plunged into such a tragic state. It is long past the time for the people to get up off their asses and take back their freedom. All who read this should know this self-evident truth. After you give them your freedoms, they'll take your soul. And they have done it quite well. This chronicle covers the precursor events, the elements of the early journey which is still underway, the destination of which is up to those with, not only the means and fortitude to stand up and fight, but the integrity. Years before Adrian Durand slithered into office, the currency of the United States of America displayed the words, "In God We Trust." Apparently God is trusting in us to help fight to reclaim our freedom.

The reader may ask how I'm qualified to write this history. The simple answer is I lived through it and I was employed as an attorney in the Department of Justice during many of the years I will discuss. My purpose is to provide a record for the future, a record that no one has revised for the political safety of those in power. My purpose is to provide a warning, if it isn't too late, and if it is, this will have to be an obituary.

In the following pages, I devote many words to the period of roughly 2008 through the year 2020, as this was the catalyst for dire changes taking place in the years that followed. These weren't solely the years of liberals fighting conservatives, they were the days when both philosophies lost sight of their purpose—the country and freedom. These were the years when the people gave away their freedoms cheaply and then lost their souls.

The 2008 United States national election was a milestone in our downward spiral, a spiral seemingly filled with record setting variations of political filth. Political greed, lies, and corruption spelled death for the country, and culpable in this travesty was a once free press. In addition, the bourgeoisie and proletariat, the country's populace, surrendered and submitted to a moral virus that deceit and corruption composed an acceptable behavior for leaders in pursuit and performance of their public office, even to the extent that complicity and responsibility for deaths could be overlooked as if no longer part of the perceptible world. I have no shame in hoping that the representatives of the people, those who were responsible for the country's demise, ultimately went to hell or eventually will go there. The source of corruption of legislator's souls and those of the presidential cabinet seems to have been some black mystical force. It is something unseen that swallows government legislators when they are bestowed with the hopes and unbridled trust of their constituents, and take *their seats faraway in the anonymity-bestowing distance of Washington. They suddenly believe they are above all laws, free to ignore the Constitution, free to change it, free to pass legislation to the detriment of the country, free to ignore a responsibility to protect the republic, and free to disregard their responsibility as custodians of the country's financial future. This lack of moral fiber must surely be scribed on their ledgers, which await a final reading when they meet their maker for judgment. And one simple question begs the cosmos for an answer. What right does any legislator have to change our country from a constitutional republic to one of communism or socialism?*

As a matter of background, the reader should know the definition of a variable doctrine politician. It is an NFP member, a person and party holding ambivalent views that are, shall we say, based on a self-centered benefit, and not necessarily bound to any lofty principle or ethic. Their party was once the National Progressives Party, which they later named the National Freedom Party or NFP. The conservatives were the CLP, the Constitution Libertarian Party.

Leading up to the 2008 election, during the last months of a CLP president, Benjamin Warner, the NFP played a devil's opus on the heartstrings of the ill-informed, the uneducated, the poor, minorities, and the complacent American voter, promising to solve all the country's problems, if only they were given the freedom to act as they deemed necessary. Compounding their sin, the NFP took advantage of the young forming minds of children in grade schools, spreading their propaganda as if God handed it down in person, the hope being that the children would influence their parents.

To understand better the dynamics at play, we should scrutinize a picture of the electorate of the nation during this period. A large percentage of the people were so ignorant that they couldn't identify the vital issues facing the nation or the candidates for which they were blindly voting. They were only interested in thirty-second sound bites on the radio or television (vid-net type technology), which spooned the twisted facts of political-pudding into their lazy brains. Colleges and universities, predominately infestations of communists and socialists, pounded students with fanciful easy solutions and enslaving ideas, and these young people spread the poison further by voting to give away freedom. The older generations, factory workers and professional people were too busy to seek in-depth information from multiple sources of political opinions to perform an objective analysis, and consequently they fell in line with the mindless masses.

During 2005 and 2006, the CLP held a slight majority in the House of Representatives and they had become bloated from feeding on government power, just as their predecessors, and sadly, their successors. The political climate in the country, with the help of the liberal-bias information media, began shifting from conservative principles to an evangelical NFP point of view, a vision called the progressive view. However, there wasn't anything progressive about it. Some said it was a national socialistic view (equal sharing of wealth.) In their propaganda they claimed the CLP had caused all the country's problems by allowing capitalism to operate too liberally on free market fundamentals, and that more controls were needed. They did their best to create bitterness between the rich, middle class, and poor, purposely forgetting the way companies operate and that the average, and sometimes the poor person who is eager for a better life, were the people who essentially formed small companies. People had forgotten the lesson learned in Russia when it experimented with socialistic collective ownership and a classless state. A vast portion of the American electorate couldn't extend their mental power to visualize what a social system would be like if everyone was a worker and workers were paid by need and not accomplishment. They never bothered to ask who would be the executive at the top giving directions for such a country. Likely, another despot would fill the void born out of people without courage and intellect.

As an aside, I'd like to point out that even the educated voter faced an uphill battle in acquiring competency on all the candidates and their backgrounds. The primary impediment to this discovery process was a failure by a large portion of the national broadcast news press, which were those organizations utilizing television. The failure came in the form of orchestrated bias on behalf of the NFP candidates. Any coverage on non-NFP candidates was always negative while the NFP always got positive articles, and this pertained to looking into their backgrounds to determine their fitness for the office. Ironically, the press supported people moving the country toward National Socialism, which ultimately would control everything the press presented to the public. It was strange, the press supporting change that would cause the demise of their own small world.

As campaigns moved forward in time, the NFP provided only vague specifics about their proposed remedies. The questioning observers were scalded by various emotion-inflaming labels, such as being insensitive, being obstructionists, being unpatriotic, being part of the problem, being for the rich and not the poor, being racist, and of being members of a radical movement organized by the CLP. This was clearly an effort to stifle freedom of speech. Protecting our own sovereignty, our borders, and saving our capitalism became the crying violin of the CLP minority and conservatives in the country. The NFP lied to the people to get votes, knowing that after the people elected them they would have carte blanche to do something totally opposite to their campaign promise. They could deny having made the promise in the first place. It was the election dance, the 'old lust for power' two-step.

The country's politics were heavily influenced by socialists with extraordinary personal fortunes and with voting fraud (ignored by the press.) These socialists funded misinformation campaigns on the broadcast media and the Internet, making certain the public mainly heard their story and their candidate's accusations against the CLP candidates. The NFP used clandestine maneuvers such as breaking campaign donations into small pieces, circumventing the funding regulations, having their minions contribute untraceable amounts of money using one-time credit cards, using money laundered from foreign contributors, using phony community groups, having people turn in fraudulent absentee ballots, and by registering voters who didn't exist. The NFP's massive amount of campaign money allowed them to acquire more and more control, as if setting up a chessboard so pieces could tactically strike. To protect their plan the NFP, in years prior, used their control in the House and Senate to confirm malleable judges in critical voting states. They also pressured the major television news and print media. As I eluded above, voter fraud was rampant, supported by local unions and supported by NFP judges who ruled on the validity of questionable absentee ballots. Every congressional and senatorial election turned into a confrontation between the NFP and CLP forces, armies of attorneys, everyone trying to muster the most votes, which would ultimately face the court of an NFP-purchased judge.

For the reader's background, I need to define voter fraud. Simply, it is an election vote made illegally. It occurred when people who were not valid to vote, voted. An invalid voter could have been a nonresident, one who had not registered, didn't have a valid identification (in some areas), or people who voted more than once. So, the game that the NFP played was diverse in the ways they submitted fraudulent votes, often simply accomplished by paying a poor person to vote multiple times for a sum of money. Despite the fact that voter fraud may have dated back to the country's beginning, 2008 brought it into monumental focus as it began to sway the election process.

In the 2008 election, the people of America gave total freedom to the NFP party by continuing their control of the Senate and House of Representatives. The NFP along with the new president promised wonderful government changes, promised improved national security, promised to save the people's retirement system, promised to provide low cost national healthcare, promised to form warm alliances with countries intent on eating us alive, and essentially promised to make the sun shine and the flowers grow. The most insidious promise they made was to equalize wealth across the population. I will explain why this was so bad later on.

Freedoms in America had been undergoing erosion in random areas for several years leading up to 2008, but it was drastically escalated and focused when the NFP candidate, Thomas Norman, won election as president of the United States. He was the first devout progressive socialist president in decades. He began quietly working in concert with the NFP-controlled houses of congress, issuing acidic executive orders, eating away at our freedoms, starting like a light snow that slowly blankets you with its somnolent hypnosis. Norman, promising to help the little guy, was largely unknown. People of power locked away his college records from Johnstown College and Dartmouth, and the press, because he was a liberal, had ignored them in its vetting process. Clearly, Norman utilized the psychological deception of big falsehoods; if a lie is big enough, anyone calling out the lie, faces the ridicule for being a fool. This applied to his credentials. The people ignorantly believed in the integrity of their elected representatives and in the utopian definition of hope, which the NFP whispered into voter's ears like a siren song. It was as if the word, hope, carried the magical power of Merlin from the King Arthur folklore. Little did the American people know or even fathom in their wildest nightmare they were initiating the precursor to the total destruction of the American way of life, removing restraints on one of the most vile political minds in the history of the world, save for Marx, Stalin, Hitler, Mao, and the man who turned every citizen into a slave, Adrian Durand. The country should have seen the handwriting on the wall when Thomas Norman filled his administration with unvetted staff who were infected with an assortment of unorthodox communist thinkers, radical semi-revolutionaries, and people seeking the destruction of our democratic republic. Right from the start, Norman's socialist-Marxist strategists began an incessant drumbeat, repeating the use of the same old villain, building a rhythm aimed at making the people focus its hatred on the wealthy and any group advocating keeping the government lean, efficient, maintaining minimal debt, and adhering to the Constitution. This theme connected well with their promise of making things better once the people gave Norman and the NFP more control. Norman and his NFP surreptitiously used their unchecked freedom to take the country in a catastrophic direction—and it will continue unless the people stand up and fight. It's nearly too late now! The clock is counting down to total and brutal slavery.

Dear reader, I know some of these facts can be tedious but please read on to learn more of the steps they used to fundamentally transform the country away from a constitutional republic.

William lifted is eyes, allowing them to reach into the blankness of the fabric covering the mattress, down into the threads woven one over the other. The reference to unchecked freedom triggered a connection. When he was a young boy, the world was small and his little portion was an island isolated from problems. He emptied waste paper and fed their dog . . . what was his name? . . . Charlie. Doing his chores was his ticket to freedom, exploring the woods, tinkering with an electric coil and train transformer, or carving trigs with his trusty pocketknife. What brought that memory back? He remembered going in the car to see grandma and her small farm. Beucher didn't kill that part of his brain. He found his father's words again.

During the election of 2008, I was taking a class in law school and doing a research paper on the nineteenth amendment. I spent some time at a polling station where citizens voted, my objective being merely to observe the voting process. A man walked in, looked at the sample ballot taped up on the wall, and marched over to the people responsible for monitoring voters.

He said, "Why is my name on the ballot under the CLP party?"

An elderly man pushed up his glasses and replied, "Because you filed as a candidate, I suppose." Then he grinned as if it was the silliest thing he'd heard.

He replied, "I never filed or registered as a candidate. In fact, I'm an independent, and not for either the CLP or the NFP. Someone has perpetrated a fraud to cost the CLP candidate votes so they'll lose the election."

I thought the trick was quite clever, but sick. I never heard if the authorities prosecuted anyone.

The use of money for buying favors is perhaps one of the dirtiest parts of the political process. The method used to repay large contributors is more of a window into the soul of the manipulator-in-chief. Upon taking office, President Norman pushed for infrastructure improvement funding to be sent to the states for repairing highways, bridges, and public facilities. Coincidentally these projects were largely dependent on union labor for completion, the same unions that had helped fund Norman's election machinery. So, through the work projects Norman paid for his votes with the public's money. This wasn't redistribution of wealth, it was corruption.

On the floor of the House of Representatives, the NFP claimed they could use the election mandate, the people's permission, to guarantee everyone would be living in harmony, everyone would live in total security, everyone would share the wealth equally, and they claimed the Constitution was a laughable document and no longer relevant. Furtively, the NFP began implementing their rulings using out-of-sight presidential cabinet czars, making new regulations that punished one business at the expense of another such as manipulating labor regulations in favor of unions and regulating where companies could expand their business. This repaid unions, gave them more control over workers, enslaving workers in a form of collective, abridging their right of self-determination, their right to control their own work value.

Like a thief in the night, they began stealthy steps to regulate radio and television programs that were carrying political content, setting down regulations on programs that carried political discussions such as complaints about administration policies. Working with their local organizations, which started during the campaign, the NFP declared the private news media had too much freedom to satisfy their listener's desires and such dangerous content needed to be controlled. They promised they could make all political broadcasts present arguments that were fairer and equal. One of his non-cabinet appointed administration people, a man with a communist organization connection worked at converting the private broadcast companies to public broadcasting, which meant the government and President Norman would soon control what they said. Norman used licensing to push broadcasters to his political viewpoint, and if the broadcaster refused the NFP content suggestions, Norman's people would reissue the company's broadcast license to someone more sympathetic to the NFP. He also would have the Internal Revenue System of the government perform an exhausting and costly investigation into their tax records. Norman and the NFP pushed a legislative bill named with the oxymoron, the Fairness Doctrine, which aimed to make broadcast's content less caustic to Norman and the NFP. There was nothing fair about it. The rumor crossing political tongues declared a non-cabinet man created the bill and the speculation identified it as Durand's brainchild.

They issued regulations to control any internet system functioning as an information channel, including social networks operating on the internet. The first thrust came at the mere postings on the internet and then later the monster swallowed everything. Their regulation stipulated what they allowed regarding disparaging comments about the Norman administration, claiming the need to watch for threats against the president. Their virus infection aimed at control and censorship. If they didn't like something—they could make certain only their opinion found its way to the people. This allowed the NFP to control and hide news of corruption, crimes, and removal of other freedoms in the future. This was the first major onslaught to control the flow of information exchange and dissent—to blunt the free speech part of the Constitution. The first amendment within the Bill of Rights in the Constitution stipulated that Congress shall make no law abridging freedom of speech. The public grumbled but under a barrage of the NFP's public propaganda announcements dispelling rumors of control, the weak-minded and lethargic public acquiesced. The public outcries from minority conservatives arguing vociferously against this freedom abridgement were ignored.

The act of the government shielding information from people gripped William for a moment, broadening his understanding, exposing further the poison of the despicable vid-net screen violating his home. It was the SAC's hypodermic for injecting a daily dose of mind-distorting toxin.

William read on about the country clamoring for change, the burdens of terrorist threats from Islamic extremists, the worries over climate change, and the people depending on intelligent solutions from snake-oil politicians who were only interested in enhancing their fortunes by preying on people's fears. More of the poison appeared to him as he read how Norman created regulations so friends could profit from restrictions on coal for electricity production and how, with his sleight of hand, he funneled millions in grants to former campaign contributors so they could form companies to develop uncompetitive solar panels and electric cars, companies that ultimately failed.

William quickly scanned over a discussion on immigration, people illegally entering the country from Mexico, which he learned had caused problems with governmental social systems, but won the NFP a sea of untapped voters—a headcount his father emphasized, that had helped the NFP acquire more control. His father's reasoning surprised him; once the NFP had a larger number of voting bodies they could push the CLP completely out of existence and usher in a single-party-government—a step toward total government control. It was another small tile to the mosaic of trends clawing at the country.

He kept seeing the word, control, over and over. It had to be part of his father's warning.

Reading on, William plowed through a section covering trouble with the labor force, unions and how the union collectivists, who were communists in disguise, had pushed for so much control and large wage concessions that American companies were no longer able to compete in the global market. As a result, they began manufacturing outside the country. Then his father's argument struck him. If Norman's government had allowed free enterprise, not including unions, to evolve naturally within global market forces, in-country manufacturing would have grown. His father hedged his argument with a comment that when the foreign countries manipulated their currency and subsidies they were creating unbalance in the natural economic system negating free enterprise. This cheating required stern reprisals for which legislators lacked the stomach.

William laughed to himself when his father wrote of the stealthy growth of unemployment and the resulting loss of homes by homeowners, and that it was like boiling a frog. Then he read how the NFP enhanced their control over the country in a different manner. They increased the worker's servitude to the NFP party by promoting forced arbitration on all contracts between unions and company owners. They used NFP populated review boards to manipulate proposed employee dismissals and to expand regulations making companies pay contributions to laid off worker's unemployment benefits.

The chronicle pages seemed to bring William to a halt for a moment as his father backtracked to explain a nasty recession taking place in the middle of 2008. His reason for discussing it, William learned, was to show how the NFP's ravenous hunger for votes from the electorate caused massive financial collapse. It seemed, in the NFP's insatiable desire for more power, they pursued legislation promoting rules to allow people to obtain home loans for which they weren't qualified and could barely afford. The power-hunger NFP pursued this expansion under the pretext of the progressive nanny state, the government's obligation to help everyone get a home, as if it were a right dictated by the Constitution. Their attempt to acquire more political power and control, combined with the recession, caused a massive investment securities failure. Numerous CLP members, who were part of the minority in the House Financial Services Committee, asked for a tightening of the loan qualifications. In front of cameras, the sycophantic congressional representatives wagged their fingers and pompously blustered away regulation attempts at control. As a result home sales soared and the greedy jumped into the government sponsored feed trough. Prices soared. Home mortgages became the golden goose as an investment security.

Ultimately, when home prices fell because of unemployed workers, the investment packages of mortgage securities sank in value like a rocket falling out of the sky. Banks holding large portfolios of these bundled securities needed billions and billions of dollars to cover their losses, which they didn't have. All hell broke loose—the most severe recession since the Great Depression. And it was caused by people greedy for votes, power, and control.

William thought of the boiling frog and how he had been that frog and the SAC had been the fire under him, slowly cooking his brain.

Continuing with comments on the 2008 recession, his father referenced the press, which had been nonexistent in William's world going back to before he started college. But as William read on, it seemed he hadn't missed much. During the inquisition on the financial collapse, the broadcast media, internet press, and printed newspapers, exercised blatant and gross bias, and failed to pull back the curtain of deception to expose those of the NFP who had caused the failure. Instead, they only shined the spotlight on members of the CLP, and the CLP president, Benjamin

Warner, who was just leaving the Whitehouse at the beginning of the financial collapse. William paused at his father's comment.

I beg the reader to bear with me through these very subtle abuses of our economic and political system. Trust me it gets worse.

William pulled his eyes from the chronicle, letting them fall despondently on the bed sheet as if in an unfocused daze. The corner of Lynn's pillow tugged at his heart. In his memory, he saw her hair splashed in waves across it as she slept. He saw her head turned toward him, smiling warmly. He felt a quiver in his chest and looked away. His eyes yielded painful tears onto his cheeks. He took in a long breath. He had to stick to the purpose, he told himself.

Thinking again about the chronicle, he affirmed that only a short time ago he would have laughed at such a story, would have considered it purely wrong-thinking, considered it a product of the ethereal underground, and considered it treason against the SAC. He laughed silently, sourly, vengefully. During the early years of his tenure with the SAC, he had looked at Durand as a savior who had helped to form a country after the years of President Norman. Now his father's words were wiping away the SAC propaganda fog. It was as if his father's words were implanting a new reality into his memory.

He looked at his torch and checked his blanket for shielding against any leakage of light. His head ached a little, high up above his brow, but he wasn't about to stop reading. He knew Beucher's torture caused it and most likely, he had an implant in his head causing it. And if there was an electronic device inside his head it could kill him at any time. He had no time to waste. He returned to the chronicle determined to learn his father's secret.

Thomas Norman's soldiers, his cabinet, and his front men, figured heavily in his plan. He enlisted into his administration some of the most radical Marxist, campaign and platform strategists of the time, and without a question one of the most audacious and dangerous of this staff was a twenty-eight year old Harvard graduate of government theory, Adrian Durand. Who in the country could have predicted that political madness would come on the pale horse of total NFP control of the House, Senate, and presidency? And it was bestowed by a populous longing for the gossamer-nation, shining brightly high on a hill. The NFP's massive control gave them an insatiable zeal to broaden the government's influence over the nation's illiterate and incapable populace. It also set the country irretrievably down the path to national socialism mixed with Marxism, however they seemed inclined to leave room at the top of their classless society for a ruling group, which no doubt included them. Norman and the NFP embraced nihilism to the extreme, unabashedly doing as they pleased.

For the reader who has no reference to the past, I must clarify the meaning of fascism, Marxism, communism, and socialism, at least to the best of my memory. At the time of this upheaval, fascists believed that culture is created by the collective nation and its state, and that cultural ideas are what give individuals identity, and thus they reject individualism. A fascist believed a nation is a collective community and shuns pluralism as destructive to society. The totalitarian state is accepted as a means to represent the nation in its entirety. The Marxist wanted productive capabilities in the possession of the collective, to facilitate removal of materialization from life, and in so doing form a classless society and eliminating inequality between humankind. Communism is a combination of a revolutionary and socialist movement aimed at creating a classless, moneyless, and stateless social order. This order is based upon common ownership of assets to produce goods, as well as a social, political and economic ideology that aims at the establishment of this social order. According to Marxist theory, communism comes after socialism, which is considered merely a transitional phase. Socialism took as its heart the idea of a social organization producing and distributing goods owned collectively or by a centralized government that plans and controls its economy. There are obvious perils associated with all these. One case in point is the National Socialism under Hitler that caused the demise of Germany in the 1940s.

Therefore, dear reader you should see a glimmer of structure forming like brushstrokes to an artist's canvas, building from unrecognizable splotches of the NFP paint into a picture of imprisonment under the SAC. Perhaps you are still confused about why you should read on or why you should care. The answer is in the most wonderful words we have, liberty, freedom, and choice. These words are the white angels given to us to destroy the darkness of oppression and to save society for future greatness. It's ironic that those same words, when not valued, causes the creation of the dark angels of human suffering.

His father's words were sliding into nearly virgin areas of his brain, attaching to thoughts and feelings he had had over his years with the SAC. The words were like food and air into his lungs.

Moving on, it only took a few months after the 2008 election before the public began to witness and read about changes the NFP and Norman were instituting, and when the public began asking questions about the alterations, asking about the massive spending allegedly to solve the recession, asking about the new taxes, expressing concern regarding the planned massive increases in the national debt, expressing concern regarding the communistic backgrounds of the people working in the Norman administration, the NFP and the president screamed in horror that they were being unfairly attacked. The Norman administration and the NFP labeled the people asking questions unpatriotic radicals. Some analysts began to see Durand's National Socialism fingerprints on Norman's policy.

Reading on, the description of protest marches surprised William, as if it were a sparkle of sunlight through the clouds. He found it remarkable that people freely and openly shouted angrily against the encroachment of the government into people's lives and complained it wasn't responding to the people's wishes.

The disturbances popped up around the body of the country like festering sores. To deflect the fire of examination, the Norman administration and the NFP accused gray-haired sixty, seventy, and eighty-year-olds attending rallies of being right-wing radicals and a threat to the country. The public cried out that Norman was breaking a promise not to increase taxes on the middle class. It proved he had talked out of two sides of his mouth— and that he had been lying from the time he began campaigning.

One day I was sitting in a coffee shop, while I was studying law at Georgetown University, when two of my fellow students came in and began discussing the new taxes Norman was legislating and the massive debt. The ensuing discussion became carved into the stone of my memory.

I was with Angelo Conti and Luke Backus. I said something like, "I don't understand why you can't see how Norman's destroying the country's credit rating with his massive debt. He's projected to add one trillion eight hundred billion to the debt in just one year."

"He promises that he'll improve the economy," claimed Angelo.

Luke stared at Angelo and me. "You heard he is only allowing his favorite news reporters at his news conferences, didn't you? Do you know what that will do?"

I replied, "It will coerce those who want the privilege to keep reporting to avoid making any disparaging comments about him. Their news organizations will overlook anything negative about his administration."

"They wouldn't do that," Angelo said.

"If our press fails to use an objective eye, he will be free to make changes outside the review of the House and Senate—and the public," Luke replied.

Angelo laughed. "That won't happen. He's promised total transparency for his administration. He's going to tell us everything he's going to do. He's going to post it on the internet, too."

"Where did you get that?" Luke snapped.

"It was on a campaign pamphlet."

Luke frowned at both of us. "Have you done any other reading?"

"Didn't need to."

Luke stared sternly at me and then gave humorless laugh. I can still see that laugh if I close my eyes—because it scared me. "So Angelo," I said, "how are we going to reduce the nation debt?"

He grinned at me as if I didn't have any brain. "We don't have to worry about it. It's not real. It's funny money."

Again, William marveled at his father's description of the unprecedented power bestowed upon the NFP by the gullible and illiterate electorate, and how the NFP began their plan, fundamentally moving the country toward wealth redistribution, one of the steps toward a classless society. He said it was like four angels of death swooping down to consume the country. The first angel was the bogus economic stimulus legislation, the second was the budget and job destructive national healthcare legislation, the third came in the form of the tax-laden carbon fuel environmental legislation, and the fourth came as relaxed regulations on qualifying for welfare. These formed the American economic apocalypse. The NFP and Norman marched the four evil horsemen toward a goal of building and increasing every citizen's dependence on their government control.

William read on voraciously.

The NFP surreptitiously enlisted help outside the government from national socialists, union operatives, and communist elite in crafting the massive legislative spending bill. The spending also served to repay election supporters. The NFP legislators acted with impunity as if the people's taxes were in their personal piggybank—and the people weren't to question them. Promulgating at every opportunity, they cited fear of a growing recession, demanding urgent support for passing stimulus legislation for jobs. They increased the taxes on families who made over one hundred fifty thousand dollars income. This was their effort at generating class hatred and their attempt at creating an inequality of wealth in the country. Despite many people understanding the need for a wealthy person to generate jobs so those with less could pull themselves up, the argument struck a sympathetic nerve with the non-thinkers. What legislation the NFP produced was an incomprehensible pile of paper littered with pustules of kickbacks and special favors. Chief among these were grants to so-called alternative energy companies started by campaign contributors. The NFP- led House and Senate forced the parasitic bill forward, stealthily passing it in the late hours of the night, out of sight of the public.

Again his father mentioned the media, that the printed news, newspapers, and broadcast news, which were decades earlier the watchdogs of democracy—willfully abdicated their responsibility covering the stimulus bill in favor of their own political philosophy, choosing not to expose the excesses of phony budgets targeted toward fraudulent projects, projects sponsored by the NFP's election campaign contributors. William had never imagined how important a news reporting function could be to maintaining an ethical government.

Then he read his father's description of the healthcare angel of death, the angel riding on a black horse. His father echoed the loss of freedom, that information emerged slowly about the legislation, and that it contained hidden within its thousand shadows, dark mechanisms stealing a person's control of their own medical treatment and records. In addition, the healthcare program was a poisonous national socialistic system. It required every person to enroll in the national healthcare system. It destroyed constitutional freedoms, such as taking away choice, taking away self-determination, and reducing the privacy of personal information. It made one group of people to pay money to offset the costs incurred by another group. Private insurance companies evaporated with the stroke of a pen, sentenced to either fold or focus on other forms of insurance. The legislation violated of the Constitution by making it mandatory for a citizen to buy a service, and to beat that argument the NFP and Norman had the Supreme Court declared it a tax. With it stipulated as a tax, the government could force people to buy health insurance, even if the people didn't want it. Secondly, it gnawed at religious liberty by requiring church affiliated hospitals and treatment centers to carry out activities in opposition to their religious beliefs. The people who couldn't afford to pay became part of the NFP sphere of influence as the government gave those people subsidies for their payments. This unfunded liability added to the national debt. William had to pause at the comment that the healthcare legislation started a downward movement in the nation's credit rating, which placed the nation in financial peril with a looming debt of trillions.

The uninformed public sang the song that the NFP had implanted into their recently washed brains, a song that said the CLP wanted was to protect the rich. The mindless public missed the inescapable fact that they were losing another piece of control of their own lives, surrendering to become part of a collective that would take the product one person's brain and sweat, and give it to a person unmotivated to—or unable to exert similar life-negotiation skills. The people didn't see the calculus, the impossibility that the NFP couldn't lower medical insurance costs when more people would need government assistance under the plan, in essence the government paying for their care. The angel-of-death-legislation gave the government control of everyone's medical information, people who might need treatment for a given malady, and at what age. It was like facing the dark angel. Strangely, after the healthcare became law, the president and the NFP, gave government subsidies to an ever expanding list of special groups, such as House, Senate, Supreme Court, and union members, which seemed to violate the equal protection clause of the fourteenth amendment of the Constitution. The liberals cried that the insurance companies had caused the need for the socialistic healthcare because they kept raising prices, but they ignored the fact that a company tries to make a profit for its stock holders and that they only averaged three and a half percent in 2009 and later they occasionally got above six percent.

Another harbinger of death appeared, the grand stimulus, supposedly applied to stimulate the economy. He found it incredulous that after the stimulus was enacted, the recession continued unabated along with the massive unemployment. As the USA became more national-socialistic or perhaps Marxist-socialistic, his father described, the governments across the ocean in Europe reaped the whirlwind of their own failed socialistic controls.

The first country to taste the bitter fruit of unbridled socialism was Greece, defaulting on its sovereign debt, needing massive money injection from other countries of the European Economic Union. Greece was flushed down the socialistic sewer by a wave of poisonous actions, such as special benefits to unions, early retirements, and the reduction of work hours. Spain defaulted on its debt and Italy followed, causing massive panic in the European stock markets and the bleeding of the International Monetary Fund. It also caused France and Germany to approach China for support instead of the U.S., slapping President Norman in the face for causing such massive debt. It was a world-power slap in the face for Norman. They were indicating the once world economic leader, the US, couldn't help them—as the United States had for decades in the past.

William started release a satiric laugh and remembered he had to be silent in the dark as well as invisible. He was slowly seeing the thread his father was forming. He read on.

As the recession grew, the government gleefully took over banks and investment companies, supposedly to help the flow of credit and to prevent the collapse of banks holding debt securities with plummeting values. Many of these companies held billions of dollars in the grossly devalued packages of mortgages. They also restructured automotive companies by taking over their debt—abridging the bankruptcy law. The first level bond holders, the people entitled by law to get their money back first, were threatened by the government if they didn't acquiesce to taking pennies on the dollar. With the complicity of the Congress a legislative bill was passed which allowed the president, without any congressional oversight or study, to take over any financial institution he deemed a potential problem for the country, and this included banks. Of course, this opened the door for dictatorial powers and the potential for the president to influence how these companies were operated. All he had to do was cast a disappointed eye in their direction and he could change their business decisions, such as how much cash liquidity they should maintain. The government promised to extricate itself from these economic spider webs as soon as possible, but it didn't happen. Norman's involvement in the web of banks and security financing was surreptitiously pursued largely for the sake of unions, so the unions wouldn't lose their retirement funds, so the unions would continue their political support. In effect, the administration paid the unions for helping get it elected, but the unions didn't know they were dealing with a snake that would turn its head and bite them.

A voice in William's head cried out for understanding the stupidity of the populace that allowed such actions.

Norman continued implementing his (and possibly Durand's) Marxist-socialistic changes, forming a new office to make the country depend more on the government for all forms of energy, trying to eliminate private industry from providing cost-effective energy solutions, axing the coal industry, instituting another of the dark angels of the economic apocalypse, the carbon tax. William smiled at the SAC-like trick, the NFP using a furtive regulation associated with the environment to make all companies pay a tax to use hydrocarbon fuels such as coal, natural gas, or oil. No one knew who got the collected hydrocarbon fuels tax money, which was routed through a circuitous brokering system structured to effectively make money from nothing, tantamount to charging for the use of air. Businesses closed because of this carbon consumption tax. Norman, having earlier purchased leases on western lands through the front company, Sayfe Solar, now directed government grants to the embryonic energy company, Sayfe Solar. Unemployment increased. Norman blamed the economy on Warner's presidency.

The miniature tiles kept forming the mosaic for Norman's takeover of the country, but what about Durand? Norman lied about saving jobs and unemployment dropping, even counter to numbers published by the Bureau of Labor Statistics. William had to laugh to himself again at his father's exposition, that Norman's government had its nose up capitalism's ass so far they could see through the eyeballs. What he read next brought tears.

Thomas Jefferson said, "A government big enough to give you everything you want, is strong enough to take everything you have." The event Jefferson warned about was taking place with the Norman presidency. The reader of this chronicle might ask why we should lament the death of capitalism. The answer is a simple one. Capitalism is freedom! Capitalism is the freedom to create something without the fear the product of your brain will be stolen by the government, the freedom to take one's product and sell it for profit, the freedom of an individual to own property, or a person's freedom to sell their own home. The

447

freedom of selling one's home facilitates the freedom of relocation, of independence, and encouragement for creative people. A person who can own property, will in most cases, acquire pride. The person, who owns a home, owns a space where they are free from government eyes, and in that space, they can think free thoughts. The fourth amendment to the United States Constitution helped to secure a person's private space from unreasonable searches and seizures. It helped to create personal sanctuary.

William felt his father was summarizing a list from a criminal indictment, how the NFPs pushed for spending on welfare and government-provided subsistence for the unemployed and low income people—becoming another of the four horseman—and aimed at building government dependency and future voters. It was a furtive method of moving money from one group of people to another. At the same time the government created discontent, envy, and hatred between the economic classes, between the whites, blacks, Latinos, Asians, virtually any minority— and they created an excuse for the term social injustice, feeding the need for their programs. They blamed the inequities and the social injustice on the wealthy, rather than criticizing an individual's failings, an individual's life choices, or the government smothering the individual with burdensome rules.

His father's reference to Lincoln surprised him.

The NFP marshaled toward obtaining more voters than the CLP so the CLP would have to go out of existence. Sadly, as they carried out their plan, they basically told the people at the lower economic level to forget aspirations, told them they couldn't make it on their own, told them don't bother trying, told them the 'system' was stacked against them, told them to trust in the NFP government. If only the people had recalled words of our famous leaders. One of them once said, "You cannot help the poor by destroying the rich. You cannot strengthen the weak by weakening the strong." Abraham Lincoln said,

"You cannot bring about prosperity by discouraging thrift. You cannot lift the wage earner up by pulling the wage payer down. You cannot further the brotherhood of man by inciting class hatred. You cannot build character and courage by taking away people's initiative and independence. You cannot help people permanently by doing for them, what they could and should do for themselves." It seems some teachings are never too old and are never heeded.

In concert with Norman, unethical power-hungry millionaires, unconcerned about the freedom of the average citizen, pulled the democratic process through a cesspool. For more understanding on the factions participating in the democratic process, I'd like to digress a little.

Many decades ago and as far back as the founding fathers, the people who supported the political and economic positions stressing the rights and freedoms of the individual, as well as the need to limit the powers of government, were labeled as liberals. In the early development of the country—limiting the power of the government was a key ambition. This goes back to Thomas Jefferson. That philosophy was mutilated through evolution. In 2008 and 2009, the dominate viewpoint preached by disciples of National Socialism to the population was that the government should provide more protection for jobs, equal wealth, housing, medical care, and retirement. The idealistic non-critical thinking youth and people with social guilt readily accepted the idea, and they didn't bother considering the magnitude or form of the cost. It was as if the utopian change proselytized by NFP politicians had transformed into a type of religion. A thorough analysis of the potential negative effects was nearly impossible, but later, after people stood back and looked at the medley long enough, the hidden pattern and malefic purpose became visible. The NFP indirectly promulgated the philosophy that the individual citizen had to serve the needs of the government.

Seemingly, in a demonstration gesture to their world audience, the NFP initiated a downward slid in our military spending, which resulted in our defensive readiness sliding

449

dangerously into mediocrity. One of my friends thought this was Norman's first move to initiate his own secret police unit.

The words secret police grabbed hold of William, connected him with his own DPP.

The mysterious deaths sprouted like weeds. The first case involved inspectors general within the first two hundred days of Norman's administration. Two of them were involved with monitoring budget allocations, and after indictments were rumored, authorities found one the men, who worked for the Justice Department, at the side of the road in his car dead. The medical examiner's report listed traces of a strange substance in his blood, but ruled it a heart attack.

William quit reading, needing to rest his eyes and rest his head, which still ached on and off as if Beucher had connected it to a clock. He shut down his light, pulled back the covers, before rolling onto his back and looking up into the dark of the room. What he was doing suddenly struck him as funny, his comical procedure, lying under the covers with a torch and reading. He had done it when he was a kid. He laughed with a strangled whisper. He wasn't much more than a kid when he started with the SAC. The work he did when he first started at the SAC seemed very benign and he couldn't remember professing any political philosophy at the time, although the SAC demanded loyalty to the idea of the protective Father State. It was strange how things had slipped over him like some sort of mist, quiet, dark like the room now, but deadly. He had brainwashed himself into becoming a national socialist, wanting to serve the State and help those who couldn't survive on their own. Probably unlike most of those employed by the SAC, he actually felt sorry for some of the people. But that was where danger lurked for the philosophically, no, the politically immature. By acquiescing to the premise that the government needed to care for people, that it should control everything, and that it should acquire and then distribute the country's bountiful gifts to the people—he had helped open the door for the State to control him. Without checks and balances one man or a group of men can take a country down a path of lunacy and destruction. The SAC had given him a little car and a condominium where his family was safe, making him a slave to the gifts. Now he knew the SACI had spied upon them, and they probably never had any privacy. *So that's the price of national socialism, the loss of privacy—and freedom.*

He rubbed his forehead a little, pushing his thumb into his temple, feeling the skin give way until he felt the bone. He rubbed the area. *What are Lynn and the kids doing? I have to learn dad's secret.*

Time was moving on. Like a mole burrowing back into the ground, William covered his head and picked up reading where he left off.

He quickly covered several more factors. The illegal immigrant inconvenience became another cut into the constitutional flesh. Under the camouflage of humanitarian concern and sympathy for people who knowingly broke a nation's sovereignty, the NFP manipulated a crisis into an opportunity for acquiring more uncritical voters and control. By embracing amnesty with total disregard of the nation's existing laws, they passed an onerous piece of legislation again in the cloak of night, thereby acquiring the loyalty and votes of millions of illegal aliens, who with the stroke of a pen became full citizens eligible for government handouts. The bill, sponsored by the NFP, ignored the fact that ten million illegals broke the immigration law. This was another brick taken from the foundation holding up a civilized society, not the immigration law, but the fact that it was any law and the government was arbitrarily disregarding it.

Following the reference to the Norman administration selectively enforcing laws, his father included a special note, understandable for a constitutional scholar.

At this point, reader, I think it appropriate that I cite one of my favorite historians, Paul Johnson, who wrote in his book about the American people. He said, "Next to religion, the concept of the rule of law was the biggest single force creating the political civilization of the colonies. This was something they shared with all Englishmen. The law was not just necessary—essential to any society—it was noble. What happened in courts and assembles on weekdays was the secular equivalent of what happened in church on Sundays." Obviously, Norman and the NFP cared not for any lofty philosophy.

The NFP allowed the illegal immigrants to stay in the country and bring their extended families, creating additional unfunded cost to social services in many states, the financial burden adding to the national debt, and adding millions on top of massive national unemployment. It was like a mugger sticking the knife in the nation and twisting it to steal money. These new citizens didn't know the cost they would have to pay, particularly after Durand closed the borders stopping the new residents from visiting their old homes.

Curiously, neither the media nor the NFP gave mention to border crossers belonging to Islamic terrorist groups, people such as members of Al Qaeda, Hezbollah, or Taliban who tried to establish underground cells.

An additional hardship awaited the new struggling, hard-working immigrants. The NFP had a trick up their sleeve. They passed legislation to have all the immigrants get a picture ID with a fingerprint. Subsequently, in elections, the NFP kept count of their votes and when it didn't correspond to the number of immigrant votes they forecast, immigrants were threatened. Fearing the people who had opened the crossing gates would throw them out of the country, the immigrants spoke out very little. The NFP-controlled Justice

Department superficially investigated immigrant allegations, never coming to any conclusion.

William paused. He wondered if the SAC was still fighting the Al Qaeda and Taliban in the AFPAK war. In those final flashing minutes, his father had only brushed against the facts to bring him understanding, and now they were pouring forth. In those final minutes, how could his father tell him all the facets making up the disintegration of a democratic republic? It was so subtle the way the control crept over the people. He had to make himself concentrate with the focus of a microscope on his father's every sentence but he was glad. It was like looking at the individual grains of sand making up a beach. On he went.

President Norman's view of addressing the terrorists groups, such as the ones mentioned above, who were slipping into the country through our sieve-borders, was confused naiveté at best—at least at first. Norman saw Sharia law as a competing despotic system and as an alternative corrupt philosophy needing eradication. He didn't want any opposition to his goals.

Somewhere about the time I got out of Georgetown University, a discussion broke out in one of my classes on the legal ramifications of Sharia law in the midst of our "constitutional" framework. One student posed a couple questions that drew harsh declarations.

Winston, a chunky guy with thick glasses, disheveled long hair, and an easy grin asked, "As a matter of curiosity, what would a law student obedient to Sharia say if they were accused of plagiarism, clearly a form of stealing, and clearly punishable according to the brutal Sharia dictates. And how would a state attorney general view a case of a woman being buried up to her waist and stoned?"

Our professor chimed in, "Those questions are moot because Norman's strategy person, Adrian Durand, will not allow Norman to accept Sharia law in the smallest pocket of the country, and that's it! Case closed. Durand is going to be president one day and then we'll have a bright shining country. Wait and see."

William held back a muscular contraction in his throat that could have released a scream of pain and disgust. He read on, fighting the disgust for the country's failure. He read of the deaths of Latino immigrants after the 2010 mid-term election. It was a story of horror. The report documented several people lost their lives allegedly because the people didn't vote. A team of mysterious unidentified men packed the non-voters onto alleged government planes carrying out their deportation to Nicaragua. However, the local law enforcement authorities found bodies of some of the missing deported legal immigrants and missing family members, when they floated ashore near Galveston, Texas. The Department of Justice never investigated the case.

World events popped into his father's writing.

The Middle Eastern immigrants, who were part of the mandatory ID policy, became more of a growing problem for President Norman. A large Muslim population had inundated Belgium, a large part of France, and Denmark, causing changes in each country's socialism-friendly laws by substituting Sharia law. In the countries experiencing a massive influx of Muslims, Muslims took out their frustrations on non-Muslims in an escalation of street beatings. Christians, Jews, and moderate Muslims fled these countries because of religious persecution by the intolerant radical Muslims. President Norman began deporting all Muslims who were not US citizens and all he could find operating training camps scattered throughout the country. Under Norman's divergent philosophy, NFP made it illegal for Muslims to bring distant family members to the US once a member of the Muslim family had become a citizen. In Philadelphia, the police returned gunfire after Muslim snipers in buildings shot at them. A gun battle occurred in downtown New York with Muslims connected to an Islamic Jihad group out of Yemen, a group trying to build a mosque very near the World Trade Center Memorial. A protester who made an off color remark about the Muslim patriarch was shot by someone in the crowd. In the cacophony that followed the construction site was breached, two Islamic Imams were beaten near death, and several glass containers containing PCBs (polychlorinated biphenyl, a nasty chemical) and other biological waste were scattered around the construction site. No one was prosecuted.

I had bad feelings about the abridgement of the civil rights.

Norman attacked another of our freedoms, that of religion. He used his favorite tool, an executive order, which again bypassed caustic discussions with the CLP in the House of Representatives (a fruitless gesture since the CLP was the minority). He issued an executive order placing all religious buildings under the environmental control of the EPA, its regulations for carbon dioxide, making the buildings subject to the related taxes on carbon dioxide production. On the surface, Norman claimed the carbon dioxide regulations were behind his decision, but think-tank conservatives declared that Norman sought to diminish religion. Church congregations took up services in private homes—free of the government propaganda.

The NFP ripped more flesh from the constitutional body of the country by providing new power to unions, allowing unions to coerce and manipulate management decisions on company headcount, allowing unions to steal a person's private business. They facilitated this in a circuitous manner by passing legislation eliminating the use of a secret ballot by workers, which destroyed freedom of speech, the voting of one's conscience. As unions gained control of companies, private and publically owned, it became more common for the owners to sell their interests or merely to walk away from their life's work. Many of these companies that the unions took over, subsequently closed.

By now, the reader of the chronicle is probably wondering about the importance of this litany of graft and corruption, some of which may sound like trivia. The answer is simple. You want to know how your world was formed, and how the previous one, *although not without its faults, died prematurely. You want to know why your world is oppressive and totalitarian. All the subtle little steps, allegedly to protect the people— actually contributed to the slow erosion of freedoms. I apologize for my occasional rambling. I confess, although unembarrassed, that I have cried more than once as I have written this record about my once great country. Please have courage to read on.*

Continuing with their plan, the NFP began building public support for more of their speech controls. The NFP charged the CLP and other conservatives with inciting riots with hate speech. In the flurry of political rhetoric, allegedly infuriated liberals murdered two CLP members in Virginia. The FBI, working with the Virginia law enforcement, investigating political connections, and the possibilities that an individual perpetrated the crime, found one suspect. The FBI investigators gathered evidence circumstantially proving the NFP contracted with the murderer. They were still fussing with tangential investigations when I joined the Department of Justice, DOJ. Eventually the NFP contractor was arrested as the result of a plea deal by the murderer, but as the NFP member was being transferred from one holding facility to another, the FBI van plunged into a river, and coincidentally the hit man hired by the NFP never made it to his trial, falling victim to poison in his jail food.

Norman developed a deep fear and mistrust of people giving opinions counter to those of his administration. He had one of his czars issue a contract to a private security company to perform a study of opinions being expressed and speeches being made within various political action organizations. This happened around 2012. Investigators from the Department of Justice learned that one contract for one hundred million dollars was arranged with a shadowy organization. As part of the contract, a swarm of administration undercover agents spread across the country with the task of infiltrating and becoming members of public groups with the purpose of monitoring the speech and opinions. People who offended the sensibilities of the Norman administration felt its threatening financial wrath through the IRS, the government's tax collection department, or a special group within the Justice Department charged them with sedition. The infiltrators, the spies, known to the public as speech watchers, left in their path a terrible chill on free speech in the country. They exist to this day, lurking throughout the SAC country and functioning well on Durand's behalf.

How was all this revolutionary chaos allowed to take place without any sort of public outcry? The answer is simple. No one reported the truth in the news. Whitehouse operatives controlled the news media, killing all of the negative information related to Norman's administration and knowledge of Department of Justice investigations. The Whitehouse power brokers threatened to close their businesses if they didn't comply.

In the Senate, the NFP members pushed for the formation of a committee on what they called, facts and fairness, which was supposed to investigate violations identified by the FCC. Ultimately, the NFP took the people's freedom mandate for change to a result never before envisioned. Using a senate committee, they formulated the beginning elements of the current Department of Facts and Fairness, DFF. It functioned under the public's radar until it was officially formed in 2024, providing the NFP nearly total public censorship—and the capability to rewrite history. This was a major step in the destruction of the freedom of speech amendment to the Constitution.

Norman and the NFP instructed the Department of Homeland Security, now called Department of People Protection under the SAC, or commonly DPP, to track and catalog people associated with rightwing or conservative politics, people openly supporting CLP candidates. When the Norman government, via the Department of Homeland Security, began snooping into citizens exercising their conservative views, placing them on watch-lists as potential sources of insurrection, they violated the people's first amendment rights—as well as privacy. Heavily armed Homeland Security goon squads filtered across the country exercising unlawful search and seizure with phony warrants served on anyone writing negatively about the NFP and Norman.

It started early, William thought, the SAC-type control, spying, and treats. He ran a wishful finger across the lines of text, as if feeling his father's pain, and subconsciously knowing it was his own sorrow he was feeling from the horrible record.

With all the attacks on the country's constitution, the underhanded imposition of destructive laws and executive orders, you the reader might ask, where was the public outcry protesting these abuses? The answer is very simple. The public didn't see or hear information on them. The news media, in love with the Norman administration, became complicit by repeatedly minimizing any detrimental effect on the country's freedoms, especially under threat of losing their business. They failed to look objectively at Norman and the damage he inflicted upon the country.

I apologize, but I must backtrack a little in chronologically, but with good purpose. Since I'm writing this record as I remember the past, I find one event often triggers the recollection of something too important to omit, even though it may relate to activities previously discussed. That's the case with the following comments on a court case called, Magruder vs. State of Illinois.

William lifted his eyes from the paper, wondering how his father had kept track of all the bits and pieces of history over the years. He couldn't imagine himself using little notes tucked away somewhere for twenty years. William flashed on an image of playing with his own children on Christmas, playing a simple board game Lynn had fashioned from memory that required each player move an object down a path toward the prize. That was right. He remembered. The SAC discouraged the celebration of Christmas. He usually had to work on those days if they were during the week. The SAC also scared people from going to church by, interrupting services, listing those attending, and later interrogating the attendees.

However, he could remember other things the kids did when they were toddlers, things at which he and Lynn had marveled.

He turned off his torch, wondering again if the dull ache in his head was from an implant, although it didn't really matter. He was fortunate to be alive and able to read. He suddenly thought of his hate for the SAC for taking his father. The SAC needed to be destroyed. They were a disease slowly killing humanity. He realized just then he didn't have any trouble thinking that. Perhaps it indicated some of his conditioning had faded. He wished he felt better so he could read nonstop to the end, to his father's last word, to that reason for being sought by the SAC.

Chapter 26

Lynn woke to an echo filtering into her mountain room from somewhere down the tunnel outside her door. It was the middle of the night. She immediately thought it was probably the men working the nightshift, moving military equipment into storage areas or removing food supplies with a forklift, taking various provisions to the central kitchen for tomorrow's meals. The noise that had aroused her wasn't very loud, but it had found a crack in her awareness, which had been very delicate since the SACI had taken William and the underground had rescued her and the kids. She hadn't been sleeping very deeply even when she was tired. With her heart in such pain, the only thing that made her feel better was teaching Stefan and Marie, and playing with them.

In her sleep, she had been fighting through a nasty dream, trying to bring William's mind back from a deep paralyzing trance, some sort of stupor induced by the SACI brainwashing. She was in the same mind-locked state as William, seeing what he was seeing, yelling at him to wake up so they could go back home. It carried an eerie resemblance to a dream she had a few days ago, although it seemed a different chapter. It was equally depressing right down to the same dark figures controlling them.

Down deep in her heart, she felt William could stand up to the torture. She had seen his inner strength over the years, a subtle steady force that kept him working at the SAC even though he had whispered to her at night in bed that he hated every minute. Seeing his torture was the worst of all pains she had ever experienced, but she'd seen him fighting it. Nevertheless, the stories she had heard from two women in the food market parking lot, from women with whom she had formed a sort of bond, women who lived near her housing area, fed her tortured hope. At first, she had been wary, fearing they might be working for the SAC, but she could sense if a person was to be trusted, gazing into their eyes, looking for that special connection, listening to their voice, watching their body language. She was good at it, unlike William, and he never knew of her contact with these women. If he did, he would have worried like crazy and she didn't want him burdened with more worry, what with him struggling year after year, fighting the nasty Steinhoff man. It had been refreshing to talk with women and share her shopping troubles, although their conversations had to be short because of the vid-cams. Going to the market was no pleasure, searching for food to make decent meals, meals including some sort of real meat and real vegetables, the type of meals the SAC had declared should be eaten only once or twice a week . . . for the good of the country. That was totally ludicrous. They didn't have enough food supplies for the people, for the whole country.

One of the women she had exchanged greetings with regularly whispered a story to her while they were standing in an open area of the parking lot. It was about a man and wife, a story that made her cringe.

Supposedly, the SACI or the DPP, arrested couple and took them away, charging them with conspiring with the underground. A neighbor who wanted the couple's apartment turned them in, falsely accusing them. The woman telling the story swore she saw the man and woman after the SACI released them and she described them as acting as if brainwashing had taken their minds. Lynn couldn't see William that way in her mind. She told herself to see him as fully alert and alive.

Since the underground had rescued her and the children, and they were living away from home, and away from William, the hours burned like days, and the days disappeared like weeks. Even as her heart ached for him every day and she prayed every night for him to survive, she tried to put her mind on the children. She had to keep them moving forward with their studies. She didn't know how she would keep going, with the children opening the wound with their daily questions about their dad, wondering if he was okay or if he had escaped. And when word finally came that he had been released, their new questions drew more of her painful tears, tears from feeling their emptiness from missing him, and feeling their blind hope of seeing him walking down the tunnel any day. It was all too horribly brutal, wondering if she'd see him again, worrying what her children's lives would be like, and not knowing if they'd ever see true freedom. *William, I love you.*

Chapter 27

William looked blankly at the chronicle page for a moment, his eyes freezing, as if interrupted by his mind traveling on its own. A dull pressure held his head. Dark emptiness slowly crept over him. It was as if it were trying to suck the life-energy from him again. Where was he going? What was he going to do? He couldn't quit. His promise. He had to finish reading his father's words. He had to concentrate. He had to remember his dad's courage. He began reading the chronicle where he left off, trying to forget about the continuing ache in his head and heart.

My historical digression takes us back to the middle of 2009, and the case of Magruder vs. the State of Illinois, when the Norman government, with the aid of the NFP, made a change to the Supreme Court, bringing more destruction to the Constitution. The bleeding hearts pushed a law to make it illegal for a homeowner to protect their own life with force in their own home, as in the case of a robbery. The case of Magruder vs. the State of Illinois dealt with a burglar breaking into a home and killing three little girls. After killing the little girls, the burglar entered the parents' bedroom where the father shot the intruder dead. The lower court found the parent was within his rights to protect himself and his wife with the handgun he owned. The Illinois attorney general, an NFP member with lofty connections, pushed the case to the next level, where they obtained a negative opinion. The attorney general tried again and ultimately the Supreme Court took the case. The lower court was overturned by the Supreme Court, by a Supreme Court which was influenced by an NFP-placed justice, Justice Chester K. Creighton. The case was pivotal. With the reversal of the lower court's decision by the Supreme Court, the father was convicted and given a life sentence. However, the major result came elsewhere. This was a severe blow to the second amendment. It created a crack through which the NFP could begin removing weapons from the populace. Norman needed control of weapons so he could eliminate any revolutionary threat to his government and his program to remake America. Someone discovered later that the Illinois attorney general had connections with a national socialist organization, which received funding from a chief contributor to the Norman campaign.

Ramifications of the healthcare bill began to appear in 2011. As people peered through the cobwebs of the legislation and saw the government control permeating the legislation, it wasn't long before some states protested the mandated control by filing lawsuits, claiming it violated their state sovereignty, forcing them into massive debt. Of course, the poor of the Latino, black, and white communities swooned over the prospects for the promised free government healthcare, which wasn't completely free. As a means of monitoring and controlling costs in the system, councils were formed with the authority to assign treatment priorities for various types of illness, to control the flow of patients to the dwindling number of doctors, and to make judgments on who was considered to have a critical illness. In the beginning, the public called these councils death boards and because of a few incidents, they became secret. If you got a disease with a high mortality probability, the review council placed you at the bottom of the list for seeing a specialist physician for treatment. People who got cancer automatically fell to the bottom of the list and many died before they could move to the head of the line for treatment. Medical research and development fell on the shoulders of the government since the private pharmaceutical companies could no longer make a profit. The official name for the death boards was the Federal Coordinating Council for Comparative Effectiveness of Medical Treatment.

Eventually this new step toward the socialistic rapping of freedom caused problems with small businesses. They were required to provide minimal healthcare for people working thirty hours per week or more, or they had to pay fines. The unfair healthcare burden forced a small family bakery, in business for seventy-five years, to close for nonpayment. The Internal Revenue Service, IRS, badgered the owner so severely the father to committed suicide. The bereaved son, a man of forty-five, did the unspeakable. He configured an explosive in a cake and drove to the IRS determined to sacrifice himself by blowing up the building. The authorities stopped him a thousand yards from his target, but the blast wave blew out most of the windows above the first level, resulting in numerous injuries from glass, but only one fatality.

People believed this was the first resistance to despotism in America since the revolutionary war against England.

As this new war began, it was marked by more protesters with similar desperate circumstances, pushing them to the threshold of violence. Another of the initial terrible events was that of a distraught husband, trying to get treatment for his wife who had an infected cut on her foot. The medical treatment allocation council kept her pushed to the bottom of the appointment schedule for seeing a doctor, unaware and unconcerned her infection could continue to spread, which it did, the bacteria eating part of her leg and growing to the point it killed her. Grief stricken, the husband of thirty-five years, an electrical engineer at a government facility, went to the visitor's gallery of the Senate, where he sat quietly assembling the components of a chemical explosive. Apparently, he removed a detonator from a ballpoint pen, which he connected to his wristwatch, before throwing it from the balcony to explode down on the floor. A lady senator and a man, both belonging to a committee related to the treatment council were killed by the blast.

Almost a year later a similar disaster occurred. Another husband, an elderly man of seventy-five, whose wife the treatment council placed at the bottom of the treatment schedule for a pacemaker, watched his wife needlessly die. The man located the meeting

location for the treatment council from an underground information source. He waited in a
parking garage and when the members of the medical treatment council entered the garage,
he blew himself up with an estimated twenty pounds of Semtex plastic explosive wrapped
with glass marbles, glass orbs belonging to an antique collection. After the garage attack,
the government moved all meetings and gave members of the treatment councils twenty-four
hour bodyguards.

These examples of protest are important as an example of the failure of socialism in
terms of lives, humans who were treated like so much trash to be discarded. These are
sadly dwarfed by the human tragedy of today's SAC government.

President Norman pushed a second stimulus package, but the money wasn't truly
for his job stimulus package, it was for behavioral studies, which included research on
manipulating the behavior and beliefs of the population, officially benignly labeled as
population analysis. Under this program, the NFP and Norman set up a website for
good citizens to report bad people to the government. The Norman administration
encouraged citizens to report people guilty of disseminating damaging information about the
government on the internet, sending out information they deemed harmful to the positive
growth and attitude of the country.

William scanned the lines of text ahead and saw reference to
universities. He pondered what corrupted minds operated the school he
attended. His father talked about campuses being a battleground for the
concept of true freedom of thought, NFP members dominating faculties at
universities and colleges, controlling opinion, carrying out their
manipulation with scorn and punishment, punishing students holding views
affirming self-determination, chastising and flunking anyone asserting the
conservative views. Then a milestone event struck. A student at Virginia
Technical University, who spoke up in a discussion, espousing the virtues
expressed by Thomas Jefferson, was failed despite having perfect grades on

the objective tests. As William read it he smiled, that the student returned to class the next day, walked to the front of the class, repeated the words of Patrick Henry, pulled out a large caliber handgun and split open the instructor's head with one shot, splattering blood all over the chalkboard poetically washing away the instructor's bullet points on social justice. A voice deep in William's head cried out that violence was horrible. But what did the patriots have to do to break free of the tyranny of King George?

Reader, never underestimate the distorted mind as it will undoubtedly surprise you. This was the case with Norman as he found a creative way to increase surveillance and therefore, control. Allegedly, Mexican gangs, working with Islamic terrorists, crossed the southern border with plastic explosives, and blew up a section of the El Paso airport and a section of the San Diego airport, both at the same time. After it caused a public panic, the public begged for more security. Reacting to public cries, the NFP created the National Safety Surveillance Act, which caused the proliferation of cameras in almost all public places. The public didn't realize the political anarchists running the government would use the crisis to create a spying system of cameras so vast that their virus is spreading to this day. The unstoppable growing presence of the cameras destroyed the freedom of assembly, freedom of speech, and breached the search without warrant clause of the Fourth Amendment of the Bill of Rights.

Did the vid-cams start with that event? William asked himself. He could barely believe it.

Moving on, he covered his father's description of a massive unbalance that spread across the globe, the Taliban infiltrating the Pakistan military, taking possession of a 500-kiloton nuclear bomb that eventually fell into Al Qaeda's hands, the Iranians producing several plutonium nuclear bombs, and fights within the World Trade Organization over China's unrelenting currency manipulation and their supplying Iran with rocket materials.

A chill came over William. He suddenly felt as if Beucher would come into the bedroom at any second. A voice in his head cried, SAC loves us. SAC gives life. You're home now, he told himself. He desperately wanted the voice out of his head.

It was hard to grasp the immensely troubling events engulfing the period when his father was living at home and when William, himself, was growing up. He now understood the death spiral of the country and the reason his father had begged him to read the chronicle. He wondered what events and experiences had made his father study and practice law.

He turned off his torch and threw back the covers. Nothing. No sounds. Only blackness. Nothing strange, at least as far as he could see. He didn't have many pages left to read. He had to finish it and find his answer, his father's big secret. He rubbed his eyes with the knuckle of his forefinger, and returned to his reading, hoping he'd learn the secret very soon.

One of my early assignments at the Department of Justice in December 2012, after I graduated from law school, was to help in an investigation of the Speaker of the House, Marshal Becket, who received an election vote total that exceeded the number of registered voters. My colleague, Winston Packer, and I began our investigation with the Ohio election officials, who were NFP members. The unions and the NFP members collaborated in manipulating the local news media, getting them to claim the report of fraud was a case of double counting, and not a real case needing prosecution. After several records documenting the count and the vote accuracy disappeared, our investigation impotently ended. However, one day when I was working at the state attorney general's office, preparing to return to Washington, I took a call from a woman who said she witnessed the voter fraud. I agreed to meet her at a Methodist church that afternoon, and when I got there, she was gone. The pastor said the woman sat inside until two men escorted her out of the church. The woman never returned to her family. My investigation ended without anyone prosecuted.

At the end of 2012, the government, run by the NFP, established an internet agency czar to work with the National Security Agency. It arranged for all internet traffic to go through NSA servers so they could monitor for cyber warfare threats and domestic terrorism. This restructuring allowed the NFP total control all the information flowing about the past, present and what was to come. They created a database on anyone who owned property, a car, a credit card (which is like a coupon that is billed to its owner), or was active in virtually any business as a customer. Freedom of speech was again trampled into the dirt, right along with the freedom to carry out commerce privately on the internet. When a panel of industry experts spoke out and presented a simple solution that required less government control, the government administrators ridiculed their idea as that of a paranoid mind.

I watched the country reelect Norman in November of 2012 fearing the high probability of his continuing destruction of the country. He gathered the fruit of his election machinery, which carried out the usual plan, spinning and lying to the American public as he had before, promising more changes and more protection from the rigors of making a living in the world. As previously, the election had become a game of who could submit the most fraudulent votes. He won nearly the entire Latino vote, especially in the areas where immigrants were recent benefactors of the immigration amnesty. He used his attorney general to stifle voter fraud investigations. Later, people learned that Norman told the IRS to ignore applications by political policy groups seeking nonprofit tax status from the IRS (they were the tax collection arm of the government). I personally saw copies of electronic mail messages confirming this, but the Justice Department turned the other way. (Later, after the election, no representative in congress even hinted at articles espousing the formation of a special investigation of IRS criminality and possible abuse by Norman.)

The day of Norman's swearing in, he issued a deluge of executive orders. These orders established a barrage of regulations that began eating into the economy by increasing costs for businesses and the average citizen. The long-term effect was to keep stifling growth in the economy.

Early on, Hamas, a Palestinian Sunni Islamic terrorist group, attacked Israel in concert with Iran. Egypt funneled missiles into the Gaza area supporting Iran. Congress refused to get involved and Durand recommended we stay out of the trouble, but President Norman ignored Durand's advice and at the last minute issued an executive order giving a massive arms shipment and satellite support to Israel. Norman's support aided Israel enormously. That was the start of a struggle between Durand and Norman within the NFP for control of the party.

Now we arrive at the moment of tribulation in January of 2013. I denote the time because that was the month Adrian Durand was sworn in as a congressman. Thirty-three year old NFP member, Adrian Durand, a cross between a socialist and Marxist, was elected to the Congress by preaching with fluid and compelling oratory that the government must look after all the little people. He promised he could work miracles if only given freedom to act—with the people's mandate. As if it were déjà vu with the Third Reich of Hitler in Germany, the public couldn't see past the great oratory and sleight of hand to detect his real agenda—government control of people's lives. He mesmerized people with his speaking. Again, as previously, the news media was an accomplice in the mugging of America, discouraging and chastising any opposing decent aimed at reinstituting commonsense.

Adrian Durand's background, documented by researchers, was influenced by troubled minds planting ideas into his cranium, and like seeds planted on corrupted ground, they produced a troubled offspring. His bachelor's degree came from Columbia where he pursued a dual major in ethics and political science, studying under Professor Clark Millington, an outspoken proponent of Marxism and a frequent traveler to

Moscow during the 1970s. Concurrently, Durand became close friends with another professor, Geoffrey Forsyte, a devout socialist. After Columbia, Durand went to Harvard for his master's degree in political science, where he joined the People for Progressive Change Society, a pure socialist organization who paid for the worshiper of Vladimir Lenin, Russian philosopher, Victor Petrov, to speak on campus. Petrov was known to be active with the Russian KGB, which was their intelligence agency like the current SACI. After graduating, Durand spent some time in Philadelphia working in low-income areas helping people get welfare food coupons, registering people to vote, and fighting for people facing eviction. Durand traveled to Russia to visit Petrov. A year after leaving Harvard, he became a state representative and four years later Norman solicited Durand to join his political strategy staff.

William read his father's background on Durand with great anticipation, barely able to take a breath. It was like seeing the wizard's secrets.

Durand espoused the idea that a social existence nurtured securely through government safeguards was the only way to elevate the human condition and eliminate stress between classes. He was outspoken about his distrust and dislike of Muslim countries, and was a fierce proponent of measures against Islamic terrorists. Supposedly, he believed the closer the classes were to each other, the happier were the people. Whenever I read about these socialistic goals, goals aimed at leveling the classes, I was always curious whether those at the top of the food chain would also be leveled, or whether they were exempt. The elite and the wealthy socialists—and communists, always seem very willing to promote the classless society, but it is done with the idea they will be at the top directing the whole affair, leaving the poor to grovel in the dirt for a living, waiting for charitable handouts, the alms.

In a continuing effort to pull the freedom-teeth from the people, Durand pushed congress to pass a law stopping ownership of guns holding more than two bullets, which

471

pretty much eliminated all handguns. The law helped send the Second Amendment of the Constitution into a death spiral. (Dear reader, remember a populace needs guns for revolution. No guns, no revolution!)

It wasn't long before he began working on the other leg of power, the courts. He replaced appellate judges with strategic and seemingly evil intent to obtain control of the courts. The reader of this chronicle should thoroughly analyze this court action. The importance of stuffing the courts was fundamental to achieving more power. By installing judges who they controlled through money or threats, the Norman administration squashed lawsuits against his administration or he could initiate actions against private citizens. He could and did influence and abridge the rights of private citizens, and the states, as set down in the Constitution, claiming an authority based on a concocted "greater good" argument. When and if a group or legislator contested a violation in the court, the judge ruled in favor of their sponsor, the government.

By strangling the pillars of the country, the executive, judicial, and legislative branches of the government—the public didn't stand a chance at offering resistance, especially with the press buying into the socialistic changes.

September of the next year brought national disaster, another terrorist attack unparalleled in human barbarism. The attack employed an old military nerve gas. Authorities theorized the terrorists brought gas into the country through a gaping hole in the Arizona border with Mexico. One of the strongest theories suggested a group smuggled the gas out of Syria during their civil war. It was the same variety as Saddam Hussein used on the Kurds, the hellish odorless and tasteless vapor, VX gas, which kills indiscriminately. A private plane with the VX nerve agent left a small airport in Baltimore, Maryland and flew south along the coast several miles before turning west. When the two military jets confronted the plane over Annapolis, the terrorists released their package, killing fifteen thousand people over the southern half of the city. Norman countered the act of terrorism with massive carpet-bombing and bunker busting bombs, dropping them in the western areas of Afghanistan, trying to kill Taliban and Al Qaeda fighters. This also seemed to start a new frame of mind for Durand, one more negative toward relationships with that part of the world.

Durand masterfully increased his influence in the Congress, and into policies and events. About the third quarter of 2013, Durand urged the DOJ along with the FBI to investigate a corporation structured to sell and exchange carbon dioxide securities like a broker, taking a fee from each transaction. I watched from the sidelines as teams of investigators made weekly trips to Chicago to audit books and interview employees, primarily those who were in the finance department. Within a few days they learned this brokerage was connected to powerful men in both Europe and the US, and their objective was to use environmental threats, arbitrary carbon dioxide emissions limits, and a mandatory exchange of virtual securities to bring the country under a single global governing body. In a curious touch of irony, this grandiose socialistic plan didn't mesh with Durand's grand plan for a new country under his control. He pushed the attorney general to declare the business criminal and ordered all the associated people to be prosecuted for fraud and racketeering. The media lauded Durand for his stand.

In 2014, Durand became Speaker of the House and when the Chief Justice of the Supreme Court died, Durand pushed President Norman to appoint Oliver Wells, who was a product of Harvard and a student of interpretive law under Professor Wendell Kant. Durand also lobbied and got, an old friend, Terrance Packer, installed as the director of the FBI. Durand and Norman knew Oliver Wells would interpret law using the doctrine that the Constitution was a living document subject to growth and evolution, and that it should match the social attitude du jour. To the layman—this meant the court would be more likely to rule outside the strict language of the Constitution, essentially making up new rules to suit the powerful people of the government. This opened the door to all sorts of rationalization for political preferences, primarily scripted by the NFP.

Late in 2014, Durand sponsored a bill to change the retirement system. The government originally created the system called social security to provide financial security for the elderly of society after they paid money into it over their lifetime. Durand implemented a plan to provide for people who never paid a dime into the system. His plan drastically inflated the unfunded liability. His overt premise was that the people would end up on welfare anyway so they might as well be included in the social security disbursement system, but it was Durand's covert objective that people never saw coming. Durand's people used the internet media like an orchestra, inflaming the illiterate public until the public demanded passage of the legislation for the greatest good. The CLP protested the proposed bill by walking out of the senate; Katherine Roget, the senate minority leader led the departure. Of course, Durand's bill passed. This was one of Durand's covert transformations of our country toward a totalitarian state.

Government lunacy marched on. It took over the purchase of all drugs and established a department for their control, requiring all doctors and pharmacies within the government healthcare system to go through the a newly formed drug control department, which is now part of your Department of Wellbeing. Durand added an amendment to the drug program that revised the unemployment benefits. With the lingering high unemployment, he twisted fellow legislator arms and combined welfare assistance with unemployment, allowing a person to register for food assistance in the same application as their unemployment compensation. The number of people receiving food assistance and housing assistance nearly doubled. These measures made him the people's hero.

Moving like a ghost, Durand manipulated the country's finance machinery. The NFP and Durand decided they couldn't financially justify getting out of the business of controlling the banks with the lingering trillions in national debt from the financial collapse back in 2009. Of course, now the national debt included massive interest payments. On the surface, Durand convinced the NFP that the banks needed more government control, as well as more management applied to the value of the dollar, and he cunningly knew *finance was an integral element needed to complete his concept of control. In addition to finance, they began requiring companies to go through an approval process to get a license for outsourcing any labor or assembly outside the country. On the surface this looked like it was done to appease labor unions and increase jobs, but there was something hidden under the smell wafting into the air. Before the CLP had a chance to protest, my boss assigned me to look into the constitutionality, consult with constitution scholars, talk with business leaders, and visit with members of the CLP to hear their opinions. My immediate manager told me that if I were smart I wouldn't find anything damaging to the government. No sooner than I had begun to accumulate statistics and review the case law, my director terminated the investigation. I asked why. My manager told me that the word had come directly from the attorney general to cease. It was one of my early lessons in government manipulation of the law, and by the attorney general, a man I believed might have incorruptible integrity. He was just another of Norman's minions and had some curious connection to Durand. I had splashed myself on their radar as someone to watch.*

William felt a little relief from reading about the demise of his country when he read about the troubles across the world, the Pakistan government overthrown by their own Inter-Services Intelligence group, India fearing Pakistan's nuclear bomb arsenal, Durand pushing congress to ignore the situation, expressing only superficial concern about the Muslim controlled Pakistan government. It seemed crazy to him. The people in Pakistan, who lead a coup d'état, used their nuclear bombs to threaten India into giving up all of Kashmir. Additional pressures fell upon the US as Pakistan sold bombs to Palestine and Syria, aiding them with their war on Israel. At the same time, Pakistan planted a bomb in Mumbai, which the Indian intelligence force found and defused before it exploded.

What William read next conjured feelings of anger. His mind suddenly shot back to his father on the mountain, to Steinhoff's sickening approach before the mission, and then to a panorama of visions of his family's struggle under constant threats, mental programming, and the never-ending watching eyes of the vid-cams—and it all came from Durand.

Durand, who was barely past the eligible age for the office of president, executed a sweeping political campaign throughout 2016 for that year's presidential election, calling in all his political debts, reminding all the people on welfare that he was the man who helped them, and mustering an army of volunteers to carry out a blitz on internet social networks, manufacturing lies that ripped at the heartstrings of the mindless masses. Many people on the street didn't even know who he was, only that he had enhanced welfare and promised jobs.

Durand was elected president, using masterful oratory, some of which he probably gleaned from Norman, and escalating the classic political promise to new heights of shamelessness. Durand overpowered the other candidates. One of Durand's strikingly bold promises was a guaranteed income for everyone. Chief among his voting base were the recent Latino inhabitants with new voting privileges who gullibly believed he would give them promised income assistance by way of a tax refund. Durand handily won in the southwest, northeast, and Florida, taking ninety-five percent of the Latino and black vote, and taking forty-seven percent of the white vote. The people didn't know that they had just made a deal with the devil.

Durand quickly appointed his cabinet, starting with Carl Vincent, a former NFP policy officer, assigning him as the director of the CIA. He made Helmut Kauffman, a much younger man with an unusual gift for intelligence and trusted new friend, his chief of staff, and he appointed Cyrus Babcock as attorney general. Durand made a strange selection from the political point of view with Babcock, since Babcock was a lightweight with only the gravitas of being the state attorney general for Vermont. However, he was well liked within the NFP.

Where Norman was a liberal progressive as well as a communist oriented self-absorbed power grabber, Durand was somewhat of an unknown except for his prior associations in college and his bludgeoning method in the congress. When an article appeared in a newspaper citing Durand's influence on Norman and his associations prior to working for Norman, the CLP and conservative America cringed and held their breath for another ride on the spiral of the death-to-freedom rollercoaster. By the way, the author of the article lost his job at the newspaper. Even I had written a research paper back in college, and in it, I highlighted Norman's violations of the Constitution. I also mentioned some of Durand's influence, so I was aware he was radical and that I may have made dangerous enemies with my writing.

One day in early 2017, my boss came into my office and told me with a stern face, looking as if he had just received a prison sentence, that I was to attend a meeting with NFP senators and CLP congressmen. When he said the administration requested the DOJ investigate allegations of misappropriations, I suspected someone was playing a game. The CLP threatened national exposure of an NFP plot to blackmail CLP members with misappropriations of campaign money. The CLP pressured the DOJ to investigate the case. It seemed the NFP were trying to get the CLP members to switch over to their NFP party, or not run in the next election. A handful of NFP congressmen and senators thought our probe was unjustified, shortsighted, and a politically motivated witch-hunt. The NFP promised to show records, which would prove the CLP people alleging the charges only wanted to make political points. I met with a few CLP congressmen and a similar number of NFP representatives and senators, taking depositions and gathering any sort of electronic and paper documents I could. After two months, the CLP withdrew their request for the investigation. Rumors floated around that the NFP had bought off the CLP. The bosses above me terminated the case.

A month or two later, in an attempt to tighten control on the money supply, the NFP began passing a very intrusive government regulation on the individual retirement

477

accounts (IRA). The IRAs were retirement accounts individuals contributed to as savings. The Congress tried to put them under the watchful eye of the Guaranteed Retirement Accounts Department, claiming the government could better make certain that the people would be able to retire, claiming it would help the elderly and those who didn't understand investments. Numerous CLP senators boisterously complained to no avail and the NFP passed the controlling bill in late night secession. There was no media coverage. However, the same CLP senators demanded and got a constitutional review. The Department of Justice assigned me to investigate the constitutionality of the government controlling IRAs, which belonged to private citizens, just in case the DOJ had to go to court in a lawsuit. I had my doubts about the DOJ taking any case to court, not with Durand's control all over the DOJ. The DOJ assigned two other attorneys to assemble records from government computers. To my surprise, a class-action lawsuit crawled its way to the Supreme Court, seemingly riding on a wave of public opinion, opinion broadcast in rallies and speeches, the largest at the Lincoln Memorial. In typical fashion, the NFP played the media like an artist playing a concerto, and the court ruled five to four affirming the bill as legal. After that, I was assigned a new task at DOJ. However, being curious about the Supreme Court decision I made a few inquiries, and learned there had been immense political pressure on a couple of the Supreme Court Justices. Doing a little snooping, I found a collection of electronic mails hidden in the computer at the Department of Justice, emails that proved the Whitehouse had pressured the justices. My bosses knew it was wrong and were afraid to move on it, knowing the attorney general was Durand's man. That was when I learned Adrian Durand was in total control of the NFP, the House, and the Senate, and some justices on the highest court in the land. By controlling the IRAs, the welfare, the freedom of speech through the news media, and with regulations killing gun ownership, Durand had taken control of the country and moved it inch by inch to National Socialism.

Following the court's decision people marched on Washington, the major portion being seniors. Many were arrested. After Durand's first intrusion into people's private affairs, people started buying gold and hording it. Sure enough, it wasn't long before the government passed a law prohibiting people owning more than two ounces of any precious metal.

I should mention at this point in my chronicle that I have included some events, which may not sound relevant, but I believe they all help to paint a picture of the ubiquitous changes contributing to an oppressive government, all of them sucking the life breath from our freedom.

An ominous event in March of 2019 shocked many of us at the Department of Justice. Someone or a group blew up the CLP national headquarters in Washington, killing twenty-two staff members. This violence marked another milestone for the country as three prominent newspapers described the irrational occurrence as the work of a terrorist group. Of course, this explanation defied all credulity. The FBI jumped into action, supported by a team from the DOJ. The NFP used their control of the news media to spread the premise that underground Islamic jihadists caused the explosion. Coincidentally, the 2020 election campaign had just started. Within three weeks, a group or individual blew up the CLP offices in Philadelphia and Chicago, causing a broadening of the FBI's bombing investigation. Strangely, within weeks the FBI indicted the chief financial officer of the national CLP for money laundering. The FBI, with the help of a court friendly to Durand, seized all records and assets, in effect freezing the CLP campaign money. Many CLP candidates limped forward with inadequate campaign money, a few dropped out of the election hunt, electing to go back into private business, and a handful of others already in office switched their party, joining the NFP. This was the beginning of the dissolution of the CLP.

The CLP held a conference in Cleveland with a massive number of state police covering the attendees, protecting the building from sabotage. The leadership presented information that showed that the list of their financial contributors had dwindled because of growing doubt about their potential for success. After five floor votes, pushed by two senior senators, the CLP conference obtained a majority opinion that they dissolve the party. Three congressmen promised to never rest until a complete investigation was made. Senator John Warner Baird of Kansas was extremely outspoken about the bombings, openly blaming the president and his staff for being so detached and not willing to admonish their followers, coldly implying they were complicit. He called Durand a cold two-faced son of a bitch.

Neither the FBI nor the DOJ apprehended anyone for the bombings, but some of us in the DOJ saw portions of evidence archived on the computer system and it pointed to a job contracted by the NFP. Two months later the FBI identified the florist delivery van that the bombers had parked in front of the CLP headquarters and calculated it contained at least a thousand pounds of ammonium nitrate. I did a little undercover snooping around and an informant I knew quite well, and trusted, told me Adrian Durand had people arranged the hit. My naive bravery was a mistake. One night, shortly after I had poked around, I got a phone call warning me that my children and wife would disappear if I didn't stop. I stopped. The FBI never solved the bombings.

Weeks and months slid by with the nation holding its breath. By the time the news media began to see the national socialistic mosaic Durand had painted, starting back when he worked for Norman as a staffer, it was at least the third quarter of 2019. A key example of this alarmed awareness came at a conference of the Center for Progressive Social and Economic Justice. In a question and answer session, a senior member of a liberal news media organization, in an out-of-brain manner, asked a strange question of the committee on the stage: "What do you all hope to accomplish by moving the country to a national-socialist-Marxist government? That's clearly where you're going. And what does each of you expect to be doing once it has been accomplished?" I've never forgotten their answer. "We expect to convert the country to total government control of jobs, income, housing, and manufacturing." Then a man, one of the chairpersons replied, *"We all will be working in the government making the important decisions to reorganize society into a single, productive, and collective mind. We will be running the controls for those who don't have the capacity."* The liberal newspaper journalist then asked, *"What if the people above you don't want or need you?"* With that question, the conference became deadly silent. They never answered the question and quickly moved on.

William envisioned the picture of corruption and the frustration his father must have felt trying to enlighten him in those final minutes on the mountain. It deeply saddened him that people had thrown away the most precious possession in the universe, freedom. It was clear why his father wrote the chronicle, but it was too late for the country. At least it seemed so.

He paused for a moment, thinking. The question that hovered in a distance for years, and had not received an answer before, returned. The answer was his existence. He lived in a totalitarian State as an entity worse than a slave, lived under its brutal control, and he had no value. Slaves had value. The SAC dispatched citizen-comrades, slaves of State America, who had no value, to labor farms for disposal. It was SAC's method of limiting the number of mouths they had to feed. It wasn't genocide because they sent anyone. Control was a key word, a key element, a word his father had been stressing throughout the chronicle. William couldn't grasp what was in his head, but even with the devastating revelations, he still had a spark of hope. Down in his gut he felt something had to be in the remaining pages. He fanned the pages. Not many left. A voice exploded in his head. *Beucher!* He froze listening for any sound in the darkness beyond his eyes, beyond his blankets. Another voice erupted. *Did I hear Hans? Stop! You're home.*

There's no Beucher! How many times were those random voices and fears going to pop into his brain?

William snapped off the torch and lay there in the dark, remembering and sharing his father's remorse. A beast feeding on human weakness destroyed his father's life, his father's family, and now his family. Regretfully, he hadn't been as aware as his father had, but how could he— without seeing the country before Durand's destruction? His father had seen a country with promise and freedom like a sunburst, and he hadn't. He had stupidly followed a different path than his father, complicitly aiding the SAC, blindly revering what the parasitic beast did, totally missing the cost to humanity, practicing the policies no better than democide, the intentional murder of unarmed and helpless people for any reason.

The question hammered William's conscience again. Why had he gone in his direction and made the choices he made? He hated that question. He would hate the question the rest of his life. Maybe he hadn't bothered to question his world, as he should have. He heard a whispering voice in his head. *Every citizen owns the country. Every citizen is responsible.* He knew that now.

The people who had created this horror were afflicted with a god complex. If they weren't—it meant people believed in the slavery of a whole society purely as the way man should live on earth. Impossible. Every man was born by a miracle, the same as every other man. No person popped into the world with a title stamped on his head that he was to be a slave, as if decreed by God in the womb. The people of integrity who became rich did so with ideas, coming from their own ingenuity and hard work. When the hardworking people created something of value and sold it, they contributed to society because of the jobs they provided to others.

He could see how some millionaires in decades prior to the SAC, the ones who lacked ethics, the self-defined demigods, could exert perverse influence on society.

Without his father as a guide, he had gotten lost along the way, but everyman had to learn to walk. By not guarding his integrity, he had lost the anchor of his self-respect. Finally, at this late day—at last, he saw it. The NFP, before the horror of the SAC, had been an organism feeding on the integrity of its citizens as if they were food, extracting their integrity-blood, which was stealing freedom. At the most fundamental level, as his father had said, the people became a mindless mass. What his father perhaps failed to recognize was a deeper cause—the mindless mass had sacrificed their integrity seeking the acceptance of others like a parasite hypnotically accepting the NFP point of view without analysis. They valued being with the crowd, using the collective thinking of the mob, rather than risking independent action by using their own consciousness. They were selfless, giving themselves to a manufactured opinion that was not based on any critical logic or analytical thinking, like a manufactured screenplay, the product of psychological wordsmiths who were masterful in moving a collective mentality down a desired path.

With the dark filling his eyes like a blanket, as he endured a dark veil of melancholy, he went back to his college years. It had to have been then or just after college that the SAC initiated their psychological war with the people. They had to kill a person's self, the integrity to act for what was right. By forcing people to talk in unison, a collective mind, repeating the SAC propaganda, they weakened the independent person, sucking a person further down into their muck. He wished he could do it all over—

differently—not that he could make a difference, but at least he would have acted with integrity—and probably got killed.

He wasn't heroic by any stretch of one's imagination, except for his family. He hoped, somehow, before he died, he could make atonement for his lack of conscience. Turning on his torch, he looked at his wrist for his trusty cheap watch. It wasn't there. He couldn't remember where he had left it. Oh well. He went back to the words of his father.

I can still see in my mind the country of that time. I will now try to address the deadly somber atmosphere that crept over the nation at the time of Durand's horrible changes. The nearest description I can use for you, my dedicated reader, is a comparison to the feelings one would experience at the moment of consoling prior to a funeral. As I think and try to form words to express how it was back then, I can't hold back the tears. The pain rips at my heart. We faced a poison spreading through the nation's body—and the people couldn't stop it. While increasing numbers of the population were becoming alarmed, strangely some people still believed in the poison, holding on with clawing fingers to the hope that the NFP government could protect every citizen from all unforeseen dangers of the world, provide opportunities for a reasonable fair income, and respect the constitutional rights of the people. With every passing month and year, the poison permeated more of the national body, until finally it became too perilous even to attempt a cure without the final personal sacrifice. The poison was "control" and it slowly killed the body's cells of freedom. People couldn't get jobs and barely lived on the special economic survival allowance, which Durand extended year after year. People could not express criticism openly for fear a neighbor would report them to Durand's people monitoring public speech. Questions were either not addressed or brush away as too trivial for concern. Political action groups were accused of being subversive radical movements and badgered by local law enforcement or unidentified thugs, thugs who murdered members by night. People who still had guns, hid them to prevent the government from confiscating them, and if there was a gun registration and the person didn't surrender a matching gun, the authorities arrested the person whom they thought guilty, whether they had evidence or not. A black-market sprang up, supplying illegal guns from Mexico. Some people tried fleeing the country, both to the north and south. People who were out of work kept their mouths shut for fear of losing their government paycheck. If you risked talking to anyone, you only talked to very close friends whom you trusted with your life.

Fighting free speech, Durand's attorney general, Cyrus Babcock, charged an author, Ramsey J. Coulter, with sedition for a book critical of Durand's early presidency and his communistic changes. Coulter called out Durand for suggesting he would eliminate the rich from our country by making everyone equal. Some of us at the DOJ, who observed the senior attorneys working the case, were appalled when they applied the sedition charges for a book, which was protected under freedom of speech and press. For some reason the case never made it to court. It was rumored Coulter went into hiding. Coulter's book caused the Durand government to make new restrictions on books. The first change came to history books. All the new history books for schools were to clarify all the associations of previous presidents. Word filtered into the public from the revision committees that milky language had been added to the books, describing various executive orders and actions of the presidents, and these decisions surreptitiously painted them as socialists, and either a member of the NFP or a sympathizer.

With increasing frequency, posters appeared glued to buildings, light poles, and road signs, calling for someone to assassinate the president, calling him the reincarnated Hitler. And so it began, the verbal underground revolution.

In the campaign for the election of 2020, Durand crisscrossed the country espousing his usual promises. Of course, the election was a farce, a foregone conclusion from the beginning. Naturally, with only two or three holdout CLP candidates, Durand and the NFP swept around the country, vowing a job for everybody who could work, a total stoppage of jobs leaving the country, and a new national ID card so everyone could get *proper healthcare totally provided by the government. At last, he would end the ten-year recession, solving the national debt of trillions—one of the biggest economic parasites on the country. Durand used corruption and lies to push his way into office—again.*

After the election, some political dirt flew about Durand in a story on the social media of the internet. It conjectured in an itemized list how Durand would destroy the country. This drew raucous laughs from the remaining believers. It also alleged Durand planned to form a national database in which every person's life would be recorded, including DNA, if it existed, medical records, friends and relatives, a person's whole social network. He and his staff, as well as unidentified teams of men, attacked the people propagating the accusations. After a five-hour national internet failure, all traces of the internet article had evaporated, and then a related rumor spread that the mother of person who wrote the internet article claimed her son was taken by three men in gray suits and a big black car.

The quiet speculation about the NFP being responsible for bombing the CLP headquarters lingered like the smell of old fish, but nothing more appeared in the media. However, CLP Senator John Warner Baird of Kansas, who had been voted out of office the year before, and who had been a vociferous spokesman about the bombing, died in a corporate jet that catastrophically lost pressure and crashed. The pilot and two others died. Strangely, the plane had recently passed a complete maintenance checkout.

A month after Durand's swearing-in ceremony for his second term, a mass protest march descended on Washington D.C., marching from the capitol building up Pennsylvania Avenue and across Constitution Avenue. The march, which was initially peaceful, was more like a funeral procession, marked by black placards declaring the death of the country, and declaring Durand destroyer of the constitution. It was the largest march ever to take place in the city.

Four months after the election a handful of senators, previously CLP members and a bipartisan citizen action group, pressed the Justice Department to continue looking into the bombing of the CLP headquarters. Durand, with obvious confidence that no connections would lead to the NFP or to him, gave Cyrus Babcock his blessing for an investigation. A few of us at the DOJ could see Durand was playing a game. Babcock sent a group of us staff attorneys out across the country like swarm of ants scouring over the putrescent political picnic lunch. Therefore, once again I was looking into the CLP bombing, and nervously, I must say.

We executed our investigation of the bombing in conjunction with the FBI, which seemed curious since FBI Director Wade Elder belonged to Durand's inner circle of power. They had the attitude that they had sealed their loose ends and that our investigation would quickly hit a dead end. We took a low visibility approach, giving bribes to talk with gangs, throwing money at insignificant militias, crime organizations, and then we connected with an ex-CIA operative who was disgruntled with the government's direction. He pointed us to a paramilitary group for hire working out of Georgia. With the meager evidence we had, the people in the group were untouchable, and on top of that, someone alerted them to our probe, which cost the life of our ex-CIA source. I received another threatening phone call and when I reported it to my manager, all hell broke loose. The manager yanked us back to the DOJ where the FBI and a couple NFP senators admonished us as if we had plunged into the investigation as whim. The manager stood aside as if completely ignorant of the whole affair. Finally, the CLP investigation came to a head when Attorney General Babcock returned from a Whitehouse meeting and told us he was closing the case forever.

A throb began above William's left eye. He sent his fingertips at it, rubbing deep, feeling his skull under skin, closing his eyes, seeing the black chair on the backside of his eyelids, hoping the pain would subside soon. He pulled in a long slow breath, trying to relax away the pain. After a few minutes, he felt the pressure and throbbing fading. The spawn of Beucher's demented work would return he told himself as he opened his eyes. He set his eyes on the page again, finding where he had stopped, hungry as ever to take in the words.

A man who had a talk radio program, working with two citizen political action groups, sparked questions in the public, at least in the minds of those who cared and worked at the FBI and at the DOJ. He bravely, cavalierly, and stupidly drew attention to events that seemed to connect Durand with influencing the Supreme Court, of taking away gun rights, and muzzling free speech for the purpose of squelching revolution-minded groups. Risking severe repercussions from political censors, the radio person blasted the allegations over the airwaves. Then he went on with allegations that Durand had sold access to an oil producing area within territorial waters of the Gulf of Mexico and taken the money himself. He justified his argument with reports of a Latin looking man, possibly Brazilian, going into the Whitehouse numerous times and that it was a wealthy Brazilian dealing in oil. He made some other accusatory connections that one of my colleagues said could have only come from the NSA. The DOJ did not pursue any investigation and the FBI blew it off as lunatic-right ramblings. However, the Alliance for Civil Justice, ACJ, launched a private investigation. They tried tracing money and crashed headlong into a maze of overlapping companies, one owning another, finding only two connected to Durand. However, the ACJ managed to push forward with a civil case implicating Durand. Miraculously, the case made it up to the U.S. Court of Appeals, the Washington Circuit, which barely formed a majority vote in favor of Durand's argument. Three months later one of the dissenting judges, Martha Hillborn-Wyatt, a healthy woman of forty-seven had a heart attack. I got a call from a friend working in the Chicago Police Department who told me about a reporter who was murdered. He described it as suspiciously strange, as if it were professionally done. About three weeks before the murder, the reporter had written an article, and he posted it on a high-traffic internet website. In the article, he alleged a connection between the judge's death and the court's decision. The authorities found the reporter dead with a strange drug inserted into his anus. I kept the information quiet while I tried to figure out the safest route to take morally and physically. I considered going all the way to the attorney general, but that would have been suicide. He was Durand's man. The talk radio person, who was only fifty years old, also died of a heart attack. Two coincidental heart attacks caused me to back away from the case with my conscience screaming at me for weeks. Family was first.

It was probably six or seven months after his election when Durand started addressing the military. He pushed the Congress to cut military spending drastically, ridiculously cancelling urgently needed new armored troop vehicles, a new stealth fighter plane, and a massive robotics program—that was about completed. Then he gutted the NASA budget. The action disheartened many in all the ranks, causing three generals and two admirals to retire early.

About nine months into Durand's second term events began to fall on my head. I got a call at my office from a woman asking me to meet her at a coffee shop in downtown Alexandria, Virginia. She wanted to discuss some sensitive information she had. I feared she might want to discuss the court case that probably killed at least two people. The hostess walked me to a table in a back corner where I was surprised by the person sitting there. I pulled back a chair and sat across from a striking, dark haired lady, looking in her middle thirties, clutching a black handbag on her lap. Her face could have appeared in an advertisement for cosmetics, with her precision cheeks, delicate chin and nose, all touched with a minimum of feminine enhancements. She pinched her light-pink, glistening lips, into a fierce line. I have never forgotten her, not because she was beautiful, but because of the shear contrast between her beauty and the fear, she carried on her face. She wore simple glasses without rims and her fearful blue eyes pierced me to the bone. She looked as if she was on the verge of jumping out of her skin. She looked around the restaurant and out into the parking area, and then with accusing eyes she looked at me for a moment.

She spoke, her voice coming out in a whisper. "Did you drive around to make certain you weren't followed?"

"Yes."

She sipped her coffee, her hand visibly trembling. She surveyed the room again and brought her scared eyes back to me. "I work for a non-profit constitutional think-tank located in Silver Spring, Maryland. It's an organization dedicated to study and writing of analyses on the problems and issues facing the country in relation to the precepts set down in the Constitution of the United States, our loss of freedoms, Sharia law violating our constitution, influence of the UN, voting fraud, loss of a two-party political system, the encroachment of national-socialism, and failure of the president to follow his oath of office."

"What's the name of the group?" I know I sounded a little skeptical at that point.

"That's not important and it's probably better for you if you don't know. But the group isn't why I'm here."

"What's this all about? If you don't mind me saying, you look terrified."

"I can't take much time. They are probably watching me. Everything must be off the record." She studied me intensely, her breath seemingly stopping.

"Yes, yes, it's off the record. That's fine."

"Good. I'm here because I represent a group of patriots who must remain anonymous. They thought you might be someone who believes in our Constitution and liberty."

When I heard those words my heart about stopped. I knew that anything I was about be told could be found seditious by the Durand administration—and it could get me dead. After swallowing a lump in my throat I replied, "Yes, I am such a person . . . as long as it's lawful."

"Good."

"Do you have a name?" I asked her, not expecting an answer. People in that sort of business didn't give out names.

"I'm sorry, no names."

"All right, continue."

She glanced warily toward the entrance, seemingly checking each table within sight, and then she checked what was beyond the windows. "The group of patriots consists of a variety of professional people, such as journalists, business people, academics, government employees, and intelligence people. All of them have met and shared information. They all have heard of situations where men in gray uniforms with no markings have approached and threatened people in positions of authority and influence."

"What do you mean?" I understood but I guess I needed reassurance to satisfy the incredulity in my mind.

She leaned forward and whispered, "One case was taped. A man videotaped gray-suited men walking a neighbor out of his home to a waiting black van. It's very clear on the tape. The man was a government employee and audited government budgets. His wife, questioned in secret in a clothing store, said he had found billions in misallocations of appropriations. One case involved the transfer of a billion dollars to a department listed within Homeland Security, which subsequently placed large orders for automatic weapons and ammunition, and then reopened a two hundred acre army-training center. When the man checked with Homeland Security, they knew nothing about the department, the weapons, or the army base. He also found several million granted to a green energy company owned by other companies, which Durand, Kauffman, Snider, Radford, or Bruner owned. From these men some of the money seemed to have gone to various judges and law enforcement officials. By the way, the man never returned to his family. He just simply disappeared. The police said they need more time to declare the man officially missing."

I remember her words paralyzing me.

She went on. "A copy of an email-memo has been obtained confirming the existence of a secret police unit being operated by the NFP. The people in our group are certain this mysterious police unit is not connected to the FBI, CIA, NSA, or any military intelligence unit."

491

"How did you or your people decide to call me?"

"Your name emerged as someone at the DOJ who had been engaged in some important investigations supporting the law and our Constitution. They felt you were someone they could trust."

I merely shrugged, my modesty operating in full control.

"Too many people critical of Durand's presidency have had accidents."

Stunned, I stared stupidly at her for the longest time. "What do your friends want from me?"

"They want you to investigate on an unofficial level."

"Why doesn't your group pursue the appointment of an independent prosecutor?" After I offered my idea, I immediately saw panic on her face.

"Coming out into the public view is not safe, but once we get the necessary evidence we will present it to two active generals, and two of the justices at the Supreme Court who can be trusted. Once that's accomplished we'll try to get a committee, including several legislators who can be trusted to craft articles of impeachment for presentation to the Congress and the American people. But that's the major problem. He controls of the press media, the internet, both the House and Senate via the NFP, and many of the federal courts. He can shut down the social media internet sites any time."

"You'll never get an impeachment."

"There are other measures the group is considering if all else fails."

"Seizure of the government with the military?"

"Possibly."

"I'll help as long as it doesn't place my family in danger."

She checked the entrance and the windows again, and then her watch. "You cannot trust anyone. You know that, don't you? They're like body-eating bacteria, eating anyone and anything that goes against them."

I nodded.

"When you've gathered any information, get on the internet and connect to a website, Bestofshow-Shepherds, and leave a message. If we need to contact you in the future it will be about an albino German Shepherd puppy."

That was it. Abruptly, she got up, paused beside the table with her face stricken, gazing down at me as if pleading, and then she walked off toward the restroom. Our meeting ended. A few minutes later, she walked out the entrance wearing a blonde hairpiece. She climbed into a cab waiting at the curb.

Nearly numb, I sat there trying to wrap my brain around what had just happened, uncertain what I could do and—what I should do. It was clear people at the highest levels of government were fearful for the country. This fear wasn't the tepid warm candle flame that could muster a protest march; it was the white-hot precursor to revolution. Words like impeachment and coup d'état drifted through my brain, and I knew impeachment fell impotently short as a probable solution. Armed patriots were once again required, as Thomas Jefferson had foretold. When I left the coffee shop, my eyes washed over every conceivable location that could hide an agent or camera. I now watched for agents from a part of the government that had spit on the Constitution and I watched for who might be watching me.

I buried myself in an evaluation of what was happening. I found the existence of patriotic people inspirational, people sounding not unlike those first intrepid men and women of our founding colonies, people recognizing the Constitution was being torn to shreds—and they had decided to take action. Running in a strange parallel with the nation's early years, when speaking against the English crown meant peril, it also meant certain peril when anyone who spoke out against the Durand government. History was already writing the list of victims.

When I told my wife what happened, she sobbed on my shoulder and asked me to think about changing careers. She asked if we could move out west to the mountains, perhaps up into western Canada. She didn't want me to get involved, but in her usual *perceptive manner, she could see into my soul, see my pain, and she knew my heart wouldn't let me surrender without a fight. Being incredibly intelligent, she could see what was happening all around us just as I could.*

William took his eyes away from his reading. His head throbbed. He rubbed it for several minutes, remembering his mom's face and then he silently cried.

Chapter 28

William moved the pages away so his tears wouldn't stain them. The emptiness filled in chest again, but Beucher didn't cause it. In his mind he went back home and to his youth. He could see his mom and dad and his sister again, all happy sitting and eating at the dinner table. He ran the back of his hand over one eye and then the other, disposing of tears. He didn't know why his mind went back there to that time. Years later, after his father had fled, his mother had been a rock of support, never sounding depressed, always trying to emphasize the positive of any situation, as if she had been enlisted as a combatant fighting a battle on the home front. It was strange how he had been relatively happy during those hard times, and had felt extremely free. Then he remembered—the clouds, the government men in gray suits pestering his mother year after year, asking about his father. Nevertheless, the remaining family had managed to get by. One day a man stopped him and asked if his father was home or if he had been home. He knew that man was evil.

Beucher had asked so many questions. Beucher wouldn't place that helmet on his head again, not if he could do anything about it.

William turned off his torch and pulled down the covers. Inexplicably, he felt anxious about the house, as if eyes were on him. He moved to the edge of the bed, sat up, and suddenly noticed a slow pulsing green glow in the pitch-black room. The faint light washed ominously against the wall above his dresser. He stood next to the bed, cautiously observing the violator of his space, thinking the SACI had planted something aimed at playing with his mind. He lifted a foot in a hesitant unconscious movement and crept to the dresser. Electricity fired his nerves. He thought he might bolt out the door. At the dresser, he looked down in utter confusion at the pulsing light coming from a watch. The watch wasn't his. He never owned any watch with a glowing face. It had to be another SACI trick, something to entrap him. He started to reach for it with the intention of depositing it in a drawer, but couldn't bring himself to touch it. His first priority was to finish his reading and not permit anything connected with the SACI to entangle him. He didn't touch it. He made his way in the dark to the toilet and returned to his cocoon to resume his reading.

Before getting very far into my undercover investigation of the alleged secret police, the Department of Justice sent me to investigate a group in Michigan that was allegedly planning to blow up NFP offices in Dearborn. The powers above assigned Ben Halpern as my partner for the trip to Detroit on the investigation. We began looking for militia connections, trying to interface with the local FBI, local police, and the Michigan State Police, but after two weeks, the DOJ office recalled us. I got the feeling it had been a goose chase to get me out of Washington, although I had no reason for the feeling, merely one of those sensations on the skin warning me to be careful.

No sooner than I was back at DOJ, Durand fired the Chairman of the Joint Chiefs of Staff, four-star Jeffery Marshal and replaced him with General Barnaby Peters, who had been with logistics. Durand issued an executive order spelling out more cuts in the military and freezing the recruiting, even while we had ongoing operations on the ground in the Mideast. More military officers resigned their commissions and a few weeks later rumors began flying that the administration had pushed the officers out under various threats. There was talk of a severe restructuring of the military. Durand formed a special committee under his cabinet for studying military strategy and operations. Durand placed Helmut Kauffman in charge of it. Undercover discussions broke out at the office coffeepot on the ramifications of the military changes, but these talks didn't last long. Shortly after any of these coffeepot discussions started, the pensive participant's would look warily around the office, and up at the ceiling. Then they would walk away.

Everyone was on edge at the DOJ as well as across the whole country. Two television networks included commentaries about the seriousness of the drastic reorganization of our military, citing the concerns published by think tanks and senior political observers. The next day the same networks backpedaled, reporting the changes were necessary for streamlining and the evolution to a more modern military. I contacted a producer at one of the news media companies, who admitted they had been visited by two gray-suited government men who never removed their dark sunglasses, joking they could have been in a spy movie. The internet erupted with a torrent of postings calling for Durand's impeachment, an impossible task with the NFP controlling the House and Senate—just as I had mentioned to the lady in the coffee shop. The next day I got a call from a man claiming to be an executive at the news media company. He wouldn't give his name and his voice was distorted. He said Durand's goons threatened to blow up their broadcast facility if they didn't go soft on Durand.

A month later, at noon, I sat at a traffic light in Georgetown, heading toward a small restaurant for lunch when I got a strange call on my cell phone. The caller asked if I had an albino German Shepherd for sale, and if I did, please pull into the parking area ahead. Stupidly, I pulled into the shopping area. To this very day, I don't why I did it. I thought I knew who it was, but I was still scared. When I saw a large van pull into the parking area, I climbed out and stood beside my car. The van pulled up alongside, its side door opened, and I found myself staring down the barrel of a large caliber handgun. Looking out at me from inside the vehicle were two men in business suits and a fashionably well-dressed dark-haired woman with immaculately lined lips and eyes, looking like a corporate CEO. The man asked me if I was interested in preserving the Constitution and the country. I froze. My brain went into lockdown. Their crisp white shirts and color-coordinated ties told me they weren't a threat, they were far from being criminals, and they weren't Durand's goons.

Finally, I gathered enough moisture in my mouth and answered, "Yes, I'm interested." That was the moment I lost my family!

After I climbed into the van, the driver traveled to a parking garage where we switched to a large black car. From there they drove us to a second parking garage where we split up into two smaller cars. The car in which I rode with two other people went to a side street and pulled over. A tour bus with darkened windows pulled up, opened the door, and the three of us climbed in. We all rode silently and somberly down the street for several minutes to a place where more people climbed on board. The bus made two more stops, picking up people. After they completed the pickup process, the bus cruised on the parkway, while we all had a small lunch and a discussion in the lounge-like interior.

The selection of passengers shocked me. I met, Army Major General Sylvester Carlson, Marine Major General Jake Underhay, Marine Lieutenant General Harlan Wilcox, former U.S. Senator from New York, Robert McGraw, Washington Post Editor, Del Symon, New York Times Political Editor, Cornelius Hawthorne Whitney, Barkley Stoner, Justice, Second Circuit -US Court of Appeals - New York, Army General Calvin "Buck" Firestone, U.S. Congresswoman from Virginia, Paula Stinson,

Princeton Professor of Government, Stella Yates, Yale Professor of Biomechanics, Bartlet James, and Howard University Professor of Economics, Andrew Carlton. And from the intelligence area I met Senior Analyst with the Central Intelligence Agency (CIA), Charles Jay, and Senior Analyst with National Security Agency (NSA), Steven Rutenberg. The girl I had met in the restaurant wasn't there.

The discussion, led by General Firestone, focused on Durand taking over the government with the help of his NFP, the country exchanging freedoms for Durand's control, Durand using a secret police force, and the Durand administration lying and grossly violating the Constitution as well as the oath of office. None of the people mentioned the debt facing the nation, choosing only to focus on the fundamental elements of the country's survival. The attendees were in complete agreement that the primary objective of the meeting was to organize an effort to preserve the country, to take it back. As soon as the leaders announced the objective, I flashed on the year of 1776. Later in the conversation, all the members agreed for the sake of security that no one person should know all the activities of the group, mainly in case of brainwashing, which Charles Jay and the generals confirmed Durand's government was employing with new vigor—helped by his secret police. Many people in the NFP were aware of it going on during Durand's first term and had been ignoring its illegality. Everyone in the group acknowledged that if Durand's people caught us, they would execute us.

The generals, Charles Jay, Steven Rutenberg, and the two people from the press media explained what they had heard, and could confirm about Durand's megalomania, and his moves toward total dictatorship. We all agreed the people had given it to him a morsel at a time by ill-informed voters, by a lazy apathetic proletariat, by the left-leaning privileged wealthy, and by the power-greedy members of the legislature. I had never heard so many allegations spoken so openly. It was extremely scary and yet it was like a burst of antiseptic arctic air. According to the generals, within a few months, Durand would move the military under the control of a new department called the Department of People

Protection, known now as DPP, formerly called the Department of Homeland Security, which the attendees agreed was being dismantled. Rutenberg said Durand would likely suspend Posse Comitatus sometime before taking full control.

You, the reader, should understand the importance of this. Posse Comitatus was a United States federal law passed in the 1870s after the end of Reconstruction from the Civil War. It was intended to prohibit federal troops from supervising elections in the former Confederate states. It generally prohibited federal military personnel and units of the United States National Guard under Federal authority from acting in a law enforcement capacity within the United States, except where expressly authorized by the Constitution or Congress. The Posse Comitatus Act and the Insurrection Act substantially limited the powers of the federal government to use the military for law enforcement in a domestic setting.

Charles Jay added he was surprised Durand hadn't already suspended Posse Comitatus to crush protest marches. He also reported that Durand had started gutting the defense department. General Firestone spoke about DARPA, mentioning he had oversight responsibilities for it, emphasizing the lethality it had if Durand began to control it with any concentrated effort. In a grave voice, he lamented the loss of many people working there, some of our brightest engineers and scientists in the country, many of whom were fleeing to Canada. The two men from the intelligence areas confirmed similar defections. The man from the NSA said a team had, in top secret, run several scenarios in simulations on one of their big computers, and they confirmed that the path forward under Durand was unalterable unless patriots used armed force and a military coup d'état, which the simulation gave a low probability of success. If people marched on Washington, Durand and his control machinery would manipulate the press reports and characterize the march as a laughable radical movement organized by disgruntled members of the defunct CLP. There was a high probability Durand would have his enforcement-minions lockup a large number of marchers to see if they could catch the ringleaders. I asked about the probability Durand would declare martial law (control by armed forces) and would eliminate habeas corpus. (Habeas corpus, for the reader without any historical connection, is essentially the right of a person charged with a crime to be brought before a judge in a timely manner and not be subjected to unlawful unlimited restraint.) They all agreed that Durand did not need to go that direction with all the control he had obtained, but it was possible. The generals acknowledged they didn't have any people on the inside who could carry out an operation to assassinate Durand with a bomb, like the scenario attempted on Hitler. We reached a consensus for undertaking four missions, one mission to focus on forming underground resistance groups in California with people from the government installations at Lawrence Livermore, Los Alamos, Stanford University, and the Freedom Institute in Virginia, and three other paramilitary type missions aimed at terminating key people. The group didn't discuss any details, as they were secret within the team volunteering for the mission. The meeting broke up and they delivered all us to our cars with the same clandestine procedure as they originally used. When I got into my car, my hands trembled so badly I could scarcely grip the steering wheel. Before starting for home, I looked all around me for people who might be watching too intently. I knew Durand's goons could kill me at any time.

In the following months, the generals briefed three of us on a few strategies, giving us only general elements for the most part. I don't know why they selected me to hear such plans. I was scared to death and at the same time deeply gratified for the opportunity. I saw only two or three of the other members at these meetings, and never saw the same people at consecutive meetings. The people risking their lives never ceased to amaze me. I drew my inspiration from their selflessness, honor, and sense of duty. I also exchanged information with someone in the group through a website until someone discontinued the internet connection. Eventually, they replaced it with another one, which I won't mention here. However, about four months after the initial meeting, I can't remember precisely, a group of military officers walked the halls of the capitol, talking to all the representatives as *well as to the senators, making arguments about the military being irrationally and irreversibly destroyed—and too much power being given to the president. Word got out, not via the press, but by word of mouth and the internet, reporting no House or Senate committee would propose legislation to counter Durand's executive orders.*

Many months later, Adrian Durand increased his hold on the country, scaring the hell out of us, shaking the military to the core. In one of his most questionable executive orders, he placed all land-based nuclear weapons on stand-down and under review of his special committee, Military Weapons Study and Control, MWSC, totally without consulting military oversight or congressional leaders. The Joint Chiefs and the Secretary of Defense, who were operating with the new DPP, issued a letter advising him and the congress it was a monumental mistake to rely solely on a submarine based deterrent, crippling our overall defense. Durand, in a storm of anger, fired all joint chiefs and the defense secretary, and replaced them with lower level officers. He placed the country on DEFCON level two during the military transition and warned Russia and China not to make any assumptions. Again, all I could do was look into the constitutionality in my spare time, which I spread over several days, keeping it quiet from everyone, fearing my bosses would fire me. Of course, my efforts only served to convince me that my country was in dire peril, in the throes of a paranoid narcissist that would rule it like a new Russian Stalin.

Within days of Durand's move, a group of four NFP congressmen and one congresswoman approached Durand with their objection to his changes with the military, citing fears of him building too much power in his office. Additionally, the only way the public heard about the meeting was by a daring patriot group publishing the congressman's letter on the internet, which Durand's people quickly scrubbed out of existence. None of the congressmen spoke of their conversation after the meeting, but rumors told of a brutal shouting exchange. Nevertheless, through a series of strange events taking place over a span of four months, the four congressmen and one congresswoman fell upon tragedy. Two of the men were hospitalized with food poisoning and died. The authorities found one of the men, conveniently for Durand, in a car fire in a shopping mall parking lot. The fourth congressman died from a heart attack. The last of the group, the congresswoman, had a massive stroke that left her incapacitated and nearly vegetative. A warning floated on the rumor-breeze aimed at people thinking of crossing Durand. No allegations for the cause of deaths or the accidents ever officially surfaced, and no government agency initiated any investigation because of the circumstantial association of the people meeting misfortune, but everyone knew who gave the orders.

A few months later, a media blitz orchestrated through the Durand controlled information channels, praised Durand for wisely taking control of the nuclear weapons from the Joint Chiefs, the very same people who had attempted a coup d'état and were arrested for treason. The media bombardment was fabrication. No military people had attempted a coup d'état. The reports declared Durand had saved the country by taking land-based nuclear weapons from the control of some generals who had become unbalanced and dangerous. According to Durand's rewritten history, just like Joseph Stalin during the gulag days in the USSR, Durand was the savior. No one in the government and no one tangentially connected with the government felt safe with Durand in office. Making the environment even more tenuous, China flexed its muscles with its new class of nuclear submarines, which allegedly possessed a cutting-edge laminar flow methodology to achieve incredible underwater speed.

The reader of this chronicle should try to step back from the forest at this point. This history must be taken as a whole and not in terms of the individual elements, as it forms a canvas for a total picture of Durand's abridgement of our freedoms, free enterprise, freedom of speech, protection from search and seizure, and the right to own arms—the core elements of the Constitution Durand destroyed to convert the country from a representative democratic republic into a police state. I have omitted many references and details of similar destructive occurrences, limiting my comments to key examples. I apologize if I have been a *little repetitive. By no means, did Durand execute the complete transformation alone; the communists had been poisoning our bravery and the pride-of-self of our people for decades. But Durand drove the stake into the nation's heart.*

All a person had to do was look around and it was easy to recognize that no citizen was immune to Durand's onerous control. Even the CEOs of industry were subject to Durand's unrelenting ego-building rant. The leaders of industry fell under Durand's microscope after we dipped back into recession. Durand's presidency, without any question, caused the downturn with a tsunami of doubt, spreading market fear, and a major loss in confidence by the financial sectors of the country and the intertwined foreign banks. Durand went on TV like a white knight announcing his formation of the Department of Employment, which would be in charge of developing new jobs and investigating large corporations to certify they didn't avoid their social responsibility for job creation. As if passing out food from paradise, he initiated government-controlled projects in natural gas, oil production, manufacturing on-shore of flat screen televisions, cell phones, and video cameras—all to be government owned and operated. He forced the refurbishing of railroads, all of it by using the US treasury as his personal piggybank. Unions sang his praises and in less than a year, the imports from China dropped to a trickle, causing China to demand payment for the treasuries it had purchased years earlier. China cancelled agreements on climate regulations and nuclear nonproliferation. Furious with the foreign threats, Durand showed them his control. He stopped the exchange of interbank funds by the Treasury and Federal Reserve. He used the, all-ready-in-progress, NSA spying on overseas telephone calls and in a short time, he had several Chinese arrested for cyber warfare. Then in the same breath, he had five people, despite their diplomatic credentials, arrested for espionage from the Chinese consulate. Durand's control of courts sent all of them to long prison terms. Subsequent to locking away the Chinese spies, he terminated all the internet connections outside the country.

Under the category of internet control and isolation, Durand brought more changes. Despite NSA's monitoring of all communications and cyber attack prevention, Durand required the military to discontinue all use of the internet, and had them convert totally to encrypted microwave through satellites. In 2021, Durand forced the congress to put whatever was remaining of the Pentagon under the control of the DPP, just as the generals I met in the van had predicted. The head of DPP was given to a relatively unknown, Leon Fournier. Fournier had helped Durand get into the congress, and in addition to being a military historian, he was a devout communist. The country seemed to freeze in its tracks.

As if the turmoil in the United States wasn't enough, that same year Belgium became an Islamic government controlled by Sharia law, causing a mass migration of Catholics, Jews, and Asians into France and Germany."

Durand's war on the underground escalated in 2022. He assigned Cyrus Babcock to stop the growth of conspiracy groups forming in the country, trying to stop the underground revolutionists. My manager threw me into an assignment that drew scrutiny from high above, the investigation of conspiracy groups and militias. Allegedly, according to the Durand administration, the groups were trying to overthrow his government. Of course, Durand thought all groups other than the NFP were trying to overthrow him, the new despot running the country. I met with three groups whose members were a collection of college professors, Wall Street people, corporate executives, engineers, teachers, union workers, and state legislators. These weren't the people I had met previously in secret, the generals on the tour bus, and I didn't know whether they knew any of the other underground people, but I warned them to disband or face prosecution. Those were my orders and as I pronounced them, it was acid in my mouth. I hated every minute, because I was telling people they didn't have the right of freedom of assembly or dissent. I also had to inform them of a new Durand amendment on a legislative bill making the defacing of any government official's picture a form of hate crime, punishable by two years imprisonment. So all the mustaches kids used to draw on faces, Durand had made illegal.

On my way back to the office, a news announcement interrupted the music on my car radio, telling the American people that the country had defaulted on an interest payment on its national debt in the amount of nine hundred billion dollars. One of the people on the radio began to offer speculation on the problem and before he could complete his argument, his producer cut his microphone off in the middle of his sentence. No one knew what the default meant for the country since Durand held the throat of the country under his totalitarian boot.

A week later my boss assigned Carl Mayfair as my new partner and dispatched us to investigate an organization in San Francisco, Free the US, abbreviated FUS, advocating succession from the United States of America. They were also protesting the loss of a two-party political system. Its office had been bombed a week before we got there, killing one of the two staff who were in the office at the time, leaving one witness to identify the people responsible, men in a black van dressed in gray suits. When we heard the description of the perpetrators, Carl looked at me with a cold expression, pushed his chair back and stood. I stared at him, speculating if I should say what I wanted to say or just shut my mouth. I remember that experience as if it were yesterday. I told myself, to hell with the government, and I then advised the organization members to stop their public protests, if they wanted to live. If more violence fell on them, the Justice Department, although it should, probably wouldn't find justification for helping them or conducting any investigation. Their faces went blank as if they were in shock. One woman, a person of at least fifty, asked why. I told her we had entered into dangerous times. Carl started for the entrance, telling them the meeting was over as he opened the door. When we got back to our Washington office Carl wrote the report, stating the case lacked merit for further man-hours. Knowing the attorney general's corrupted connection to Durand, I didn't understand why my manager had sent us.

The way the intimidation-noose slowly began to strangle the remaining breath of freedom and spirit of hope in the country chewed William's insides. He knew how living in such a world could be and his heart pained with a sympathetic beat for those seeing it for the first time.

Back in Washington, after our California trip, Carl began asking strange questions about what I read and what I thought about everything going on. The alarm-hair went up on the back of my neck. I figured he was a mole sent to watch me. I suspected someone saw me as a threat, especially with all the assignments that had exposed me to the destruction of our freedoms that Durand and the NFP had perpetrated in the reconstruction of the country into a socialistic-communistic state of their vision. My being a constitutional attorney didn't help.

To resolve the interest payment issue on the national debt, Durand raised the debt limit and had the treasury issue bonds, which initially failed because no one would buy them. After Durand ordered the treasury to offer the bonds at a crazy interest rate, Germany took a chance. This fix was fine until we moved into 2023, when Durand devalued the dollar to resolve more of the debt, principally distressing China. After China protested, he paid them back seven hundred billion instead of the two trillion dollars in gold they were demanding. China, Russia, and Brazil immediately sold their holdings in dollars, and purchased Euros.

Later in 2023 and into 2024, the DOJ sent me, and my watchdog, Carl, all over the country, searching out the militia groups. We found two of the largest militia groups in Michigan and Kansas, and from what we could learn, these groups were nothing more than well armed farmers, factory workers, and store owners. The FBI had these groups in their sights so our visits were extra baggage and busywork. During an interrogation of two militia members in Kansas, they expressed their fear of big black sport utility vehicles. While we were in Indiana, a militia group barricaded itself in a barn outside Fort Wayne. Without any hesitation, overly aggressive DPP field operatives annihilated the militia using two rocket-propelled grenades (RPGs). When I caught up with an FBI agent, he said they were ordered to turn over the situation to the DPP and that's when the fireworks started.

Weeks later, I happened to take out some trash to our collection container at the side of the house and discovered the last bundle my wife had deposited had disappeared. I concluded Carl was taking items from our trash container at home and my trash basket at work, trying to see what I was reading or perhaps he was looking for written communications I'd gotten from the underground. Regardless, a year before I ran into Carl, I had stopped writing much of anything in encrypted emails, both at work and home. I had never used electronic media for communication, a practice ruled out in an early discussion with the generals.

The election of 2024 wasn't any sort of real election and would have been a joke if the country hadn't been lying on the emergency room operating table with the madman Durand holding the scalpel at its throat. The sick and manipulated country elected Durand again, surrendering all the electoral votes to him. It wasn't long before Durand unleashed more controls. The election told the world how sick we were, with only one percent of the people in the whole country voting.

Very soon thereafter, Durand issued an executive order making it impossible for anyone to sell a gun of any kind. Surprisingly, five NFP senators gave short speeches on the violation of the Constitution, but no other people spoke out publically on the subject. Everyone knew people that throughout the country, people hid their guns. One report after another came into the office about farmers arrested for hording guns. Two of the senators speaking against the action, in another coincidental accident, got a case of food poisoning from a fancy restaurant. Durand's people blamed an underground revolutionary group that wanted to create government chaos, but a few days later a fastidious doctor at the hospital somehow discovered radioactive matter in their feces. The material proved to be something extremely scary—a nasty item called polonium 210, a radioactive isotope that kills people *by radiation and slowly disappears by natural disintegration. Carl and I were working with two other DOJ attorneys and two FBI forensic experts, trying to track the isotope, when we were blindsided by the concocted explanation that an antiestablishment anarchist group claimed credit for the crime. Again, people at the top of DOJ ordered our investigation closed. I was going to ask who at the top stopped us, but again I kept my mouth shut. How would an underground group get the rare radioactive material and why would they care about two relatively obscure NFP senators?*

Nearly at the same time as the poisoning, someone blew up a government building in Houston. The Durand administration blamed it on terrorists who supposedly came into the country via our Mexican border with the help of a drug cartel. Being suspicious, I used a payphone to call a sheriff I knew in the Houston area and learned someone had seen a black van on a street video surveillance recording. He said the next day the recording disappeared from the police station. He laughed and said terrorists didn't have access to the police evidence lockup and the video. There was no doubt in my mind and in the mind of the good sheriff that it was another of Durand's secret police who had taken the video and that the incident had been orchestrated for elevating the country's threat level to create more control. Durand doubled the guards on the borders and began using random stops on interstate highways to look for the terrorists. The random highway searches seemed to be something more sinister, a harbinger of tighter control.

A sound startled William. *Beucher! Hans. No, you fool. You are home.* The noise sounded as if it were quite close to him. He snapped off his torch and tore back the blankets, hungrily listening, his heart thumping in his chest. Then another sound filtered through the dark, coming on a muffled ghostly voice. There it was again, but this time the character of the intrusion was familiar, infuriating him by its invasion. It was the damn vid-screen system spouting SAC announcements in his living room. He hadn't destroyed the beast, the vid-screen, after all. He heard it clearly, floating to him like a hated phantom.

One of the usual mechanical female voices from the vid-screen said, "Announcement: All citizens are requested to be on the alert for two criminals who stole a shipment of meat coupons. The coupons were to be given to needy families. The men shown here in this picture are presumed armed and are extremely dangerous. They are believed to belong to a revolutionary group dedicated to making the lives of our citizens harder. A reward will be paid for information leading to their arrest. A reward is also being offered for information leading to the arrest of a woman and her two children. The woman may answer to the name, Lynn, and the DPP believes a fringe underground group is helping her. She was last seen north of Fairfax, Virginia. Long live Father Durand. This announcement ends."

William wondered if the theft were true about the two men stealing coupons. The SAC could have created a phony story in an effort to spread uncertainty, fear, and emotional dependency on the government's nanny blanket of security, which was cloaked control. Suddenly, he realized he had heard an announcement about a woman and two children. It had to be Lynn. She had to be free. Tears filled his eyes. He felt a surge of hope, of despair, of love, of hollowness, tearing through his chest—and he felt new energy, energy of hope for his family surviving.

If only some force could assassinate Durand. No. That wouldn't work. It would take the elimination of many people in addition to him; the surgery would have to be nearly simultaneous in many areas. He had a burning hunger to finish his reading, to hear about more areas attacked by Durand's corrupted mind.

William pulled the blankets back over his head, turned on his torch, and as he looked at the pages of his father's words, disappointment gathered on the fringe of his thinking; he hadn't yet heard any great secret. The end approached within a just few pages. Sadly, he hadn't read anything that constituted a lethal threat to Durand's empire or any revolutionary idea.

Durand replaced Babcock with Coleman Lloyd as his attorney general. Lloyd had the reputation for marching as a dedicated Durand soldier. He was a solitary and vengeful man who would fall on his sword for Durand. After the change, a rash of suspicious security-threatening events erupted, seemingly orchestrated to justify implementation of more regulations related to the protection of the public and national safety. The first event consisted of a bomb placed near the Rayburn House Office Building in Washington, and although it didn't do much damage, it provided an excuse for Durand to make another move that had been predicted by one of the agents I'd met in the underground group. He organized the FBI, CIA, and NSA all under the DPP umbrella, giving Coleman Lloyd an administrative connection. Shortly thereafter, a man in the CIA leaked information to the New York Times internet newspaper debunking the terrorist attack, stating that Durand faked the attack to create the justification for grabbing control of the investigative and intelligence agencies. Special agents working for Durand traced the leak, identified the reporter at the newspaper who wrote the article, and interrogated the reporter harshly until he identified the CIA leak. Durand's stooges within the DOJ charged the reporter and prosecuted him for releasing classified materials. Later, while the DPP held the CIA person and the reporter for their trial other prisoners tried escaping from the same facility. During the confusion of the failed jail escape, the DPP accidentally shot the CIA person and reporter.

Later in the year, to my horror, Durand placed the Department of Justice under DPP. My spare time increased dramatically. I worked on a white paper covering states' rights and the constitutionality of states to have their own right to bear arms, which I was thinking about circulating on the internet, although I was scared Durand's goons would kill me. I was trying to stay busy. I think one of Durand's intelligence people saw my notes on my desk during that span of time, possibly during lunchtime. My superior reprimanded me for wasting time, even though I had plenty of time at the office. My personal mole, Carl, kept asking me where I got my ideas, and with whom was I meeting. A few weeks later somebody up the chain of command replaced Carl with Marty Gibson, who I initially thought might be an ordinary attorney like myself.

Durand took the existing communication legislation, tweaked it to his liking, and forced a bill through Congress officially forming the Department of Facts and Fairness, DFF, which I mentioned before in relation to speech control. The new law required all newspapers and media get permission before they reported anything that would tarnish morale or sentiment about the government or the country.

Then, wouldn't you just know it, on my next assignment my manager sent me to visit news and print media companies, and gave me the responsibility of checking their compliance with the new legislation, explaining the new regulations, listening to their complaints, and recording names. As a result of DFF's comprehensive control program, they began the broad review of history books written after Durand took office.

It wasn't many days before Marty Gibson's clandestine purpose began to spawn clues. He tried suckering me into discussing the likelihood of an underground revolutionary organization taking over the government. We were sitting in the office drinking coffee and he just blurted it out, as if he needed to cough up a bad piece of hotdog; he hinted with a wink that he knew I belonged to such an effort. Strangely, I hadn't given him any reason for such an allegation. He was obviously just probing. He clearly had no talent for probative spy work. He was about as delicate as a butcher trying to remove someone's tonsils with a cleaver.

Meanwhile, adding to his hit list, Durand proved there were no sacred cows. He took on the social security system, proving in 2025 that it wasn't exempt from massive changes to further his obsession for power. Durand moved the replacement for social security, the National Living Share Payment, money paid to people who didn't work, either because of disability or age, under a newly structured Department of Treasury. Durand raised the age of eligibility for the share payment to seventy years.

Carrying out his scheme for control of medical services, which was under the national healthcare system, he required each doctor to see a minimum number of people per month and he required each patient get a government voucher before going to a doctor. In addition, his government gave the doctors a fee schedule limiting their salaries that further discouraged doctors from practicing medicine, making it nearly impossible for them to pay expenses, let alone make enough income to provide for their own families. This resulted in the departure of increasing numbers of medical professionals to other countries and it sent many to work in a black market of medicine. The number of doctors dwindled from a 2008 number of 660,000 to 100,000 at the last count I had seen.

Durand clobbered another piece of the nation's information infrastructure in 2026. Television executives for ABC, a television and radio broadcasting company, were accused of broadcasting classified information on an agreement between the US and Russia. My manager at the DOJ assigned me and two other attorneys to investigate and form the government's case for prosecuting the alleged criminals. My manager hinted that we probably shouldn't find anything. When I asked him why, he brushed the question aside. The broadcast report alleged an agreement stipulating how the US and Russia planned to work together to clean Islamic extremist groups from countries in the Middle East, including Chechnya. In our investigation, Jeffery Van der Linden and I confirmed Durand's own people leaked the information. It was another piece of a surreptitious plan, creating a security breach, finding media people guilty, and ultimately obtaining an excuse to tighten controls on all the media, television, internet, radio, and newsprint. This was part of Durand's stranglehold on the freedom of the press—and the control of information reaching across the nation. I wrote the report and copied my manager and his boss. Within *hours of my submitting my report up the ladder, my manager called Jeffery and me in to undergo questioning by a team of four gray-suited spooky people from an unnamed group within the DPP. We sat down at a table in a small room with a mirrored observation window. They wanted names of the people talking and doing the leaking of details on the operation. I remember one of the spooks touching my wrist, which was a strange physical contact in that setting, and after that, my head became hazy. I woke up the next day in an alley, my clothes saturated with alcohol and an empty bourbon bottle in my hand. They accused me of being a spy. I think they tried some brainwashing techniques on me. I couldn't remember much of anything. I reported it to the police, who promised to investigate, and I informed my manager. My boss pulled me aside and whispered in my ear, "If you know what's good for you, you had better shut your mouth and go about your business. If you had just given me the report and not sent it higher, this wouldn't have happened." He then told me that they found my colleague, Jeffery, floating in Rock Creek east of Georgetown. I think they let me go so they could follow me to the underground. Marty Gibson, who they hadn't called into this meeting, pretended to be sympathetic, but he kept watching my every move.*

In January of 2027, they assigned me to handle prosecutions of violators of the National Living Share Payment benefits from the Department of Wellbeing, a do-nothing paper-shuffling job. After the drugging, I watched my surroundings like a hawk, anticipating Durand's goons grabbing me again. I figured I might eventually disappear into a river somewhere.

Russia and Durand's government declared war against Pakistan and Afghanistan in May of 2027, the AFPAK war, and Durand used the conflict to build his new army with his new team of loyal generals. It wasn't long before Iran began sending more weapons into Pakistan, a destabilization activity they'd been pursuing as far back as the late 1990s. With Durand's movement toward more isolation, helping with the war didn't make sense, except it was a way to divert attention from his increasing grip on the country's freedom, creating a point for the country to focus its energies and frustrations, and a theater in which he could test his military.

In June of 2027, a cataclysmic disaster struck our country. The chilling announcement rang out across our televisions and radios like a verbal hammer to the nation's forehead, bringing a crescendo of despair. The Durand and his minions of the NFP announced the country was now and henceforth to be called State America and that the new government was the State America Committee, the SAC. The SAC replaced the representative republic with a totalitarian government run by a group of men. The SAC was directed at the top by Adrian Durand, as the chairman. Durand picked three vice chairmen to work under him. The United States of America died that year. It was the year Durand slammed the prison door shut on four hundred million citizens. To make a visible sign of the break with the past and symbolize the change, Durand declared he was building new administration buildings, including his residence within one of them, relegating the Whitehouse to a sightseeing attraction. Rumors flew that he was going to demolish the Whitehouse, but he didn't.

Protest marches erupted all over the nation. A cross-section of young people and silver-haired old-timers assembled in cities, chanting and speaking of lofty freedoms, until armed Department of People Protection goons marched against them. The largest protests were in Washington, Philadelphia, Chicago, and Los Angles. In Washington, the DPP gave orders to disperse and when the people didn't move, they fired rubber bullets and teargas. They somehow killed five people, and as if by plan, they killed three people in Philadelphia. In Los Angeles, people set buildings on fire and the DPP arrested more than a hundred protesters. Some of the protesters never made it to the detention center alive. The real horror came at the second protest in Washington a week later. This second protest boasted eighty thousand people. When people began throwing rocks and burning bottles of flammable liquid at the DPP, military tanks rolled down the streets to disperse the crowd. The crowd set tanks on fire. As the DPP fired real bullets at the protesters, a military tank crushed two people under its tread. When people watched the news on the SAC-controlled television, the narrator described the protests as small disturbances full of racists and hate speech. None of the violence was shown. The truth leaked out by word of mouth and over the internet until Durand's government temporarily shut down the internet. British and Canadian news accounts suggested a broader protest, but offered no video footage as proof. Durand's people shut down satellite communications for British and Canadian news people; they couldn't even send pictures from their cell phones. The British claimed there were thousands of political prisoners rounded up by the Durand government. I was told Durand had collected at least two thousand people, although I couldn't verify the numbers. In the following days, the TV reports were silent on the protests. The boot of oppression came down hard and swift, quickly bringing an eerie and gloomy silence to the cities. I talked with a longtime colleague at the DOJ, whom I could trust, and learned that the British press got their information from an underground shortwave broadcast and later they obtained pictures that were smuggled out of the country when Durand ordered all foreign press out of State America.

Durand demonstrated his resentment for the people after seeing the demonstrations of blistering hate for him. He had his gray-suited secret police enter the Library of Congress, gather a truckload of books, including works from the special collections by Jefferson and Benjamin Franklin, and had them set on fire on the Capitol steps in full view of his controlled video cameras. People screamed in horror as best they could in their new Durand controlled country.

I had one of my last meetings with members of the new revolutionary underground. After plastering Durand with every cursing epithet imaginable, we lowered our heads, promising renewed drive, and promising our personal sacrifice to retake the country. We discussed a new project for a future offensive measure, talking over placing a bomb near Durand's new office, something that could symbolize the revolt, even if it only blew out a few windows.

Except for the initial protests, lasting only hours, the country's passing happened in a rather benign manner, as if the angel of death had crept in silently and smothered the country. Apparently, Durand had established the control needed to suffocate any armed militia protest, having strategically placed his chess pieces over the years.

The people who associated with the CLP and citizens registered as conservative voters were silent after the initial protests for fear Durand would collect them and imprison them. Rumors floated around about arrests of people who were once CLP staff workers, people who had operated conservative websites on the internet, and other outspoken pundits critical of Durand.

Reader, I must tell you that even now, as I write this chronicle, which is necessarily aimed at capturing some of the key events for documenting history, I feel the deepest sorrow for my country. It's as if I have lost a mother or father.

In the area of world economics, Mexico, Spain, and Greece slid into bankruptcy in late 2027, the third time for Greece. Durand loaned Mexico money in exchange for leases on a large portion of their oil and precious metals mining. As part of the bargain, Durand ran massive military raids on the Mexican drug cartels, his troops indiscriminately killing hundreds.

Under the heading of censorship, all textbooks, old and new, were revised at the college and lower levels under the premise that a tranquil society could only be achieved if the past errors were prevented from infecting future decisions. Durand established a board to review all fiction books.

It was early 2028 when Durand formed the Department of State America Protection (DSAP). Director Helmut Kauffman began running DSAP as its first officer. The new DSAP was composed of all the previous intelligence departments, the Department of People Protection(DPP), sometimes called the street police, the Department of State Protection, which was the national military that carried out foreign wars, and the Department of Facts and Fairness(DFF). Kauffman placed all intelligence organizations under the State America Committee Intelligence (SACI) group and personally handled the SACI. The SACI handled foreign and domestic intelligence.

While sitting in my office in early 2028, literally burning time by reading a tattered old magazine, waiting to hear what was going to happen to the Department of Justice, three men in gray suits arrived at my desk and arrested me. They didn't give me any reason. SACI goons took me to SACI for questioning, which was in the Washington D.C., NSA building, since Durand hadn't completed the new building. I had no idea if they would torture me and then kill met, but my answer came quickly.

Durand's unidentified goons deposited me in a holding room that had a simple collapsible bed, sink, and toilet. Then, as near as I can figure, within hours of my confinement some military officers attempted to breach the security at the Whitehouse, apparently attempting a hostile takeover. All but three of the twenty were wiped out. Sometime later that night, when the SACI agents moved me to different area, I saw another SACI team leading men in military uniforms down a nearby hall. Within a few minutes, I heard the most horrible screams from that location.

My interrogators pushed me into a room with a table and chair, both of which had straps. Minutes after my interrogators placed me in the chair and began slamming me with questions in the beam of a blinding light, they wiped something wet across the back of my neck; I assumed a drug. By the second day, I had resigned myself that I would die. I was gravely worried about leaving my family alone. Late the third day, they released me, and by that time, still had not told me my crime. My head was spinning on and off for two days. I had no idea what, if anything I told them while under their drugs. When I got back home, the SAC-operated television news reported that all the military that had attacked the Whitehouse were dead.

A day later, two disastrous events cut into my gut. The first came when I learned Durand was eliminating DOJ, and the second stabbing pain came when the SAC announced the executions of several prominent people for treason. Army two-star general,

Sylvester Carlson, Marine four-star general, Jake Underhay, former NFP senator from New York, Robert McGraw, and Barkley Stoner, the Justice from the Second Circuit, US Court of Appeals, New York, and Princeton professor, Russell Yates.

A week later, I got an encrypted message telling me the SACI had penetrated my underground group of people, and that everyone should go into hiding. My underground group gave me instructions on a location where I could hide, instructions for a final mission, and what I was to do for future communication. From what I knew, the resistance-underground had been seriously damaged, if not destroyed. Its status was unknown. The last bit of information I received from the group before I went into hiding urged the last person alive to keep the freedom-candle burning until one of us completed the ultimate mission.

When I go over everything that plunged us into this condition of slavery, I can't help thinking of something I told my son when he was very young. What we really want is often right under our nose. Freedom.

William found that sentence filled with words oddly disconnected from the general text. Could it have been a momentary lapse in his father's logic or festering depression erupting into his writing? His father had repeated the same phrase at the bunker, seemingly out of some sort of mental fixation, perhaps an artifact of a deteriorating mental state. Maybe there were more clues to the meaning ahead on the remaining pages. What was the ultimate mission?

I left home within an hour of receiving the warning. I had to go into hiding before the SAC used my family against me, and make no mistake about it, they would have tied me down and peeled the skin off my children and my wife in front of me to make me talk. I had to leave. I selected a location in the south, in the mountains, one of the three secure places I could go, if I wanted to stay alive, if I wanted to serve my country, and if I wanted to save my family, to wait with hope everyday that my country would escape its imprisonment. Leaving my family ripped out my soul.

By 2032, the world conflict hadn't subsided. For some strange reason, when a conflict arose between Israel and Iran, Durand refused to back away from support of Israel. Iran moved militarily by launching their new surface-to-surface rockets from hundreds of miles away from Israel and smuggled rockets into the old Gaza area through Egypt. The SAC reported in their controlled news that Iran launched two large rockets believed to have contained nuclear weapons. Luckily, Israel had greatly enhanced their antimissile defense, extending the technology originally provided by the US military years before Durand took over. Israel shot down both the Iranian missiles. When Israel analyzed the warheads, they found they were indeed plutonium nuclear warheads. Through a shortwave broadcast, I learned the Israelis hit Tehran with a large nuclear device. The surrounding Muslim states began preparations for conflict, but when the Israelis dropped a second nuclear device on Iran and a smaller nuclear bomb in Syria all the hostiles took a step back. Caustic peace talks began but no real truce was ever achieved. The radioactive fallout hit State America in five days, drifting with the jet stream air current. Durand's government announced they were sending inspectors across the country to check iodine-131, cesium-137, and strontium-90 levels. These are three of the major radioactive isotopes in the fallout. No one reported the findings; however, Iran and Syria suffered massive destruction and radiation.

The SAC purged more people in 2036 for conspiracy against the Durand government; one of them was a well-known writer for the New York Times, Editor Cornelius Hawthorne Whitney. Durand's people executed him for sedition. Shortly thereafter, the congresswoman from Virginia, Paula Stinson, was sent to prison. There were a couple other people executed for treason.

Durand's SAC began closing the economy in 2040, determined to make the State self-sufficient, eliminating imports and exports. This shocked China and Europe, sending their treasuries into a spin. They demanded payment for all the United States treasuries they held and they wanted payment in gold. Durand promised to continue paying the interest rate on the original bonds in gold if they canceled their demand for the total outstanding amount. If they didn't, he wouldn't give them compensation for their investments, which now belonged to the State. This threat didn't sit well with the bondholders. The most heavily invested countries convened an economic summit to address how they could force the new State America to comply, and after a lot of verbal bluster full of embargo threats and total world isolation, Durand relented, agreeing to pay back "every damn penny" over a fifty year period in exchange for cooperation on world Islamic terrorist threats. Apparently, Durand was worried about a nuclear attack by a splinter extremist organization, something he couldn't completely control. In addition to the worry over a random nuclear event, having adequate strategic minerals worried him. If Durand had all the minerals he needed he would have stopped all trade outside the country, but he needed materials like lithium, gallium, and silicon for electronics and batteries. The stock market, irrelevant at the time, was dissolved.

Durand's closed economy brought harsh changes to the country. He put people to work in government-operated companies, earning wages in dollars, which employees were required to use to buy government coupons for housing, food, and travel. The coupons became a survival-umbilical to the SAC government womb, effectively chaining every citizen to the SAC. It was simple and yet deadly. The SAC sent engineers to work on technology deemed important to the SAC. SAC told the farmers what crops to plant and how much to plant—before the SAC managers took over the farms. For a few years, there were private businesses, such as food markets, clothes stores, and some minor home supplies, but eventually the State confiscated the property and took over all commerce.

The last communication I received from my friends came by shortwave radio in the year 2045. Spread out over several days in brief broadcast bursts, the final message hurt me on a personal level. It also made me question whether the underground had a chance of *taking back the country. My friend from the underground, General Buck Firestone, was killed at his Idaho ranch while fighting off a DPP assault force trying to capture him. It reported he showed great courage with his two machineguns, well-coordinated personnel mines, and homemade napalm. I loved the general like a brother, even though I only talked face-to-face with him four or five times. He was the type of man who looked you in the eye and made you feel like a brother; he could make you feel like you could go into battle with a BB gun. I still remember the last time we talked, when we were planning our sewer project. In particular, the General made a reference that made me burst out laughing.*

He said, "I'd like to stick a warhead from one of our W-59 Minuteman missiles right up the SAC's ass." He shrugged and added, "It would only be five hundred pounds, only a little five megaton firecracker, but it would get their attention."

I asked him about the size of the Hiroshima bomb.

He grinned and laughingly said, "Oh, it was a whopping fifteen kilotons." He then gave one of his big belly laughs, almost a Santa Claus laugh, and continued, "I'll probably not live long enough to see it." He slapped me on the shoulder like an old friend, laughed again, and said, "You know, I heard the damndest thing. One of those same nukes came up missing a year or so ago." He gazed off, kind of in a trance and turned to me. "I hope Durand's world is blown to shit in a fireball. And if I can't personally do it, I hoped a man with the courage of a patriot will suck it up and get it done."

Of course, we never got to that point. They buried the big fuel oil and fertilizer bomb in the floor of the sewer and carved Norman's name on a wall opposite the bomb to identify the site. I guess they wanted to give that bastard some credit for the country's death.

Durand took the country and its people down a very dark road. At an early point in State America, the hypocrisy of Durand's relationship was exposed. The people saw Durand in the light of day, and saw that his talk of equalizing the human condition was pure propaganda. They finally saw him as just another despot thug. The glorious idealistic SAC gave people in the new SA military, the DPP force, and the SAC administration, special privileges, including special homes, special food coupons, and the best jobs. Equality of wealth and privilege did not materialize. It was a lie—as it has been with collective systems since the beginning of time. There is always a person running the collective system and all those not involved with its operation become a slave workforce.

From the early 2030s until now, the year 2054, Durand progressively implemented and perfected his police state, utilizing controls on every aspect of people's lives, assigning people to occupations, regulating and rationing food with coupons, directing where people could live, and identifying volunteers for the military. Now—instead of being willing to give away freedom, a few people in the underground hope to find an escape from the relentless dreary existence created by Durand. They hope to get back just a little bit of freedom, the liberty their father's didn't prize highly enough, the freedom their father's recklessly squandered.

According to a couple of the last information exchanges I had with the underground, Durand has initiated one of the final phases of his control. This started around 2047 under Helmut Kauffman and a perverted psychologist, Doctor Conrad Beucher. I had gotten a briefing on Beucher years earlier. Doctor Beucher, a dark creature spawned by the CIA, took his expertise in mind control to new levels of human torment and helped form the Thought Mentoring Department, TMD, within SACI. Within a few years, their work evolved into experimentation with thought mentoring via sinus cavity implants, whose function is still partially unknown. Around 2049, the SAC began implanting all babies with some sort of tracking device. Once they have implanted the total population, the human race's ability to exercise freedom of choice within State America will face its end. Revolution will have become impossible! They will have the ability to send signals to the implants to kill or mentally impair a freedom fighter. In fact, they may be able to control thought.

The first signs of nano-bot implementation was observed in 2051 and reported through the underground. The SAC indiscriminately used people as guinea pigs. They started the program with SAC personnel they considered disloyal, people who had merely questioned or complained about relocation, food coupons or an assignment. According to intelligence reports, following the initial laboratory tests they used this technique on portions of the general population as an experiment to increase work output and to engrain mental patterns. The evil doctors tormented such sacrificial subjects with the experimental devices as information specialists, analysts, supervisors, managers, and section heads who disappointed to the SAC elite. These test subjects were sent to an SAC resort spa supposedly under the pretext of a holiday, but once they were there, they were implanted with a device, which when signal-activated, caused the brain to release some combination of endorphins, dopamine, serotonin or other body chemicals. The SAC seems to have developed the most recent version of the implant for pacifying the population, reducing threats of people overthrowing the government. Once they have implemented this latest violation across the country, the world's capacity for dehumanizing people will have sunk to its lowest level. Some of the implants are designed to activate with control signals sent from vid-screens installed everywhere in the country.

Now that I've nearly arrived at my conclusion, I must fill in some important elements of the revolution against the SAC. Many years ago, patriots asked me to help with a mission coordinated by two generals, who are long dead, a mission to move and bury a bomb in the sewer under the SAC building in Washington. The reason for this operation was connected with Durand moving out of the Whitehouse and using a new office in the monstrous new SAC headquarters, a building to be built with the most modern methods, including sloped exterior stone walls designed to deflect any street-side explosions. The gleaming white marble structure positioned in the middle of blocks of old downtown Washington D.C. real estate, although only limited to ten floors above ground, was to be the ego-gratifying symbol of his new power and control. Once the plans were underway for the new presidential office, our underground resistance moved quickly to install the device before construction of the new building commenced. Since the bomb was to be located nearly right under Durand's ass, it had to be sizeable, requiring a large truck and a large sewer work crew. Interestingly, the underground group buried the bomb before the SAC broke ground for its new SAC administration building, and General Buck Firestone personally supervised the sewer crew. General Firestone said it was his 'John Hancock' signature on a declaration of freedom. Then he cited a line from that document, "But when a long train of abuses and usurpations, pursuing invariably the same object evinces a design to reduce them under absolute despotism, it is their right, it is their duty, to throw off such Government, and to provide new Guards for their future security."

Going on from here, the future is destined to plunge more deeply toward a fiery hell when Bernard Ivan Gordon Bruner, the sociopath, replaces Durand. Once Bruner takes over as SAC chairman, the nation and the people will be pushed to the lowest extremes of slavery, where death on the job while working for the SAC will be the norm and not the exception. Everyone will be on food rationing and the Bruner will use the present food coupons as psychological torture. The State will consist of slaves and masters, although the current status isn't much different. The slaves will have TS-V implants. The TS-V derives from the terms, total solution, version five. The TS-V will give them total electronic control, even instant death at the push of a button and a microwave signal. In addition, programmed euthanasia is included in his agenda, with the possibility of assigned dates for termination. The euthanasia derives from an old United Nations program called Agenda 21, which President Thomas Norman attempted and failed to push past his own NFP people.

Reader, I know what I'm telling you will be discovered by the SAC, most likely when they brainwash who ever reads this. One of the last messages from my contacts told me that I was one of the last alive with special knowledge, and it was my responsibility to make the final sacrifice for the country. As I pass away, I hope with all my heart my sentinel time hasn't been for naught and someone will pick up the flame, and carry it into the future.

This is the end of my chronicle. In these last few words, I offer my assessment of what caused this horrible condition to befall the world's great experiment as a constitution based federal republic. I've asked myself a thousand times how it happened and why people didn't see the lies and deception. Specifically, I believe the failure was threefold. First, and maybe the most significant was the total failure of the printed and broadcast journalistic media to report objectively the facts about events, policy, human greed, and corruption. The journalistic media of the time failed to ascend to the lofty definition—writing characterized by a direct presentation of facts or description of events without an attempt at interpretation. They were the guardian eyes and ears of the people and they failed! The second failure came from an uneducated populace, people stupidly happy, people too willing to accept simple solutions wrapped in grandiose platitudes and grand oratory, people too willing to accept hollow political promises without a modicum of analysis, and people totally ignorant of the blessing of the Constitution. The people, acting as a mob, were too willing to trample the Constitution that had served so brilliantly since its creation. The SAC took away people's ideals by allowing them to live like a parasite off the host government. People were too willing to take the easy government handout, surrendering to greed—from the wealthy elite voter right down to the poorest voter in the country. As this infection of mind and soul grew, cutting into the flesh of the proletariat, down to the working heart of the nation, it was easy to observe that the nation's soul had lost its moral code. The people surrendered their self-respect and conscience for favors, instead of using their freedom and pride to make their own way. By not nurturing the higher purpose of ideals and not urging people to improve themselves, and fight with self-respect for a better life, and by people not fighting the addiction to State welfare, the people lost their souls. If you give away your freedoms, the looter will steal your soul!

Third and last, the representatives elected by the people failed their oaths to the people and the country. Our lazy populace, trusting them, elected them to office. Sadly, too many people, the voters, who sent men to raise up the country, did so seeking the greedy favors of looters. The people sent politicians to represent them who lacked commitment to any moral code, who then looted the nation's future of achievements by exploiting power to satisfy personal greed and to repay their looter benefactors—instead of doing their proper job rendering judgments consistent with their oath and moral code to move the nation upward along the best evolutionary path. The press ignored the representatives. And for their punishment those representatives and members of the press should burn in hell for prostituting their souls and our country for power and money. The people gave away their freedoms!

The single factor that gave birth to these diseased children of society (the collective-preaching progressives, the detached uneducated voters, and the pocket-filling elected) was a crisis, the crisis of principles—morality, ethics, and integrity. People of virtue failed to stop the growing hollow mob who coveted incompetence and admired the dispensers of the unearned. When used as a virtue the term, 'integrity' refers to a quality of a person's character. When the mindless masses and the mob's integrity slid into the abyss of slime and corruption, without the people of virtue holding the mob unaccountable, the virtuously courageous bequeathed the only product possible—the destruction of the country by political cannibalism.

I sincerely hope I have given you a picture of the slow metastasizing cancer that crept over the country, turning what was the light of the world into a dark prison of despair. I urge the individual patriot still alive to rise up, not for the faceless mob, but for himself as a free spirit fighting for his own freedom against a many-headed monster. By this patriot visiting the monster's sewer near SAC headquarters, locating Durand's picture on the wall, bringing that despicable face down, returning hope with moral code in hand, writing the alpha to cause an overdue omega, maybe he can release the cleansing light of a thousand suns.

I hope for a new beginning.

527

Chapter 29

His father's words painted a picture William never could have imagined and even as he reached the end of the long chronicle, they were unfulfilling, leaving him thirsty for more. With his emotions soaring and plunging, up with pride for what his father had done, and down with disgust and anger for the people who had abdicated their duty to protect the freedoms of a once free society, and anger at the people who had stolen his opportunity to live in a once fine land. They had cheated him of a legacy. He then remembered his promise.

Turning off his torch, he pulled down his covers, trying to think of his next move. Rolling onto his back, staring into the darkness surrounding him, allowing his mind to go back over his father's words, he analyzed and tried connecting a few subtle and curious references. No doubt, his father had employed a cryptological awareness when preparing the chronicle. The words repeated in William's brain, undergoing his dissection, hopeful parsing, and reassembly from what he thought his father might have considered important. Certainty of message and ultimate purpose were ghostly at best. He now faced a critical decision.

The jackhammer promise chiseled his brain, a commitment he had made with a subconscious belief the opportunity would never occur, loomed before him. The vision of visiting a sewer, fulfilling a promise to his father, standing in front of Durand's picture came to mind. It seemed purely a spiritual act on his father's behalf, one he intended to complete out of his debt to his father. He gazed off past the room, as if through the walls. Yes, he had to see the picture on the wall. *What we want is under our nose.* His dad didn't say under our nose at the last, he had specifically said under 'the' nose.

Other words continued to stir in his mind. An element of what he had read lingered on the edge of an idea. It troubled him. It was something other than the overall content of what he read, something beneath the surface—the information vital to the SAC as well as the underground. Even though his father hadn't written the chronicle specifically for him, it seemed quite possible his father had been trying to convey a hidden message to whoever read the pages, especially since his father couldn't continue much longer. Another reason to suspect there was a message entwined in the words was the way the SAC still considered his father a threat after so many years. He didn't know why, but he had one of those indescribable feelings that he had missed a message buried in the words. However, having endured Beucher's brain manipulation, he knew his thinking could be way off balance.

His father mentioned weapons. The way his father had discussed the bomb openly without any attempt at deception seemed strange. Again, he thought of his father saying that old adage. Why had his father requested him to visit Durand's picture in the sewer as one last remembrance? He had asked the same thing in the last portion of the chronicle. Perhaps his father had been isolated too long and was trying to be poetic. *No! He was sane.* William considered the last sentence and its references. On the far fringe of his thinking a realization formed. He grinned. He liked the reference to the brightness of a thousand suns, it seemed quite appropriate for the whole government.

He rubbed his forehead and then his eyes. All the history, all the acts of human depravity, all the subtle acts that slowly stripped the freedom-flesh from the nation body, were more than he could have fathomed. Why did people embrace the idea they should be in control of another human? Why was there a collective of the population, a majority, willing to settle for selfless sharing of government handouts, the payment for which was the sacrifice of their integrity and ultimately their soul? Were the capable and prosperous people sucked down into the muck out of a sense of guilt, because they had risen above the less capable, or were they sacrificed by the mob because they had fought the fight to keep their soul? It seemed persecution and control would be unavoidable at this time in the SAC's evolution. Curiously, despite being initially disguised in candy-promises of good intention, the reign of dictators always mutated into whips and chains as if by some mysterious cosmic law. That seemed to be the answer. Regardless of the SAC sending him to capture his father, the brutality of the SAC would have eventually come down on his own head and his family's.

With his eyes becoming wet with tears, he suddenly felt anger and then pure hatred. How could he fight back? He felt like he understood his father's words and feelings. With the SAC intent on persecuting him, he now conceded he had been born too late to taste true freedom, but his wife and children still had a chance to savor its sweetness.

The pain was growing again in his head, beginning to pound with every pulse of blood going through his veins. He pushed it away from his thoughts.

Lynn and the kids. He saw them in his mind. They came at him like a marching drumbeat for a cause, the only cause there could be for him now, their survival. He desperately wanted to know they were alive and doing well. He remembered Stefan's weird note about finding his watch, and a reference to Stefan's friend Russell, a boy Stefan had never brought to the house, much less mentioned.

He collected the papers, slid them under the mattress, and sat up, swinging his legs over the edge of the bed, immediately feeling dizzy and tired. He sat there waiting for his head to clear, slowly rubbing his eyes and breathing easily, listening to his own breath, waiting for strength to come. He was still exhausted from Beucher's chairs, and he still felt soreness in his back and stomach.

The watch!

He had almost forgotten. With his hands poking through the dark, he felt his way to the dresser, where he let his fingers seek out objects. There was a coin, then a key to something, and then the watch. When he touched it, the digital face suddenly glowed red. It was nothing like any watched he had ever owned. He held it up and studied at it, and just as the face started to dim, tiny words appeared.

It read: Location of first kiss?

William didn't move, stunned by what he saw. Then suddenly realized he had to protect it from any vid-cam that might be looking through a hole in the wall. He cupped a hand around the side of the watch.

The watch's display winked out and returned. The watch displayed three choices to the question, displaying them one at a time: 1-front porch, 2-backporch, 3-dancefloor.

The screen then showed three numbers and a flashing cursor. He pushed a button on the side of the watch, finding it moved the cursor left, the wrong direction, and after trying the other four buttons he managed to highlight the number one. He pushed the fifth button to submit his selection. The display then asked him his favorite dessert. He selected banana cream. The display asked his wife's favorite dessert. He selected raspberry pie.

He thought for a second. Wait a minute—how did they know these questions? The SAC couldn't have known such details.

The display asked him how many rooms were in their first apartment. He answered two. The display then told him that his wife and kids were safe and they were several hundred miles from him. The watch display asked if he was okay and gave him a grid with the alphabet. With the cursor and enter button he answered, yes, but watched. He looked around the dark bedroom and then asked the people on the other end of the mysterious watch about the safety of the communication connection.

"Very safe," they replied.

"Can you escape?"

"Watched too closely." He swallowed hard, thinking of his family. He typed, "Now know secret. Have a big job to do."

"What job?"

"I have my father's chronicle. Russell knows where hidden.

"What is job?

A hollow feeling gripped William, robbing his breath as his eyes filled with tears. He entered the words, "Freedom for my family." That was, if his theory was valid.

"Get people clear of Washington Wednesday PM, tomorrow."

"What will happen?"

"Do not know for certain. Hope."

"Can we help?"

"Tell wife and kids I love them more than life." His heart hammered in his chest. He only had a feeling.

"Will do. Please destroy watch completely."

He typed, "Goodbye." Standing there in the dark, he sighed as if he had crossed a threshold.

He shoved the unique watch in his pocket, amazed and grateful for word on his family. It was curious, but in a way, that word removed the remaining shackles on his heart. He removed the chronicle from under the mattress and made his way in the dark to the kitchen. He opened refrigerator door and with its light found Lynn's sugar canister sitting on the counter, a simple metal can with a twist-on lid. At the trash container, nothing more than a simple plastic bucket with a lid, he hunched over its top, emptied the sugar and inserted the chronicle with as little motion as he could manage. He went to the garage for a shovel, and silently he crept out to the edge of the short back walk. At the location where he told Russell to look for instructions, he shaved off the layer of sod, buried the chronicle, and replaced the sod so it looked nearly untouched, at least as near as he could see in the faint glow of light bouncing off the overhead clouds.

Cloaked by the dark of his garage, he searched his workbench, feeling random shapes until he found his hammer and a rag for wiping floors. He laughed to himself. He had only used the hammer to hang a picture or two for Lynn, and now he would use it for something he never would have imagined in one of his craziest dreams. Pushing away a Beucher-inflected pain in his back, he knelt down on the concrete floor, wrapped the watch in the cloth, and laid it out flat. He slammed the hammer repeatedly onto the cloth encapsulating watch, beating its fragments until they felt too small for study. Even if the watchers heard him hammering, they wouldn't find anything to study. He went into the bathroom next to the kitchen, and dropped the contents of the cloth into the toilet. He flushed the toilet, turned on the light to check for any residual parts and flushed it a second time, making certain the toilet had completely swallowed the evidence. Staring at the swirling toilet water, feeling relief from the excitement, he thought he felt invigorated from knowing his final objective.

Suddenly a voice popped into his head. *Confess to Beucher. You made progress. You need to join Father Durand's family.* His stomach began to churn. What had they done to him? *You are home. Fight it.*

Chapter 30

A knock on the door awakened Lynn and as the webs of sleep dropped away, she heard a woman's voice, low and muffled filtering through the dark. She glanced at the small clock on the little night stand. Why would someone come to her door at three in the morning? She slid to the edge of her bunk, coming fully awake, grabbing her robe from the back of a chair, wrapping it around her as she padded across the cold stone floor. When she cracked the door, she found Claudia. Claudia looked at Lynn solemnly, her mouth drawn and her eyes betraying to Lynn the seriousness of the visit. Claudia's brow furrowed as her eyes glistened. Lynn's breath stopped in her chest.

"Sorry to wake you at this horrible hour but I had to give you the news," Claudia whispered in an unrushed voice, as if emphasizing her hating to pass the message.

Lynn covered her mouth with a tightened fist. "William?"

"He's alive and home. He found our watch and we exchanged some information. He says he's okay but can't escape because he's closely watched."

"Thank God, he's okay. But . . . you . . . there's something else . . . isn't there?"

"He said he had a job to do and to tell you that he loved you and the kids dearly."

Lynn shook her head incredulously, her face growing pale. "What job?"

"He said his job was to give you freedom."

Lynn gasped. "That can't be."

Looking bewildered, Claudia replied, "All we know is he advised our people to get far away from the SAC headquarters. We don't know why." Claudia pulled out a handkerchief and dabbed her nose. "My man is there somewhere. I hope he can escape."

Lynn began to cry. "My William's going to do something crazy. I just know it. Isn't there something your people can do?"

"Lynn, he's being watched by vid-cams in your home, he's being watched by a v-tran outside, and he's probably been implanted with a tracking device. Our people would get slaughtered trying to extract him. If there was a way the generals would do it."

Claudia pushed the door open a little, stretched out her arms, and hugged Lynn. Lynn felt as if she might collapse, her head feeling light, her eyes filling with tears, as her throat grew tight. She couldn't swallow. Her legs weakened. Lynn clutched Claudia, weeping into her shoulder. Claudia dropped her head next to Lynn's as they held each other. They both sobbed.

Through her tears, Lynn knew William was fighting the monstrous SAC for her and the kids. He was being strong for her and she needed to be worthy and strong for their children. She pulled back and looked Claudia, stiffening her chin. "We mustn't cry. We have to be strong for him. Thanks for your love and the sympathy, I needed it."

"No you didn't. You're stronger than you think."

"I hope so. I'll pray that your man makes it back."

"Mom, what's going on," Stefan murmured from his bunk.

"Go back to sleep, I'll tell you in the morning."

"If you're okay, I'll get back to my watch," Claudia whispered, giving a quick glance down the tunnel.

Lynn clasped Claudia's hand and looked at her with a warm smile, thankful she had such a friend. "I'm okay. We'll be fine. Thank you so much. I know you'll let me know if any other word comes through."

Claudia gave her a kiss on the cheek, "You bet we will, honey. Go get some rest and take care of those kids."

"Thanks, Claudia."

As Lynn lay down on her bunk again, allowing her eyes to search the blackness of their mountain room, she couldn't help but wonder what William had up his sleeve, what he was doing at that very minute. He wasn't one to set out on a course without some sort of purpose or a target to reach.

Chapter 31

When the yellow morning light knifed past Lynn's precious drapes covering the bedroom window, sleep still held William in its vaporous arms, allowing him to savor rare moments mentally drifting. Then his awareness brushed away the vapor, replacing it with sharply defined thoughts and developing scenarios of what he might do. Strangely, he had slept quite well, resigned and content with his decision. The badgering visualizations had not recurred in several hours.

After showering in wonderful hot water, shaving, and dressing in a warm sweater Lynn had given him for one of his birthdays, he found an apple in the refrigerator. He sat down at the kitchen table, running his gaze around the kitchen, remembering the important parts of his life, seeing meals with his family, all the moments speckled with the laughs, and his children's small but milestone discoveries.

The apple's tart freshness captured his mouth, tasting intricate and precious, as if he'd never eaten one before. He took a few minutes to prepare a cup of instant coffee, and while slowly sipping it, he looked at the pictures of his family in his wallet, kissing each of them before shoving the wallet into his trousers. He sipped his coffee, taking time to taste it and smell it. He felt an unusual calm as if drugged to see every movement with anticipation and purpose. He looked around the kitchen at what had been his life, thinking that in the future the house would not see their lives taking place within its walls. The house would be hollow and dead. His family had really been his life—never the property of the SAC. He drank the last of his coffee, looked at the bottom of the cup, and set it on the table.

I'm ready.

William went to the small closet near the front door and reaching for a coat, he realized his head felt much better than it had since arriving home. It was simple, but very pleasant, not having the throbbing in his head, although his back and stomach still felt as if a medieval torture machine had stretched the fibers of his muscles to near the breaking point. Pain shot from his shoulder into his back when he pushed his right arm into the coat. He stopped, grimaced, and fought the pain as he inserted his left arm into the sleeve. William sucked in a breath and walked out onto the front porch. He stood motionless for a second and then he pointed a finger at the black v-tran across the street. He gestured for them to come. He laughed to himself. This was where he would try controlling them. He walked to the edge of the driveway near the garage.

A vision of him sitting in one of Beucher's chairs popped into William's mind. He grabbed his head with one hand as throbbing started behind his left eye. He grabbed the corner of the garage with the other hand and held himself up. *People need father Durand. Damn the pain! Beucher's programming. Lies! Think your own thoughts.* There were still the power-hungry and the greedy who wanted control people as if they were cattle. *Wrong thought. No it wasn't.* They stole the country's wealth, abused power, and enslaved humans like cattle. The SAC wasn't altruistic. It was human sickness. He had to keep fighting the implanted programming. *It's my thought. It's truth!*

The v-tran pulled up in the driveway with a man staring sternly at William through the open front passenger window, his gaze spearing William with accusations, as if William were a deranged monster.

William pushed the pain away from his thoughts and walked over to the v-tran. "I'd like to see Section Head Karl Steinhoff," William said, wincing once from the throbbing back in his head. "I want to give him more information. I think I remember more about the conspirator." He hoped his dangling worm of information would entice Steinhoff to take a nibble.

The protectors stared at him incredulously for a moment and then the man who was driving grudgingly talked into his com-link as if he were straining to open his mouth. The man was silent for a moment and then nodded his head and gesturing with his hand, as if getting clarification. He then turned to his companion on the passenger side of the vehicle. "They want us to bring him in."

The second man immediately stuck his head out the right-side window. "Get in the back. Section Head Steinhoff has apparently granted your wish."

A short time later William found himself going into SAC Building Two, where he was handed off to two security guards, patted-down over his entire body, and then escorted to a place he never thought he'd go, to Steinhoff's office. A guard swung open the office door revealing to William the only man in the SAC government he had ever despised. William stood there, just inside the door, relieved his head felt clear again and satisfied he had made the first step in fulfilling his promise. A guard nudged William in the back and they moved forward toward Steinhoff, an armed guard on each side of him. He didn't take his eyes off Steinhoff. William and the guards stopped a few feet from Steinhoff's desk. Steinhoff's mouth, pressed into a line, moved slightly as if he were fighting a thought of amusement or satisfaction of his superiority over William. Steinhoff folded his arms and he leaned his chair back, tipping his head up, looking through squinty eyes and down his nose at William. William no longer feared the man in the chair.

"Well, what do we have here?" Steinhoff sneered. "What's going on in that new brain of yours, the one Doctor Beucher allowed you to keep?"

"I've been trying to remember," William began, contritely, with his hands clasped behind his back. "I've been trying to remember something the conspirator told me, but it won't come to me clearly. I get an occasionally flash on a vision of a sewer, but then it fads. I think I might be able to remember more information if I could go down in the sewer where the bomb was hidden. And, if I could, I would like to see the place I identified the bomb . . . to save our Father Durand. I . . . I really want to help . . . to make up for my mistakes and wrong thinking. I want to serve our family."

"Whose family?" Steinhoff asked tauntingly, as if the question made no sense. "You don't mean Father Durand's family." His voice became soft. "Whose family?"

"Durand's family, of course. The SAC family I love."

"You love?" Steinhoff snapped, laughingly, throwing his head back, his question sounding more like a declaration.

"I admitted my mistakes to Doctor Beucher," William said, pitifully. "I'm trying hard."

"Very interesting, Manager Rinehart. Oh wait, I'm sorry, you're patient Ninety-nine," Steinhoff replied in his superior manner. "Why should I believe you? Why should anyone believe you? This is probably some figment of your imagination, perhaps an artifact from Doctor Beucher's treatment?"

William held out his hands, palms to the sky, gesturing as if making an appeal. "Call Doctor Beucher and ask him? I have nothing to gain by wanting to see the Father's picture in that sewer."

"What do you mean? Durand's picture is in a sewer?"

"I think I remember being told his picture was in the same sewer as the bomb. I really feel if I could go there I could help with more information . . . remember more of what's been flashing through my mind in spurts."

"Okay, I will do just that . . . call Doctor Beucher," Steinhoff snapped. He turned toward his vid-link screen. "Vid-link on," he snapped.

"Vid-link, ready."

"Call Beucher."

Beucher's image came on the screen.

"Section Head Steinhoff, I see you have a guest," Beucher said, sounding pleased with the surprise of seeing William.

"Yes," Steinhoff snapped. "Your patient, Ninety-nine, wants to visit the sewer where he identified the bomb's location. He thinks it might help him remember more information. He says maybe by paying homage to a picture of Father Durand that he thinks is down there—he might be able to pull more information from his brain. What's your opinion? Is this worth our time? Or should I just send him back to you? Perhaps he needs more time in one of your chairs."

"Oh, I suppose it's possible . . . but . . . yes, he could be correct. During our thought mentoring procedure, we discovered a similar memory. Therefore, it's quite possible there's a picture down there. It could connect to other repressed memories. You should have my report on your desk by now. Whether going there will help him remember something missing or not, is a good question. That's problematic. However, you can't bring him to my department again."

"Why?" Steinhoff snapped.

"Director Kauffman wanted to avoid further deterioration of his faculties."

"Yes . . .yes, that is correct. You're correct and I agree with Director Kauffman." Steinhoff looked behind him at the corner of his desk. "I see I have the report you mention. Okay, what about the question at hand? Will it help him remember or not? Straight answers please."

"It could very well help remove a psychological block . . . something I didn't uncover due to the abbreviated treatment schedule."

"So I have your recommendation?"

"Yes, you do. I'll be glad to participate if you like."

"Thanks so much, but this will be a security operation," Steinhoff replied. "Oh, Citizen-Comrade Beucher, I'd like your agreement in writing in a net-message. Is that agreeable?"

"I'll be glad to do that," Beucher replied abruptly, sounding agitated.

Steinhoff spun around, facing William. "Vid-link, off." Steinhoff folded his fingers and sent his eyes off across the room, for a moment of silence his mouth changed from a tight line to a strange grin and back again. He returned to the Vid-link. "Vid-link, on."

"Ready."

"Call Director Kauffman."

Steinhoff's vid-link showed Kauffman just turning to face the vid-link camera and screen.

"Yes, Karl, what can I do for you?"

"William Rinehart is in my office, claiming he thinks he might be able to remember more information if he's taken to the sewer where he helped us locate the bomb. Doctor Beucher agrees that the visit could have beneficial results, helping to pull out deep memories. I thought I'd inform you before making my decision."

"Did you have him brought in or did he initiate the request?" Kauffman tilted his head skeptically and squinted.

William looked at the vid-link with only his eyes concerned not to reveal to the vid-link camera any facial character that could unlock his charade or proffer warning. He sensed a violent warning in Kauffman's testing question, and wondered if Kauffman's manner was part of an old intelligence director's gifted awareness of potential danger and his cautious respect for the unexpected.

"Sir, the idea was his. He approached our surveillance vehicle and asked to come here," Steinhoff replied, his tone carrying apology, while the lines around his mouth looked tight.

"If that's the case, I'd think we should avail ourselves of the opportunity to gather new fruit. I assume you are going along to supervise and scrutinize and verbal revelations."

"I wasn't . . . uh . . ."

"You were not going to miss it. Isn't that what you were going to say?"

"Yes, sir."

"Karl, I want you there to keep track of everything . . . the usual armed guards accompanying, of course. Karl, there are to be no accidental shootings."

"Yes, sir."

"I want this man kept alive, Karl—for a long time and under our constant surveillance. In fact, when you're done with this little excursion I want him placed in our Lewisburg high security facility."

"Of course, sir. I planned on attending and I will be accompanied by Doctor Beucher."

Kauffman smiled. "Excellent, keep me informed. Vid-link, off."

Steinhoff ended the vid-link and turned back to William with a superior curl to his mouth that told William the man thought he had finally extracted the ultimate vengeful reward. "Section Head Steinhoff," William began, "I'll be glad to write a report for you so you can present it to Director Kauffman."

"You are to address me as, sir. Is that clear?"

"Yes." A voice echoed in William's head. He would play Steinhoff's game. He didn't care what he had to do as long as he got down in the sewer, visiting the picture his father had described, fulfilling his promise, and discovering what his father surreptitiously cloaked in the chronicle's puzzling words. The look on Steinhoff's face, bitterness chained by his own fear of Kauffman, seemed on the threshold of breaking. Steinhoff sneered at him as if he were a festering sore he had to lance. Steinhoff's resentment and poisonously infected brain confirmed again the soul-crucifying nature of State America and the virus running it at the top. It was clear as the sun in a blue sky above a January snowscape; even if William hadn't been Henry's son, he would have lived as a slave. He wondered if Steinhoff knew that he was also a slave. Durand was a living icon, but in the near future, his infected legacy would mutate further under Chairman Bruner. William thanked his father for his extensive analysis of the precursor events.

"Since Director Kauffman wants to make certain we extract all the cobwebs lurking in your brain, I'm obliged to use whatever means possible to facilitate your memory. I will accompany you to this underground shrine and personally watch you pay your respects to Chairman, Father Durand. And I expect your memory to be reborn—before you are dispatched to Lewisburg, one of our particularly nice facilities. In fact, I'm surprised you weren't sent to one of our labor camps in northern Minnesota. Of course we wouldn't want you to die."

William lowered his eyes and spoke softly. "Thank you, sir."

"I want you to be silent."

William nodded, still averting his eyes.

"Guard, bring a v-tran to the front of the building and take this patient down to it," Steinhoff snapped authoritatively with a stabbing gesture toward the door. "I'll be down in a minute. Have another v-tran pickup Doctor Beucher and bring him to the sewer entrance. We should have two guards who have guns."

A few minutes after William got into the v-tran at the entrance of the building, Steinhoff climbed into the front passenger's side, disgust distorting his mouth, as if he were bored. William sat erect with his eyes obediently straight ahead, barely able to believe what was happening, but displaying a face that Steinhoff would consider penitent. He didn't want Steinhoff sidetracked by any excuse.

"Protector Stevens, drive to the entrance of the sewer where the bomb was excavated," Steinhoff directed. "Do you know that location?"

"Yes, sir. Very good, sir."

Steinhoff turned to the guard sitting next to William in the back seat. "Protector Crane, you do have your sidearm with you?"

"Yes, sir."

"Protector Stevens, do you have your sidearm?"

"Yes, sir."

Steinhoff twisted his head enough to see William in the back seat, maliciously staring at William out of the corner of his eye. "If the patient tries anything strange, the two of you are to shoot him . . . to kill him. Oh, wait, we can't kill him. In that case, you are to shoot his legs, his arms, anything none-vital. I'd say his head but the Director wants it."

"Very good, sir."

William descended the stairway, plunging down into a massive sewer tunnel. As he stepped into the tunnel, he noticed two vid-cams monitoring the stairway and tunnel like two silent watchdogs. Crane walked alongside him and Stevens walked a few feet walked in front. Steinhoff and Doctor Beucher followed Crane and him by several feet. They had all entered through a fenced-off steel door at a street-level concrete maintenance access, an entry point William never would have suspected.

"Okay, let's get the lanterns on," grumbled Steinhoff.

William didn't know what to expect and thought the feeble light was adequate for trudging down a sewer tube.

Crane and Stevens snapped on their yellow battery-powered lanterns to augment the dingy yellow glow given off by the ancient incandescent bulbs enclosed in protective glass globes strung down the ceiling like dirty pearls. The light from the bulbs failed to stretch the distance between globes, leaving the sewer predominately in shadow with tiny stepping-stone pockets of light, except for the two lanterns.

William had no idea what he might see in the sewer stretching out before him, or what he was going to do. He only wanted to keep his word and fulfill his promise to his father. It now looked as if he would have to do a little playacting along the way, and it looked as if Steinhoff might shoot him before the final curtain descended to the stage. However, he had formed a hunch from his father's writing. Despite the armed guards and the indeterminate prospects for his future, he felt electrified—and unbelievably free.

Overhead, along the ceiling of the concrete tube the usual vid-cams kept popping out of the shadows, overtly displayed seemingly as much for a warning, as for observing. The SAC eyeballs covered every angle, obviously protecting against any sort of sabotage.

William caught their footsteps echoing from somewhere down the underground tube, as if they had released phantom visitors walking along with them. Dampness flavored the air with an earthy odor and something putrid . . . perhaps something dead. Splotches of dark indistinguishable matter coated the surface of the tube and an infinite tangle of roots snaked across the surface trying to suck in nutrients.

"First, can you please take me to where the bomb was excavated?" William asked with a thoughtful inflection, trying to sound like he was absorbed in an effort to remember and likely to offer new revelations.

"This is your show, Ninety-nine," Steinhoff grumbled. "You had better make it good."

"This place really stinks," Crane mumbled.

Stevens laughed. "It's only the dampness. This place hasn't seen rain water or raw sewage in a million years."

"Stevens, do you know where to go?" Steinhoff asked.

"Yes, sir. It's to the right, just up ahead at the junction."

The size of the sewer surprised William and he now understood how a group could hide very large objects down there. It was easily large enough for the passage of a small powered vehicle, possibly a small truck, or for someone to bury something like a car, given the right equipment and the time to do it. A very creative mind had selected it for the fertilizer bomb. It ran through the heart of the city, and most importantly, was only a short distance from all the SAC buildings, although, William suspected, the SAC had likely closed off all other connecting arteries that approached or ran close to their imperial structures.

As they came to an intersection of their tunnel with one crossing at right angles, William remembered they needed to go to the right. Several yards after turning right, they came to a large hole in the floor that looked like a festering wound, with the scattered concrete, old bricks, and piles of dark clay still lying around.

"Why hasn't this been filled in?" Steinhoff barked. He turned to Beucher, who returned a sheepish glance before looking off down the sewer. Crane and Stevens merely shook their heads.

"No one was assigned to do it," William said plainly with a sense of satisfaction.

"Silence, you," Steinhoff barked. "Get on with rejuvenating your memory before I march your ass out of here and over to Beucher's thought mentoring room. Right Doctor Beucher?"

"Yes . . . uh . . . we could do that."

"I thought I was going to Lewisburg," William said plainly.

Steinhoff glared at William. "You may not make it out of this sewer."

"Yes, sir," William replied, laughing on the inside. He closed his eyes and grabbed his head acting as if he were concentrating. Concerned that his acting needed a more convincing character, he squeezed his head and grimaced with a little groan. Then he noticed the wall. What was it? Sure enough, under what looked like someone's attempt to smooth over the wall with some sort of surfacing cement he saw indentations for letters. It was the name, Thomas Norman. It was just as his father said.

After a moment, Steinhoff shook his head disagreeably. "Are you making any connections or is this a big damn waste of time?"

William jerked his head. "Uh . . . there . . . I just had a flash. I need to go back the other way, to see Durand's picture." William tried sounding distant and detached. He closed his eyes, swayed a little, and shook his head, manufacturing a grimace again for good measure. "I think there's something in the other direction. We should go the other way. I think I remember something that's back there . . . something important."

"Okay, let's get going, then." Steinhoff leaned close to Stevens and whispered in his ear, "Stevens, keep your eyes on him."

"Yes, sir." Stevens unhooked his handgun. Stevens motioned for Crane to do the same.

Pausing, William looked at them with his head slightly tilted, as if listening to music, his face marble smooth. "Steinhoff, you can kill me, but then you might miss information vital to Father Durand's State America . . . and . . . what about the director?"

Steinhoff laughed with a sinister tone, as if he knew a horrible secret. "You could have a little accident while we're down here. You've always been a pain in my ass with your attitude, so unpretentious, so pure, and so damn eager—even if you were being duped so the SACI could maintain surveillance on you and your family."

"You still might miss vital information," William muttered. "Besides, I've only been a manager and no threat to you for years. Why invoke Kauffman's wrath by killing me? It doesn't sound like a profitable venture for you." William doubted Steinhoff cared about Kauffman's wrath; he was too unbalanced with his hatred. He thought he'd go easy on Steinhoff the rest of the way to make certain he had a chance to see whatever it was his father wanted him to see.

"Okay, get going," Crane said, pushing William in the back with the barrel of his handgun.

They walked back toward the intersection and into the left portion of the sewer, where William hoped to discover his father's secret. He hoped he could satisfy his father's curious request. Up ahead he saw more sentinel vid-cams keeping their never-ending vigil. Feeling electrified, William wanted to dart forward toward his father's mystery. He caught himself. He shortened his stride, trying to avoid looking eager or anxious, trying to quench his excitement even as his heart raced with anticipation. He threw his eyes out at everything, scanning the walls to the left and right ahead of

551

him, searching for something concealed by the dirt on the walls. Suddenly, he remembered. He cursed at himself for not counting the steps.

In the distance, on the edge of the light, William saw an object on a wall. *What is that?* Was something on the left wall? It was lighter than the surrounding sewer wall. It seemed to be almost reflecting light. He took a long slow breath. *My God, I've found it!* His father was right. On the left wall was a white square with a picture of Durand. Years had covered it with dirt, random splotches of mud, and the runners of fine roots. Some sort of dark mold appeared to be eating the edges, almost giving the appearance of a picture frame. A heavy patch of dirt hovered above Durand's head. The picture was easily three-feet square and from the heading, *Elect The Country's Savior*, it appeared to be an old plastic political campaign banner. At its corners circular rust spots indicated some sort of metal anchors had attached it to the wall.

"Here is where I needed to come," William murmured, as if in a daze. "Let me work on my memory." He grabbed his head with both hands.

Steinhoff and his goons stood back several feet down the tube, smugly watching him as if William were an idiot going about some insane ritual. William stood opposite the deteriorated picture of Durand. He thought of his father, remembering all his pleas for final actions.

Suddenly, William's face flooded with warmth, as if his face were flushing with blood. His head grew fuzzy as a sense of elation flooded over him. The somber reverence for his father gave way to a flashing thought of praise for Durand, and a tranquil feeling of satisfaction. *Durand had rewarded me.* The heaviness in his thoughts from minutes ago, his resignation to his final days left him. *Will Durand love me?* He turned to Doctor Beucher standing behind Steinhoff. He could almost feel Hans pushing him down the hall toward his cell, his one-piece suit filled with the stench of his own feces. He had hated that . . . hated it terribly. He closed his eyes and saw an image of Beucher, grinning at him hideously. He pushed his eyes open. He grabbed his head with both hands, thinking of Durand.

Steinhoff turned to Beucher. "What's he doing?"

"He may be having flashbacks," Beucher muttered. "It's normal."

William caught himself. Wait a minute . . . all of it didn't make sense. *I'm here for my father. My father . . . not Father Durand . . . my father warned me . . . the implants . . . the control.* That had to be the cause. The damn implant. His head throbbed, this time at his left temple, and he seemed to hear a high pitch whine. He had to fight it, fight looking at the picture of Durand. He dropped his head, fighting the throbbing in his ears, anguishing over his enslavement, gazing blankly and dejectedly at the floor. *I'm still their damn slave!* He grabbed his head, squeezing with his hands over his ears. On the floor, a few inches from his shoe, he saw something that didn't belong there, a piece of wire, a remnant possibly something left behind after a repair. It fired off an idea. He bent over and picked it up.

"What are you doing?" yelled Stevens, freezing where he stood, his gun gripped tightly in his hand, but pointing at the floor.

"Be very careful, Ninety-nine," Steinhoff declared in a low deliberate warning tone. "We'll shoot you if you breathe wrong."

"It's just a piece of wire," William replied, his voice detached, thinking back to his father, trying to break free of the effects in his mind and the hypnotic effect of staring at Durand's picture. Beucher's brainwashing must had programmed a response to pictures of Durand. It had to be the brainwashing. He turned toward the wall, looked at the wire in his hand, and pushed it into his left forearm. The sudden piercing pain sent an electric wave crashing through him. Blood oozed from the puncture in a sanguine rivulet. William felt his head clearing as the throbbing diminished. He pushed the wire in his arm again and gasped from the pain. It excited him that he broke through Beucher's conditioning, winning a battle for freedom. He looked determinedly at the Durand's picture, recalling his father's words.

"Isn't this picture glorious," William announced, struggling through his pain, thinking he needed a little time. "I can't believe I actually helped preserve Father Durand's country. I think I'm feeling a memory returning."

Again, he thought back to his father's guidance. Despite how silly it was, he had to scratch his father's name on the nose of the picture. He'd promised to do that. He reached up and pushed the wire into the panel displaying Durand's smiling image, right into the nose. The wire pierced the think plastic sheet to a hard surface behind. He pulled the wire back and tried again. As he worked the wire, the plastic revealed its age, tearing a little and producing a hole. *Wait! What is that?* In the opening, he saw the edge of a gray metallic object extending out from the wall a fraction of an inch. He tore the opening a little more and stopped. A circular disk four or five inches in diameter protruded from the surface of wall. Fearing an approach by Steinhoff and his lethal associates at any moment, he hastily expanded the opening and peeled it back so he could see the more of the surface.

"What are you doing?" Steinhoff barked warily, standing fifteen feet away with Crane and Stevens who were poised to shoot. "You're defacing an image of Chairman Durand for which you will be imprisoned. Now you have done it! Social treason."

Not looking at Steinhoff, William replied, "I love Father Durand. Do you?"

Steinhoff stared at him, taking a step closer.

William leaned in close to the wall, looking through the hole. In the center of the circular plate was a small square pad of nine buttons, each button with different letters of the alphabet. As he was about to read the print at the top of the pad of buttons more of his father's words returned. There were those strange words about wanting what is right under our nose. What was next? Yes, yes, he needed to return hope, moral code in hand, writing alpha to bring a proper omega. He rubbed the dirt from the words at the top of the plate, paused, and grinned. "I'll be damned," he muttered. He thought of his family and touched the button with an "A", the "L", the "P", the "H", and then he stopped. This was what he had felt in his soul he would find—somewhere. He whispered, "God forgive me for the innocent lives that will be taken to save the many." Suddenly, it struck him that he was no longer powerless; he had found his courage, and he approached his freedom. He thought of his father's words carved into the wall. After you give them your freedoms, they will take your soul. Perhaps he was answering that plea.

"What is that?" Steinhoff yelled, his voice carrying desperate confusion and a fearful final warning. "Don't move one inch. Stevens, place him in restraints, immediately. Shoot him if he doesn't comply. Doctor Beucher what is he doing?"

William turned and grinned at Steinhoff as he pushed the "A" button.

Stevens squeezed the trigger of his gun, filling the tunnel with the deafening explosive reverberation of the discharge.

William felt something slam into his left side and then a piercing pain as it thrust him to the sewer floor on his right side. Slowly he pushed himself up on his hands. His head began to float. He reached toward the location of his burning pain. It was wet. Blood was coming out his left side, coating his hand. He looked up through the hole in Durand's nose. His face felt relaxed. His mouth curled with pride as his eyes showed serene determination and the knowing that he had achieved what no one else could have done. He saw a flashing row of red lights, illuminated buttons cycling through some sort of sequence, some sort of countdown. William watched the lights, grinning, joyous, knowing his family would live. "Durand, here's Buck Firestone's firecracker up your ass," he snapped. Then his face became motionless and serene. "Here's freedom for my Lynn, Stefan, and Marie. Thank you, Dad. I love you, Lynn, and my wonderful kids."

William saw a microsecond of the brilliant white light of the sun.

Chapter 32

On top of a ridge in the Allegheny Mountains, west of Harrisburg, Pennsylvania, two sentinel observers for the FUS underground saw a white glow expand from the horizon upward into the clear southeast sky. One of the men jumped to the telescopic rangefinder and activated the digital video capture. The glow seemed to inflate like a bubble of white light, competing with the morning sun, slowly changing to yellowish orange before the distance and the edge of the earth swallowed it.

The moment the light faded the man on the rangefinder spoke into his headset microphone. "Control room, this is observation, Browne, reporting."

"Control room."

"Better send someone up to get the video we just shot. If I had to guess, someone blew up something really big—down to the southeast."

"Someone will be right up to get it."

"Observation, out."

"Control, out."

Ten minutes after the observers reported seeing the light, heavy footsteps came from the hall of the excavated mountain habitat that had become home for Lynn and her children. A shadow ran across the floor, pulling Lynn's eyes from the book she was reading with Stefan and Marie. A figure stood in the door. She had only recently met the man.

"Mrs. Rinehart," the man said in a heavy voice, "I believe your husband has just saved our country."

"Excuse me, General Wilcox, what did you say?" Lynn asked, her eyes large with alarm, her brain trying to reach for a pleasant word she had missed or a reason behind the visit that didn't mean sorrow or fear. Claudia stood behind the general crying into her handkerchief. Lynn dropped the book on the floor as she rose to her feet. Her breath shuddered, refusing to release. "Oh, God. What happened?"

Stefan jumped up and wrapped his arm around his mom and Marie leaned against her, looking up at her as if begging to understand.

"What's wrong, Mom?" Marie pleaded, pushing her head into Lynn's waist.

General Wilcox took Lynn's hand, looking down at her with his wrinkled and worn eyes. His voice came soft in a heavy whisper. "Mrs. Rinehart, we have just confirmed with one of our agents in Virginia that a large nuclear device has been exploded in Washington. We believe it eradicated all of the key people in the SAC government. I also just got word that the SAC military command transmitted a message on one a television frequency, their vid-net, and on several shortwave frequencies, giving their surrender. The whole government, including the intelligence and military command structure has been eliminated. Your husband severed the head of the snake and saved the country."

General Wilcox looked up at the ceiling, the lines in his face tightening, as if he were fighting with himself. He gathered a breath and then turned softly to Lynn. His throat moved oddly with his swallowing. His eyes glistened with tears. "Mrs. Rinehart, we're pretty certain your husband used information given him by his father. We are pretty certain he detonated a five megaton warhead that was buried by another hero, General Buck Firestone." He paused, his voice catching as a tear ran down his cheek. "Mrs. Rinehart your husband sacrificed his life to destroy the horror that has gripped this country for too many years. We have believed for quite some years that it was the only way to decapitate the SAC monster with any sort of success. Your husband gave us back our freedom." The general took her hand, glanced at it and then kissed it. "Your husband and his father helped to stop the despot and megalomaniac Durand from implementing his final transformation phase with the sociopath Bernard Bruner. The man we had inside until the SACI caught him and brainwashed him, discovered Bruner and Durand's plan was to implant every person with an electronic control device so the SAC could make a single-mind society of slaves. The SAC would have controlled everything. They were going to control births, and take the babies from their mothers, who would then be subject to the State's discretion. They were going to control the race by artificial insemination, closely checking all DNA. The SAC would have flushed away or used for hard labor, those people not measuring up to their standards either racially or medically. Everyone would have been a slave, physically and mentally. No free thought and no free speech."

Lynn's thoughts stood still with the general's numbing ramifications. She wrapped her arms around General Wilcox, laying her head on his chest, sobbing, needing to feel his strength, needing the compassion in his arms. Stefan and Marie clutched her, both of them crying. Her William was gone. Her love, her best friend was gone. As her heart sank as low as it could possibly descend, she thought she couldn't go on without William, but then she reminded herself why he had made the sacrifice—so his children could be free. Possibly, he had felt patriotic, but it was mainly the children. She knew it. That was William. The pain of losing him would linger with her for the rest of her life, like a hole in her heart, but their Stefan and Marie were going to be able to live in a country where a person could chose their own path.

"General, did Claudia's man make it to safety?" Lynn asked, her breath shuddering.

"Yeah, Russell made it out, barely, but he made it."

"That's wonderful."

"Yes it is. It's fantastic. Now, maybe they'll get married and have some kids."

Lynn looked down at the floor as she wiped away her tears. She then looked at the general, drawing on inner courage that she had only recently started using, sending him a solemn gaze. "General, tell me William's deed wasn't a wasted gesture, that the country will never come to this again," she said, stiffening, her words like hammering steel.

"I can't promise you anything. In a free society people can only trust in the safeguards."

"Well, the failure of those goddamn safeguards cost me my husband—and probably millions more!" She fought her sobbing, holding up her chin. "Why would people let such a thing happen?"

Wilcox sighed heavily. "I have wondered on occasion if it wasn't God's lesson for man, a punishment for surrendering integrity and humanity for greed and power."

"I hope we've learned something."

"Lynn, we are going to make some major revisions—when we get this mess totally cleaned up and this place brought back to a constitutional representative republic. When we start over we will protect the Constitution as inviolate. The first proposed revision to receive a lot of consideration is a constitutional amendment prohibiting one party from holding a majority in both the Congress and Senate at the same time. That will probably cause a few battles but it might also demand the parties cooperate for the betterment of the country. A two-term limit for members of both the House and Senate will be implemented. We may discontinue absentee ballots, but voter photo identification will be mandatory, especially since voter fraud helped with our disaster. Special voter provisions will be made for military personnel." He stopped. "Have you ever voted?"

"For what?"

"People in the government."

"No, there was no voting when I was old enough. My parents mentioned it once or twice. But they were afraid to say much."

"I forgot how long it had been since it was stopped."

"I would love to vote. Please tell me more."

"The presidential qualifications will be reviewed and confirmed by the Supreme Court working with the FBI and the Justice Department, prior to

Craig L. Andrews

any political campaign—including a psychological profile and thorough background check of all associations. We are still twiddling about handling the Attorney General, trying to keep that office independent of party. The political campaigns will be changed. There won't be any socialistic nuts in office with an agenda of changing us from a republic based on Judeo-Christian principles. Executive orders will require consent of both the House of Representatives and the Senate. All children and adults must be educated on the content of the Constitution and pass a test, either in school or after school. Most likely labor unions will be changed or abolished; they have too much socialistic collectivism baggage. Several old timers think we've had enough of the faceless collective brain, which has destroyed enough lives. The press, the journalistic media engaged in reporting on the government and people in politics, may undergo a yearly review by a rotating committee of private citizens of equal numbers from all political parties. Of course, this will be hard in view of the freedom of speech. However, the new process won't be to limit speech, but to expand it. This may be a bit naive on my part, but perhaps such a system could keep journalism reporting only the facts and not biased opinion. I've heard there's some support for keeping a closed economy for a couple years. We need all the jobs we can muster. The brains have had many years to think about our mistakes." He gazed at the floor in thought. "I'm sorry for belaboring my answer to your question. Now, in your sorrow, is not the time for details of the future."

"Respectfully, sir, I think it's an excellent time."

"We're going to need people with your spirit."

"General, what about other countries?"

"For quite some time we've been in touch with elements in Germany, Russia, Sweden, and Japan, accomplished by shortwave and ELM, but they could not interfere without catastrophic consequences. No. It was up to us to haul our bacon out of this fire. They were supportive because of their interest in global stability and getting back more money on all the treasury notes they bought from us years ago."

"What was the difference between the country you remember and the poison of the SAC?" Lynn asked, sounding skeptical, the corners of her eyes looking haggard, a little fearful, and skeptical.

"A lot, Lynn. The SAC did nothing but suck the life from us and control us. The republic we used to have, at one time, provided and maintained freedom. We didn't protect the freedoms very well. We tolerated too many narcissistic egos, pursuing greed and power at the expense of the average citizen. We allowed billionaires to play games with national socialistic groups to erode our system from within. Some of that manipulation may fall under sedition in the future, although we have to watch trampling on freedom of assembly and freedom of speech."

"God, help us, General," Lynn said and then she looked down at her children, hoping they'd truly be free. She looked off with a distant gaze, not really seeing the ceiling of the mountain tunnel, thinking of William. "William, I love you."

The End

Craig L. Andrews is eclectic when it comes to writing genre, connecting his creative wires to whatever sparks a great story and take the reader somewhere memorable. In the creation process he is shackled to the goal of developing characters and stories driven by logic, plausibility, and giving the reader a deserved adventure. In writing Chronicle of Stolen Souls, the Legacy of Fathers, he tried to raise a warning torch for those taking the complacent path through life and endeavored to highlight our precious freedom. He holds a B. S. degree in physics from Findlay College and an M.S. degree in physics from Bowling Green State University. He has authored both physics and automotive engineering papers. The author has two loves, art and science, and despite a focus in physics his writing includes The Ninth Martini, a Clancy-type thriller, The Godmanchester Stone and The Bed and Breakfast, in the horror genre, and Silent Conscience, a politically oriented thriller. In the area of nonfiction he authored Broken Toy, A Man's Dream, A Company's Mystery, a biography of a man whose company trademarked a mouse named, Micky, two years before Walt Disney. The biography was a major reference used for the 2005 PBS History Detectives program. When he's not writing he dabbles in photography and video animation.